A Casual Brutality

Also by Neil Bissoondath

Digging Up the Mountains

A Casual Brutality

by

NEIL BISSOONDATH

Clarkson N. Potter, Inc./Publishers
DISTRIBUTED BY CROWN PUBLISHERS, INC. NEW YORK

Published in the United States in 1989 by Clarkson N. Potter, Inc.,
225 Park Avenue South, New York, New York 10003
Originally published in Great Britain in 1988 by Bloomsbury Publishing Ltd.
Originally published in Canada in 1988 by Macmillan of Canada
CLARKSON N. POTTER, POTTER and colophon are trademarks of
Clarkson N. Potter, Inc.
Design by Cliff Morgan

Manufactured in the United States of America

Library of Congress Cataloging-in-Publication Data

Bissoondath, Neil, 1955-
A casual brutality.

I. Title.
PR9199.3.B457C37   1989   813'.54   88-28951
ISBN 0-517-57202-8

10 9 8 7 6 5 4 3 2 1
First American Edition

For
Anne Marcoux
who has taught me
among many other things
perspective

The author wishes to thank
the Canada Council and the Ontario
Arts Council for their financial assistance,
and Macmillan of Canada
for their understanding and encouragement,
during the writing of this book.

Sur La place un chien hurle encore
Car la fille s'en est allée
Et comme le chien hurlant la mort
Pleurent les hommes leur destinée.
Jacque Brel
Sur la place

"Only God gives and takes life.
But God is busy elsewhere, and we're the ones
who must undertake this task . . ."
Argentine miltary interrogator
Captain Beto to Jacobo Timerman
Prisoner Without a Name,
Cell Without a Number

T*here are times when the word* hope *is but a syn-*
onym for *illusion*: it is the most virile of perils. He who cannot
discern the difference—he whose perception of reality has slipped
from him, whose appreciation of honesty has withered within
him—will face, at the end, a fine levied, with no appeal, with only
regret coating the memory like ash.

Grappler lays his hand lightly on my shoulder, glances at me,
his handsome, aging face still in the half light. He says, "You're
sure, Raj?"

I nod, once, my lips tightening against one another as they do
when I wish to demonstrate determination.

His dark eyes, hooded by thick brows, search my face, rest for
a moment on the compressed lips; then there is the faintest soft-
ening, perceptible only to those who know him well, in the lines
that fan out—thought lines, he calls them—across his temples
from the corners of his eyes. Acceptance, this: Grappler knows
me well.

My grandmother, veil fine and diaphanous—as if spun by a

spider—pinned tightly to her hair by a golden butterfly, says, "Son," and stifles a sob in her crumpled handkerchief.

This irritates me. My grandmother is a woman who has built much of her life on public and private display: witness the jewellery, the bangles and beads she drapes on herself even in grief; witness her dislike of slenderness, proof to her not of physical health but of emaciated wealth. And despite my knowledge of her, despite my familiarity with her personal theatre, despite the fears of abandonment and endless evenings I know must be running rampant through her, I find my sympathy short. I expect greater fortitude, expect her still to think only of me, even though I know she probably never has. I am being unfair—the word forms in my mind, materializing like a distant accusation—but I am, at this moment, beyond fairness; it is too conscious, too practised an attitude and, right now, it is only to the visceral that I can react.

Grappler squeezes my shoulder, says, "Take a look, then. One last time." His hand insists at his words and he turns with me, slowly, completely around, until we are gazing back out from where we have come.

At the final, hazy pallor of sunset casting shadow into the world. At the parking lot, unusually empty, the few cars widely dispersed, the lights along its perimeter ineffective still, greenish glows high up on their metal posts. At the wire fence, from here a fading, ashen mesh; and beyond it, marking the far edge of the narrow asphalt road that girds the airport grounds, a mass of sugar cane black against the deepening evening sky, like an immense shadow hugging the ground, a slice of the approaching night detached and sprawled heavily across the near horizon. The thin, tangy brine of invisible gasoline fumes hover here at the unbarred entrance to the terminal, here where the grizzled edge of the steady fluorescent light behind us mingles with the dusk and holds it at uneasy bay.

I look at Grappler. What does he expect me to do? Sigh? Whisper bittersweet words of farewell? And I wonder, too, what *he* is seeing. Merely a parking lot? Or the darkening rubble of shattered dreams?

But these are questions to which I do not wish to know the answers, for I will not perform, and I cannot grieve. Yet.

A car drives slowly into the parking lot, its headlights brash and attractive. With hesitation, red brake lights blinking nervously, it manoeuvres into place beside Grappler's little red Honda. The brake lights flash the car to a standstill, lose their sharpness to a steady glow; but they do not, as expected, snap off. Instead, there is a shout, words brief and indistinct jarring in the silent dusk, and the figure of a man runs from the attendant's booth towards the car. He is mostly all shadow, but my eyes see more of him, see the green of his uniform, the squared heaviness of his helmet, the black slash of moulded metal and plastic that hangs by a strap from his shoulder. The silhouette of his right arm gestures with impatience as he shouts once more. He watches as the car jerks forward, lunging to the edge of a stall and, with a timid growl, sucking at power, moves to open space ahead, coming to rest at an angle. Satisfied and without another word, the man swivels around and retraces his steps in a long, easy, loping gait, a man, it seems to me, at ease with his power.

"Order," Grappler says. "Is this what it's all about." His voice is flat, the question not a question.

My grandmother comes up behind me, touches me on the arm. I do not look at her, but I hear her sniffling.

"Maybe now we have a chance." But he speaks in a voice drained, a voice that expresses at best an impotent optimism. Then he continues: "Of course, they haven't helped anybody else. Jamaica. Grenada. Ferdinand Isle. They've just kept them in line, that's all." He gives me a weary grin. "But that's all behind you now, isn't it, Raj?"

I ignore the tincture of sarcasm. Because it is true: it's all behind me now. Or, at least, it soon will be, as much of it as is possible.

"Let's get you checked in," he says, turning abruptly into the white fluorescent light.

My grandmother says, "Son."

At her whisper, the word *anguish* comes to me, but as just a word, without context, without essence.

Grappler slips my passport and airline ticket from my shirt pocket and walks rapidly into the large, bright hall. There are few people around. His leather heels clap loudly on the scuffed terrazzo floor, and the sound echoes up along the white walls into the high, empty ceiling.

It is like the first time.

Then, too, my grandfather had not been here. His little store, the final stage of what, in my eyes, remains an epic on the smallest, most personal scale, demanded during business hours—for as far back as my memory will go, unvaryingly eight to five, Monday to Friday, eight to one-thirty on Saturdays—his hovering presence and sly attention. He was, in his taciturn way, a happy victim of the dictatorship of small business. So then, too, as now, Grappler and my grandmother had accompanied me, he as solid and dependable as she was not.

And standing now beside Grappler at the airline counter, watching mutely as he goes through the motions of checking me in, it occurs to me it is as if I were again eighteen, about to take the plane alone for the first time, and incapable of showing my ticket or choosing a seat. But his solicitude pleases me, calls up briefly, vaguely, a time of tense expectation aggravated by my knowing nothing of the place to which I was going but the name Young Street, picked up the week before my departure from an airline radio advertisement. It is a pleasant memory, even as it brings back the foolishness I felt when I first saw the name correctly spelt; it was several puzzled moments before I realized this Yonge was my Young, and that it had nothing to do—as I had feared—with a trendy youthfulness.

So it is like the first time.

Yet, it is not. There is, outside, none of the cacophonous chaos of cars rakishly parked to disgorge overdressed passengers and voluminous luggage; none of the thin boys and ragged old men crowded about offering taxis or porter's services; none of the bustle and noise of relatives, immediate and more distant, seeing off in dramatic fashion departing family members.

Now the terminal is almost deserted. Little groups of two or three sit scattered around on the chairs of hard orange plastic; they keep to themselves, speak little and then in whispers, quietly watchful, eyes diffident and wary of contact. The concession booths of corrugated iron painted sky blue and hung with hand-painted signs—Newspapers and Magazines, Flight Insurance, Casaquemada Crafts—are unlit and locked, gates of heavy wrought iron, painted the same blue, chained tightly into place. The gleam of the lights high overhead, searching out the empty corners, the unpeopled seats, adds to the sense of desolation.

My grandmother says, "But Son, who going to cook for you? Who going to clean your clothes?"

On the second-floor landing, strolling slowly in from the waving gallery, are two of the men in green, low-brimmed helmets concealing their faces in shadow, belted around their waists holsters of polished brown leather that move in weighted rhythm with their steps. Their hands—skin an almost imperceptible pink, impressionistic, colour caught only at a glance, this so unlike our local whites, who, of an inert yellow, seem always unaffected by the sun—are startling and foreign in the light. Behind them, the glass wall of the airport lounge, where in my early youth my grandparents would bring me to eat club sandwiches, drink Coca-Cola and watch the activity of infrequent planes, is solid and unreflective, revealing only the darkness trapped behind it.

I say, with irritation, "Ma, I'm thirty-five years old—" But I stop myself. For, as I follow the black boots of the men in green descending the stairs in synchronized steps, as I wonder where their unseen eyes are sweeping, my grandmother comes, unsought, into my view; and that part of me that I have, in the last few days, brought under strict control flickers with panic at the shrunken, tremulous age that has only recently come over her. I falter, then, my gaze frozen on this sudden apparition.

"No luggage? What you mean, no luggage?" The man's voice, a mixture of incredulity and irritation, is directed at me. It is with relief that I turn towards him, to his thin, worried, young man's face and crumpled white shirt, epaulettes crushed and collar long unwashed. He says, as if personally offended, "Not even a bag?"

Grappler says, "Not even a bag. He travellin' light." He pauses for a moment, studying the young man's face. "Somethin' wrong with that?"

"No," the young man says unhappily, slapping my passport, ticket and boarding pass on the counter.

Grappler says, "But you ain't give him a seat number."

"We not botherin'." He shrugs unconcernedly and makes a face. "The plane ain't even half-full, he could sit anywhere he want." Then he turns back to me, repeats in a skeptical voice: "No luggage?"

No luggage: no clothes, no books, no medical bag, not even a toothbrush; just my passport, a one-way ticket and, in a canvas moneybelt strapped around my middle, U.S. bills and traveller's cheques and my Canadian citizenship and social insurance cards—the paper and plastic that, in our little island of Casa-quemada, are in themselves a definition of freedom. I reach for my papers on the counter: "Is that all?"

The young man nods, sucks his teeth, folds his arms high on his chest, hunching his shoulders into a bony fragility. He looks away with feigned indifference towards a middle-aged couple now emerging from the shadowed world into the light, each labouring with two bulging suitcases belted and marked for identification at the handles by swatches of red ribbon. They walk with studied slowness, yet give the impression of bustle, of people who want to run and manage to restrain themselves, as they must, but only with transparent effort.

I know them, the Lals, patients of mine. I turn hurriedly away, but it's too late.

"Dr. Ramsingh."

"Mr. Lal."

They lower the suitcases to the ground and, for a moment, seem to consider their choices. Then, hand extended, Mr. Lal covers the space between us in three rapid steps. He takes my hand in his, moist and warm and with a gentle grasp. "We heard." He blinks with nervousness and licks his lips. "We're—"

"Thank you," I cut him off, maybe a touch too abruptly. But ceremony, with its artificial imposition of required words and gestures, has always aroused my antipathy: the handshake I appreciate; the words are meaningless. I withdraw my hand.

He clasps his hands, small and smooth, feminine, before his ample stomach and rubs the palms one against the other. Glancing quickly at Grappler and my grandmother, he says, "You seein' someone off, or—"

"Travelling," I say. The words *going home* come to me, but I resist them. "And you?"

"Going." He becomes more agitated, his lower lip trembling out of control. "Just going."

"Toronto?"

"Only passing through. To New York. We have our green cards."

His wife, standing still some distance off, face lowered, looks drawn and tired. My eyes flicker from him to her and back again. "How is she?" I ask. The question is sincere.

"Holdin' up, Doctor. You know."

Only too well, I'm afraid. The conversation disconcerts me, and I wish there were another flight for me to take in anonymity. But there isn't; there are no schedules left in Casaquemada; taxis are idle, buses don't run, the port is closed and here, at the airport, planes arrive and depart at the behest of unknown authorities with their own, private priorities. I am here now, ready to board this plane, only because the Canadian High Commission in Lopez City called, urging me to take it. "We can't guarantee anything if you don't take this flight," the man said, "and we don't know when they're going to authorize another one." So here I am, in this condition I hate most of all: choiceless.

"We'll see you on the plane, then," Mr. Lal says to my silence.

"Yes. On the plane," I reply as he returns to his wife. But then I realize there is little to worry about. We will avoid each other; that much, it seems to me, we have understood.

I turn, suddenly exhausted, to Grappler.

He shrugs and smiles sadly. Glancing at his watch, he says, "It's early yet. Let's go upstairs."

"The bar's closed."

"Just to breathe," he says, taking my arm, reaching for my grandmother's and leading us both past the men in green to the stairs.

Grappler says, "Because you're leaving with nothing."

Night knits its strands tightly around us beneath the tin roof of the waving gallery. My grandmother, eyes closed, sits quietly on a bench of untreated wood, right fist, clenched around the balled handkerchief, resting tensely against her chest: her pose of controlled distress. Grappler and I stand together at the low metal railing. We are alone. The air, stagnant, prickles with an unsubtle mixture of gasoline fumes and burnt oil.

He adds, "As far as he can see."

On the tarmac before us, the lone aircraft gleams red on white in a brilliant spotlight. Men in dirty white overalls bustle about, tugging at thick orange cables, tinkering at open hatches in the silvery underbelly, tossing boxes and suitcases from an open trailer to the yawning hold.

"But he's not wrong, Grappler, is he."

Beyond the tarmac and its illuminated activity, the taxiing lanes and runways stretch into the dusky distance, ending far away in hazy, dimly lit hangars and, farther on, the hills in regularly peaked silhouette against the darkening sky.

"But don't you see, Raj. He concludes that you can afford to leave with nothing, and then to buy everything new." He pauses, eyes narrowing so that, even in the gloom, his thought lines can be seen fanning from the corner of his eye out across his temple. "And he's not wrong, Raj, is he."

Again, that tincture of sarcasm: it stings. But it is, too, once more, a statement of simple truth. I say, "No," and my voice retains its neutrality.

He takes a deep, rasping breath, slips his hands into his pant pockets. "Look there," he says, with a slight jerk of his head to the left. To a corner of the tarmac where, beyond the reach of the spotlight, the smooth, grey concrete shows hazy and aquatic; where five helicopters, olive skins going black in the smoky light, sit like dragonflies at rest.

"That changes nothing," he says. "The resentment remains."

My eyes travel up and away to the distant hills, featureless in the dark; above them to the sky glossy yet with the trail of the sunken sun.

"You have a one-way ticket, Raj, and a foreign passport that says you were born here. You can escape. He probably never will. And he knows it." He looks directly at me, the thought lines running deep now. "Tell me, Raj, can a man who's warm really understand a man who's cold?" He gives me a moment to contemplate the question, then he continues. "I once read that somewhere, and I've wondered about it ever since. I think it's one of those fundamental questions that most people would rather not grapple with. One of those 'maybe' questions." He chuckles and looks away, back to the helicopters. "*No luggage!* You can't expect him to like you, Raj, not when you have everything he wants."

"That's always been the problem here, Grappler. Everybody's got something somebody else wants, and there's never enough to go around."

"But a lot of people have what they want. Like your Mr. Lal. You'd be surprised how many of my neighbours have their green cards or their landed status in Canada. Casaquemadans yesterday, Americans or Canadians today. People who change countries like they change clothes. When it gets too dirty—"

"What would you have them— No. What would you have *us* do, Grappler? What are *you* going to do?"

He shrugs, removes his hands from his pockets and methodically, rolling one curled palm against the open face of the other, cracks his knuckles. "Carry on. As usual. What else?"

It is the answer I expect, the essential Grappler. He is a man who fights his way past fear and despair by simple perseverance, a man who will go to a funeral just to be there, strength even in passive numbers, presence a palliative.

My eyes return to the illuminated body of the clean, sleek aircraft, my own essence, it seems to me now, and, for the briefest moment, I envy Grappler his strength.

From behind us, my grandmother calls my name, her voice a brittle whisper.

I turn slowly, "Ma?"

"Come sit, Son."

I move towards her unwillingly, sit hunched on the bench beside her, my fingers curling around the smooth, warm wood of the seat.

She looks at me with damp, reddened eyes, handkerchief in her veined right hand clutched now at her throat, mouth working behind compressed lips at excess saliva. She swallows, and when she speaks her voice is subdued. "Raj. Son. When you comin' back?"

"Ma, I haven't left yet." The question, not unexpected, is so like her.

"But you comin' back, not so?"

"I don't know." There is no hesitation, but my voice falls to a whisper.

"To see me?"

"Maybe you could come see me, Ma." But my voice betrays me, at least to myself. They are words that offer a lie as possibility, words that cloak like cellophane the truths of her uncertain heart, her diabetes—"I sufferin' from sugar" is one of her proudest lines of autobiography—and the pains of indeterminate origin that require regular coconut-oil massages of her legs.

"I don't have long to live, Son."

To which there is no reply. She has not had long to live, by her own estimation, for over twenty years.

She sniffles, raises the handkerchief to her nose. "And I frighten, Raj."

"Of dying?" It is not a fear I feel myself. Not any more.

"I goin' to be alone."

"You still have the family—" I stop myself. We have already been through all this.

She dabs the handkerchief at the corners of her eyes, tightens her veil with a gentle tug, the golden butterfly shuddering on her head as if caught in a spider's web. "Don't go, Raj. If you go, I never goin' to see you again."

To which, once more, there is no reply: she is probably right.

"Stay with me, Raj."

I look away from her, to Grappler silhouetted against deeper silhouettes and against the sky. "You don't understand," I say. I look to the right, to the spotlight shining down on the tail of the plane seen, striped, between the thin metal bars of the railing. "You never really did, Ma."

"But, Son—"

"Time for the departure lounge, Raj," Grappler says. He does not look around, does not move a muscle.

But I immediately get to my feet. I think: It is like the first time.

Grappler comes over, takes my grandmother by the arm. We walk slowly back through the darkness to the light, down the stairs. The Lals are gone. The young man leans on the wall behind the counter, absent-mindedly chewing at a toothpick. He does not look at us. The hall is empty. The lights are bright.

I think: It is not like the first time.

She takes my face in her hands, tips of her fingers pressing steadily on my cheekbones, pulling the flesh, constricting my breathing. Her hurt, liquid eyes look up at me, look up through me, and her chin trembles. The muscles in the back of my neck stiffen, but suddenly, with a force unexpected from arms so thin and flaccid, she tugs my head downward and presses her lips to mine in a wet, fleshy kiss. I think: Like crushing raw meat against your lips. I try, gently, to pull away but she holds on more tightly. And it comes to me that this is a kiss not just of farewell but also of betrayal, each of us the Judas, each of us not.

She releases me, pulls back as I straighten up. There is, on her face, a startling look of childlike defiance.

Without thinking about it, I draw the back of my right hand across my lips, wiping away the moisture that coats the skin with the consistency of light moss. Behind her, over her shoulder and through the half-open glass door marked, in red paint, PASSEN-GERS ONLY, a man in green sits behind a high, wooden desk, elbows on the desktop, chin resting on clasped hands. He looks straight ahead, in our direction, but the shadow cast by the wide brim of his cloth cap hides his eyes. I wonder, just for an instant, what he is thinking, and I see us as he must see us.

Grappler grasps my shoulder, steps in front of me, hugs me, kisses me on the cheek, pulls back. It is all determined, all quick. He looks away, and I think: But, Grappler, you're crying. Yet I say nothing. His special quality, which I have always thought of as mythic, asserts itself more strongly now, this sense of a self contained, of thought formed but left unspoken. Grappler, a man of education, of understated confidence, has spent his professional life in government service. He has laboured in various ministries, has advised ministers, has travelled abroad in official delegations, has occupied for the last few years a room in the vast web of the prime minister's office. He is said to have whispered into the ear of the old man himself, to have travelled with him in the days before the emergence of the threat recently realized, when the old man still travelled without fear, secure in the knowledge of his return to his position of power. Through all this, through the allegations of corruption, the rumours of collapse, Grappler has served without demur, revealing nothing, keeping without ostentation the confidence of his office. And it is this that I now feel rise in him: this ability to retain. From his pant pocket he takes a little black notebook—the kind with a hard black cover, white blue-lined pages and a strap of black elastic to keep it closed, that we called a "police book" for its resemblance to policemen's notebooks—and from his shirt pocket his gold fountain pen. He slips them into my shirt pocket. "You're your own best listener, Raj," he says. "Use them."

I nod, but vaguely, through the shock of realizing that Grappler has grown old, that his hair is greyer than I've noticed, his face more lined, his eyes distanced.

He steps aside and, with no further ado, I walk straight ahead, through the doors that are for only me, up to the man in green who wordlessly takes my passport, flicks through it, spreads it out at the identification page. Fleshy face remaining impassive, he compares my face with the photograph, examining me feature by feature—seeking in the trees, I think, the look of the forest—from the tousled black hair with its part low on the left side, to the startled eyes and the rounded nose below which sit the small dark lips parted as if in expectation.

As I stand there, eyes wandering to the waiting room beyond, where other passengers, singly or in secretive groups, lounge on chairs and sofas of black leatherette, I make a conscious effort to not turn around. I have no wish to see them, the old man and the older woman, peering at me even as I retreat.

The man in green, satisfied, stamps my passport and passes it back to me, my boarding pass stuck into it, his fingers short and pudgy and pink. He motions me through to another man in green who stands beside the metal detector, a scaffold of wood forming a door that puts me in mind of a bladeless guillotine.

I walk through without incident, and the man in green pays no attention to me. I am in. Through the glass wall to my right, the plane glows bright and immense in its spotlight. And it is now that I cannot help myself, it is now that I turn around to face the entrance, and it is now that I see that they are gone, the distant door a rectangle of bright light. My disappointment—surprising and, in itself, a disappointment—is brief. But only because—and this I acknowledge—I do not wish to examine it, will not listen to it, dismiss it with a mental shrug. This refusal to entertain the uncomfortable, I see it as a kind of strength.

I turn back, quickly, to the waiting room, low-ceilinged and sombre, fluorescent lighting losing its edge in the grey carpeting and pillars of smooth, raw concrete. The duty-free shops that line the wall on the left are all shuttered or barred. The silence is brittle, as if a word or a sound misplaced would open a crack to hysteria.

The Lals are sitting in the far right corner of the room, both looking out, seeing—if they are seeing—the swatches of lawn and flowers that line the concrete walks to the tarmac. They appear not to have noticed me, and, following instinct, I become furtive. My hands work their way deep into my pant pockets; my elbows hug my waist; and with short, stiff steps, I wander over to the wall of glass, look through the spectral reflection of myself to the aircraft and the darkness beyond.

He says in a low voice, "She had long hair. All the way down to her ass."

The smell of whiskey recently drunk hovers like fog around his every word.

"And black and shiny, like the mane on a well-groomed horse."

He says he is a friend of the family; he says he might even be a distant relative, "from a chopped-off branch of the family tree." I admit, to my instant chagrin, that his face is familiar, and I wish silently that he were a relative more distant than he is now.

"The kind of hair only country girls have nowadays, know what I mean?"

He has told me his name, but I have already forgotten it.

"Know what does do it? Soap and coconut oil. No shampoo and conditioner for these girls. Soap and coconut oil and rain water from a barrel."

He is short, dressed in white right down to his shoes, wavy hair greased carefully into place.

"So the fella—in fact, the same fella who just checked us in— asked her where she wanted to sit, the window or the aisle. Well, she threw her hair over her shoulders, thinkin' about it hard-hard."

Two men in green emerge from the open door of the aircraft and trot down the metal stairway. Through the small cockpit window, the headphoned head of the pilot is just visible.

"Her mother was standin' to her left, her father to her right, and I was just behind her. So I was hearin' everything that was goin' on."

The men in green, moving with long, loping strides, head across the tarmac towards us. The hills in the distance have now merged with the sky at the horizon; but higher up, directly overhead, a lighter, softer blue prevails.

"So after a minute of hard thinkin', the girl threw her chin in the air and announced loud-loud, 'Gimme the aisle, man. I doesn't like too much wind blowin' on me'!" He cackles lowly, an ugly, hacking sound that resembles a needle rasping back and forth across a nick in a record.

The men in green march side by side up the concrete walk to the wall of glass, open the doors and stand each to one side facing one another, legs apart, hands clasped behind their backs. There has been no announcement—I still expect convention—but it is like a signal. A muted rustle fills the room: of people getting to their feet; of seats, unburdened, sighing; of bags being picked up. The room suddenly feels crowded, with people, with sound.

My distant relative walks rapidly across the room, to where he has left his bags, I imagine, and disappears into the crowd that is growing more animated with each second. It is my opportunity to escape and I take it, rapidly making my way to the door and out into the warm air.

One of the men in green blocks my way and curtly demands my boarding pass.

I show it to him, and, with a cursory glance, he turns away, to those who are following closely behind me. I hurry across the tarmac, the remaining heat of the day radiating up from the concrete, penetrating my shoes, tickling up my legs. I begin to perspire. The plane, sitting in its white light, looms not far ahead.

And then, on an impulse and without breaking stride, I glance around and up, to the waving gallery. It is dark. I see, in the light of the spotlight, the posts and railing, a faded blue. There are no faces. By the time I reach the silvery stairs, I am running.

From my seat on the left side of the aircraft, I see the front edge of the wing through the scratched window, my eyes dancing along the rivets to the wing-tip and, farther on, to the terminal, dimly lit and sobered by the lightless, lifeless waving gallery, the shadow of the control tower, squatting above it, ending in the squared green glow of its windows.

The aisle buzzes with people seeking seats, storing bags in the overhead bins. My distant relative, looking fatigued in the cabin light, shuffles in behind a couple bickering vigorously with hands, eyes and silent, furious lips. Over one shoulder he has a flight bag, over the other a garment bag. Squinting, he does not see me.

My hand fumbles at the already-buckled seatbelt, tightening it around my waist. My head leans back against the seat, turns away from the aisle. My eyes close. The lids, quickly, grow heavy and for a long moment I am lost in the insubstantial, the creamy cushion between awareness and oblivion.

Then a hand on my shoulder startles me into a breathless wakefulness, and I am looking into Mr. Lal's intense face only inches from mine. Through clenched teeth, he says, "I just want you to know, Doctor. My car. I left it in the parking lot. Open. The keys in the ignition." His breathing is laboured; perspiration shines like a moustache along his upper lip.

I open my mouth, in surprise, to respond, but nothing comes out. He suddenly pushes himself away and is gone, down the aisle, an apparition that leaves my heart thumping in my chest. I think: He's not going to make it, he's lost already.

I close my eyes once more, work my body into the seat. But that sweet zone eludes me. I hear the silence settle on the plane. I hear the engines whine to life. I hear the preflight instructions. I feel the gentle tug as the craft begins taxiing, feel it curve its head after several minutes of soft rocking into the runway, unconsciously steel my muscles for the burst of power and speed that will come after this brief pause during which the weight of the loaded fuselage seems to settle into the tires in solid, delicate balance.

And when it comes, in a disconcerting roar and a sense of power barely restrained, my elbows lock and my fingers tighten on the cool arms of the seat. I wait for that moment of uncertainty when the craft hangs precariously suspended between sky and earth, no longer of one, not yet of the other; that moment when the thump of undercarriage withdrawn announces commitment sealed; that long moment stretched thin and taut when my breath seizes and my brain scans the fury of sound for hesitation or uncertainty.

I wait for this moment to pass before I open my eyes to the cabin angled sharply upward, to the No Smoking sign winking off, to the gradual levelling, to preoccupied flight attendants bustling along the aisle to and from the galley, to an unhappy old man—a tourist, I surmise, holiday curtailed with tan only at the stage of a painful redness—unsteadily making his way to the washrooms at the back.

The window beckons and I watch, mesmerized, as we leave night behind and reach for the twilight above the thin, high clouds.

A flight attendant—young, fresh-faced, blond strands escaping from her tightly pinned hair and falling across her forehead—offers a drink. I ask for a bottle of red wine, and the simple act with simple words said almost in reflex is, to me, a marvel of normalcy long absent.

The plane banks sharply to the right, the left wing pitching upward, tip sweeping past a sky beginning to change in aspect, growing less placid, acquiring sheen and hints of colour. As it levels off, my window fills with the unseizable splendour of the sky split in two: the lower half a field, infinite and alive, of blazing orange; the upper half, separated from the lower by a line unnatural in its precision, a profound, luminous, metallic blue broken, higher up, only by a spirited star flashing over a lustrous half-moon.

Natural scenery, whether of beach or of mountain, water or vegetation, has never attracted me except in the briefest, most superficial of ways; I see it, and then I forget it. But now I gaze out, spellbound, trying to etch it all—the shapes, the colours, the intrinsic purity—into my memory.

Yet even as I stare and stare, I know that it is impossible to retain it all, that I will recall even in minutes nothing but a powerful impression of beauty.

A female hand, workmanlike, with nails short and unpainted, reaches down and unlatches my tray. The flight attendant, stray hairs tucked back into place, deposits on it a napkin, a plastic glass and my small bottle of red wine. She does not look at me, concentrates on the task at hand. I am grateful for her absorption.

For, in the last minute or so, gazing out, my eyes have grown moist and I have become aware of the emptiness of the seat next to mine.

I reach for the bottle, open it, the metal top spinning out of my fingers and falling soundlessly to the floor. I pour the wine, take a sip, turn back to the window. And the show is gone. Already. All that remains in the darkened sky are the star and the moon, and even they are being rapidly left behind. I reach for what I have absorbed and find it there, but fading, without the edge.

Memory: that is the problem. The threshold between remembering and forgetting is but a membrane of transience. Yesterday was. Now is—but only for a second.

I uncover Grappler's pen, spread the notebook open on the tray before me.

Time kaleidoscopes. The past is refracted back and forth, becomes the present, is highlighted by it, is illuminated by it, is replaced by it. In this rush of sparkle and eclipse, only the future is obscured, predictability shattered. Yesterday becomes today, today steps back from itself, and tomorrow might never be.

I think: Sharpen the edge.

2

✦

This is what I was thinking about as I sat that
day at my desk in my office.

That medicine is the juggling of possibility and impossibility. It
is much of the time a science, precise and predictable; and it is
also—more than one may wish and, certainly, more than one is
trained to admit—an informed guessing game, a spectacular version of a television game show. Its only art is to make it appear an
art, for the medical doctor is little more than a white-coated tech-
nician, trained to varying degrees, bringing to the skill varying
levels of perception and intelligence. Our certainty—"This is
what we will do, and this is what will happen"—is often just a
mask for the bewilderment—"This is what we might try, and this
is what we could hope for"—that we learn to hide, from our
patients and from ourselves. It is how we develop the necessary,
overweening confidence of our profession, the arrogance to inter-
vene on behalf of a teetering life, the audacity to plunge into a
living body to fix or excise a malfunctioning organ.

There is, of course, a therapeutic reason for all this. The positive patient puts up a better fight than the patient who, deprived of hope, cannot rally his resources; and it is easier for us, too, in the dark, quiet hours, to let our minds wander to a patient who is almost cheerfully—whether through genuine high spirits or in pure anger—holding off death than to one who seems eager to open the door to it.

But it remains a lie, and there comes a time, always, when one must acknowledge this to oneself, even though the temptation is to embrace the theatre and turn away from the inevitable despair.

To accept the impossibility of possibility: that is the challenge, to make a logical decision that the only option is an act of desperation. In the end, it has less to do with the intellect than with the emotions. To accept the impossibility of possibility, and to transmit it in a form neither brutal nor bogus: this is what I was thinking about as I sat that day at my desk in my office. For I have never, even through hours of imagining the situation, hours of silent rehearsal in the sleepless hours of the night before, succeeded in finding words adequate to the situation. How was I to tell a woman old enough to be my mother that, from this moment on, her life was to be measured in months?

During her last visit, when I had managed before the tests to offer possibility and at least a question of hope, she had spoken, curiously, of Christmas and of her punch à crème. She had, in a transparent, even pathetic attempt to deflect the conversation, described how she made it, specifying amounts and order of mixing. And in the silence that I, with difficulty, offered her, the thick, sweet drink had taken on the aura of icon, as if the need to put it all together—the eggs, the rum, the condensed milk, the crushed ice—would somehow pull her through; would, through some kind of bizarre logic, banish the cancer that had insinuated itself throughout her body.

I knew, thinking of that conversation and of the one to come, that I could never again enjoy that drink.

Her only obvious symptom had been abnormal fatigue, and she had brought me this along with her own hopeful diagnosis of a lack of iron, a touch of the anemia she had briefly suffered as a child. She had seemed embarrassed to suggest it, and I was reassuring. But that was before the tests. The memory of comforting words, of easy banter, of a frivolity even, was then, is now, a disquieting one. I was, am, diminished by it.

With a sigh that was a gulp of air, a sucking at courage, I reached for the telephone on the desk. But my hand hesitated before touching the white plastic, retreated to the tan file-folder that lay neatly in the middle of the desktop that I had, in my nervousness, cleaned and neatened. My fingers tapped at the folder, fidgeting, delaying, buying time in the hope that the words, the words that would tell all yet soothe where there could be no soothing, would present themselves.

I could not open the folder. It was all in there, the entire report that was a signpost to a dead end. I had been through the typed pages too many times, searching. Hope comes from doubt, or from the possibility of it, and in this report, with the cold hieroglyphs of technicality in which we have learnt to communicate with each other and with which we have built an effective wall around ourselves, there was but inevitability. I knew socially the man whose signature flourished across the bottom of the final page, lending the report authority and credence, and I wished, even as I recognized the professional heresy of it, that he had scribbled, along with his name, a hint of the personal, a brief expression of regret, perhaps.

My eyes fell on my name, typed onto a label stuck on the folder: Dr. Raj Ramsingh. And the title, as always in the aura of death, seemed cast in letters that mocked.

Slowly, the tips of my fingers inserted themselves under the cover of the folder, raised it; then, with swift determination, palm opening out and flipping over, closed it, pushing down on it as if to seal it.

Pushing with the tips of my shoes, I wheeled the chair away from the desk, swung around and stood up. A dull tension sat, compressed, in the muscles of my upper back.

The venetian blinds behind me were, as usual, closed, the air conditioner—constant hum creating a kind of heightened, corralled silence—completing the final insulation of the room. Open windows, the casual noises of everyday life, were distracting to me; there was, to my mind, a touch of obscenity in discussing disease, its cause, its progress and its treatment, in the glare of natural sunlight, to the blare of car horns and the yapping of dogs. It introduced an element of the erratic, this clash of the normal and the abnormal, and in its alchemy reality softened, seemed to swim in air suddenly rarefied.

So I had cut off the office with the hum and occasional cough of the air conditioner, with the venetian blinds and the cold, neutral light of fluorescent fixtures. In this atmosphere of sparsely decorated walls—only my various diplomas with their red seals broke the monotony of unpatterned, blue-grey paper—and spare, grey easy chairs with chrome arms, I could conjure up a sense of control. It was a way of combatting the sense of incapacity that my medical training had engendered in me, that awareness of impossibility that had grown slowly through the years of probing and revelation, that sense of how little control I, or anyone else, exercised over the basic ultimatums of life and death. And when it had come time to set up an office, I found that by banishing life, by constructing an almost hermetic cave, I could deal more easily with the multifaceted permutations of disease.

Yet now, on impulse, I reached for the cords of the venetian blinds and, with a gentle tug, opened them, the strips of grey plastic, long undisturbed, rising like opening eyelids.

Through the glass filigreed by dust and splattered rain, beyond the vertical waves of the black burglar-proof grille, past the spirals of branch and leaf of the sparse thornbush, the midday sun dazzled with the whiteness of fire, hurting the eyes. It was several seconds before I could make out the strip of balding lawn that fronted the building; and then, as my eyes travelled up, they were dazzled once again by the low, whitewashed fence that enclosed the property. The pressure of the light eased only as I focussed on the gas station across the street.

My mind emptied, and for a few moments I observed the pantomime of automotive service: the cars pulling in, the cars pulling out, the raising of hoods, the concentrated inspecting of hot engines, the casual unfurling of gas-pump hoses, the sauntering nonchalance of attendants, the finger-tapping impatience of drivers. And, as I watched, I found myself envying the simplicity of the activity. In the service bay to the right, glistening machinery elevated a car with powered precision. Two mechanics, stripped to their waists, one in shorts, the other in baggy jeans that seemed on the verge of falling to his ankles, shambled from the shadowed background, glanced up at the exposed underbelly of the car, gestured with indifference, spoke briefly to each other. Then, shambling still, with limbs so loose I could hear them rattling in my head, they retreated to the shadows from which they had come.

I recognized the one wearing shorts, from the week before when I'd had my tank filled. Waiting in the car for my change to be brought, I had been approached by this mechanic, from far a young man, closer up even younger. "Mornin', mister," he had said, a wrench held casually in his grease-smeared right hand.

"Morning," I replied.

"Hot today, eh, mister?"

"Very hot."

He leaned over, until he was looking directly at me through the open window. His face came close to mine, and in the sudden intimacy he said, "You can't help me out?"

I said, "Pardon?"

"I say, you can't help me out?"

"How?"

"I thirsty."

"And so?"

"My pocket empty, man. Help me out, nuh."

I looked away from his bright, brash eyes. "No."

With a suddenness that must have been practised, he glared and, between clenched teeth, said, "You must remember people watchin' you." He held my gaze for a second or two, gauging, it seemed to me, the effect of his words, turned abruptly and sauntered away, the wrench swinging loosely in his hand.

The air in the car, already thick with the smells of the gas station, grew close. I had been momentarily thrown by the threat, by its indirectness, by the almost sophisticated wording that seemed to offer warning rather than to promise violence. But, of course, that was what had been intended: a veiled promise of violence delivered with carefully weighed calculation, an offering softly spoken of a casual brutality. Understanding, I began to see the threat as an expression of failure; a dollar would have bought off his anger.

Two or three days later, once more buying gas, I had been ignored by the mechanic, hadn't even, it seemed, been recognized.

The car in the service bay was lowered back to the ground by the same powered precision that had elevated it. I watched it settle onto its tires, the black rubber puffing out a little to either side, until my view of it was blocked by a police jeep pulling to a stop before the service bay.

A sudden determination formed in me, and with a sharp tug at the cords I shut the blinds, the strips of grey plastic snapping sharply against each other. In the abrupt darkening, the fluorescent lighting went cobwebby. The room seemed full of a thin smoke. I lifted the telephone receiver and settled back into the chair.

Mrs. Lal was a stylish woman, her clothes, always bright and well cut, classic and understated rather than fashionable. At fifty-five, she looked her age, but in a healthy, satisfied way, few strands of grey showing in her hair, her skin unravaged. Only under her eyes—and this a recent development—were there signs of distress in a darkening of the skin.

But now, after the words, simple, direct, employing sparingly but indispensably the technical language of the report—I had stood back from myself, listening with a third ear to what I was saying, observing with a third eye how I was saying it, marvelling at the emotional neutrality my determination managed to effect, and at the same time hating it, wanting to rid myself of it—now the strain on her face, evident from the moment she entered the office, visibly tightened. Her eyes settled on me, immobile.

Her husband, seated on the edge of the grey easy chair next to hers, feet widely spaced, elbows on knees, hands clasped before him, stared wide-eyed at the carpet beneath the desk. Only his right index finger moved, jerking up and down in an arhythmic spasm. Age—he was no more than two years older than she—

showed more clearly in him, and it was his face, immobilized in shock, eyes contemplating already the void to come, that I found difficult. I felt, curiously, as if I were punishing him.

In the silence, the hum of the air conditioner seemed to grow louder. And in the stillness—air thickened, room contracting— even breath seemed to have stopped.

Then the air conditioner coughed, and, seizing on the opening, I said, "I'm sorry." Instant regret. At the sound of the words I thought: Stupid.

There was no reaction. Mrs. Lal stared at me, without seeing me. Mr. Lal stared at the carpet, without seeing it. They might not have heard the words, and I was grateful.

The call button on the telephone flashed. I watched it, the little yellow blinking light and, for a moment, failed to understand its purpose. Then, in a sudden fit of irritation, I seized the receiver and hissed "Not now!" into it. The receptionist's voice, a kind of squawk, was cut off only when I hung up.

Mrs. Lal's eyes had fallen to the carpet at her feet. The veins in her neck, tightened by tension, bulged.

Mr. Lal looked up at me with eyes reddened by invisible tears. He parted his lips to speak, but nothing came out. Finally, with effort, he said, "I can pay—" but his voice trailed off into a silent acknowledgement of hopelessness.

I sighed, shook my head gently from side to side. The grey flatness of the wall behind them looked, through unfocussed eyes, like ashen rain.

Again the call button on the telephone flashed. I reached for the receiver but now almost with gratitude, Mr. Lal's unanswerable plea echoing in my ears. "Yes, Shirley, what—"

The office door opened and quickly banged shut, cutting off Shirley's high-pitched protest. I glimpsed, in the seconds that it had been open, a male forearm, wrist ringed by a large silver watch, hand wrapped around the doorknob. Through the telephone, I could hear Shirley's voice, thinned, distant from her un-cradled receiver: "No, Doctor is busy, you cannot go in."

I said, "Shirley, what's going on out there?" But no answer came, the only sound now that of the abandoned line, like the passage of gently running water. Then a chair scraped on the floor, and that was all.

In front of me, oblivious to everything, Mr. Lal turned for the first time to look at his wife. His hands unclasped and, tentative, with a slowness that reflected a reaching out to the insubstantial, he wrapped his fingers around her forearm in a grip that seemed as appealing as it was encouraging.

Mrs. Lal, eyes closed, let her head hang loosely forward. It was as if her husband's touch had unnerved her.

My stomach hollowed.

The door opened once more, but this time barely an inch.

The receiver pressed still to my ear, puzzled, tensed with an urge to protect the silence into which the Lals had settled, I peered curiously at the door, watching as it was slowly pushed open by the same hand I had glimpsed earlier. Now an arm, covered to the elbow by a navy blue jersey-like sleeve, came into view. I put the receiver down on the desk, pushed myself out of the chair and walked quickly across the carpet. Almost in a whisper, I said, "What's going on here? I've got a patient—"

Suddenly I was caught up in a confusion of arms and stumbling as a man fell heavily against me. I grabbed at him, my knees buckling under the weight, and in the clutch smelled a biting mixture of perspiration and blood. He groaned, went limp. I felt myself falling backward, crumbling; and then the weight was lifted from me by two strong arms unconcerned with gentleness.

Regaining my balance, I looked up into a navy blue beret cocked high on one side, a swatch of silver lightning pinned to it; and below the black leather band that framed the forehead, a face thin and tapering, with squinted, close-set eyes, a face I knew but to which, in that flash of memory, I could not put a name.

I crouched beside the injured man—he was shirtless, wearing only khaki shorts caked in black grease—and straightened his legs, stretching him out on the grey carpet. I could feel my professional mind clicking in, and it was the untrained part of my brain that thought, with surprise: the mechanic.

Black boots of a military cut, laced halfway up the shin, crowded the doorway.

The untrained part of my brain perservered yet, offering me the name: Madera. And with it, glimpses from years distant of school uniforms, gloomy classrooms and youthful faces.

"Shirley." My voice was sharper than intended, and when she appeared at the door, ushered through the group of blue-uniformed men, her eyes were large with fright. "Open the door of the examination room, please, Shirley." I struggled to make a conscious show of calmness, asserting my authority, reclaiming my control.

She hurried across the office to the wallpapered door almost invisible in the far wall. She paused briefly, unsure, before the Lals. He now had his head on her shoulder while she, eyes closed, stroked his head.

"The door, please, Shirley."

She hesitated still, between the Lals and the door. Then, moving briskly, she reached for the doorknob. The examination room, walls of white, cupboards of white, high table sheathed in white, was brilliant in the fluorescent glow.

The mechanic's eyes glittered brightly at me, alert, angered, with no trace of alarm. He worked his mouth, licked lightly at his lips, said, "Leave me alone, don't touch me."

"Can you stand up?"

"Yeah, man." And he made an effort to sit up, supporting himself with his hands. A line of blood cut rapidly down his chin from the left side of his mouth. He fell back, chest heaving, light reflecting on his perspiring skin. "I awright," he said. "I just a little dizzy."

I checked his mouth. Bad teeth, but unbroken. The blood had come from a cut in his lower lip, bruised and growing puffy. A bump was rising on his forehead, but the skin was intact.

"Let's get him on the table," I said, hooking my arms around his knees. Madera slipped his hands, fingers long and slim, under the man's armpits, and we lifted him, fresh blood surging from the cut in his lip. His head lolled back onto Madera's stomach.

As we carried him past the Lals, Mr. Lal looked up, eyes wet and reddened, following us with a stare of incomprehension. His face, unexpectedly, distorted: I expected tears. Instead, his teeth gritted into anger, and, disengaging himself from his wife's arms, he began to stand up.

Alarmed, I opened my mouth to speak, but before I could say anything, one of the men strode over from the door and placed a hand on Mr. Lal's shoulder. Mr. Lal reacted as if attacked, spun around to face the man. He found himself staring at the perforated barrel of a submachine gun, froze, sat slowly, eyes riveted on the weapon. His wife reached out for him.

"Go home," I said. "I'll call you later." My shoulders were beginning to ache with the weight of the mechanic. "Shirley?" With a nod of my head, I motioned her to the Lals. She moved quickly, nervously, to them.

Grunting with effort, we placed him on the table. Blood coursed down his cheek, splattered onto the white sheet, and the contrast, scintillating red on pristine white, was startling even to me. Blood was part of the game, and I had long stopped noticing it except in the course of duty, with technical eyes: it carried no emotional weight. But now, in the disorientation of rush and noise, guns and uniforms, the blood on the sheet showed with a brutal beauty.

The mechanic, with a sudden movement, brought his hand to his forehead and groaned.

Madera flicked open the flap of his black leather holster.

I said sharply, "I don't think that'll be necessary," and I glanced at the hand on the loosened flap, the right hand on the back of which a small, round scar, shiny skin of a darker brown, confirmed memory and provided a further spur to it.

Madera grinned, teeth long and white picking up the harsh light. "Eh-eh," he said with a touch of the delight of discovery. "So is you, man."

"Yes. Madera, right?"

"Right. So you's a doctor now, I didn't know."

"What happened to him?"

"Nothing, man, nothing. Just clean him up a little for me. So how long you been a doctor?"

"Look, Madera, don't tell me 'nothing.' Somebody beat this man up."

"What you mean, beat him up? He try to get away."

My fingers probed tentatively at the mechanic's face, at the skull that had—it became clear in the bright light—taken a pounding.

"It ain't no big deal, man," Madera said in a mock whine that, in its pitch and its railing quality, prodded once more through years—sixteen? seventeen?—at memory. "Is just a little bruisin' up he get. Just wipe off the blood, put some plaster on him and we done."

My fingers continued their work, reading with their tips the subcutaneous contours of the mechanic. I wiped the blood from his mouth, checked the bruises on his ribs, the welts on his shoulders and neck.

Madera said, "Come on, hurry up." He was standing at the foot of the table, a slim solid figure almost sheathed in his dark blue uniform.

As I continued to feel and probe, stopping occasionally to daub antiseptic on tiny cuts and strips of scratched flesh, other blue uniforms, other berets, crowded the door to the examination room, looking in with a kind of passive curiosity.

Madera glanced at the watch hanging loosely on his wrist. The gesture caught my eye, and again my memory twitched. I remembered the watch, or one very similar to it, on Madera's wrist back then; it had seemed, on the sinuous arm of the sportsman, short sleeves rolled even higher to reveal veins and biceps, a too-obvious declaration of masculinity. But that was Madera, as I recalled him: too obvious, in too many ways, subtlety a stranger.

I was working automatically now. No serious damage had been done, at least not as far as I could tell in my brief survey, and a more thorough examination would have required more time than Madera's obvious impatience offered. Still, indicating the stomach, I said, "Inside. He might be—"

But Madera cut me off. "Don't worry, man," his tone so relaxed, so conversational, we might have been discussing the weather. "We're professionals, we ain't want to kill him." He chuckled, patted the mechanic on the leg, with the affection, I thought, of the hunter for his prey.

I said, "He should be in the hospital. Some X-rays, a few days' observation."

"Right," Madera said, and it was like a word of dismissal.

I forced a smile—this distressed me then, distresses me now—in an act of obsequiousness that I could not suppress. I said, "Then he ready to go." And, falling into the dialect, I felt unclean, not because it was concession—it wasn't—but because this was how we spoke to our maids and yardboys, as if we felt that, with their splintered grammar, they would then understand us.

Madera, as I could see in a split-second freezing of his features, did not miss it.

I moved away from the table, just a step backward but enough to establish distance, the conclusion of responsibility, and for the first time—viewing the mechanic's face and not what had been done to it—I was struck by what an unremarkable face it was, features and form indistinguishable from thousands of others, hairstyle—in an island in which varieties and designs of male headdress ran from heads shaved in patterns to long-unwashed cascades of liana-like braids—a simple patting down of the tight curls; it was the look of an accountant, or an insurance agent. It was in the eyes, dark slits of disquiet sandwiched between bunches of swollen flesh, that there was a story. But, then, there were thousands of those.

Madera said, "Khan," and one of the men, submachine gun dangling from the strap around his shoulder, walked from the door and placed himself at the mechanic's head.

"You should take him to the hospital," I repeated, knowing the words to be nonsense, and wondering, even as I spoke them, who I was trying to help: the mechanic, now, or myself, in the future?

"Right," Madera said.

Shirley had left, probably with or just after the Lals. The waiting room was empty, the other patients, the last of the Saturday appointments, having probably taken fright. After the unusual rush and activity, after the sense of crowding during which, unnoticed, my breathing had gone shallow, the deserted office seemed drowned in a silence sharpened by the drone of the air conditioner.

A string of dots, darkening on the grey carpet to a dark burgundy, led from the main door to the door of the examination room. I walked slowly to the desk and sat down. Before me, like a package of forgotten fright, was the folder containing Mrs. Lal's limited future. It seemed hours before, distress now dimly distant, that I had been speaking to her.

Both doors were open. On my left, exiting from the brilliance of the examination room, a rectangular column of light threw itself into extinction on the grey carpet. Through the main door, I could see a corner of the waiting room, lined with plastic orange chairs, upper half of the exterior wall glass-louvred, cutting the sharpness of the sunlight, giving the room a shadowed coolness. The burglar-proofing, like giant strands of wavy hair mounted at regular intervals, threw indistinct shadows onto the panes, shadows that, earlier in the day, in the directness of the early morning sun, had a presence that was as sharp and as solid as the metal itself.

I reached for the phone lying yet on the desk, still connected uselessly to Shirley's phone in the waiting room. I switched to another line and dialled the Lals' number. It rang ten times before I finally hung up.

The air in the office had grown warm, air conditioner grinding ineffectually against the open door. I was exhausted. Strands of tension knotted into my shoulder blades, rippled up my neck; I could feel, on my forehead, a frown tightening into a headache.

I slipped Mrs. Lal's file into a desk drawer, went into the examination room and took two aspirins, switched off the light and closed the door; switched off the air conditioner and the office light and locked the office door. The comfort of the routine and familiar.

Shirley had left her desk in disarray, telephone receiver uncradled, appointment book open, file-folders forgotten, and I spent a few minutes straightening things out. The building, unpeopled, exuded its age, felt heavy and dull. Its dust was beginning to settle, the dust that every morning Shirley had to brush from her desk and from the orange chairs. The floorboards creaked drily, screeches of splintering, as I moved around to the file cabinet beside the desk, the sound making me edgy, as if I were an intruder in my own place.

The front door swung open just as I locked the file cabinet. No one entered and, unsure, headache pounding now in the heat and tension, I hesitated before speaking. "Yes? Who's there?"

A voice, tremulous, said, "Doctor?"

I was relieved. "Come in, Sagar." A few more seconds passed before the little old man came in. Almost comically short, he nevertheless carried with him an air of passive tragedy, as if life had done all to him that it could and all the rest was but a futile footnote. His clothes, rumpled like his silver hair, were long un-washed; the shower I had had installed at the rear of the building behind his room was infrequently used. "Hello, Sagar, you've been sleeping?"

"Yes, Doctor. Tired." His red, wet eyes refused to focus on me, looked instead at the desk, at the floor, wandered along the walls.

"You haven't been drinking, have you?"

"No, Doctor, no drinkin'." He spoke with a touch of de-spondency.

"You've been taking your pills?"

"Yes, Doctor. Every day."

"Any problems?"

"No, Doctor."

"Everything quiet?"

"Yes, Doctor."

"Well, then, do you need anything?"

"No, Doctor."

"Okay, then."

He nodded, acknowledging the dismissal, and hurried out.

I thought: Some night watchman. But I was the only one, at this point, to cling to this illusion, I and possibly Sagar, if he ever had.

When, double-locking the front door behind me, I stepped out-side into the stinging early afternoon sun, Sagar was nowhere to be seen. He had probably returned to his room. Across the street, the activity in the gas station continued unabated, cars pulling in, cars pulling out, hoods being raised and gas hoses being unfurled. At the entrance to the service bay, the other mechanic sat looking out at the road, his baggy jeans pulled up to his knees.

I walked quickly to my car parked at the side of the building, my headache intensifying as I entered its even greater heat and, without stopping to fill the almost empty gas tank, pulled out into the fast, heavy traffic.

And this is how it began. At least, it was one of the beginnings. There seem now to be so many, each decision, each event like a catalyst, yet also like a consequence. But this, the reappearance in my life of Douglas Madera, strikes me as the most fateful. As a beginning it was decisive; as a consequence, capricious. And before it, everything had at least seemed manageable.

3

I *am, by birth, Casaquemadan; by necessity dis-*
guised as choice, Canadian.

In my study, across from the book shelves, red thumbtacks
pinned three maps, all set well below eye level, to the white wall.

The largest, in the centre, was a relief map of North America
and the Caribbean with Canada and, lower down, Casaquemada,
highlighted in red. To its left, slightly smaller, was a map of
Toronto, with Mississauga, in the lower left corner, hidden by a
glued-on maple leaf flag. To its right, of approximately the same
size, was Casaquemada, the island's flag, a flaming torch on a
field of green lined on either side by thin strips of blue, affixed to
a slice of sea in its lower right-hand corner.

The maps were my idea, mounted without reason or justification. It was simply that I liked them, enjoyed letting my eyes roam
over their intricate topography, discovering names that brought a
chuckle—Mt. Tip Top, Ontario; St. Porcupine, Casaquemada—
or evoked wonder—Lake of the Woods; Dedo Cortado. Following, or even during, times of stress, I would seek respite there in

my study, in front of the maps. Several weeks ago, for example, a young man was brought to my office; he had fallen from a coconut tree, was shaken, dazed, but seemed otherwise unhurt. I gave him a pill for his headache and told him to rest for a few minutes on the table in the examination room while I took a phone call from a colleague at my desk. When I went back fifteen minutes later, he was dead. It was a death of the most difficult kind: here one minute and, unforeseeably, gone the next. That evening, at home, I lost myself on the roads, rivers and names of the maps the way one can lose oneself—the past, the present, the future, one's very being—in the slow, steady, mesmerizing movements of fish in an aquarium.

It was only when Jan asked me about them, a glimmer of derision underlying her curiosity, that I said, "For Rohan, so he knows where he is and where he's from."

She looked balefully at them, from one to the other. "And how the hell's he goin' to see all the way up there?" she demanded with her quick exasperation.

Point: Rohan had just learned how to walk.

But I could not simply say to her, They're for me. That would have been too revealing, even, maybe especially, to her, my wife. While part of me—the part that sought at times to lose itself— was delighted by the maps, another saw them as slightly garish, juvenile even.

This second part reminded me of my brief flirtation, when I was thirteen or fourteen, with armchair radicalism. I had obtained, through an older school friend known for his intellectual exasperation, a few books banned in Casaquemada as being deleterious to the moral and political health, both fairly consumptive, of the island: Eldridge Cleaver's *Soul on Ice*, Che Guevara's *On Guerrilla Warfare*, three tattered copies of *Playboy*. The mere knowledge that I had in my possession material considered dangerous fired my imagination. I drew a poster showing a clenched fist between a quotation from Guevara—something about dying happily—and another from Cleaver, along the same lethal lines. I taped the poster, done with a black marker on white bristolboard, to my bedroom door and awaited reaction. My grandparents saw it, failed to understand it, said nothing. Grappler saw it, chuckled, said, "By the way, Raj, his name is Eldridge, not Elridge." Instant deflation. A few minutes later, I overheard Grappler, chuckling still, say to my grandparents, "It's nothing to worry about. He's young, idealistic." I quietly took down the poster, more embarrassed than hurt, hating that forgotten *d*, feeling my foolishness in this ignoble end to radicalism. I returned the books and magazines to my friend, and I like to think that, when his family emigrated to Vancouver the following year, he took them with him, securely secreted in his suitcase.

It was this memory of embarrassment, still surprisingly warm and volatile, that the second part of me offered as I watched Jan watching the maps. I could not bring myself to claim them as my own.

Yet, I thought, she knew. Or at least suspected. And she used this suspicion to humiliate me. "So put 'em lower," she said. "Down there." She was pointing to the baseboard.

So, on my knees, I lowered them.

She brought Rohan in, showed him the maps. He slapped at them a couple of times, laughed, beat on them with his tiny palms. She took a red felt marker from my desk, drew a thick line around Canada. "Your home, Rohie," she said to him. "Canada. Say it. Canada." He gurgled, laughed, grabbed at the marker in her hand, fell in his attempt, began to cry. She picked him up and took him to his room.

Crouched still beside the maps, I reached for the marker she had let fall to the floor and circled Casaquemada. The island, a dot, was lost in the red splotch.

Casaquemada. It was, even on its own map, small, shaped vaguely like an inverted teardrop or a plump sperm, so small that when, some time after our arrival, Jan asked to go for a drive in "the country," I didn't quite know how to respond. There were beaches, there were underdeveloped resort areas, there were sugar cane fields and banana plantations. But there was no "country," as opposed to "city." The island was too small, too meagre, to accommodate the concept as it existed in other, larger places. It was a geographically simple island, the northern coast dramatically rocky, with a chain of mountains extending across the top, from which the rest of the island skirted out into a plain the two sides of which met farther down in a kind of attenuated tail. In the northwest, just below the capital of Lopez City, the ground was still unformed, dank and marshy. It had been partially filled in to accommodate the highway that ran down the western coast then swung east and eventually north to link up, at the north-eastern base of the mountains, with the highway that ran east from the capital and along the base of the range. The housing development where we lived was halfway along this eastern high-way, named officially for King George V but since the Second World War popularly called Hershey Highway for the chocolate bars liberally dispensed by the soldiers from the American base farther up.

The island must have seemed a precarious piece of real estate to those who first set foot on it. Columbus, on his fourth voyage, old and sick and nearsighted, sensing time growing short and Spanish imperial indulgence dissipating, had deigned neither to stop nor even to grace the island with a name. That had been left for several decades later when a malcontent aboard a Spanish ship was marooned on the little, uninhabited island. The Spanish captain, a man not totally devoid of compassion, ordered that a hut be constructed of tree branches for the malcontent, a man of dis-putatious character named Lopez. The ship then sailed away, without fanfare, according to the captain's log, leaving Lopez to the island and the island to Lopez.

Three months later, the captain once more put in at the island to see whether the malcontent had learnt his lesson. He found that Lopez had set fire to the hut around himself, his blackened skeleton propped up, as if lounging in comfort, against a scorched beam in the centre of the ashen ruins. In his log, the captain had penned a brief entry: "Casa quemada." *House burnt.* "Lopez muerto." *Lopez dead.* And so, from these simple words, brutal in their brevity yet inconsequential among the thousands he had scribbled in his impatient script, the island got its name and its embryonic myth.

How different from Trinidad, I thought, discovered by Columbus on the same voyage and named for the three southern peaks spotted by a sailor: the Father, the Son, the Holy Ghost: *La Trinidad*, the Trinity. It seemed, in the face of our own conception in insolence, violence, fear and despair, an attractive, hopeful beginning.

Yet, in the end, despite history and myth, the particulars of genesis made little difference. The islands, along with others, followed similar paths through the centuries, changing imperial hands—Spanish, French, English—and acquiring, along with names of objects and places in three languages, a fluidity of culture.

Lopez City, a collection of wooden huts established at the edge of a swamp, grew slowly, creeping up the mountain slopes. Sugar and slavery came and, with them, revolts, burnings and the peculiar frenzy born of fantasy stirred in the nighttime cauldron of oppression, a frenzy that offered illusion as balm, magic as greater reality than the daytime struggle under vicious, watchful eyes.

Slavery went, abolished by minds that were higher than pockets were deep, the disappearance of its cruelties marking the appearance of Chinese and, in short order, indentured Indian labourers, among them the, to me, anonymous men and women who were to become my great-grandparents.

Villages sprang up in the flat middle of the island, adobe huts dusty in the dry season, muddy in the wet. Vegetable gardens, rice paddies, pottery shops, family cows, Hindu priests: an entire society established itself, transplanted from a land too large, in a life parallel to and distrustful of the former slaves, a people now wary of the sugar cane plantations in a land where the only industry of note was in those graceful, impressive, enveloping seas of green. Perceived grasping on one side, perceived indolence on the other: a mutual contempt settled in, a contempt that would mark forever the possibilities and hopes of the island, which seemed small even on its own map pinned to the wall.

Jan referred to the maps ever afterward as "Rohan's maps." But they weren't. He never paid any attention to them, and neither did she. The maps were all mine.

I was born thirty-five years ago in my grandparents' house, in the bedroom at the front that, for years, has been thought of as my grandfather's prayer room. It was, then, my parents' bedroom, the room in which I was, possibly, conceived, in which I was, certainly, born, and from which, after a year and a half of marriage, they were planning to move, to a house they had purchased not far away.

They say that my Aunt Sylvia, Grappler's wife, bears a close resemblance to her brother, my father. This may be so. Everyone who knew my father, who knows my Aunt Sylvia, says it is so. It was difficult for me to see, for I never knew my father. He and my mother, driving back to my grandparents' home late one night from a party, were hit head-on by a car driving the wrong way in the wrong lane. They were killed instantly, about a month before we were to move into the new house.

When I was younger, I spent much time studying my Aunt Sylvia from afar, trying to fit her with my father's haircut, his glasses, the greater squareness of his face. But it was difficult. Of my father I had only the photographs in my grandmother's album: shadowy, ill-focussed views of my parents' wedding; stiff studio shots of them in their wedding outfits, my mother in a sari, my father turbanned; more relaxed shots taken a year later in the same studio, before the same painted backdrop of broken Greek columns overhung by coconut-tree branches, my father now dressed in a suit and tie, my mother in a slightly tight—she was still overweight from the pregnancy—fashionable dress of the fifties with me, recently born, in her arms.

They were difficult photographs to assess. Their calculation made them unexceptional and this lack of singularity made them inaccessible.

So I studied my Aunt Sylvia for the ways my father might have been. I knew, instinctively, to look for the little things: the spontaneous laugh, the inadvertent frown, the impulsive gesture. And there were many of them, too many, for my Aunt Sylvia was a nervous woman, with a brittle laugh and edgy reflexes. I had no idea where, in her confusion of signals, I could find my father.

She, unmindful of my attentions, frustrated my every attempt. All the photographs of my parents were, as was the norm then, black and white, many of the studio prints with softened, serrated borders as if edged in lace; and they were aging, the black acquiring a glaze of limpid milkiness, the white tarnishing into a light, slightly smoked yellow, making my parents appear jaundiced.

My mind could conjure them only as two stiff, yellowish people. My skin, I knew, was darker than theirs; at least it was darker than my father's: my grandmother, with her finely honed sense of shading, frequently fretted over the fact. I was under her order, as a boy, to play only in the shade; playing cricket in my grandparents' yard with Grappler, my grandfather and various cousins, I was allowed only to bat and keep wicket, for these roles took place in the spacious garage, while the bowling and much of the fielding was done from the gravelled driveway that sloped, sunlit, gently upward to the road. My grandfather would relay the words of reminder occasionally tossed down to him by my grandmother from the dining room window one floor above: "Stay out o' the sun, Raj," he would say wryly. "Orders o' the manager." It was his only hint of irritation but, for him, it was like rebellion, and he spoke lowly. Days in the sun—as were unavoidable at the beach—were followed by evening rubdowns with coconut oil, my grandmother's panacea, for she entertained an inexplicable belief in its ability as bleaching agent. None of it helped. In the blazing Casaquemadan sun, my skin darkened, and there were times when my grandmother would consider me almost mournfully, only barely containing a click of regret. It has often occurred to me since that my grandmother would appreciate the snow and ice of the Canadian winter if only because, in the weak, indirect sunlight, my skin fades to a lighter shade of brown. I become, in my grandmother's words of admiration, "fair-fair."

Seeking to infuse my vision of my father with a colour less ominous, I turned once more to my Aunt Sylvia. I had already tried with my grandmother, but her skin, though fair, lacked youth, and it was no secret that she admired her daughter's. I once heard her say, with tangible relief, "I so t'ankful all my chil'ren fair, yes. They all get my skin. God is good." They *all* get my skin:

that meant my father, too. So I turned, after my grandmother, to my Aunt Sylvia, only to be disappointed once more.

For she was, too, a woman insecure in her appearance, with a fabled cosmetic collection. All the creams and oils and packs of one kind or another had, however, left their mark on her face. In bright light, her ravaged skin showed like smoothed beach-sand beneath the carefully patted-on powder. It was like a betrayal, and for a long time I secretly blamed her for denying me the ability to resurrect my father in imagination.

I had no such problem with my mother. She was a photograph—just that—because there never was any possibility I might be able to reconstruct her. My father's parents kept me jealously to themselves. Only once did I ask my grandmother about my mother. "Your mummy?" she said, her bustling over the stove taking on a nervous edge. "She was always readin'. Lyin' down, standin' up, at the table, in the car. Always runnin' off to the library or the bookstore. I ain't know how much time and money she waste on books. And it wasn't even as if she was studyin' something, no, she was just always readin', readin', readin'." And where were my mother's books? Did she still have them or had my mother's family taken them away? "No, your granpa sell them in the store. They was takin' up too much space, man. And the dust! He had to sell them off cheap-cheap. Books that she pay three, four dollars for he had to sell for fifty cents because she spoil them by writin' her name and your daddy's name in every one."

The message was clear from both her words and her attitudes. My mother was no business of mine: I was the only son of their first son. My father's younger brothers, one a doctor, the other a lawyer, lived abroad with their families and visited Casaquemada infrequently. Of his sisters, Indira, the eldest of the siblings, lived with her husband and four daughters in the south of the island, appearing only for weddings, funerals and, rarely, family get-togethers; Emma, the youngest, lived in childless but wealthy widowhood in her house in Lopez City; and Sylvia, Grappler's wife, had had only one son, my cousin Surein.

I was the only grandchild still in Casaquemada to bear the family name. It made me precious to them, especially to my grandmother. In this way I was brought up in the house of my father's parents, my mother's family distant, forever strangers.

I grew up with my grandparents—in what I felt to be a temporary arrangement, in a house in which, to my eyes, I belonged only peripherally—aware all the while that not far away down the road that ran past the front gate stood another house that was to have been mine in ways I could not, then, begin to imagine. It was a small house, washed in a creamy white, that I knew only from the road, its interior, never seen, intimidating in its vanished possibilities.

Grappler had rented it out to an American oil company, the income comfortably paying the mortgage and taxes, with a little left over for the savings account my parents, with one dollar, had opened for me at my birth. This money helped, years later, as intended by my parents, to send me to medical school. But that little house, and the larger one in which I lived, haunted me for years: I did not belong to one, could not belong to the other.

It is the losses I remember best, not the triumphs. Many people have entered my office, both in Casaquemada and, before, in Toronto, with complaints trivial or serious, and the vast majority of them have, in the end, been successfully treated. But recovery, always slow, is only quietly gratifying; it carries with it a strong element of relief, and not only for the patient. Death, though, with its overwhelming connotations of loss, of defeat, is intrinsically dramatic, even when it is slow and painless.

Loss. It stays with you, informs your every attitude, your every decision, your every act.

It is why I put the maps up on the wall in my study. For me. And, I suppose, for Rohan, too.

4

Rohan was asleep in his bedroom. The gates, at the front and at the driveway in the back, were chained and locked. Jan and I were sitting on the porch in the softened air of evening, she on her chair, I on mine, between us an indirect shaft of fluorescence from the small kitchen window behind us. We had been drinking, the wine bottle, sitting empty on the white tile floor, turning glacial with sweat in the heat.

Jan said, "I don't know, Raj." Her voice was weary with a complex amalgam, long familiar to me, of an unremitting exasperation and bad theatre blended by alcohol.

I waited, knowing that when she was ready she would speak. In this silence that always followed the phrase, I could picture her mind gathering the words, scooping at them and lining them up in logical order.

Finally, she said, "My mother always wanted me to marry a doctor or a lawyer. Did I ever tell you that?"

But she knew she never had.

"And if I couldn't manage that, she hoped I could be a secretary at the United Nations, of all places."

I grunted, wondering already how much of this was truth, how much dissembling, for my wife had, over the years, told tales of slippery reality.

"You see," she said, "she had high hopes for me."

"Well, you married a doctor."

"Yeah." She paused to drain her wine. The glass, grasped around the long stem as if it were a beer bottle, glinted insubstantial. "The princess married a doctor, but she sure as hell didn't get the magic kingdom."

"I don't want to argue, Jan."

"Me neither, but this wasn't in the plans, was it, Raj. Men waving guns around in your office, I mean. Jesus!"

"No, it wasn't in the plans." And the words, representative of so much, reverberated in my head. I pushed them away: "I don't want to argue, Jan." I struggled for dispassion.

She coughed into her cupped hand. She said, "My discussion"—raised her wine glass in her other hand, at me, as if in greeting or farewell—"your argument." Opened her fingers, releasing the glass.

It drifted slowly down in the thin light, inclining to the left as it fell, bursts of radiance flickering from its rim.

Her eyes, scintillating in her shadowed face, were riveted on me.

The glass righted itself as it neared the floor, the round base alighting flush onto the tiles, shattering, the stem cracking, the bowl toppling over into the shimmer of flying shards and striking itself into three heavy fragments.

The crack of disintegration cut jagged at the quiet night.

She said, "Fuck you, Raj."

And I was saddened. In the distance, through the darkness, beyond the glimmer of the streetlamps, the tires of a car screeched and, immediately, two car horns squealed angrily at each other. I tensed for a crash, a frequent enough occurrence at the crossroads where our subdivision met the highway, but none came.

She said, "I'm thinking about taking a trip. Home. See my folks."

"Just a trip?"

"I want to take Rohie with me."

"How soon?"

"Soon."

I sipped at my wine, now thick and warm, my mouth seeming to crinkle at its touch.

She took a cigarette from the pack on her lap, fixed it between two fingers; removed a match from its box and drew the sulphur head in a dry rasp across the side until it snapped into flame, spitting a minute meteor into an arc away from her. She held the end of the cigarette to the leaping flame, watched as it blackened, her face—fleshy, with squinting lashless eyes and rounded nose— intent on the task. She put the cigarette to her lips and sucked. The tip glowed red. The smoke, expelled with leisure, clouded the light, drifted steadily towards me, billowed past my face. My nostrils felt singed.

She said, "I don't feel safe here, Raj."

"Well, instead of a trip, then, how about enclosing the porch in burglar-proofing? It's the latest thing, everybody's doing it."

"I'm talking about this fucking island of yours, Raj."

"But that's partly why we're here—"

"It's why *you're* here."

"—to help clean things up for—"

"For Sagar? Your pet project?"

"—for everybody."

"Jesus!"

A plane roared by, heading for the airport.

I hadn't known how to end the sentence. I had grasped at words and offered them without conviction.

Shaking her head, she stretched out her left leg, her foot, thick ankled, red nailed, startling in its whiteness, moving slowly towards the broken glass. Her toes nudged at the pieces, jostling around the larger ones so that the light sparkled off their irregular shapes.

"You see, Raj?" She pulled more smoke into her lungs. "The fire's out. I think it went out the moment we landed."

"Not really. It's just—" But I was lying, and the lie could not sustain itself.

"It isn't what I thought it would be."

"I know that. It isn't what I thought it would be, either."

She let her head fall back, as if looking up at the ceiling. But her eyes were closed. When she spoke, she spoke slowly; and not to me, not even to herself.

It sat smooth and round in the middle of her outstretched left palm, the size of a tennis ball, sparkling in the way of a single water droplet irradiated by sunlight. She couldn't feel it; it was as if devoid of life.

Yet, it was enough.

For many minutes she contemplated it as it formed itself in her eye, impeccable, immaculate.

After a while tiny threads of silver lightning began shooting from its surface, minute, jagged bolts of incandescence that hurled themselves without sensation into nothingness against her palm. In their white light—a light that, even in the brilliance of the day that she knew surrounded her, took on a startling presence of its own—she could see every wrinkle and crease in her skin, flickering light and shadow deepening the grooves, highlighting the lines, the multiplicity of them giving her hands an aged look. A palm-reader had once said to her, "You have an old soul, you have been through this world many times." But then she had added, "Wisdom has eluded you, though. You have gone through each one as if it were a different ride on the same merry-go-round. The core of your soul lies inert."

Jan had not been bothered by this. The words *wisdom* and *inert* held no meaning for her; but the remark about the age of her soul had made an impression. It seemed to make sense: she had always felt old.

The sparks increased, forming a fuzz of light around the ball. Now, instinct told her, was the moment to throw it. Her fingers curled—she could feel that the ball had grown, yet retained its firmness—her arm straightened, stiffening at her side. She bent her knees and, with a sharp snap of her arm, tossed the ball forward. The momentum brought her open palm, empty now, directly before her eyes: how clean it looked, how transformed!

Then she looked ahead, to where she had thrown the ball. A field of white, snow-dusted evergreens of painted symmetry, a cabin beyond of newly varnished logs, its chimney of bleached river stones gently puffing white smoke into the cold, flawless blue above. Beside the door sat a large white sphere, the little ball she had thrown grown in volume.

She looked around. To her right the pines fell away with the land, sloping sharply down to the river, grey water, glimpsed through tree trunks, sluggish with ice floes. To her left the trees thickened, trunks blending into a wall that blocked from view the paved road she knew lay past them.

She took two steps forward, and in the movement was frustration. She knew the air to be cool, cold even, but she couldn't feel it.

She continued on.

At the sphere she crouched, both hands sweeping together into the white ground, emerging with yet another ball, which she set down on the undisturbed white beside the hole she had dredged. Scooping and patting, she set about enlarging it, the new ball swelling more rapidly than her hands could move, maintaining with magical precision its perfection of form and colour.

When it was half the size of the first, she hoisted it with ease, it weighed nothing, and—

"A snowman? You daydream about building a snowman?" I wanted to tease, to lighten the air.

The broken glass sat on the tiles like spilled ice.

Her chest heaved and air rushed as she took in and then expelled a deep breath.

I said quickly, "It doesn't matter."

But it was too late. When she looked at me, she was crying.

It was this way from the beginning: misunderstanding, miscalculation, miscarriage, mistrust.

She stood up, unmindful of the scattered glass, flicked the burnt butt past me into the darkness of the lawn and walked inside, through the open dining room doors.

I remained where I was, seated in the chair, wondering at my stupidity, but briefly, dismissing the questions to which, helpless, I had no answers and no file-folders full of technicalities behind which to hide. My mind emptied, seeking instead the silence of the night, retreating to the blended buzz of undefined sounds. From the empty lot next door—a plot of land once cultivated by a sullen, anonymous farmer, the tomatoes, okra and eggplant now overgrown by thick, vigorous weeds—came the cautious rustle of a scavenging dog.

I picked up the pieces of broken glass, thin and wet like shards of melting ice, held them in my palm, looked out into the night: into its stillness and the crushing hush of its darknesses.

I thought: She is over-reacting. But only part of me believed it.

The grass in the lot rustled again, the sound of soft paper being ripped not far beyond the fence.

On impulse, I stepped quickly over to the fence, the lawn soft under my sandals, the grass licking with fresh dew at the edges of my feet and toes, and I flung the broken glass into the darkness, realizing only as the pieces left my hand that this was not a casual gesture, that with my ear I had taken aim.

The dog yelped, crashed away farther into the lot.

I leaned on the fence, fingers clasping at the cool chain-link, and, for a moment, I didn't know which side of the fence I was on. I didn't even know what purpose it served.

Asha said, "God exposed himself to me." She pulled her veil— of crimson silk lightly patterned in waves by golden thread— more firmly around her head. A swatch of her hair, dyed the red-dish brown that for a time found favour with many of the "fair-fair" Indian women of the island, showed on her forehead. "God is like a movie director with a script. He will give the actor some leeway, but in the end the actor will follow the script. Of that, He will make sure."

"And free will?" I glanced at Jan. I knew she didn't approve of my challenging Asha.

"Yes, there is free will," she said without hesitation in her clipped, precise, almost robotic voice. "But it is in exercising our free will that we do what we must. We decide on our own, without knowing it, to fulfill the dictates of the script."

"Lights, camera, action, eh?" But I knew there was no provoking Asha. She was, in a stunned way, imperturbable.

Jan, her hair pulled untidily into a ponytail, took a cigarette from its pack. She hadn't slept well, looked drained in the diffused light, an uneasy mixture of the dull day coming into the living room through the half-opened windows and the yellowish glow from the small glass chandelier.

I said, "Freeze will."

Jan found my eyes and, defiant, lit the cigarette.

Asha looked from her to me. "Her smoking does not matter, Raj."

So Jan had told her about my attempts, gentle and unobtrusive, to persuade her to stop smoking.

This irritated me, disturbed me even; for it seemed, as frivolous as it was, too great a revelation of the personal. I was guarded with Asha—her religion, so all-encompassing, unsettled me— and part of me wished that Jan would be the same, or at least a little more so than she was. I said, "Ever heard of lung cancer, emphysema—"

"Words, Raj," she said calmly. "What she does will not matter. If she is to die of one of your diseases, she will, whether she smokes or not." Her thin, unpainted lips stretched into a slight smile. "The script is written."

Heavy raindrops, from the grey clouds that had been creeping in and thickening since midmorning, spattered down onto the roof, each at first identifiable, like a single clap of hands, then blending in a sudden surge into a thunderous roar. Beyond the swirls of burglar-proofing at the half-opened windows, through the electric shimmer of the rain, the sky hung a dark grey above the mountains shrouded in cloud. A mango tree, towering in a distant yard, seemed sanded into a solid, dark green mass.

I said, "So even suicide—"

She nodded, once, her large, dark, beautiful eyes, rendered theatrically mysterious by black eyeliner, shining on me with a touch of the fanatic.

I said, "Free swill."

Jan turned sharply towards me, said my name with a tinge of exasperation that I recognized as warning.

Smiling at her, I got to my feet, offered drinks and headed off, not without relief, to the kitchen. Rohan, bare-backed, small for his three years, was squatting on the carpet in front of the television in the little family room just off the kitchen. "Hello, Ro," I said. But he did not respond. "What's on?" He seemed not to have heard me; not even an eyelash flickered. I turned my attention to the drinks, wine for Jan and me, water, as usual, for Asha.

Outside, the rain continued falling through the grey light. A chill built up in the air. Before searching for the corkscrew, I put a shirt on Rohan. He was watching taped highlights of the previous week's NBA games. As I pulled his arms through the sleeves, crouched before him and did up the buttons, his eyes did not waver. I brushed the hair back from his forehead. He pulled his head back, looked past my arm to the television screen.

I went to the kitchen. On the counter, the wine bottle was beginning to sweat and the ice cubes were already loose in their aluminum tray.

Jan, in a rare moment of transport, once said of Asha that in her eyes danced the ghosts of the past and the phantoms of the future.

I thought it excessive, but said nothing. In the three years that we had been in Casaquemada, Asha was the only person with whom Jan had been able to form a friendship.

Asha and her husband Raffique lived across the street in a house not unlike ours. We met them the day we moved in, she quiet, pretty in an inexacting way, he older-looking with wavy, greying hair and a gregarious manner. They struck me from the first as a curiously mismatched couple. She, with her eyes of disquiet, suspicion and a repressed touch of the manic, was difficult to converse with. Raffique, though, fuelling himself on an unlikely mixture of beer and fine whiskey, could talk about anything, even a topic totally foreign to him, by listening closely and developing instantaneous questions, views and opinions. Talking to him was, at times, like conversing with a critical self, gently challenging. I found this quality attractive; he reflected yourself back at you, but with a slightly different shading; it was a powerful, subtly seductive tool that he used to its fullest in his flourishing import-export business. I grew quickly to like Raffique. With Asha, though, right from the beginning, I was more circumspect. Jan went the other way. After an initial suspicion, she warmed to Asha, but a certain tension—she didn't trust him, she said—remained in her feelings about Raffique.

For the first while, we met fairly frequently for dinner, at our place or at theirs. But then, as was probably inevitable, we began seeing them individually. Raffique would come over for a drink or Jan would go to Asha's for coffee on the porch. During this period, Jan's distrust of Raffique sharpened, and I came to realize that we were probably hearing different sides of the same story.

Raffique's side I knew well. From me, at least, it was no secret that he was bored and frustrated after fifteen years of marriage to a woman who, he said, considered a bed a place for sleeping in, "the snoring kind of sleeping, I mean." He spoke, with anguish, of their attempts at love-making, constructing in my mind a picture of Asha under him in bed, her teeth gritted in duty, her eyes shining with a mixture of fright and that unreadable mania. He admitted to several affairs throughout the years, breaking them off when the women demanded more than weekly trysts, divorce for whatever reason being cause for scandal in an island the size of Casaquemada, forever tainting in a way that affairs, no matter how public, were not. He had built up, too, an extensive collection of pornography—a growth industry during the island's oil boom, several private clubs springing up as lending libraries— mostly video cassettes acquired on business trips to New York. He would watch them late at night, after Asha had gone to bed.

He offered to lend them to me, but I declined, pushing away the inevitable image of his self-gratification.

It went on like this for just over a year, their estrangement becoming more and more evident, Jan's dislike of him at times bubbling close to open hostility. Gradually Asha changed, not in her manner—she remained as withdrawn and as reserved as ever—but in her dress. She began wearing plainer clothing, left her jewellery in her bedroom, dispensed with all makeup save for the eyeliner. Her self-effacement, in a strange way, said something cautionary to me; it reminded me that in every tale there are two sides, each self-serving, each self-justifying, each a truth, each an untruth.

Raffique's visits became a burden and proved a strain in my relationship with Jan. We never spoke to each other of what they told us, both guarding the secrets with what I began to perceive as an unhealthy loyalty; somehow, in being loyal to our friends, we were being disloyal to each other. I felt the gap growing between Jan and me, a gap in which swirled the substantial ghosts of Asha and Raffique's words; and one afternoon, feeling the chill from Jan's latest coffee session on the porch across the street—Asha had, at this point, taken to drinking only fruit juice—I attempted to bring up the subject with her. My words, offering to reveal Raffique's confidences if she would share Asha's, were guarded, maybe too much so. I tried to explain that we, Jan and I, would be better for comparing their stories, we would see more clearly where they each stood and where we should stand.

She reacted as if stung, spinning on me with a spitting fury. She accused me of wanting to control her, to strip her of the little that was left to her.

Stunned, uncomprehending, I mumbled inconsequentially about strangers coming between us.

"Strangers!" she shouted. "Tell me about it!" Ignoring Rohan who, playing with a truck on the floor beside us, was beginning to whimper, she blazed her unhappiness out at me. "Your island, your family, your friends. Even your skin colour. I stand out here like an albino."

I said, weakly, "But they're all—"

"Raj, I don't belong here. Everything that is mine, everything that is me, is up there in Toronto, don't you understand that?"

"But what does that have to do with—"

"Everything!"

Rohan, banging the plastic truck on the carpet, began crying. She glared at me. I waited for her to continue. But no words came. She turned, went into the bedroom, closed the door behind her. I hesitated between the door and Rohan. Then the key turned in the lock. I reached down to Rohan, picked him up. The truck fell from his hand as I hugged him to my chest, softly said his name. But he continued to cry, clenched fists beating at the air. He would not be comforted.

Everything, I had come to understand through my medical training, eventually resolves itself, sometimes for the better, sometimes for the worse, but usually for neither; not solution, then, but resolution almost mathematical with inevitability. Maybe this is what, cloaked in the mystical, Asha meant by the script.

Their rupture came, not in Casaquemada but—in a story that winged itself as if by telegraph back to the island—in Trinidad. Raffique had been on a business trip, visiting suppliers in various islands, and had arranged for Asha to meet him at the Hilton in Trinidad, his last stop. They'd planned to have a short holiday visiting friends. Raffique was to arrive on a Thursday evening, Asha the following morning. But at the last minute, Asha, on a whim, decided to go one day early. We drove her to the airport on Thursday morning. She sat, quiet and tense, in the back seat, terse in conversation even with Jan. I thought at the time that she was nervous of the flight, a slow, unsteady ride on a small regional carrier; but I've wondered since if there was not more, a clearer sense of purpose than was evident that morning.

In Trinidad, at the hotel reception desk, she identified herself as Mrs. Ali, apologized for arriving early, and requested the key to the room reserved for her husband and herself. The desk clerk, checking the reservations, wrinkled his forehead. "Mrs. Raffique Ali?" he asked. She nodded. "But Mr. Ali checked in two days ago," he said, "with Mrs. Ali." She insisted that there had to be a mistake, maybe a different Raffique Ali? She showed him their address in Casaquemada, and demanded to see the registration card. She immediately recognized Raffique's handwriting and noted, before the clerk could snatch back the card, the room number. Maintaining her composure, she thanked the clerk, said there'd been a mistake, and made her way to the elevators. The room was not difficult to find and, at her knock, the door was immediately opened, by Raffique, behind him the half-dressed nineteen-year-old daughter of his Barbados supplier. It is said that Raffique, calm, said simply, "Good morning, Asha," while the girl, reaching for her bra, demanded who the hell Asha was, to which Raffique replied, "My wife. She's early."

This conversation, repeated in every eager retelling of the story in Casaquemada, has the ring of invention; it could easily be a tacked-on ending of machismo; certainly the men, and some of the women, who repeated it did so with an edge of admiration. Those who expressed sympathy for Asha did so in a roundabout way: "When the poor girl walk into the upside-down hotel"— so-called because the lobby was set at the top of a hill, and the elevators went down to the rooms—"her whole life turn upside-down."

But whatever their conversation, when they returned to Casaquemada it was separately and to different places, Asha to the house, Raffique first to a hotel and then to a rented townhouse. A few days later, when I was, mercifully, at work, Asha spent an hour at our house with Jan while Raffique loaded his clothes, video machine and tapes into the car. I wouldn't have wanted to see him; I wouldn't have known what to say.

It was not long after this that Asha piled her clothes on the lawn in the back yard, doused them in kerosene and set them ablaze. Alarmed by the muffled explosion and the oily, black smoke that rose genie-like into the sky, Jan and I hurried over. Asha greeted us at the gate. She was serene, so much so that I thought her drugged. She had draped her red veil over her head and wound a red sari tightly around her body. She smiled, not so much at us as to herself, but said nothing.

Jan asked if she was all right.

"But of course," she replied, as if surprised by the question.

"And the fire?"

"Liberation. I'm burning skins." She smiled once more. "Fancy clothes," she said, her voice subdued but tinged with the automatic, as if she were repeating words given to her. "Expensive clothes. The immorality is evident. In different clothes, you are a different person. But each person is a lie." She caressed the edge of the veil. "Simplify, simplify."

She opened the gate and while Jan took her into the house I went around to the back to check on the fire. She had chosen the spot carefully; there was no danger of conflagration. Small pieces of charred cloth, some trailing flame, rode into the air, hesitated, floated back down to the grass. I fetched the hose, curled on a metal wheel at the side of the house, and dampened the lawn all around.

Inside, Jan and Asha were sitting in the living room, the drapes, of a heavy, red velvet, drawn closed, the room lit only by a square of white, fluorescent light from the rectangular recess in the far corner where the fish-tank used to be. I approached them. Jan stood up, placed herself between Asha and me, said, "She's all right."

"I should take a look at her," I said.

Jan put her hand on my chest. "She just needs to be alone." She spoke firmly, protective of Asha.

I said, quietly, "This isn't normal, Jan."

"I'll explain." I waited as she went over to Asha, placed her arm on her shoulder and had a whispered conversation with her. As they talked, my eyes wandered around the living room, rarely used, formal with varnished wood-panelling, heavy furniture upholstered in the same red velvet of the drapes, ornate lamps of brass and crystal. It had the feel of a museum set-piece, even the parquet floor gleaming as if newly set. And my eyes came eventually to the brilliant recess in the wall. There, on a wrinkled piece of the same red velvet, sat a framed print of Jesus, a multiarmed Hindu god in brass, a tattered copy of the Koran and, in the centre, displayed with prominence, a double picture frame holding two black and white photographs, on the left a portrait of a young man with Indian facial features and negroid hair, on the right a close-up of a pair of bare feet.

And as Jan and I left, she didn't have to explain to me what had happened. I already knew.

I saw Raffique only once after this, late one Thursday afternoon when he came to my office. The last patient of the day had left and I was preparing to go home. I had just replenished the stock of syringes in my black bag—the bag that had become an extension of me, going where I went, always at hand—and was searching in my desk drawers for my keys. He knocked at the door, came in.

I stood up, surprised and embarrassed.

He said, "Hello, Raj." He had lost weight, looked tired, but the smile of gregariousness was still there.

"Raffique." I managed a smile just as my fingers, groping nervously, discovered the keys in the pocket of my white coat under the folded stethoscope. "I was just about to leave."

"Let's go have a drink," he said.

"I can't—"

"What happen? Jan won't like it?" He shook his head, snickered. "We're friends or not?"

I slipped off the white coat, hung it over the back of the chair, picked up the bag. "You tell me."

"Come on, man, Raj. I know this really nice place down in Lopez City." He glanced at his watch. "At this time o' the day the road's empty. Is a fifteen-minute drive."

I picked up the phone, called Jan and, without quite knowing why, on the spur of the moment, lied. I told her one of my patients had just been taken to Lopez General Hospital with a heart attack and I'd be home late.

Raffique was pleased.

We took my car, leaving his locked in the driveway at the office. The last of the sunset showed an orange streaked with black on the horizon above Lopez City. As we sped along the deserted highway, the last project to be completed before the oil money dried up, Raffique spoke little. He said he was happy, business was going well even with the difficulty of obtaining foreign currency in the shrinking economy. But mostly we just listened to the radio, to the news and the local music that the station played at this time of day.

He directed me to the northern section of the city, into the low foothills, an area unknown to me of narrow, unlit roads, grassy hillsides and widely spaced run-down houses. High above us, the mountain towered black against the sky scrubbed of orange to a luminous dark blue; at the summit I could just make out the dull glow of the spotlights at the ruins of the British fort that looked out, uselessly, over the Caribbean approaches to Lopez City.

"Pull in there," he said, pointing to a small driveway dug into the side of the hill, overhung and almost hidden by trees.

"Here?" I said. The headlights picked out, in the thickness of the vegetation ahead, a rough footpath heading up the side of the hill.

"Here." He got out and stepped towards the path.

Hurriedly I switched off the engine, locked the car door and, stumbling in the darkness, followed him. We walked uphill for a couple of minutes until, from behind a stand of trees, I made out the dull lights, from kerosene lamps, of a house. "What's this place, Raffique?" I asked, but he did not answer, just told me not to worry, that I was his friend, it was his treat.

It was an old wooden house, effectively hidden from the road by the trees and grass. The door opened to his knock, and a woman's voice greeted him with a jocular familiarity. We entered a small room, a parlour of sorts, crowded with two worn sofas to either side, a battered coffee table with a kerosene lamp on it between them, faded calendars and Christmas cards pinned to the walls by large-headed brass tacks in which shivered sparks of the unsteady light.

"This is my friend Doctor Raj," Raffique said.

The woman, plump, middle-aged, her long hair, dyed black, recently washed and hanging loose around her shoulders, shook my hand with a damp, firm grip.

Raffique said, "On my account, Mammy."

She smiled, tight-lipped.

Raffique, looking around the small room, said, "Quiet this evening."

She sucked her teeth, the rush of air expressing regret. "Business slow, man. People ain't have the money to pay."

"You tellin' me, Mammy!" He chuckled. "But not to worry, I not goin' to let you starve."

She laughed, briefly revealing the gap of her missing upper incisors. "Listen, man." She took him by the arm. "I have a new one for you. Just your type. Not too ripe."

"You too good, Mammy."

"Have to keep the customers happy, not so?"

"Is the secret to a successful business, Mammy." He glanced at me, ignored my puzzled frown. "Listen, nuh, Mammy, since nobody else here, we could stay out here? The rooms kind o' small out in the back."

She turned to me. "Here awright for Doctor Raj?"

"Here's just fine with me."

Raffique was settling himself onto one of the sofas.

The woman offered a rum and Coke. "Is all we have," she said apologetically and pushed her way through a curtain to the next room.

I sat on the other sofa, uneasy. The sounds of the forest floated in from the night, filling the room with an arhythmic symphony of clicks, clacks, croaks and screeches. I said, "Raffique, what—"

"Raj," he interrupted me. "You're my friend. I want to do something nice for my friend."

The curtain to the other room was pulled aside and two girls, of no more than fifteen or sixteen, came in, each carrying a large frosted glass. A glance told me that they were of the countryside, with long, lustrous hair, dark skin and a thinness that came of early undernourishment.

One of them came over to the sofa, sat beside me and gave me the glass.

The other sat beside Raffique. He took the glass from her, took a sip, slipped his right arm around her shoulder.

The girl beside me moved closer.

The girl with Raffique put her hand on his thigh, moved it slowly to his crotch, unzipped him, dug her hand into his pants. As she lowered her head to his lap, I put my drink hurriedly on the floor, pushed away the reaching hands of the girl next to me, got up and walked out of the house into the noisy darkness.

When I got to work the following morning, his car was no longer parked in the driveway.

"We never simply dream of them," Asha was saying to Jan. "They come to us from their higher plane, and never without a purpose."

"Who does?" I held the silver platter before her and she took her glass of iced water.

Jan said, "The dead," as she reached for her glass of wine.

"No, not the dead." Asha held the glass poised at her lips. "They are alive, all of them, but in a different form."

I took my glass from the platter, laid it on the round brass table in the centre of the room, sat down across from them.

Asha said, "And when they come it is to deliver a message, oftentimes a warning."

My last evening with Raffique had left me with a sympathy for Asha. But as her mysticism grew, as she started claiming psychic power, my sympathy thinned, grew intermittent. "How disappointing," I couldn't help saying. "Phantom delivery boys. It hardly seems worth the trouble of dying."

Jan took another cigarette. "Raj, sometimes you're so—"

But Asha would not be perturbed. "They have fun, too, Raj. Where they live, it is literally a garden of Eden. Trees, flowers, birds, rivers."

"You've seen it?"

"Yes."

"You visited?"

"My mother came to me. She was standing in front of a waterfall, happy and smiling. She looked younger and slimmer than when she was on earth. As if—"

"As if she'd been jogging a lot?"

Jan barely suppressed a smile.

Asha, as always, remained unperturbed. "You are a doctor, Raj. You know the secrets of the body, but you know nothing of the secrets of the soul. I do not expect you to understand."

I considered her answer for a moment. "You see, Asha, the physical is hard enough to deal with. I don't trust realities that exist only in the mind."

"Because you're not ready to accept the spiritual side of you. One day you will be. You will grow. You will learn."

"So might you." She had stung me with her suggestion of immaturity. "Maybe one day I'll accept the idea of gods and goddesses. Maybe I'll even understand how people can worship a man who might have existed two thousand years ago. But I'll never be able to worship a living man."

"Not a man," she said with a hint of passion. "A saint."

Jan said, "He's raised the dead."

I said, "It's been done before."

Jan said, "He promises eternal life."

I said, "Can't these people promise something simple, like a car?"

Jan said, "Raj."

Asha touched her on the arm, silencing her.

Outside the rain had lessened considerably. The sky, clouded still, had brightened. The rounded, wistful sound of a conch shell being blown came in through the window. Asha sat up, listened. "I must go," she said, standing up and giving the water glass to Jan.

I unlocked the living room door and we walked out with her onto the porch. Jan offered to lend her an umbrella but she refused. The street was now lined with parked cars; various men and women dressed in white or, like Asha, in red, were hurrying through the rain to Asha's next-door neighbour at the corner. I walked her through the gently chilling rain, the drops large and soft, to the gate, unlocked it and let her out. She thanked me and, as she turned to go, looked me directly in the eye and said, "Watch out for lightning."

I said, "I can't even hear the thunder."

That evening, the television news told us of two burnings, a cinema and a jewellery store. As the screen flickered with black and white images of leaping flame and falling timber, the modulated voice of the news-reader spoke of speeding cars and Molotov cocktails, of shadowy young men scampering away into darkened side streets. Jets of white water played on the dancing shadows. Helmets glinted in the light. And, on the edge of the crowd, well-built men in tight uniforms stood serious and immovable, submachine guns held across their chests, berets pulled low on their foreheads.

Jan and I finished the bottle of wine and, later, after dinner, while I went through the new issues of the medical journals in my study, she spent the evening playing with Rohan.

5

My *grandfather's prayer room looked out onto a* patch of lawn, the grass, originally dug up from the roadside, thick and wide-bladed and of a deep, dull green. It ended, not far ahead, at the fence, four feet of concrete bricks, painted cream, topped by three bars of metal piping, each a foot apart from the other, painted a silver that shone dully in the sun. Just beyond the top railing was the narrow asphalt road that seemed to me the only line of defence from the forest that sat, dense and sullen, on the other side.

When I leaned just a bit through the window—cautiously, for instinct, if not memory, recalled an early tumble to the grass several feet below—the rest of the front yard came into view. To the right, the gnarled mango tree, its permanent shadow keeping the ground beneath dank and musty. To the left, a concrete path, covered with an oxblood red, paint laid on so thickly that it tickled at the soles of bare feet, linked the front gate—a frame of thin metal piping swathed in chain-link—to the porch. Between the path and the gravelled driveway that, sloping downward along the grey brick wall, separated my grandparents' property from Mrs. McLean's, was my grandmother's "flowers garden," as she called it, a little square of earth delineated in brick and crowded with fragile plants that flowered infrequently. It always intrigued me, this garden, for it was the only part of the front yard that went largely ungroomed, except for the occasional weeding that my grandmother insisted on doing herself.

It intrigued me because the rest of the front yard inspired in her a passion for neatness. From the porch, she would survey her domestic domain with a double vision, the one private, the other public; and when, as invariably happened, she spotted a problem—a chip in the painted walk, say, or a few unruly blades of grass—she would mumble tersely, "Look at that, look at that! But what people goin' to say?"

The lawn was kept short, tight, carpetlike with weekly trimmings by Wayne, a boy six or seven years my senior; he lived with his parents farther down the road in a house of weathered wood and adobe, mysterious in the grip of vegetation, a house that seemed forever on the verge of vanishing into an embrace of leaves and branches. Every Saturday morning at five o'clock, when the sun was not yet up, the air still fresh and the sky a cool luminescence, Wayne would arrive with his cutter, a slim blade set at an angle at one end of a long wooden handle, sit on the steps in front of the porch, balance the cutter on his knees and sharpen the blade. Often, the soft, rhythmic rasping of file on metal insinuated itself gently into my sleep, nudging at me like a whisper, bringing me softly to wakefulness in the webby darkness of my room; and, for a long moment or two, I would imagine that I was hearing the wheezing breath of the house, dust seeping through the cracks in the floorboards and the wooden walls that divided the concrete shell into rooms. I would ease myself out of bed and tiptoe through the darkened house to my grandfather's prayer room.

The room, small, crowded with boxes and a trunk that seemed always to have been there, exuded its own peculiar smell, a thick odour of dust, perfume and burnt oil. It hovered most strongly at my grandfather's altar in the corner behind the open door. A two-level stand draped in a thick green brocade busy with vines and leaves in silver thread, it was, to my eyes, a confusion of brass plates and brass vases; brass gods, multiarmed, and pictures of gods, monkey-faced; wilted flowers and tapering mango leaves; and *deeyas*, the small earthenware lamps, cottonwool wicks burnt halfway down, from which rose the smell of burnt oil.

Enveloped in the smells, I stood always about a foot away from the window and watched as Wayne, wearing only a pair of ragged khaki shorts, a shadow in the dim twilight of the coming dawn, set about cutting the lawn. He held the cutter in his right hand, arm stiffened, blade resting lightly on the grass, as if measuring with the wooden handle the distance between his hand and the ground. Then, after a slight movement of the blade to the right, he described a circle in the air with the cutter, elbow loosening slightly as his arm stretched vertical, locking tightly once more as the blade, gathering speed, descended to the lawn, shaved swiftly through the grass and, without pause, swept into the air for its next approach; it was at this moment, as the blade reached vertical, that Wayne took a little step forward, bringing a fresh swatch of lawn into the path of the sweeping blade. And so it went, mechanical, controlled, swift, with a mesmerizing precision. As the sky brightened, the defined muscles of his arm and back would stand out in relief, his dark skin lustrous with perspiration; the whetted edge of the blade, wet with dew, flashing in the air, the shavings of grass, dark still, flying like slivers of stiff silk.

I stood at the window and watched as he covered the entire lawn, pausing only if the blade bit into a stone. There was something in this act—an act, it seemed to me, of holding off jungle, of beating back an insistent interloper—that I envied; there was something in it, a determination casual in its execution, that I longed to emulate. My grandmother, of course, would not hear of it, looked at me in horror, inquired quietly whether I had gone mad, and told terse tales of decapitation and dismemberment by inexpertly handled cutters. "Go and study some arithmetic," she said the one time I dared ask. "Is in your books you going to find your future."

"And Wayne?" I said. "Where he going to find his future?"

She did not reply, just turned back to the stove where, in a black iron pot of sizzling oil, she was frying chickpeas into spicy *channa*.

Of Wayne I knew little. He had been to school—he could read and write—but had been withdrawn early in order to add to his family's income. His elder sister, a store clerk, lived in Lopez City and visited Salmonella—the name of our little town, bestowed by a piqued Canadian missionary doctor, the meaning of which I discovered only much later, when I was in medical school in Toronto—as infrequently as possible. His father, a sullen, distant man with a reputation for bouts of incoherent outrage, drove a taxi between Salmonella and Lopez City; his mother, a woman of ample size, quiet, and acknowledged as a "hard worker" by my grandmother, was a washer of other people's clothes, including ours. Wayne, as a young boy, would sometimes accompany her to my grandmother's, sitting idly beside her during the two or three hours that she spent at the large concrete sink beneath the house. My grandmother took to sending him on little errands and, eventually, for lack of anything else to do, he fell into a part-time job. When, as was inevitable, he was taken out of school to look for work, my grandfather hired him.

But his job went undefined. He was an employee of the store and spent his time there stacking boxes, washing the sidewalk, sweeping the floor. But my grandmother had first call on him; she could summon him away whenever she wished, and at her phone call he would make the half-hour trek to the house in order to run a five-minute errand to the store or to behead a chicken. He would arrive sweaty but good-humoured, trot down the driveway to the back stairs and, rubbing one bare dusty foot against the other, wait for my grandmother to call down her orders. She would begin, without fail, by berating him for his slowness in getting there and then, in the tone of impatience she reserved for the hired help, give him his instructions. He would look up at her, hands clasped behind his back, listening intently.

And staring down at him from another window, keeping myself concealed behind the curtains of white lace, seeing the beads of perspiration glistening on his forehead, seeing his eyes squint against the glare of the sky, noticing the neatness of his worn clothes, I felt a kind of embarrassment, for him and for me. For I was required in my grandparents' house to perform no duties. Only occasionally did I sweep the porch, carefully guiding the broom up and down the rows of tiles in search of every speck. But this was a game with my grandmother: she would ask me when there were visitors, to show her control of me; and I would comply, with a confusing mixture of shame and pride, humiliated at fulfilling Wayne's function but anxious to prove myself equal to the task.

And I wondered at this difference between Wayne and me, this difference that permitted me to watch him but not to help him. I was disturbed by it, for him and for me, and tried without success to see myself through his eyes. I thought he must be angry with me, must view me with a certain contempt. Observing him, though, being wary of him, I could not get far beyond his easy friendliness. It was as if he considered us equals, almost; and if I considered us equals, or even felt myself in some way challenged by him, it had to be kept secret from my grandmother, for not only was Wayne poor and hired but he was also black, reason enough for my ambiguous feelings to cause scandal.

One Saturday afternoon, as I was reading in the porch, my mind drifted, the printed words fading away in midsentence, and it suddenly came to me to exercise my authority. Across from me, in the wooden chair she claimed was good for her back, my grandmother was making her way through the newspaper, painfully, her weakened eyes squinting, lips moving silently from word to word. In the yard, his bare back shining in the hot sun, Wayne was painting the concrete path. He was drawing the paintbrush, bright with the usual oxblood red, slowly along the edge of the concrete, careful to avoid the reaching blades of grass. On impulse I rose in the still, thick air, leaned on the bannister and called out, in a voice thinner than I'd wanted, "Eh, Wayne boy"— the "boy" borrowed from my grandmother—"you can't work faster than that? Your father is a snail or what!" And as soon as I heard myself, as soon as I recognized the voice as that of my grandmother, my face went warm with shame and I understood that I had crossed a boundary I had not wished to cross.

My grandmother looked quickly up at me, noncommittal, and went immediately back to her newspaper.

I laughed hollowly, trying to make light of it.

Wayne did not respond, did not even look up, just quickened ever so slightly the strokes of his brush. It was after this that I detected in his attitude towards me a shy, embryonic deference, as if he sensed that, one day, despite the difference in our ages, he might be dependent on me for his living; he assumed, as did others in the family, that I would one day inherit my grandfather's store, as my father had been meant to do.

This responsibility seemed then, at the age of ten or eleven, awesome. And unwanted. Yet it seemed, too, only natural. I comforted myself: such was the way of the world, such was the life into which I had been born. We hired them; they depended on us. We, they: that was the way it was meant to be.

But I never again gave him an order and, deep down, never lost the shame that had come to me as I stood there that hot afternoon, at the bannister, on the porch, the tiles, cool under my bare feet, suddenly, and irrevocably, chilled.

I held the mango leaf lightly by the stem, between thumb and forefinger. It was wide, tapering gradually to a point, of a deep green shining as if waxed.

Angela said, "You have to do it slow."

I said, in irritation, "I *know*. Stop botherin' me."

We were sitting crosslegged on the cool concrete floor beneath the house. Spread before us on a piece of cardboard was a bed of earth, dug up from the anthurium bed that lined the back fence then shaped into a square and patted down tightly. On the earth, damp and dark with the cow dung that made it ritually acceptable, I had traced circular patterns in flour, placing in the centre a *deeya* lifted from my grandfather's altar, two half-wicks, damp with oil, twisted together to form a whole. Along the border, we—in this, I allowed Angela to help—carefully arranged the various flowers we had gathered from around the garden. With a can of water and the mango leaf, we were ready to perform a *pooja*, I the pundit, Angela, a kitchen towel draped veil-like over her head, my helper.

Angela, a year or two younger than me, was the daughter of my grandparents' neighbour, Mrs. McLean. She was fatherless, Mr. McLean having, according to my grandmother, "taken off" to Trinidad in search of work. We had long been playmates. Her mother, young, neat, smelling always of a sweet powder, was a teacher at the Salmonella Presbyterian School, in charge of the five-year-old newcomers. Patient, strict—qualities she carried with her even at home—she had what was to me a fascinating talent for sharpening pencils, shaving them with a sharp pen-knife, exposing the fresh, bright wood under the paint and creating a point of needlelike impeccability. So entranced was I by the blurry flash of the blade, the tiny woodchips spitting onto her desktop, the magical paring of the lead point, that at times, bored with scratching the alphabet or cardinal numbers in my copy book, I would purposely snap the point and take the pencil sorrowfully to her. This came to an end one day, however, when, after four sharpenings within an hour, she took away my pencil and gave me a ball-point pen. There was no scolding, just the firm imposition of a solution to the problem. But to me it was like punishment.

I was about to dip the leaf into the can of water when it occurred to me that something was missing: fire. I had forgotten to light the *deeya*. Just as I put down the leaf and reached for the box of matches in my pant pocket, Wayne trotted down the back stairs, a cutlass in his hand.

He grinned at us. "Hello, pundit," he said.

I glowered at him and waited until he had walked past, making his way to the chicken coop behind the garage. He was going, I knew, to slaughter dinner.

I struck a match and held the flame to the wick. It caught, burned for a second or two, and went out. I tried again, exposing more of the wick, but again failed. Frustration, for I associated with all Hindu ceremony, in addition to the dirt and the cow dung, the flowers and the water, a thin smoke and the smell of burning oil. I compromised. Into the *deeya* went ten match heads, the sticks arranged in a grid on top of them. I threw in a lit match and pulled back. Nothing happened. I leaned cautiously forward and grinned in triumph as there came a sizzle and flash of flame, and a meagre braid of black smoke wound itself into the air between Angela and me.

"The water now," she said, more intent than I.

"I *know*!" I reached for the leaf. "Who's the Indian here?"

From the chicken coop came the flutter and cackle of panicked poultry.

I dipped the mango leaf into the water.

Angela said, "Two hands, Raj."

I sucked my teeth. She was not Indian, she was black; she was not Hindu, she was Presbyterian; and, usually, neither fact was of any consequence to me, as they were to my grandmother, who, on seeing either Angela or her mother, would say a coy "hello" or "good morning," twitter nervously and pretend to be busy. But at this moment, I resented her—of all people—being right. It was with a distinct lack of enthusiasm that I sprinkled the water over the little altar. The fire in the *deeya* died, the smoke disappeared.

"You have to say the words, Raj."

"I ain't know the words, awright?"

The panic in the chicken coop increased. A cacophony of squawks and flapping wings filled the drowsy afternoon.

She said, "Is easy, man, Raj."

"Oh yeah? It not like the Lord Prayer, you know." That would have been easy. Every morning at school, the free-standing blackboards that divided the building into classrooms were removed so everyone could see the central stage. Led by a teacher, we would sing a hymn or two, listen to a blood-curdling biblical tale from the headmaster—hundreds of thousands were enthusiastically massacred in his retellings, religion as gripping as the war comics I often read—and end the "worship" by chanting the Lord's Prayer. Then the blackboards, either side offering chalked-in information on Civics or Hygiene or The Kings and Queens of England, were put back in place and we, sufficiently fortified, scared witless, got down to the work at hand.

Angela said, "It does go like this, not so? Oooommmmm, Shanti, Krishna, oooommmm, bugga-bugga-bugga, ooommm..."

I sucked my teeth again. "Shut up, you soundin' like the chickens."

"You could do better?"

But I couldn't. I threw down the mango leaf.

The panic in the chicken coop had subsided. Wayne had found his victim. Now only one bird screamed, a hoarse, crazed cackle that tickled like cold needles up my spine. I knew he would be bringing it over to where we were, to the garden tap that sat on a length of vertical pipe not six feet away, looking like an alert grey flamingo.

Angela said, "You not goin' to make the mud balls, Raj?" It was normally our favourite part, mixing a bit of water into a handful of the soil, fashioning several balls from the paste and placing them with care among the flowers. It seemed always an important part of the pundit's function, this relished moulding of rice or earth with the fingers and palms. But I had lost interest.

The squawks of the chicken grew louder. I looked around. Wayne emerged from behind the garage, the cutlass swinging from his right hand, the chicken tucked under his left arm, its neck grasped securely in his hand to prevent pecking.

Angela said, "Oh gawd, he goin' to kill it?"

I said, "What you think? The cutlass ain't for ticklin' it, you know." I uncrossed my legs and swung around, preparing for the spectacle. But inside, I was nervous.

The back yard before me, hidden from prying eyes, had been left largely untended. The lawn, patchy, broken by occasional mud puddles—the depression in which the house was set levelled off here, the ground, undrained, remaining permanently moist—was shadowed, crowded by a couple of orange trees, a spindly lime tree with mildewed branches and, at the back where it ended at a concrete wall growing mossy at the base, a towering breadfruit tree in the corner to the left, the anthurium beds in the middle, several banana trees to the right. Beyond the wall, massive trees of a dark, wet green, leafy and liana-draped, marked the plot of land, enclosed by a wooden fence, that was my grandfather's private retreat. It was there, after lunch on Saturday afternoons and attired in a frayed white undershirt, worn, baggy pants and rubber boots, that he would disappear with his cutlass, his hoe and rake, emerging two or three hours later mud-splattered and sweaty, a self-satisfied grin on his face, the veins on his arms swollen into bluish cords.

Angela said, "You not goin' to watch, eh, Raj?"

"What happen? You frighten?"

She hesitated. "No."

Wayne, ignoring us, crouched beside the tap, gently lay the cutlass across the shallow drain and, the chicken still firmly grasped, turned on the water. Milky with chlorine, the water crashed onto the drain, darkening the smooth concrete, highlighting the slight gouges made in its surface by previous blows of the cutlass.

Angela slipped the kitchen towel from her head, twisted it into a rope, began winding it tightly around her hands. But her eyes were as mesmerized as mine by the falling water, its splattering thud onto the concrete, its droplets spitting onto the flat, black blade of the cutlass.

Wayne lowered his left knee to the ground. Slowly, his right hand replaced his left around the chicken's neck, while the left slipped back and wrapped itself around the legs, yellowish spindles that jerked spasmodically. With arms tensed—knots and strands of muscle straining through fine, dark skin—he pinned the chicken to the ground, trapping its flapping wings, the right under its own body, the left under his left hand; the head and neck he positioned on the lip of the concrete drain. The bird, immobilized, went strangely silent, but its head continued to wriggle and fight, as if reaching for air, its left eye, wet and glittery, jumping wildly in the socket.

I was suddenly cold, as if fevered, and a droplet of perspiration oozed from under my skin, tickled its way down my neck and chest. I thought, chilled, of a centipede.

Wayne reached for the cutlass and with a quick movement

raised it into the air. It twitched once in his hand, then twice, as if impatient to strike, but each time the chicken writhed in frenzy.

The perspiration hesitated as it reached my stomach. Angela, behind me, exhaled strongly, as if with effort. I forced saliva down my dried throat and the movement, like a shuddering of my body, jarred the perspiration into a rapid descent to my navel.

The cutlass fell, a blur that took me by surprise.

I thought of my belly opening up, flesh sliced open by the perspiration.

The cutlass clanged sharply on the concrete.

I thought: He missed.

Red liquid spurted.

I thought: He's cut himself.

But no. The head of the chicken, beak closing slowly, lay in the drain, pink water swirling around it. The neck, stiff, shot blood.

Behind me, Angela retched, choked. A burning sourness rose from my stomach to my mouth. I clapped my hand over my lips and clamped my teeth hard together.

Wayne removed his hand from the body of the bird, held the blade of the cutlass out to the falling water.

And suddenly the chicken was airborne, wings flapping, claws opening and closing, neck spurting blood. It headed towards us, flew over our heads, hit the ground behind us hard, ran, took to the air again, thudded down onto the gravelled driveway and trotted, its movements swift and mechanical, into the garage.

Wayne, stunned, looked up in dismay. His mouth fell open. The cutlass clattered to the drain. Disbelieving, he followed the chicken with his eyes, looked down at the head lying at his feet— the beak now opening, but more slowly than it had closed—and up again. Then he jumped to his feet and ran past us to the garage.

A warm liquid coursed down my chest. I turned to Angela. Blood was in her hair, blood streaked down her cheek, soaked into her dress. Warm liquid dripped from my hair onto my forehead. I wiped at it: blood. And across our little altar—on the patterned flour, on the *deeya*, on the flowers—splotches of more blood.

The chicken, slower now but agile yet, dashed from the garage and up the driveway, Wayne in desperate pursuit.

My grandmother, in her precarious way, as if always about to fall, hustled down the stairs. "Wayne boy! Wayne!" she shouted. Then she saw us.

Angela began to wail.

My grandmother, horrified, screamed. "But what all-you children doin'?"

I pushed at the altar with my toe. "Playin' *pooja*," I said.

That evening, as we ate the chicken, now stewed, my grandmother said, "You like playin' pundit, Raj?"

My grandfather, slicing a chunk of boiled plantain with his fork, chuckled to himself.

I did not answer. All my concentration was going into chewing the chicken: I had decided, for pride, to force myself.

My grandmother said, "You think you want to be a pundit when you grow up?"

The piece of chicken between my teeth went viscid. The severed head came to me, its beak opening and closing, its eye glazed and sparkling.

"Eh, Raj?"

The thought horrified me. I did not like the men who were pundits. I did not like the way they were catered to by tittering, subservient women; did not like the way, seated after the ceremony in the company of men, they shovelled enormous amounts of food from banana leaves into their mouths, the juices running from between their fingers down to the elbows; did not like the furtive way in which they pocketed their payment before hurrying off to another prayer meeting or a wedding or a funeral. And it was well known that to be a pundit one needed an overweening fondness for rum, so that one could collect enough bottles to hold the various liquids—the water, the perfumes, the clarified butter—of the calling.

My grandfather, picking up his glass of the strawberry pop that we called red swee' drink, said, "You goin' to have to learn Hindi, you know."

Hindi. Angela's *ooomm-bugga-bugga*. The language my grandparents used when they wished to keep their conversation confidential. The tongue pundits used for their unintelligible chanting; but even when they switched to English, their words, individually recognizable, added up to nonsense.

My grandmother, clearly enchanted by the idea, said, "I could teach you."

The chicken sat heavily in my stomach. In my head, it was flying again, spitting blood. I said, "No."

My grandfather grinned, sipped his pop. My grandmother looked regretful, said, "Pundits does make good money, you know. People always marriedin', people always deadin'."

"No," I repeated. "I doesn't like eatin' with my hands."

"Your hands?" My grandmother sighed. "But you have to. People does eat Indian food only with their hands. Especially the pundit."

"I like forks, Granma."

She went wordless and, after a moment, I thought she would cry.

When, several years later, it came time for me to leave Casaquemada, my grandmother asked if she could arrange a *pooja* for me, to call down celestial blessings and for luck. I refused, harshly, but it took Grappler, with the quiet backing of my grandfather, to convince her to leave my luck to chance.

6

━◆━

It was at the shopping mall about a week later that Jan and I ran into my cousin Surein.

We had been to the supermarket, a game, at the best of times, of guessing and hope. Just as the previous week, there had been no butter, chicken, eggs or cheese, but the sugar shortage of the last couple of months had been relieved by an emergency shipment from Guyana. Pushing the shopping cart along the aisles, between shelves packed with canned Japanese fish, British biscuits, Danish cookies, local rums, California whites, French reds, Portuguese roses, potato chips and candies, chocolate bars and maraschino cherries, I couldn't help but wonder at the strangeness of it all.

The oil money, so easily acquired, flowing to the island not from effort but as a consequence of distant events, had given Casaquemadans cosmopolitan tastes. We came to prefer the frozen to the fresh, paper to peel. Crystal was imported from Italy, glassware from Germany, leather goods from Brazil. The roads became clogged with Fords and Chryslers, Mercedes Benzes and

Rolls-Royces, Toyotas and Hondas, Suzukis and Hiaces. Fortunes soared. Women flew to Miami for day-long shopping trips. Champagne was bought not by the bottle but by the case.

And in the midst of all this, as the electric can-openers buzzed and the microwave ovens hummed, as supply helicopters clattered to and from the off-shore oil rigs and laden container ships lined up off the Lopez City docks, sugar—long the mainstay of the Casaquemadan economy, the crop that lent the island value in the first place—tumbled casually into agricultural ignominy. Oil climbed in importance from third place, after sugar and tourism, to first, while sugar tumbled to fourth or fifth and tourism fell to inconsequence. Only the hotels missed the tourists, but surely I was not alone in my disbelief as every morning I spooned an artificial sweetener—*Product of the U.S.A.*—into my coffee.

We made our way past idle bagboys waiting at the entrance, lanky young men with nervous, watchful eyes grouped before stacked boxes of Arawak, the local beer produced, it was popularly claimed, in a stable at the racetrack. Another bagboy strolled along behind us, pushing a trolley with our paper-bagged purchases from the lightly cooled air into the greater heat outside. Past the armed guard sitting at a table leafing through the newspaper. Past a middle-aged woman selling sticky homemade sweets from a tray. Past a cluster of youths, male and female, overdressed, overloud, standing aimlessly in the afternoon sun. To the carpark clotted with cars and vans, various vehicles creeping along the lanes in impatient search of a vacant spot.

We wound our way to the centre of the lot, to where we had left the car. I opened the trunk; the bagboy lifted in the groceries. Jan, balancing Rohan on her left arm, dug into her purse for the tip.

A voice from behind me said, "Here, boy, catch!" And the spinning silver disk of a coin flew over my shoulder into the suddenly juggling hands of the bagboy.

Jan, looking over my shoulder, said, "Surein." The tone of her voice told of a barely unspoken expletive.

"Hello, Jaaan." He clapped me on the shoulder, said my name in greeting.

Jan took another quarter from her purse, gave it to the bagboy.

Rohan slapped Surein's hand away.

The bagboy, pocketing his money, headed off among the cars back to the supermarket.

Surein said, "Fifty cents, Jaaan? But you going to spoil the natives, girl." With one hand he seized both of Rohan's flailing arms and, with the other, roughly mussed his hair. Rohan yelped in protest.

I said, "Take it easy, Surein. He's tired."

He laughed, released Rohan's arms.

Jan, defensive, said, "I always give them fifty cents."

Surein turned to me. "You have a generous wife, Raj."

I nodded, smiled thinly. With Surein, reticence came naturally to me. My junior in years, he had seemed always my senior in every other way, with a cunning barely concealed yet unreadable dictating his every word, his every action.

He said, "All-you going home now?"

Jan said, "We have to give Rohan his bath."

But Surein, true to himself, ignored the message. "We'll follow you."

Jan frowned, her broad face, grown fleshy recently, tightening into unhappiness.

I said, "Lenny's with you?"

He nodded. "He just pick me up at the airport." He looked around. "Now where that damn boy gone?" He spotted him six rows of cars away, peering with several others into the exposed engine of a Lamborghini. Surein shouted his name twice, and finally, Lenny, thin and wild-eyed, with a shock of wavy, unruly hair, looked up. Surein, walking off, said, "See you at the house." In passing, he slammed our trunk shut, the sound dull and hollow in the thick air.

Jan soothed Rohan, agitated still, his hands pushing hair away from his forehead. We got into the car, its interior heated to a torrid breathlessness. Jan settled Rohan on her lap as I eased the car out of the spot into the lane and began snaking through the lot, past the tightly parked cars to the outer lane, past the little stores and boutiques dark behind large show-case windows crowded with objects gaudy and shiny, past the cinema—garish posters advertising kung-fu movies and Bombay film-factory musicals—in front of which idled groups of young men in challenging, audacious pose, past the private security jeep with two armed men permanently posted since violent robberies of the cinema and the supermarket, past a gaggle of ragged children, seven- and eight-year-olds unkempt and unwashed, their oily hair cut as if with a dull knife, bare feet cracked and dusty, vociferously offering for sale tomatoes or cucumbers or clutches of spotty bananas, cautiously to the exit through which, in nonchalant defiance of the large sign, cars regularly entered. The road was clear and, manoeuvring carefully around a wide pothole, I pulled out and started for home.

Jan locked herself into a charged, angry silence, gazed out the window at the passing fences, neat lawns and shuttered modern houses.

There was no point, I knew, in talking about it. We had been through all this before, many times. She was as aware as I that there was no preventing Surein's visit, for it was the way of the island, intrusive, irresistible. People—friends, family—would turn up unannounced, expecting to be entertained and, if the time were appropriate, also fed and watered. We would have to close the books if we were reading, turn off the water if we were showering, arise if we were sleeping, and offer the unexpected visitor coffee, cake, cookies, wine or a meal, all accompanied by smiles and reams of inconsequential chatter.

It was to Jan an intrusion, this privacy that held always a public element, while to Casaquemadans, to my family and friends, it was a right they could not imagine being denied. Jan at first made no secret of her feelings, accepting with equanimity the inevitable unpopularity that her frankness attracted. Mine, with the possible exception of Grappler, was not a family that appreciated honesty; it was one that demanded games.

We were still at my grandparents', sometime in the early months after our arrival, when Jan first encountered—and I was reminded of—the importance of social and familial submission.

It was a sultry Sunday afternoon and we were asleep in bed, drugged by the heat, the eroding power of which, distant in my memory, had left us stunned. We had opened the windows, drawn the curtains in vain attempt to effect at least an illusion of cool in my childhood bedroom, and the effort had lodged itself in my dream: of frost, of ice, of wintry sparkle. In the grip of the subconscious, cool and delicious, I heard my grandmother call my name, softly, once. I held on tightly. She called my name again, and my grip loosened. She said, "Raj, you awake? You awake?" Jan, pressed lightly against me, stiffened as my grandmother's voice nudged at her. I awoke, remained still, and with my hand, unseen in the webby darkness, urged Jan not to move. Then, through my closed eyelids, the ceiling light flashed briefly. My grandmother quietly called my name. I did not react. The light flashed again, and again she softly said my name.

This time I gave in. "Yes, Granma?"

"Oh!" she said in feigned surprise. "You not sleepin'?"

What was there to say? "No."

"Good. Your Auntie Indira here. You comin' out?"

"Coming."

She closed the door.

Jan said, "Shit, I don't believe this."

"Welcome to my grandmother," I said, as she grew angry at my ambivalence and I, sitting up in the bed, was reminded of childhood and of being obliged to kiss remote aunts and vague uncles, strangers whom I neither knew as people nor cared for as relatives, but whose cheeks demanded an affectation of affection.

That first time, unsure still of herself, unsure still of my grandmother, Jan complied, shyly, kissing my father's youngest sister, her absorbed husband and all four daughters, each as primly pruned as a pampered poodle.

In our own house, though, Jan became more severe, never turning anyone away but unmistakably displaying her displeasure with a reticence and a withheld smile. It was with Surein—following now not far behind in his low, red Corvette mysterious with windows of smoked glass—that it first broke into the open. He had helped us move, providing an open-trayed truck with Lenny, his companion, his helper, his employee, his friend, as driver. He was enthusiastic that day, in good humour as he lifted crates and hefted boxes; he seemed genuinely pleased that we had come to Casaquemada, never actually saying so but demonstrating it with a lighthearted expansiveness in which I could see strong glimmers of Grappler's personality. At times, as he railed at Lenny or teased Grappler about his frequent rest breaks, he even sounded like him and, overhearing their banter, it was at times difficult to tell just from the voices who was speaking, the father or the son.

In the following weeks, as we settled in, Surein became a constant visitor, stopping in now and again for a drink, turning up at lunch or dinner time and seating himself at the table. When he took to arriving at odd hours, midmorning or midnight, taciturn, complaining of souring business deals, smelling of alcohol and demanding more, we grew guarded. I hid the alcohol. Jan began greeting him coldly, withdrawing to the bedroom the moment his horn blared from the road.

This put pressure on me. I could not turn him away, for he was family. Yet I did not relish his visits, either. So I put up with them as best I could, chatting with him, keeping him on the porch, longing for him to leave but doing my best not to offend him. Jan couldn't understand me, and, truth to tell, I couldn't understand myself, either: this urge to not offend. But why? Within me were vague stirrings of reason, all couched in the emotional even as my mind, with logic, rejected all justification. In my confusion, I felt myself powerless.

Finally one evening, Jan confronted Surein. Edgy with anger, she accused him of violating her privacy.

"Violating your privacy?" he responded in an aggrieved voice. "But what the hell you need privacy so for?"

Quickly I said, "She means, just give us some warning—"

Jan said, "Can't you call before coming?"

Surein, agitated, jumped to his feet. "Is-not-our-way," he said, all ten fingers thumping on his chest at each word.

In the shadows behind him, Lenny too stood up, tentative.

"In Canada," Surein continued, "is your way, keepin' people away. But you livin' in Casaquemada now, here the doors always open, we ain't 'fraid o' the neighbours." He began pacing along the tiles, the heels of his boots rapping in rhythm with his words. "Up there in your little rat race, people does hide from each other, people 'fraid each other."

Jan, coolly, said, "So tell me about all the burglar-proofing. Everthing's so open here, everyone's so friendly."

Surein paused; in the silence, a frog croaked from the lot next door. Lenny slowly took his seat once more. "It ain't the same thing," Surein said. "You have to do something to keep the niggers out."

And from the darkness behind, Lenny joined him in quiet laughter.

The conversation ended. Nothing changed. Surein continued to drop by as he wished, and I knew that word had spread among the members of the family the day my grandmother called me at the office to inquire delicately after the state of Jan's nerves.

Surein's Corvette, red and shiny, filled the rearview mirror as he pulled close to my bumper, fell back, pulled close again in a game of impatience.

Jan glanced back, stared for a moment, said, "Asshole." But there was no bite now to her voice. She looked out again at the passing fences, the neat lawns, the shuttered houses, and her chest rose and fell as she fought the touch of claustrophobia she had acquired not long after our arrival in Casaquemada.

I said, "Surein will never change." I eased the pressure of my foot on the gas pedal. The car slowed. Surein fell back. We were not far from home.

Even when we were children, when Grappler, my Aunt Sylvia and Surein visited on the weekends, or when I went to them for a week or two of my summer holidays, Surein seemed constantly to be testing me, but for what I never really knew. It was clear, though, that I failed to measure up. With this awareness, tacit but tangible, every word he spoke came to me cast in mockery.

It puzzled me even then that he was so different from his parents, coarser, more physical, a kind of glare in his eyes distancing him from them and from me. I once overheard my Aunt Emma whispering to my Aunt Indira that Surein seemed to have taken, unfortunately, after Grappler's father, a man long dead who was said to have spent much of his life haunting, and being haunted by, rumshops. It was not difficult to see that Surein felt these differences. I sensed a certain desperation in him. He once said to me, in a rare moment of candour as we talked late one night, that he thought he had been adopted. I knew this to be not true: in his face, square and fleshy, was Grappler; in his hands, long and narrow, slim fingers tipped by broad, deep-set nails, was my Aunt Sylvia. He had inherited too his mother's emotional brittleness, but longed for Grappler's solidity, seeking it, I could see, in the physical.

During my summer visits I shared Surein's bedroom, sleeping beside him in the large bed that he had stiffened to an earth-like rigidity by inserting two plywood planks between the mattress and the box spring. He said he found it more comfortable, that it reminded him of bivouacking at jamborees—whatever that meant—with our school's troop of army cadets. I never trusted him enough to reveal that I had once considered joining the troop, that I had even gone so far as to stay at school one afternoon after classes in order to do so. The sea cadets in their white flat-top hats, white uniforms and knee-high socks did not attract me; their shorts struck me as feminine, and they all seemed to be members of the Society of Joseph and Mary, serving as altar boys for fun. The army cadets, on the other hand, wore berets of green felt and khaki uniforms with trousers that tucked, businesslike, into heavy black army boots: there seemed a certain romance to them. That afternoon I watched from the second-floor balcony as, down below, the troop, with rifles shouldered, marched up and down the deserted parking lot of the school. The afternoon sun, coming in at a steep angle, threw shadows of the concrete fence and the thick coconut trees onto them. The hoarse orders of the drill-sergeant echoed up the walls to me like the growls of a hacking cough: "Hup-two-t'ree-fo-hup-two-t'ree-fo . . ." He was a member of my class, a student of below-average ability who sat in a corner at the back, sleepy and emaciated, with a face that looked eternally stunned, retreating behind spectacle lenses so thick they reduced his eyes to blinking buttonholes. And it was here on the balcony, watching, listening to the metallic tramp of their boots mingling with the raucous scream of a throat that betrayed its youth, a throat that sought authority but achieved only hysteria, that I lost the romance. I turned away, embarrassed for them, made my way down a stairwell to the other side of the school and caught a communal taxi to Salmonella. All the way home, squeezed in the back seat between a bejewelled young man exuding cologne and an absorbed old woman exuding perspiration, my bared elbows clinging stickily to the transparent plastic that protected the seat, the cadet troop continued tramping through my mind, stern faces staring steadily ahead, right arms swinging stiffly at their sides, boots crashing forward to the barked commands of one who could barely see. By the time the taxi let me off into the incandescent gloss of twilight, I knew I could not join them, I knew I could never belong.

I could tell none of this to Surein. He spoke always with enthusiasm of the cadets, was at pains to maintain the sheen of his uniform and boots, told fervent tales of shooting practice at the military rifle range. He would not have believed me, would have taken my rejection of the cadets as a rejection of him, would have seized on my refusal as a failure, as grist for further mockery.

So it suprised me, one evening as we were preparing for bed, to see him slip a kitchen knife—the stainless steel blade glinting dully in the gossamer light of the bedside lamp—from his pant pocket to under his pillow. He did it quickly, sitting on the bed, while I changed to my pajamas in the corner. I said nothing, slipped into my side of the bed, and waited, waited for him to begin his calls into the night.

As the house plunged into darkness and the quiet settled in, Surein would call out to his parents: "Goodnight." They would reply, with vigour. Then he would lie quiet for five, ten, fifteen minutes, his breathing gradually getting louder until, as if it came bursting out of him, he would again call, "Goodnight." And Grappler would reply, his voice heavy with sleep. Surein's breathing would subside, for five, ten, fifteen minutes, then build again, rapidly, to another call through the darkness to the room across the corridor: "Goodnight." Getting no reply, he would repeat it, with greater urgency: "*Good*night." And eventually Grappler would answer, sleepier yet, his voice a patient growl.

After several nights of this, a pattern emerged: when the rattle of Grappler's snoring reached us, Surein was content with a single *goodnight*; when there was nothing but the sounds of the night, the frogs and the crickets and the constant buzz of nocturnal silence, he would indulge in his night-calling, displaying what I thought at first to be an excessive politeness, and began worrying about only later, as it went on. I said nothing, though. With Surein, I thought it best not to probe.

But that act, that surreptitious slipping of the knife under the pillow, was revelation to me. The darkness, the silence, became oppressive; in my mind, the knife glinted still in its hiding place.

He called his first *goodnight*.

The replies came.

I waited, tensed, listening to the sharpening sigh of his breathing.

He called out for the second time.

After a moment, the reply came, slow and drowsy, floating on the stillness.

Surein coughed lightly, shifted uneasily under the blanket.

I waited.

Grappler's snore, light, like a constant bubbling, drifted across the corridor into the room.

Surein stirred, turned onto his stomach. The shadow of his arm slipped under the pillow.

My mind drifted, thought receded, images grew indistinct, lost colour in dissipation.

Then suddenly, a snap: senses fused and I was awake. My eyes stared unblinking into the darkness of the ceiling, and my ears, straining into the cadaverous silence, answered my unformed question: Grappler now made no sound.

Surein sat up, his breathing quickly audible.

I could hear him sweating, could feel his fear in the unmoving air.

His tongue worked around his mouth in a soft, sticky fizzle, like oil beginning to boil, and an attentuated choke—the *goo* of his third *goodnight*—escaped his throat.

"It not so bad if they dead, you know, Surein." The words, quietly spoken, came of themselves, could not be held back.

He leapt on me. His left hand covered my mouth, the warm blade of the kitchen knife pressed painfully into the gristle of my throat. "Shut up," he whispered. "Shut up." And droplets of warm water—sweat? tears?—splashed onto my forehead.

Gradually he released his grip, fell back onto his side of the bed. With a cracked voice he said, "I ain't want to be like you."

I turned away, fearing his fear, hating his contempt; and when sleep came, I dreamt of earthquake: of trembling ground and precarious footing.

The next day Surein fetched from his closet two pairs of boxing gloves, red and bulbous and strung with long white laces. Grappler was at work, my Aunt Sylvia at play with her cosmetics in her bedroom. He pulled me out into the back yard, led me past the swimming pool to the very rear of the house, to where, in the unpierced shadow of a giant avocado tree, garden tools leaned rusting against the lawnmower and humming machinery filtered impurities from the pool water.

In the damp coolness, he threw a pair of the gloves at me, slipped his hands into the other and stood waiting.

I knew nothing of the sport, but could not refuse the challenge. I inserted my hands into the gloves, drew the strings tight with my teeth as he had done, and raised my arms, the gloves before my chest, as I had seen boxers posed in newspaper photographs.

He moved in quickly, feinted at my stomach with his right and, as both my gloves dropped to block the blow, struck with his left at my face. The glove filled my vision; I jerked my head back; he caught me on the chin with a powerful, glancing blow. I stumbled backward, shook the right glove from my hand, felt my chin: wet. I glanced at my fingers: he had drawn blood.

Slowly withdrawing his hands from the gloves, he came up to me, raised my chin with the tips of his fingers, examined the cut. "No big thing," he said. "More blood than cut." He picked up my discarded glove, removed the other from my left hand, tied the strings together. "When you goin' to learn to defend yourself, Raj?" he asked. Rhetorically, it seemed to me.

Today, in the right light, from the right angle, the scar, small and elliptical, remains visible under my chin, Surein's mark indelibly etched on me.

Our last open disagreement several months later did not attain the physical, but, maybe for this, it helped more than all else to explain Surein. We quarrelled over his refusal to support the West Indies cricket team that was at the time beginning a test series in Jamaica against the touring English team. Everywhere, all over the island, radios were tuned to the cricket broadcast; men walked around with transistors held to their ears; women carried them in their bags; at school during the lunch break, boys in the classrooms and teachers in the staffroom clustered around radios, the transmission more gripping for being distant and fuzzy with static. When a West Indian batsman hit a six or reached his century, a collective cheer went up, the school sounding from the street like a hive of suddenly stirred bees.

England came in to bat. After losing an early wicket, and filling the school with cheers, their batsmen settled in to an unruffled period of scoring. A hush fell as we listened to the commentators in Jamaica, themselves now subdued, as they gave the unremitting tale: two runs here, three there, a ball swept for four. A dropped catch: groans and lowly uttered oaths. Boys began drifting away to the corridors. A ball smashed for six: the cheer, tentative at first, then growing to full blood, of a single voice. I looked up: Surein. He was grinning. "What I tell all-you! What I tell all-you! Is the Englishman game, he's the best—" He was cut off, chased out, by a hail of pens, pencils and erasers.

I wrote it off then as simply a bad joke on Surein's part. Cricket, the only area in which the term West Indian acquired any significance beyond the geographical, was taken seriously, often to the point of fanaticism. Violent arguments were not unusual, and I heard of one couple, the parents of a school friend, who refused to speak to each other for a week because one had declared that the other's favourite batsman couldn't "bat no-arse."

But Surein kept it up for the five days of the test match. There were heated words, the occasional scuffle. Several boys, even a teacher, asked me what was wrong with my cousin. Someone suggested that maybe he thought he was white, and, for a while, he was referred to as the Englishman. Anyone else in a Casaquemada not yet six years independent would have been mortified. Surein, glorying in the passions he had stirred, was delighted.

I found myself in an uneasy, and unusual, situation. It was as if Surein, the perpetual insider, and I, always most comfortable on the periphery, had switched positions. It seemed unnatural.

I didn't want it.

I couldn't stand it.

I confronted Surein at the first opportunity, the following weekend during Grappler and my Aunt Sylvia's Sunday afternoon visit to my grandparents. I cornered him under the house. "What this nonsense is you playin' at school?" I demanded.

He grinned. "I ain't know what you talkin' about."

"You damn well know what I talkin' about. You know they callin' you the Englishman? You know some o' them sayin' you think you white?"

"So?"

"You not shame? It ain't easy for me, you know, people thinkin' my cousin's a traitor."

"Is your problem, Raj. Besides, if it have a traitor here is not me, is you."

"What the hell you talkin' about?"

He flicked a finger at the scar on my chin, pushed me away from him. "You take a good look at that West Indian team o' yours?"

I said nothing, waited for him to go on.

"How much Singh or Khan or Nath or Ali it have on it, eh? Five? Six? Where all the Indian players gone? How come they ain't get pick, you could tell me?"

"Maybe they ain't good enough—"

"Bullshit."

"So you sayin'—"

"I sayin' that it ain't have enough Indians on the team to make it West Indian. I sayin' that they pick people for their race. And I sayin' that if you support that team, you sayin' is all right to do that, and that make *you* a traitor."

And it was at this moment, standing there in the shade under the house listening to him, the sun beating down clean and hard on the gravelled driveway close by, that I understood: Surein needed something to fear, he needed someone to hate, and it was only through these passions, their stir and their consequence, that he could fashion an image of an unassailable self.

It was to me, at age fifteen, a terrifying vision. The faces of my school friends—black, white, Indian and Chinese—crowded in at me. I thought of Wayne, of Angela. And I wanted to say to him that he was wrong, that his premise was warped, his equation false.

But at that moment my grandmother called to us from the window above and he walked rapidly off.

It would be years before I would see that I had confused school with life—the naivety of childhood with the reality of adulthood—years before I would perceive the theorem of race that informed every attitude of our little Casaquemada. In this, too, this vision of the cynical, this vision of victimization, Surein went before me, never seeing it, being enmeshed in it.

It is tempting to say now that Surein and I drifted apart. But this, in its implication of initial closeness, would be inaccurate. On the surface nothing changed. We continued seeing each other at school, saw each other during family visits, still spent vacations at each other's houses. But I, at least, learned a greater reserve. I turned more inward, skirted around the distant, inexplicable pain that I felt, left unexamined the sense of aloneness that was germinating in me, and hitched my imagination to the adventure fiction of lands foreign and fantastical. If Surein's response to our world was to lash out, mine was, characteristically, to withdraw. It seemed the only intelligent alternative.

We eventually went our own ways, Surein to England, I to Canada, he to law, I to medicine.

I married, stayed on, established a practice.

He returned to Casaquemada at the end of his studies, with his degree, with twenty pounds of superfluous weight, which he would never lose, and with a bubbling hatred of the English, of their food, their weather, their country and their racism. He was embarrassed by his acquisition, enthusiastic at first, of English slang and an English accent and worked hard, on his return, at ridding himself of both, at reassuming the island accent, at reclaiming island attitudes.

Surein himself said little about his time in London, save for the occasional expletive coupled with the word *Brits*. What I know of his experience there—one, it seems, of battle both verbal and physical—and of his actions upon his return to the island—he never practised his profession, became instead an importer of odds and ends, of whatever was in temporary demand—I learnt from the letters written to me in Toronto by my grandfather and by Grappler. Their skepticism was never made explicit; their loyalty was too great for that. But in their writing about him, it was not difficult to see that they exercised a discretion that was like kindness.

By our return years later to Casaquemada, Surein had distilled himself into a desperate, dizzying font of island virtues, so that Jan's need for privacy, our discomfort at what we saw as intrusion, what he saw as right, was an affront to him. He responded in his usual fashion, at times going out of his way to drop in, and we realized after a while that he enjoyed provoking Jan's displeasure. She accepted the challenge, reigned in her resistance in his presence.

But it was an adjustment she never fully made, an expectation she never quite accepted. She would rail afterward, releasing at me the fury that, during his visits, I could see building in her growing reticence of speech, her increasingly spasmodic movement, her voracious sucking at cigarettes.

In this, as in so many other things, I was of little help to her.

While part of me shared her resentment, another—the part that, in my youth, submitted to kissing unfamiliar familial cheeks— gave me pause, warned me that to challenge family was to alienate family—friends forgave, family fumed—and that in this lay an evil and a sadness that would forever oppress the soul. So I tried to placate, submitting to both, and, in my vacillation, betrayed both, betrayed, without knowing it, even myself.

I said, "Miami, New York, Rio?"

Surein took the beer that I held out to him, tipped the neck towards me in thanks, took a long swallow. Bubbles swam up the bottle, his larynx leapt in his throat like a beached fish. "Miami."

He and I were on the porch, Jan in the kitchen scrambling the eggs that Rohan, in his irritable fatigue, insisted on having. Surein had ordered Lenny, diffident, minimalist in movement, to bring the groceries in from the car, and he, wordless as usual, occasional passion visible only in a passing frown, was complying.

"Buying trip?" I sat across from him. The sunlight, brightness diffused, sat like a hazy cloud of luminous dust, shadowless on the hills and trees, houses and lawns.

"Buying trip." With quick flicks of his thumb, he undid the two top buttons of his shirt, of snug fit and military cut; with a sigh, crossed his legs, the fat on his thighs bunching under the tight grip of his trousers; removed his glasses, a recent and still-resented acquisition of black plastic frame, and drew his right palm across his forehead, wiping off the oily sweat that habitually slicked his skin.

"More cowboy boots?"

His face, plump—a delight to our grandmother, who rejoiced at the rotund, recoiled at the slender—and unshaven, clouded at my question. A few years before, Surein's business instincts had led him to import two thousand pairs of cowboy boots. "Everybody want to be Travolta," he had exclaimed over and over in excited justification. My grandfather had silently shaken his head; Grappler had gently suggested that, possibly, he was stretching the principles of supply and demand rather taut: there was no demand, so why supply? "I goin' to create one," he'd responded, transported by his first attempt at leading the market and not following it. "You know Casaquemadans. Once they was Bogart, then Johnwayne, then Clinteastwood, then Brucelee. Next is Travolta. Man, they already dancin' like him in the discos." And his hip dislocated itself, his right arm stiffened into high theatrical wave.

But he had miscalculated. Casaquemadans had found other cinematic moulds—Sylvesterstallonie, Charlesbronson, Chucknorris—and he was able to sell only a few dozen pairs. In a pique, facing a storeroom full of large white boxes, he'd sworn to wear every single pair himself. Birthday and Christmas gifts, though, became predictable, became even a family joke. Only Surein failed to find humour in the situation.

He said, "Tires."

"Car tires?"

"People don't ride bicycles no more."

Lenny approached from behind Surein, uneasily lowered himself into the hammock that hung between two of the wooden columns. Aware of his status, or lack of it, he had not followed us through the living room, had come instead around the house.

Surein said, "Finished, Lenny?"

"Yes, boss." His cowboy boots, battered and oversized, sat primly together on the tiled floor.

Through the window to the kitchen behind me cans and bottles banged on the countertop as Jan energetically unpacked the groceries.

Surein, slipping his glasses back on, looked up. "How you goin', girl?" he called.

"The girl"—and she said it as he had, *gheeul*, in the island accent—"doin' jus' fine."

He chuckled. "You never goin' to get that right, *gheeul*. You still soundin' like a Canadian tryin' to talk like a Casaquemadan."

"Well, Surein," she said, in feigned regret, "I guess I just don't have your education."

"Is not everybody who could be a lawyer." But he was disgruntled.

From the window, the knock and clatter of bottles and boxes took on a greater desperation.

With controlled anxiety, I offered Lenny a drink.

"No beer for the boy," Surein said. "You have any orange juice?"

In the kitchen, as I shook the juice bottle, Jan crumpled up the paper bags and stuffed them into the garbage can in the cupboard under the sink. She said, quietly, "For Prince Phillip or for the Queen?"

I poured the juice. "The prince." We exchanged quick smiles. It was a private joke, a private revenge: Lenny habitually walked or stood a pace or two behind Surein.

Rohan, sitting at the dining table, bits of egg flecked around his mouth, demanded some juice. I half-filled his plastic cup, wrapped his buttered fingers around it.

Surein's voice boomed through the window: "Ey, Raj, how 'bout another bottle o' horse piss?"

Lenny took his juice with a nod. Surein reached for his second beer. I said, "Fresh from the horse's—"

"Never mind," he cut me off, pulling the bottle from my hand.

Lenny giggled, choked on his juice.

Surein sat back in his chair, slouched, ran the tip of his index finger up and down the neck of the bottle. He said, "Things gettin' hot out there, Raj."

"About eighty-five?" I played at naivety, for he was about to engage his favourite topic, tales of vehicular mayhem, graphics of robbery and mounting murder. His most cherished stories, the ones he delighted in recounting over dinner, involved a bicyclist dismembered by a car and a motorcyclist beheaded by a truck; he relished the details, of body parts gleaming and red along a quarter-mile of road, of the man's head trapped still in the helmet twenty feet away from the rest of his body.

He said, "You hear about the murders last week?"

"The family?" It had been all over the newspapers, a man, his wife and their young daughter had had their throats slit by thieves.

"They was sleepin' in their beds, Raj! Them fellas didn't have no reason to kill them." He sipped his beer. "And what about the bank guard? They shoot the man in the head for no reason at all, they had his gun, he had his hands up." He grew agitated. "You not safe anywhere in this island now. In a house. In a bank. Even your car. You hear the latest? Now they hittin' your bumper, you stop to check the damage, they pull a cutlass on you. Money gone, car gone, and if they feel like it you gone, too."

"Why are you telling me all this, Surein?" His intensity irritated me. I would have liked to believe that his words were sharpened by a personal paranoia, but all that he spoke of and more was reported in the newspapers, on the radio and television; it was the hushed talk of the island. Yet a part of me didn't want to know about the multiplying violence, was unwilling to acknowledge it.

"Businesses closin' down," he continued. "Jobs disappearin', money gettin' scarce. And people gettin' desperate. They not just thiefin' now, they killin' for no reason. No reason! Like if they crushin' ants, cool-cool."

I repeated my question: "Why are you telling me all this, Surein? What's the point?"

"Broken dreams is the most dangerous thing in the world, Raj. People ain't know how to let go. They taste the easy life, and they ain't want to go back to the hard one. Once sugar was king. Then oil become a bigger king. Look at the oil price now: it ain't have no more king, it ain't have no more easy money. And people goin' to take it where they find it. And you know where they findin' it? Here"—his finger jabbed at the open living room door—"and there"—his finger jabbed towards a neighbouring house—"and there"—his finger picked out another house—"and here"—his thumb pounded on to his chest. "What left, we have. What we have, they want."

"That's why we have burglar-proofing, that's why we have police."

He laughed. "Yeah, man, Raj. Sure. The burglar-proofin' goin' to stop the bullets and the police goin' to stop servin' and protectin' themselves long enough to arrest the sons-o'-bitches. Now tell me 'bout Ali Baba and the forty thieves."

Lenny giggled.

Surein looked quickly around. "What you laughin' at, boy? Eh? You not laughin' at the doctor, eh?" There was true menace in his voice. "Don't forget yourself, you hear me, boy? The doctor is a brahmin like me, he ain't no cane-cutter like you, so watch who you laughin' at."

Lenny fell silent, his face frozen into a kind of blank negation.

"Maybe it wasn't me that he was laughing at, Surein," I said, lightly.

"He know better than that. Right, Lenny?"

"Right, boss." And he stared away, past the fence, past the grassy lot, above the houses to the distant hills.

"What we need, Raj," Surein continued after a swallow of beer, "is protection. Self-protection."

"Condoms?"

He sucked his teeth, looked around in exasperation. "Ey, man, Raj, I talkin' serious now." And his gaze came around to me, rested, liquid and sombre. "You ever wonder what go happen if somebody break in here? What you goin' do?"

He had stirred one of my spectres: I could make no reply.

"Stick 'im with a needle? Hit 'im with a stet'oscope?"

Behind him, Lenny grinned, soundless, but making no effort to conceal it from me.

"And what if you at the office? They hittin' during the day, too, in broad daylight. Jan and Rohan . . ."

I said, weakly, "Life is full of risks."

Surein looked back at me in a merciless silence.

I said, after a moment, "They're going to Toronto on holiday, anyway. Soon."

He sipped his beer, tilting his head back but keeping his eyes, narrowed, on me. "That's nice. And afterward?"

That was the unspoken question: Would there be an afterward?

He reached with two fingers into his shirt pocket, extracted the car keys, tossed them to Lenny. "Go bring the canvas bag from the trunk." As he clattered off, Surein reached down, put his beer on the floor and tugged his right pant leg up to his knee, stuck his fingers into the boot and withdrew a small knife. He held it up to me with thumb and index finger, displaying its small wooden handle, its scarred and shining four-inch blade. Finally, with an upward flick of the wrist, he grasped it in his hand, settled back into the chair. "Under my car seat it have a axe-handle. Under my bed, it have . . . something with a bigger bite."

The display: Where ended the facade? Where began the reality?

"And I not just jokin', I tell you. Somewhere in them streets out there, it have a grey Toyota with smashed headlights and a black man who never goin' to call Indians *coolies* no more."

"What happened?" Listening to him, something went dead within me. I heard his words but could not weigh them; my defence, I think, against despair.

"He cut me off at a corner and—you know how these people bold-bold—he call me a stupid coolie. So I take off after him, force him off the road, smash up the headlights."

"And the man?"

"These people brave when they runnin'. He lock the doors and stay in the car." He lay the knife on his lap, picked up his beer. "No big deal. Stand up to them and they does go quiet-quiet. Is just like dealin' with a bad dog. Slap 'im twice and the tail does curl up between the legs." He chuckled, perspiration glistening along his upper lip.

"Surein, you're going to end up dead one day." I spoke lightly, a laugh trembling through my words.

He poured a bit of beer through his parted lips, worked it around his mouth, swallowed. "Perhaps. I ain't going to be the only one, though."

This was a transparent fiction. Surein, like so many others, had prepared his way. In his incautious boasting, prompted usually by alcohol and that resurgent urge to humiliate, he had shown me, at various times, an inch-thick wad of U.S. hundred-dollar bills, a savings passbook for Citibank, a moneybelt fat with U.S. and Canadian traveller's cheques all endorsed by the tourists and foreign engineers, in the island on contract, from whom he'd acquired them at inflated, irresistible rates. He was rumoured—to ask was socially unacceptable—to have invested in a shopping centre in Miami, in an apartment building in Coral Gables.

Lenny reappeared, slowed, his boots shuffling across the tiles, a bag of faded brown canvas hanging by a leather strap from his hand.

Surein stood up, took the bag from him, undid a couple of buckles. His breathing was now a shallow rustle, his tongue flicked rapidly at his lips. Lenny, standing just behind him, peered intently over his shoulder at the bag. Surein threw back the flap, dug deep with his right hand and, spilling a crumpled shirt and a pair of balled socks, tugged out a neatly folded white towel. Thrusting the bag into Lenny's hands, he stepped close to me and put the towel on my lap. "Unfold it," he said.

I picked up the towel, felt the concealed weight of it, sought with my fingers the concealed shape within it.

Surein, impatient, said, "Is not a damn Christmas present, Raj."

I threw aside the careful folds of furry cotton. Lying on my lap, stark against its field of white, was a large revolver. My vision, unbelieving, unwilling to grasp its form, swam before the butt of polished wood, the machined perfection of the black metal.

Surein said, "It pretty for spite, not so?"

And he was right: an object of peculiar beauty, it mesmerized with the quality of broadswords under glass, of sabres crossed on a wall of chiselled stone, deadliness on display.

He said, "Made in the U.S. of A. Packaged protection. Just point and pull. It does shoot a hurricane."

The phrase—*It does shoot a hurricane*—pleased me, ran itself again through my head, offered, in its very sound, the thrill of ultimatum.

"Go on, pick it up. See how it fit in your hand."

My fingers reached out, dark over the powdered field of the white towel. Then: they went cold.

"I could let you have it wholesale."

Stopped.

"Pick it up, Raj. Feel it. Hold the eye o' the hurricane in the palm o' your hand."

Darkness and sparkle. Shards of hard light tinkling and tumbling down from the tattered treetops. We move forward in the brimming silence. It is like walking underwater. The hesitant crackle of twigs and dry leaves under the crepe-rubber soles of our shoes. Muscles tensed. A worm of sweat wriggles from my right temple down the side of my face. Surein, face for the first time razored clean of childhood fuzz, holds the pellet gun lightly before him in both hands.

Stop: a gentle flutter of wings, the rustle of soft leaves. Look: up among the spindly branches of a nearby sapling, in among the sparse and struggling leaves. A little grey body almost a shadow.

Silence. Breathing. The blood pulsing in my temples, in my wrists.

Surein raises the pellet gun, stock against his shoulder. Takes aim. Waits.

The tiny grey head rises, beak opens: a thin cackle.

My throat constricts: I cannot draw breath. Lips go dry.

The gun cracks.

My eyes close and my ears listen for the sounds of panic, for wings beating back leaves in escape.

Nothing.

I open my eyes to Surein. He is peering up into the branches.

The little grey body is still there, hasn't budged. Then, as we watch, it begins to move, to topple over, falls between the branches, through the leaves, lodges unseen in the clutch of the greater thickness lower down.

We wait, watching for further movement. Step forward, un-mindful now of disturbance. Surein probes at the grey body with the tip of the gun barrel. The head hangs to the right, the beak open, the neck feathers crimson. But the eyes jump and glitter yet with life.

Surein says, "Kill it."

I pull back, instinctively.

"Kill it," he repeats. "Break the neck."

"You start it. You finish it."

"You 'fraid?" But the sneer in his voice is lost in his own ten-sion. "Kill it!"

The crimson drips now, onto a leaf of light green turning brown at the edges, runs in a thin stream across the fine veins, hesitates, pools, then breaks over and falls to the damp ground.

Surein breaks the gun open, inserts another lead pellet, snaps the barrel back into place with a flick of his right hand, holds the gun out to me. "Make sure you get 'im in the head," he says.

The gun is heavy in my hands, the wood warm to my touch. I bring it to my shoulder, take aim: the head of the bird fills the tiny triangle. Squeeze the trigger as Surein has taught me to do at distant tin cans and Coke bottles. The gun jumps in my hand, my heart pounds. The pellet cuts through leaves to the upper right of the bird.

Surein, in disgust, sucks his teeth. Steps forward. Slips from the leather sheath belted to his waist the hunting knife that Grappler, upon discovering one morning the kitchen knife under the pillow, had given unquestioningly to him. Reaches resolutely through the leaves for the bird, grasps it in his left hand, places the brilliant blade on the crimsoned feathers—

I turn away, lean the gun against a tree trunk, walk back the way we have come.

Later, Surein turns it all into a humourous tale, his the heroism, mine the humiliation.

But I do not mind.

"Where'd you get it?" My voice was thinned, speech rapid and chopped.

"You mean *them*." He chuckled. "This is just one of the bright cousins in the whole big family I bring in this afternoon."

Lenny bent to the floor, picked up the shirt and socks.

Surein said, "You not going to see how it feel?"

I shook my head slowly: no. Folded the towel over the solidity of the weapon. Hid it.

"What happen? You ain't like it?"

I picked up the white bulk, held it out to him. "What's going on with all these guns, Surein?"

He ignored the towel. "Ever hear 'bout the law of supply and demand? Well, I supplyin' the demand. Everybody want to be Charlesbronson again."

"Not everybody." Still I held the towel out.

Still he ignored it. "Almost everybody. Everybody you know, and a lot o' people you don't know."

I put the towel back on my lap.

Lenny said, "Everybody buyin' guns, Doc. Is a big business."

Surein said, "I'll throw in the bullets for free."

"So I can protect my family."

"If you have to."

And I thought, with sadness, of how far the island had gone in less than a generation, from the proudly unarmed to the aggressively armed, guns from the exotic to the commonplace. Police nightsticks had turned into revolvers, semiautomatic rifles, submachine guns; constables with the look of tropical bobbies had evolved into officers hermetic with the manner of the military. Armed robberies, once affairs of knife or cutlass, now often ended in lengthy exchanges of gunfire, the ambulance as busy as the Black Maria, the cemetery as crowded as the cell.

I said, "There are too many guns in this island."

Surein said, "You mean not enough. You have to fight fire with—"

"Water."

He laughed. Lenny stared blankly at me.

I said, "Catch." Tossed the wrapped towel at him.

He caught it, passed it reluctantly to Lenny. "I'll hold on to it for a while," he said. "Think it over. If you change your mind . . ."

I walked them out to the car at the back. Lenny got into the passenger seat, the canvas bag at his feet. I pushed Surein's door in. "How do you get those things past customs, anyway, Surein?"

He put the key in the ignition, looked up at me with a grin. "I have a lot o' friends," he said. "Little gifts does go a long way. A bottle o' whiskey here, a few dollars there. People does go blind real easy."

The engine roared. I pulled back as he screeched off. I chained and locked the back gate, bolted and locked the front door. On the kitchen table lay Rohan's plate, on its orb of hard red plastic a lump of drying egg and a half-eaten slice of bread. Flecks of egg dotted the varnished surface around, and in the air above two flies circled and buzzed like miniature vultures. Rohan was curled asleep on a pillow in front of the television; his lips and cheeks shone with grease. The door to our bedroom was closed. I opened it, went in.

It was shadowed, the drapes drawn tight; cool, the air conditioner humming its mechanical mantra. Jan was lying in bed, the blue comforter pulled to her waist, her left breast, large and white and pendulous with retreating orange nipple, hanging to the side and resting on her arm, her right breast flattened under the pressure of her right arm that reached across her stomach, the hand, concealed under the comforter, swirling between her parted legs.

She opened her eyes to me, looked dazed at me, said thickly, "You did good, Raj. Damned good."

I said, as I undid my pants, "You didn't want it, either?"

She threw back the comforter with a movement of her left hand, opened her legs farther, increased the vigorous swirling of her right hand, said with shortened breath, "But I did, I did!"

I let my trousers fall to my ankles, kicked them away; removed my underpants, freeing my arousal; climbed onto her, entered her. And as I did so, she screamed in self-pleasure.

7

With relief we left the old beach house behind, driving rapidly down the narrow gravelled lane, tires sputtering along hard-edged gouges, jogging into and out of stone-studded ruts. Grass, long and narrow-bladed, of a rich, succulent green, showered thickly from the hill on the left. From the verge on the right that fell off the paved road below, thin-stemmed weeds reached elegantly in through the open windows, nodded their tapered heads, caught on the frame, flexed with innate ease, swayed back out undamaged into the still, salted air.

Rohan, kneeling on the back seat, laughed at their movement, snatched without success at them.

Jan said, "I once knew a girl from South America. From Venezuela or Colombia, some place like that. The kind of place that makes you think of drugs and oil and easy violence."

"Like Casaquemada?"

"Like Casaquemada."

I braked at the bottom of the hill, peered to either side along the undivided ribbon of asphalt, sounded the horn as warning to the trees and the grass and the empty road. And as farewell, perhaps, to the house that stood in growing dereliction farther up the hill behind us.

"Her name was Leda," Jan said. "Short, plump, a teddy bear of a girl. About seventeen, but she acted younger. Giggled all the time. Lived on potato chips and French fries and Coke. The all-American diet."

Forest fell away on the left and the land opened out to a small grassed plain that ended at the sea, rough and uninviting here on the northeast coast. We never swam in this water—it was said to have, in the lowering tide, a dangerous undertow—preferring the slow river that wound its way, cool and clear, from the hills not far away. From the house, from its open porch and wide covered gallery that ran outside the bedrooms all along the second floor, we could just see past a sparse stand of coconut trees to where its mouth, direction ever-changing, cut through the beach to the sea. With binoculars, in the late afternoon light, we could sometimes spot on the far riverbank the large faces that Grappler had taught us to form with wet sand: grinning faces, sad faces, devils and clowns. In the slanting yellow light, through the distortion of lens and shadow, the faces seemed to come alive, glowering grotesque in the desertion of water and sand. By the next morning, though, they were always gone, noses flattened, eyes erased, washed by the high tide back into the anonymity of shapeless sand.

"One evening she got a terrible pain in her side. Couldn't stand up, couldn't lie down. Went white as a sheet, couldn't hardly talk. Kept saying, 'Appendeceetees, appendeceetees.' We called an ambulance. She couldn't even lie down on the stretcher, they had to pick her up direct from the chair just like she was sitting, with their arms linked behind her back and under her ass. In the ambulance—I went with her—she managed to lie down on her side, without stretching her legs out. Kept groaning all the way to the hospital downtown."

From the house, Grappler would sometimes lead us, Surein and me and whichever cousins happened to be visiting, on long walks to The Point, away from the river, along a narrow beach strewn with stones and pebbles, whitish red at first, black and moss-covered later on where the beach grew even narrower, past expansive clusters of smooth, soft graphite overhung by towering trees with exposed roots, to the outcrop of rock and boulder, which in its isolation, in its ruggedness, gave the illusion of the untouched. While Grappler tossed his fishing line into the water, grey, choppy, perilous with shark and barracuda, Surein and I would search among the rocks for stones turned by tide into cloudy crystals of intricate form and velvety touch. And when this ended, in delight or exasperation, Surein would go off on his own, his hunting knife slashing at vegetation or whittling at driftwood, while I sought out a dry rock as a seat and stared into the distance, past the whitecaps leaping on the grey water, to a tiny islet, thickly forested and said to be alive with snakes, that sat, unattainable, a tease to the imagination, just off the coast. When, after a while, my imagination would no longer take me there to battle serpents, to construct the unassailable, I would open my book and burrow deep into worlds far removed.

"They wheeled her straight into the examination room. I gave them her name, address, insurance number and all that shit, they gave me her hospital card, and then I just sat around waiting and watching the slime drip in—"

"They're people—"

"—the drunks and the druggies and the guys with broken arms and smashed-in faces—"

"And Leda?"

"They looked her over, asked her a few questions. And found out she hadn't taken a shit for two weeks. Two weeks! All those goddamned potato chips and French fries and Big Macs and Whoppers and Cokes and Pepsis and chocolate bars bunged up inside of her like junk in a drainpipe! It didn't take them long to stick a tube up her and flush it all out. We took the subway home. She giggled all the way. And the next morning she had a bag of corn chips for breakfast."

Call it arrogance. We had given him a name, Polloli, and he learned quickly to respond to it, to the foolishness of its sound, in the only way he seemed able, with a grin—red gums, white teeth—touched by the manic. He appeared out of the night with an unpredictable frequency, a boy of thirteen or fourteen, half-naked, barefooted, his entire body filmed in a fine dust. Where he came from, where he went back to late at night, remained a mystery; out there after sunset, the nocturnal was complete, nothing existed but the night and its siren insect calls; it was many unlit miles to the nearest village. His obvious retardation—he spoke in slack-jawed grunts, nodded with an uncontrolled vigour—caused us to fear him, and from this fear, unacknowledged, came mockery. We would stand at the railing of the second-floor porch, the concrete under our bare feet still warm from the day, looking down at him standing in the yard, half lit by the light shining from the kitchen downstairs. We would shout down to him: "Ey! Polloli! You is a stupid ass, right?" "Ey! Polloli! You does like eatin' dogshit, not so?" "Ey! Polloli . . ." And to every line of shouted invective he would grin, his skittish eyes looking searchingly up at us, his head nodding in friendly, fervent assent. Call it cruelty.

Whenever he came, my grandmother would send my grandfather or Grappler out to him with a cookie can of dinner scraps. He would crouch down beside the wall of the house, settling himself onto the rock, black and shiny, shaped like a large brick, on which Grappler cleaned the fish he caught, and, in our fascinated, malevolent gaze, devour the food with a noisy relish. We came to call the rock "Polloli's stone," began viewing it with a certain distaste. It was Surein who somehow discovered that the cleanliness of the stone mattered to Polloli, and who first noticed, with resentment, his growing proprietorship of it. We began sprinkling sand on the stone, observing with amusement his puzzlement, the cautious flutter of his hand as he dusted it clean. It became, as the thrill of verbal abuse faded, our new game, from pinches of sand to handfuls and, finally one evening, a bucketful. When Polloli came three or four nights later, we were waiting on the porch, expectant; watched in fascination as he emerged from the darkness, waved loose-armed at us and then froze, stupefied, before the pile of sand. He bent slowly, warily, reached his hand out towards it, grunted. Then, his head suddenly frenzied on his shoulders, he began sobbing, a choking guttural that rose like a rounded echo into the night. Grappler came out onto the porch, gazed down, called his name. Polloli withdrew his hand, clutched it tight against his stomach, looked around as if in fear, his eyes large, his cheeks wet with tears. It was as if we had unwittingly unleashed his demons. Spittle dribbling from the side of his mouth, he turned away and darted off into the night. Even Surein, for a few minutes at least, maintained a stunned silence. Polloli never returned. Call it youth.

"Mrs. Mazankowski's was Leda's second house in Toronto. I'd just started waitressing at the Riviera when she moved into the room next to mine on the second floor. I suppose we became friends, in a way. At least we talked, which is more than I can say for the other girls. There were six of us boarding there, me, Leda, a U. of T. student, an Eaton's salesgirl and a couple of Jehovah's Witnesses who worked as secretaries and spent their weekends doing the door-to-door bit. Leda told me about her family in Panama or Mexico or wherever the hell she was from. Rich. Filthy rich. The kid had her own credit card, for God's sake. And daddy paid all the bills, thank you very much. But she was a nice kid, though. Generous, in small ways. Always had a pack of gum to give you, or half a bag of cookies. Every day she went to her school to take English classes, and on the evenings I wasn't working she'd ask me to help her with her homework. The stuff she had to learn! What'd she call it? The conditional? Did you know that 'If I would have known it' is wrong? At least, so her teacher said. It's supposed to be 'If I had known it.' The work was a real bitch. I made more mistakes than she did, even if she went around saying things like *berry, berry gude*. How're you doing, Leda? *Berry, berry gude.* D'you like Toronto, Leda? *Eet ees berry, berry nice.* Once in a restaurant she ordered a *Cock* to drink. The waiter almost passed out. But she stuck with it, though. Worked her plump little ass off. Wanted to be a secretary, that was her ambition. Back in Uruguay or Paraguay or wherever the hell she was from, English was gonna make her real special. And with daddy's help it was gonna be top job, top dollar. But the strange thing is, none of this is why I remember Leda. I remember her because Mrs. Mazankowski's on Spadina, where I met her, was her second house."

Although it was rented, I always thought of the beach house at Manzanares as Grappler's house, as an object almost of his own creation. It reflected so much of him: large, unfettered, rambling in an uncomplicated way, yet sure and solid up there on the plot of land sliced from the side of the hill. Comfort: it is the first word that comes to me when I think of the house and the summer weeks spent there in its sparsely furnished spaciousness, reading in the second-floor gallery among its dusty wicker armchairs and its rickety rockers, playing ping-pong in the kitchen at the table that, lined by wooden benches, doubled for dining. My relations with Surein were, for the most part, tranquil. If we fought, it was usually over my refusal to put aside my book—no surprise this, for in Casaquemada reading was considered at best antisocial— to accompany him on his forays up the hill at the back of the house to hunt birds and lizards among the orange and mango trees. But the discord, his hectoring, my recalcitrance, were infrequent. He was quieter here, less aggressive. He seemed, unlike me, soothed by the sea. To me, its blue-grey expanse, heaving, alive, offered suffocation; to me, it spoke not of freedom and possibility limitless but of confinement and possibility limited. I dreamt not of sailing towards its horizons—they led nowhere— but of escaping them in the more secure reaches of printed worlds.

Surein, truth to tell, surprised me. In the early evenings, while my grandmother and Aunt Sylvia prepared dinner in the kitchen downstairs, while my grandfather read the newspaper and Grappler worked at his fishing gear, while I, with a controlled desperation, clung tenaciously to the images of greater certainty that formed from the words, Surein would drag a wicker armchair out to the porch, sit just beyond the reach of the light with his back to us, and gaze fascinated out at the very spectacle that frightened me most: at the misting of the sea in the descending night, at the melancholic merging of water and sky into a wistful extinction. At these times I admired Surein, envied his strength and wondered, with no answers, what soft part of him was touched in his unapproachable absorption there at the edge of the big, open, comfortable house. Later at night, in the sky overhead, in its blackness rent by the undimmed dazzle of countless stars, we sometimes saw a satellite floating rapidly by, a travelling point of light lower than the others but as bright. It was this, metal, man-made, more than the stationary stars; more than, for all their spectacle, the shooting stars; more than even the lunar eclipse we witnessed late one evening, the slow and inexorable darkening of the full moon to a circle, defined by the lightest of coronas, only a little less dark than the surrounding night, then its crowing revelation of received brilliance; it was this, the fashioning hand of man in the distant vastness, that seized me, mesmerized me, thrilled me, took me, with my books, beyond the suffocation of the limiting, imprisoning sea.

"Leda's first house in Toronto was in the High Park area, at the southern edge of the park, so that from one side you could see the lake and from the other the trees. It was one of those big old houses that had had its guts ripped out and its red brick peeled, the kind of renovation your Aunt Sylvia would probably like to have done on herself. Then they'd brought in an interior deco-rator and had the place done up in chrome and pastels. Like, I mean, it was *Architectural Digest* time. Leda was just blown away by the place. The school told her it was the best house they had, the nicest couple, he was a lawyer, she was in real estate, young, rich, friendly. So why'd they take in a student? They sure as hell didn't need the money. Because they were *interested*, wanted to get to know young people from different parts of the world. Your perfect Canadian couple. Only, they didn't get in until ten or eleven at night, and were gone the next morning by eight. Most of the time Leda found herself alone in the house with their two Siamese cats. She had free rein, any teenager would have loved it. But not Leda. The house terrified her, and she asked the school to move her. It was a question of security, she said."

A question of security. Grappler hadn't rented the house in years, and its owners, aging, family dispersed, had left it largely to its own devices. Several times over the years it had been bur-glarized, vandalized. They had tried to sell it, but its isolation, once so desirable, now counted against it: here, crime could be leisurely. So they had bricked it up. The gallery above was now sealed behind a wall of grey brick and dripping mortar; the kitchen below, once airy with the light and breeze that came in through a wall of tropical brick, was concealed with the solidity of rough, reinforced concrete; the door of wood was now sheathed in metal, its single bolt and lock tripled, a bar of thick, flat iron across it like a stiff belt. Only the porch, its iron railing rusting, its concrete corner posts peeled and exposed, remained free, like a tongue stuck out in impotent defiance. Walking around with Jan and Rohan, looking, mind reeling with the irreconcilable, my memories froze, my stories stuck on my tongue: the house had become a box of captured darkness. And when I spotted Polloli's stone still sitting in the corner where it had been years before, I hurried them into the car, locked the doors, and drove off without looking back.

"You see, when they redid the house, they'd opened up the windows, turned them into large, double-glazed picture frames. There was a painting of Lake Ontario, only it wasn't a painting. There was a painting of the park, only it was real. Leda's room was on the ground floor, looking out onto the park. Great room, right? But not for Leda. She couldn't sleep at night. The windows were too large, too open. They weren't like her windows in Peru or Chile or wherever the hell she was from. There, the windows all had bars on them, burglar-proofing. No way anybody could break in. And in her first house in Toronto she was awake all night listening for the sounds of breaking glass. Poor kid. The wind in the trees outside was enough to rub her nerves raw. And that's why the school moved her to the little room with the tiny window on the second floor of Mrs. Mazankowski's on Spadina. There weren't any iron bars, but it was high and it was small. Nothing could get in, not even the sunlight."

We left the coast behind. The road, hemmed in on both sides by vegetation, divided down the middle now by a broken white line, widened a little. Occasionally we passed a shack, this one of rotting wood, that one of dried earth, another precariously knocked together with the oddest of ends, all set far back from the road in patches of land cleared roughly of forest; sometimes, in the over-grown front yard, would be a goat or a cow or a group of ragged children. The sight of them, of the collapse of habitation and human, angered me, frightened me. They were both emotions of impotence.

Jan said, "Do we have to stop at your grandparents'?"

"They're expecting us."

From the back seat, Rohan called his approval: he knew that he could barter a simple kiss for cookies and a soft drink.

Jan retreated into silence.

My grandmother said, "It so nice to see all-you." Her left hand grasped my arm, her right caressed my cheek. "Nobody does come, you know." She sighed. "Chil'ren." Her hand slipped behind my neck, tugged my head forward, towards her lips. I twisted away, placed a brief kiss on her cheek: the scent of perfumed powder, the alarming yield of flesh without firmness. She fought back with a tightening grip, but I would not let my lips meet hers, would not give in to her unspoken insistence on a direct embrace that was like pressing the lips to a raw steak. She released me, turned to Rohan.

Jan, standing just behind him, pulled back, said, "Hello, Ma."

My grandmother smiled, unnaturally, with effort, too obvious the unease. "Jaan." She bent over to Rohan, who, playing the coquette, reached back and circled an arm around Jan's leg. My grandmother said, "You going to give me a kiss, Ro?"

He shook his head: no.

She reached her hands—wrinkled, veined, skin greying—out to him, and I saw how age had shrunken her. No more the plump, imposing woman of memory, no more the woman so bulky that she would call me into the bedroom after her shower to help her into her brassiere, cups overwhelmed, straps strained to link in the middle of her back.

She said, teasing, "But what going on here, Ro? You ain't want to give me a kiss?"

Again he shook his head: no.

Jan disengaged herself from Rohan's grasp, sat in one of the plastic-covered armchairs that ringed the porch, stared sightless out at the fence, at the road, at the vegetation beyond, at this scene that had not changed since my childhood. She sucked agitatedly at a cigarette.

I said, "Give Ma a kiss, Ro."

He ignored me, eyes alone looking up at my grandmother, daring her to play his game.

She took his left arm in her hand, caressed it with her fingers. The arm remained limp, uninterested. She said, "You want biscuits?"

He nodded: yes. There was the slightest shadow of a smile on his lips.

"With jam?"

Another nod.

"And a swee' drink?"

"Yeth."

"One kiss?"

He puckered his lips, held his face up to her. She clasped his cheeks in her hands, squashed her lips against his.

And watching them, listening to the trade of barter and blackmail, I felt my grandmother crushed against me, gagged at her perfumed powder, saw from close the too-white perfection of her dentured smile, heard the jingle-jangle of the gold bracelets on her arms as she said: *Give me a kiss or I not leaving you anything when I die.* I gave the kiss, as Rohan did, but he was smarter than I, he demanded immediate payment.

My grandmother straightened up, happy, the smile subdued, genuine.

"Where's Pa?" I asked. He would normally have sauntered out by now, slightly removed, with glazed, aging eyes, recognition slow, smile hesitant.

"In the back."

"He's not working, is he?"

"No, jus' dreaming about it."

I nodded, with some relief. My grandfather, after a stroke, in the enforced stillness of a slight partial paralysis, had found his strength evaporated, his body betraying the instinctive dictates of a lifetime.

My grandmother offered something to drink.

Jan chose a Coke. I opted for coffee, my mouth anticipating the thick, steamy sweetness of instant coffee and condensed milk that my grandmother conjured up. She went inside, Rohan, legs busy in the thrill of victory, following closely behind her.

I sat across from Jan in my grandfather's padded rocking chair, the cushions sighing under my lowering weight as if expelling breath, marking the silence that fell in behind Rohan's fading footfalls.

Now, I knew, would come the hard part: to fill the minutes that we would spend here. The minutes that would pulse with the tension of Jan's silence. The minutes that would grate gently with the shuffling of my grandmother between kitchen and porch, conversation muted—inconsequential question, inconsequential answer—in the greater requirement of mere presence. It was this that Jan could not grasp, could not bear: visit not as exchange but as simple testimony of existence. It was here, in my grandparents' house, that her inflexible difference became most painfully obvious. While everyone, even I who grew up here with a feeling of apartness, managed to fit into the tableau of shadow and settled dust, she stood out in relief, extraneous, as if strayed from a different painting; it was not that she could not, but that she would not fit in, and not only here but in Casaquemada itself. She was as if determined to resist.

I looked out: the mango tree, never conquered, grizzled but healthy; the lawn, as clipped as ever but patchy close to the fence where a colony of worms, so far resistant to every poison tried, was nibbling its way through the roots; the fence, metal bars showing rashes of rust through the silver paint. Everything was as it had been, but with signs of slippage that my grandmother blamed on a lack of competent help. Wayne's parents had died years before, their house taken over by strangers, and he, in the inundation of oil money, had gone off to Lopez City, to another job, more lucrative, less demanding, in the government's job creation scheme. Now my grandparents could get only the occasional day worker, young boys who filched whatever came to hand or aging drunks seeking enough money to buy the next bottle. Often my grandmother would bemoan the loss of Wayne: "Nobody want to work these days," she would say, hoping in vain that the recent and accelerating government "retrenchments" would send Wayne back to her.

Jan stood up, restless, looked down into the yard, her knuckles rapping soft and arhythmic on the low concrete wall.

I got to my feet, nodded at the lawn. "Did I ever tell you my parents are buried out there?"

She glanced at me, questioning, unfriendly. "Where? In the yard?" The cigarette glowed close to the filter.

"There." I pointed to the left, to my grandmother's little "flowers garden," long untended, her own growing frailty helpless against the swift burgeoning of weed and wild grass.

"You mean that's a fucking grave? I thought you told me they burnt them."

"They did. Beside a river."

"And they threw the ashes into the river, right?"

"All except for two handfuls, one from my mother, one from my father."

"Shit." She flicked the burning butt into the lawn.

"Wayne, the former yardboy, told me about it. My grandmother mixed the ashes into the soil, put the plants in and banned everybody else from touching it."

"That's sick."

"I find it strange that she never told me about it."

"Well, it's not exactly something you go around boasting about, I don't think."

"I wonder why she did it. Just to keep a little bit of them close by?"

"Didn't you ever ask her?"

"She doesn't know I know."

"So ask her."

"I don't think I can. I've known her secret for too long."

"That's stupid."

"Is it?" And I thought that maybe it was, yet the thought of asking, the thought of revealing what I knew, disturbed me. It would be to strip away part of my grandmother, to see beneath. She would resent it, I feared; she would feel betrayed.

"Raj, Son," my grandmother called from the door. "Go get your granpa. Tell him to come inside."

Jan said, "Ask."

I said "Don't," turned and went through the door, past my grandmother into the living room.

My grandmother said, "Jaan, you want to come in the kitchen with me?"

"Sure, Ma." The litheness in her answer worried me.

I hurried through the living room, enclosed and unlit, my shoes rapping on the dark wooden floor, echoing past the plastic-swathed armchairs, the doily-covered coffee table, the glass vases spouting plastic flowers. In the dining room beyond, brighter, sunlight coming in through the open windows, Rohan was sitting at the Formica table—another, older, of wood painted green, adjoined it at one end—devouring a plate of crackers and jam. I mussed his hair and he grinned wide-mouthed at me, sticking out his mush-encrusted tongue. My eyes moved quickly around the room, marvelling at how little it had changed since my childhood. From the latticework up above where my grandfather once battered to death an owl, bird of ill omen; to the refrigerator, of rounded edges, repainted now but bubbling rust at the corners; to the sink, too small to contain the water pressure, that imitated a fountain when the tap was turned on and, above it, the mirror now speckled green as the silver lining degenerated into a semblance of skin disease. One corner, left as a small alcove when a section of the larger room was partitioned off for a bathroom and toilet, was still used as storage space: an old Singer sewing machine, its mottled top piled with newspapers neatly folded and fresh-looking. A large trunk on which sat several closed boxes. And, leaning in the corner, a faded Union Jack furled around its pole the day Casaquemada got its independence, my grandfather never able to throw it out, never able to replace it at his store with the new and unfamiliar. Standing there, examining the frozen past, with Rohan sitting at the table crunching crackers, the odd-est sensation came to me: of having stepped back more than thirty years, of watching myself sitting alone before a plate of crackers in my grandparents' dining room, unmindful of a past, unaware of a future, only vaguely conscious of a silence deeper than the ordinary. The vision, sudden, reality shifting, unsettled me, moved me.

I opened the back door to the concrete stairway, which, stuck railless to the side of the house, led down to the driveway and garage. As I stepped out onto the landing, my grandmother, en-tering the dining room with Jan, called out, "Yes, Son, go tell him to come in. He going to get too dark out there."

"Okay, Ma." And as I trotted down the stairs, a sadness came to me. I thought: *Orders o' the manager.*

The back yard, though, had changed. The orange and lime trees, always unhealthy, had been cut down, the stumps left to rot. The grapefruit tree still stood in the far left corner, but the anthurium beds and banana trees had been cleared away, opening up the wall now mildewed at the top in black streaks, heavily mossed at the bottom in creeping green.

My grandfather was in his private plot on the other side of the wall, the spot marked yet by the thick, reaching vegetation. I walked carefully past the garage, the moist earth oozing up the sides of my shoes, past the chicken coop now doorless, wire ripped and rusted, odour long washed away, to the craggy breach in the wall, its irregular shape reminding me of an unfilled space in a jigsaw puzzle. And as I passed through it into my grand-father's garden, my grandmother's voice, heavy with hysteria, muttered across my memory: "One day he going to kill himself, one day he going to drop dead alone down there and nobody going to know . . ."

I paused just inside the garden. I hadn't seen it in years, had never really examined it, and it was a surprise not to be con-fronted by trim rows of tomato trees and lettuce heads, cucumber vines and cassava shoots. Maybe it was simply the passage of time, maybe the incontinence of age and infirmity, but my grand-father's garden, the little plot of land in which he had laboured so

long and so intensely, showed no signs of ever having been cultivated. Its weeds were thick, its flowers clustered with an almost
deliberate disorder. Banana trees reached their long, floppy leaves
into the lower branches of a centrally placed pomme-cythere tree,
which, tall, dense and spreading, effectively blocked out the sun
while, behind it, in the greater gloom, the narrow stalks of papaya
trees merged hazily into each other. Under my shoes, the ground
was soft and damp, springy with dead vegetation.

I took two tentative steps forward, called out, "Pa?" There was
no answer. I edged cautiously along the almost overgrown path,
blades of grass brushing against my pant legs. "Pa?" I made my
way to the far end of the garden, to where it ended at the wooden
fence, boards grey and rotting at the base; and the more I walked,
the farther into the contained wilderness I went, the more obvious it became that all of this, the trees, the plants, the weeds in
variety and profusion but in no confusion, had been planted here,
studiously, by a fevered imagination and controlled hands.

A flash of chalky white caught my eye from among the papaya
trees in the greater gloom. "Pa?" There was still no response. "It's
Raj." I moved towards the trees, brushing past banana leaves,
stepping over clumps of grass. A damp mustiness surged from the
earth into the air.

He was sitting on a little bench of rough-hewn wood, knees
neatly together, a newspaper tightly folded in two on his lap.

"Pa." I kissed him on the cheek, skin leathery, flesh inert, but he
seemed not to notice. His eyes, dimmed, covered constantly by a
film of water, looked off into the shadows. His fingers, broad
nails untrimmed, drummed rhythmically on the newspaper, first
the little finger, then rapidly the next and the next to the index,
then around again, rapping sharply like a tight drum, marking
time with the precision of a metronome. Young, I had been fascinated by the rapidity of the fingers, the resonance of the sound,
but had never been able to reproduce it. Once I asked him to
show me how to do it, but he'd had no idea what I was talking
about. "Pa, it's Raj."

The fingers continued drumming on the newspaper.

"Come, Pa. Let's go inside." I placed my hand on his shoulder.

At my touch, the drumming stopped and, although the sound had not been loud, the silence that came after was deepened by its absence.

"Raj," my grandfather said.

"Yes, Pa."

"How you, Son?" Still he looked away into the shadowed distance.

"I'm fine. And you, Pa? How're you doing?"

But he did not answer, slipped away into silence.

And I remained where I was, beside him, my hand on his shoulder, listening with him to the whistling sigh of the sombre shrubbery.

My grandfather was not born in this century: the thought, when I was of an age to assess the tapestry of time, staggered me. At his birth, aviation was embryonic, the automobile still a curiosity in early evolution. The Boer War was yet to come, as was the Boxer Rebellion. The Kaiser ruled in Germany, the tsar in Russia, and in England, Queen Victoria still burdened the British throne. He was, by the middle of the first world war, old enough to enlist; by the beginning of the second, too old.

But my grandfather, born in a mud hut in Casaquemada to unlettered parents more at ease in Hindi than English, lived on the distant periphery of world events, seeking in his way to push back the parameters of peasant poverty. He refused, early, to follow the path taken by his three older brothers, each of whom had traded Hinduism for education, and Presbyterianism, at the Canadian Mission School. Briefly instructed in reading and writing, he spent his days immersed to his shins in rice paddies while the youth of Europe fell dead into the ranker water of sandbagged trenches. All his life he displayed the splayed toes of feet unformed by shoes, toes that, in my imagination, I could see squelching confidently into bubbling mud.

As crumbling economies convulsed Europe and turned much of North America into societies of transience, my grandfather took a job as clerk and stockboy in a small store in the village of Salmonella, urged on perhaps by pride stung before his brothers' successes, two as teachers at the same school that had educated them, the third obscurely employed in an office of the colonial administration in Lopez City.

By the end of the second war, my grandfather had opened his own store, at first little more than a long and narrow hole in a wall, offering trinkets and baubles. But postwar Casaquemada, with American money floating in the air like green incense, was a heady time for trinkets and baubles; and slowly, with prudence, my grandfather expanded his store, little by little adding merchandise, adding floor-space, until it rivalled the one two streets away in which he had first joined a quick mind to simple business skills.

The last expansion remains, vaguely, with me. My grandfather had acquired the adjoining snack bar and on a Saturday afternoon after the close of business had Wayne sledge-hammer half of the dividing wall to pieces while my grandmother, fearful of flying brick, held me tightly a safe distance away. I was aware that afternoon, watching the head of the hammer crunch into the wall, watching the dust of pulverised concrete coat Wayne's skin, that his was the physical work, ours the financial profits. I sensed, held in the grasp of my grandmother, a troubling unfairness, but I remained, too, helpless before the unruffled certainty of life as it existed in Casaquemada.

My grandfather dressed carefully for work, in dark pants and a white shirt, long sleeves buttoned loosely around his wrists, a tie of conservative colour knotted around his neck. In Salmonella, where the poultryman across the street wore a blood-splattered undershirt, where the grocer around the corner wore day after day the same sleeveless sweater, it made him conspicuous; and it was only later that I came to understand the importance his attire held for him, when I realized that this was how his brothers, the two teachers and the civil servant, dressed every day. It could have brought him ridicule, but did not, largely because of his reserve and the dignity with which he carried himself; he was familiar with no one, polite to everyone, in contrast to my grandmother, who sought an insincere familiarity with many and was polite to few.

Only once, as far as I know, was my grandfather's reserve openly tested. A customer, unhappy with his purchase and angry at my grandfather's unwillingness to refund his money, came to the house one evening to press his demands in confrontation. He stood on the verge of the road outside the front gate, a stone in each hand, screaming coherent threats in a voice that had staggered from one of little Salmonella's four rumshops.

I crouched in the living room, peered out a corner of the opened glass louvres as my grandfather slipped a shell into his twelve-gauge shotgun and, without locking the barrel into place, went out onto the porch. My grandmother, concealing herself in the dining room, called out to me, ordering me to join her. But I stayed where I was, and she was too afraid to come and get me.

The man, bravado challenged by the group of friends who'd trailed along with him, gestured menacingly with the stone in his right hand. Then, staggering backward onto the road, he flung the stone: it bounced and clattered on the corrugated iron roof. My grandfather, unperturbed, clicked the barrel into place, raised the gun to his shoulder and fired above the man's head into the darkening forest behind; he calmly cracked the gun open, removed the spent shell and inserted another. But the man was already in flight, following his friends down the deserted road. My grandfather waited a minute or two, came back in, bolted the door behind him and spent the next half-hour or so at the dining table oiling and cleaning the gun, his face calm, his hands steady, as if he had just used the weapon, as he sometimes did, to bring down a cluster of coconuts. My grandmother trembled through the dinner preparations in the kitchen, broke two glasses and a bowl, while I, sitting across the table from my grandfather, my little finger inserted into the spent shell, regarded him with awe. He made no secret of his dislike of the gun, of his owning it, but he recognized its necessity to a store owner, understood why the police, unarmed and not particularly famed for courage, had urged it on him, issuing his licence with almost palpable relief. Despite this unease, though, his resolve in using it when necessary was stonelike, and to me all the more impressive for its understatement.

But even more than my grandfather's resolve, I marvelled at his patience, the silent self-control he displayed when driving with my grandmother, a woman who took back-seat driving to new heights. When, in the stretch of empty road ahead, a car appeared in the distance coming towards us, she would begin her chant, lowly at first but sharpening quickly: "Pa! Pa! Slow down, Pa! You goin' too fast! Go slower, Pa! Oh God! Oh God! Don't drive so fast, Pa! You goin' to kill us! Slow down, Pa . . ." And she would continue, desperation growing to terror even as my grandfather dutifully braked almost to a standstill, until the offending car had gone safely past; then she would gasp for breath, pat the perspiration from her face and chest with a perfumed handkerchief, and mumble a quick prayer to whichever deity happened to come to mind. A thirty-minute drive with her could turn easily into sixty, but my grandfather never complained, never resisted.

If I viewed my grandfather as a man of heroic, if quiet, achievement, I took a somewhat different view of my grandmother, in a vision that went a long way back, to when I was six or seven. We were at the beach, not Manzanares but one of those on the north coast now ruined by gobs of sticky tar floating in from the offshore oil rigs. I was in the water, shallow and sandy at low tide. The sky was grey with rain cloud. My grandmother, bulky in her swimsuit and plastic cap, stood on the beach with a towel about her shoulders keeping an eye on me. I squatted in the water, splashed at it with my hands, felt the gentle tug of current and sand, fine and granular, rushing around my feet. A soft rain began, an infinity of droplets visible only in aggregate, spattering warmly onto me, bringing the surface of the sea to leaping life. My grandmother tugged the towel over her head, trotted in alarm to the edge of the reaching water, called out: "Raj, Raj! Come out, come quick. Run inside the house, it raining, you going to get wet." My astonishment did not deter her. She stalked into the water, seized me by the arm, dragged me out, pulled me along at a panicked pace. My grandfather, rocking on the porch with his newspaper, grinned without looking up when I stamped past him in a huff. Later that day, as the storm raged in on wild winds, as lightning licked at the sea and thunder hammered across the sky, the old radio in the living room crackled the news of the death of a pope.

So the vision was formed, of a woman set in her own foolishness, a woman determined in her fears.

The story of her marriage to my grandfather when she was sixteen, he eighteen, did little to improve my view of her. It was a story my grandmother relished; she never spoke of her childhood, as if her marriage to my grandfather marked the beginning of her life, as if it was only in matrimony that she acquired form and being.

Their marriage, as was normal then, had been arranged by their families. Throughout the ceremony, elaborate, traditional, she kept her eyes lowered, as was expected of a good Hindu wife, respectful, submissive, unchallenging to her husband. Then, conforming to tradition, she spent the first night of her married life as the last in her father's house, her new husband to return the following day to claim his bride and take her away. The next day at the appointed hour, my grandfather, accompanied by his three brothers, arrived to take possession of her. They waited in one room while she, with the help of the aunt who would accompany her to her new home to chaperone her through the first days, prepared in another. When, finally, she and her aunt made their entrance, my grandmother looked up from the floor to four unknown male faces. And she didn't know which of the four she had married. In a panic, she whispered to her aunt, who pointed out my grandfather, second from the left. It was the first time my grandmother laid eyes on the man to whom she had already been married for almost twenty-four hours.

Relating the story, my grandmother, laughing, never shrank from admitting her disappointment at having married the darkest of the four brothers. But he was a young man of prospect: the pundit had astrologically seen money in his future, and a life of great comfort. "Never mind that he dark," he had told my grandmother's father, assuring him that the stars approved the match.

My grandfather, in his reserve, was not generally a man of wit. But whenever my grandmother told the story, he would listen with unabashed pleasure, waiting for the end to add his comment: "They does say marriage is the tie that binds. People should remember that love is the tie that blinds." So uncharacteristic was this of him that, when my grandmother started in on the story, I began finding myself waiting impatiently for the end, just to hear my grandfather drawl his lines.

It was a kind of wit, too, I suppose, the Sunday he sent me off to the Salmonella Presbyterian Church. I had been fighting with Angela over something trivial, and my punishment, as meted out by my grandfather, was to accompany her and her mother to the eleven o'clock service. I suffered through it, through the singing and the sermon, the taking of the collection. Sunday mornings after this were tranquil as, for several weeks, I secreted myself in the prayer room and watched with relief Angela and her mother, frilled and powdered, wearing identical straw hats, walking past my grandparents' house on their way to church. My grandfather never again mentioned his unique punishment—it had clearly been effective—but it was a month before my grandmother ceased fearing my possible conversion to Christianity. "People going to say we not good Hindus," she would declare daily at dinner after a day spent brooding on it. "Here we always having *pooja* and Raj going off to church on Sunday. Eh-eh! But look at this *jhunjut*, nuh!" My grandfather never replied, and I, in my fantasies, toyed with the idea of asking permission to attend church again, just for the pleasure of seeing my grandmother's reaction. I never did, though, for fear of having the permission granted.

In the admiration, distant and respectful, that I had for my grandfather, and perhaps because I spent so much more time at the house with her than at the store with him, I came to understand my grandmother as a woman of failed dreams.

I went through a stage, as does almost every young child when confronted with future responsibility, of denying any possibility of future matrimony. My childish protestations upset my grandmother more than I realized. She would say, "One day I going to find you a nice Indian girl . . ."

Spiteful, stung by the threat, I would retort: "And what if I meet a nice Moslem girl first?" To my grandmother, Hindus were Indians, Moslems amorphous and, in this way, threatening.

Her smile would tighten: "A nice *Indian* girl . . ."

"I ain't want no wife anyway."

"And how you going to have chil'ren?"

"I not going to have chil'ren."

"But if you ain't have chil'ren, who going to look after you when you get old?"

And there it was, her final frightening refrain—*Who going to look after you?*—recognized only later, with age and experience, as the entire key to my grandmother, to the marriage she made, to the children she bore, to the unhappiness of shattered dream that came eventually to be hers. For my grandmother's dream of life was one that reached back into time to a life lived off the land, lived precariously, with all the smallness and closeness implied by the daily struggle. Like her mother before her, and her mother before her, she cherished a dream of matriarchy, pictured herself as a kind of Hindu Queen Victoria, the central, cementing image of a numerous and expanding family, honoured by sons, daughters and their spouses, catered to by grandchildren—one to caress her aching head, another to massage coconut oil onto her tired legs, a third to brew bush-tea, a fourth to fetch a can of Indian sweets or butter cookies—indulged, pampered, fussed over, her whims fulfilled, her advice sought, her orders heeded. She would be loved and feared, would dispense charity and chastisement, would inspire respect, her bed a dais, her bedroom— shadowed, air pungent with creams, perfumes and coconut oil— a throne room of awe and mystery.

But there was to be none of it. The world had changed, opened up. The family had freed itself from the twin tyrannies of land and weather. Her children travelled, married not through arrangement but for love or unplanned pregnancy, and they found their niches not, as always before, in or close to the parental home but far from it, in England, in Canada, in Lopez City, at Malbaie in the south of the island. Apart from me, come to her by accident, Surein was the only grandchild she saw with regularity, and he was not one to run and fetch.

So my grandmother, unwitting, was left with her large house, living room long unused, four empty bedrooms developing a haunting echo of desertion. Slowly, over the years, her dream disintegrated, defeated by a world evolved out of her reach and by possibility created by the success of my grandfather's store. He could afford to send his children away to foreign universities, to expose them to the wider, more promising world beyond Casquemada. In fulfilling the predictions of the stars, my grandfather had helped defeat the dream of my grandmother. And the defeat had left her bitter and complaining, rendering even less frequent the already infrequent visits from family. Only Grappler and my Aunt Sylvia continued to come, and that, I suspect, was more Grappler's doing than my aunt's; there was something in the house—the inanimate quietness, maybe, or its sense of ageless isolation—that he seemed to relish. My grandmother's complaints— "Nobody does come to visit, nobody does call, nobody does write"—never fazed him; he treated her gently, as if he understood her pain, even felt it himself.

Changes came slowly to my grandfather as the years passed. At home, he continued reading his newspaper and, with greater frequency, his holy books, of small format, hard-covered and tattered, with yellowed pages of thick, fuzzy paper; continued labouring in his private garden, performing his devotions early every morning in the prayer room. His vigour diminished, movements slowed, hair greyed, but he was a man of habit not easily swayed, not even by the erosion of his own body. At work, though, he grew querulous, distrustful of employees and customers alike, spent much time obtrusively eyeing their actions and their bags. When a customer left without making a purchase, he would berate the attending clerk, insisting that the clerk, if she were any good, would have sold something, *anything*.

The town was growing, slowly, but with deliberation. New stores appeared, larger, brighter, grander, with illuminated signs and lines of chrome and plastic. My grandfather's store lost its lustre, its hand-painted sign fading, acquired a dinginess. The displayed goods, accumulating overnight the settling dust of the old building, quickly lost their freshness. Competition heightened. At Christmas, my grandfather gave free pens and calendars to his customers; the furniture store down the street gave transistor radios and T-shirts. My grandfather extended credit; the appliance store around the corner offered low-interest loans. My grandfather declared them mad and predicted their financial ruin. It was when their success could not be denied, when the furniture store expanded and the appliance store announced, with fanfare, its new outlet in Lopez City, that my grandfather, stripped of his certainty, was for the first time in his life left at a loss. He had been able to create something out of nothing, but age had dulled his edge, hardened the flexibility of his inventiveness. He wished the new away, could not respond to its challenge. He dressed as he always had, went to work every morning—the store still provided an income—but there was nothing distinctive about him now, except in the way of the anachronistic. He was ruled by necessity, and by the force of habit.

Back in Casaquemada, I found the store, once bright and bustling, a sad, dark place. There was no life to it, no sense of a future, little of a present. Only the past remained, caught in the corners, seeping from the walls. The store had been left behind.

Then, a little under a year ago, the store that had performed miracles, the hole in the wall that had educated my two uncles and me into professions unattainable a generation before, was burnt to the ground. It was a deliberate fire, two Molotov cocktails thrown at the front, one at the back, the flames meeting in a joyful, crackling dance in the centre and roaring high into the dark night in a consummate, consuming passion. My grandfather's was the second business in the town to burn, the rash of arson that had begun a few months before in Lopez City touching now the smaller towns; politics, as Surein said, spreading like wildfire. The crowd that night, flame dancing on sweaty, excited faces, cheered at the leap and crash of embers, the sparkling showers of red and orange. There was no malice; they were simply enjoying the show, as they would the Independence Day fireworks at the soccer field. Regret and commiseration would come later, before the blackened ruins. As the firemen, slow in arriving from the fire station not six blocks away, uselessly played their arcs of water into the inferno, Grappler and I held my grandfather's arms, partly in unnecessary restraint, partly in unnecessary support. I could not read his face. Was that retreat, there? Was that a touch of relief? But to me, every crash of flaming timber, every sheet of corrugated iron that curled, red-hot, like a disdainful lip, was an experience in pain. The store was not a place I had known intimately, but it was so inextricable from my grandfather, so central to the adventure of his life, that watching it burn was like watching him burn.

The loss stunned my grandfather, as we saw in the following days. He would awake, pray, dress as usual in his white shirt and dark pants, knot his tie, then spend the day, his working hours of eight to five, sitting in his rocking chair on the porch, removed, face set like a mask, fingers drumming on the wooden arms of the chair. My grandmother said, "Is as if they burn out his heart, Raj." He could take no solace, as could my grandmother, in the large insurance settlement that would keep them in comfort for the rest of their days. He grew morose, even less communicative than usual.

After his stroke two months later he lost his interest in the newspaper, began turning directly to the death announcements at the back, the only column that now spoke to him, the only place he now encountered old friends. His prayers continued, intensified, even as his pace around the dew-mottled garden to pick flowers slowed to a shuffle; but his gardening tools remained stored under the house, rusting away in their cobwebbed corner.

As his faculties slipped from him, my grandfather began occasionally to speak to me in Hindi, the language of his childhood. It was a language of secrets to me. I understood none of it, this my ancestral language, but I felt no loss, no nostalgia, little curiosity. As I listened, without interrupting, to my grandfather's incomprehensible mumblings, I understood that, in the migration of my ancestors, I had been not so much unmade as remade. Much was gone, much was new; and the resemblance I bore to those people who, almost a hundred and fifty years before, had crossed the seas to a land unknown, was restricted to the physical. I did not, like so many, cling to wooden sidetables etched with elephants. I felt no special affinity for Indian miniatures; was bored by Indian music; caressed no dream of visiting India. There was in me no desire to resurrect the ancestral. That I understood nothing of what my grandfather said in his periods of forgetfulness was of little consequence to me. It failed to move me. I had been taken too far.

If, in the end, I knew neither of my grandparents, if they never became people, if they remained as mysterious to me as my parents, I remained strangely at ease. I had somehow slipped onto a different agenda, become a mere witness to the end of what I saw to be a disintegrating culture.

Deep within me, I sensed that I had moved on.

"They had a dance contest."

"Pa?"

"They block off the whole street."

"Who, Pa?"

"No cars. No bikes. They ain't even let in donkey-carts."

He paused at the end of each sentence, puffed a little breath.

"They set up a record player. On the bonnet of a jeep. The music was loud-loud."

His speech had slowed, grown flat, was without inflection, simple pronunciation exhausting enough, strength too ebbed to flourish emotion.

"Anybody could try. Almost everybody try. Little chil'ren. Big people. Men. Women. Gran'mothers. Everybody dancin' in the street."

He went silent, breathed, ran his tongue slowly around his lips. He was as if savouring the dance of images in his mind.

"When it finish a long-long time later. They give first prize to a man. With one leg. And a crutch."

He smacked his lips, flicked at them with the tip of his tongue.

"They give him a brand-new bicycle."

I expected a chuckle. None came. Instead, his fingers began their drumming on the folded newspaper.

A sharp, sickly stench, like that of a fish ripening in the sun, suddenly materialized into the still air. I knew it well, recognized it from my childhood: this tropical smell of snake. I froze, body involuntarily arrested, eyes skirting along the undergrowth. But, of course, one never saw anything, just smelled it, sensed its slithering presence until the moment it chose either to withdraw or to strike.

"Come, Pa, let's go inside." I took his old man's hand, the drumming fingers stopping with reluctance in my grasp. With my other hand, I picked up the newspaper; then, gently, firmly, pulled him to his feet, gripped his arm and, struggling with the story, his brutal tale of useless endeavour, resisting its message of absurdity and negation, walked him back through the breach in the wall, away from his realm of cultivated chaos, back to the house.

He sat in his rocking chair, ignoring the newspaper I had placed on his lap, staring out beyond the fence to the road. His fingers drummed sharply on the wooden arm of the chair, cadence dramatic, like a horse galloping on a hardened track.

My grandmother, the brimming coffee cup held gingerly between the tips of her fingers, led Jan back out to the porch. As she passed the cup to me, swirls of steam rising from it, I glanced at Jan's face, trying to read what might have happened in the kitchen. But she would not meet my look, walked to the chair across the porch from my grandfather, sat with her glass of Coke, half empty, the ice cubes tinkling.

My grandmother said, "Pa, you thirsty? You want something to drink?"

At the sound of her voice, he seemed to awake into a febrile awareness; he turned his head towards her, eyes blinking, focussing with difficulty.

I sipped at the coffee: hot, thick, sweet, as always. His gaze, less bleary, made its way over to me. "Raj." He smiled uncertainly.

"Hello, Pa, how you feeling?"

He turned to Jan: "Hello, Jaan."

"Pa." The ice tinkled in her glass. She cleared her throat.

He said, "How Rohan?"

She said, "He's fine." There was unease at the end of her voice. We had walked past Rohan playing among the chairs in the dining room, my grandfather pausing briefly to examine him before moving on, puzzled but wordless, to the porch.

I said, "He's here. Do you want to see him, Pa?"

But he had already returned to my grandmother. She repeated her question.

"Jus' some water, nuh," he said. "No ice."

No ice. My grandparents had always been judicious with the temperature of liquids. Drinks, for themselves, were cool or warm, the extreme of either abusive to their stomachs; the water-heater beneath the house—a box of white enamel mounted on the wall and linked to twin gas tanks by lengths of brass piping, the entire unit bizarrely modern in the setting—remained unlit during showers, hot water being corrosive on the skin and taxing on the heart.

My grandmother made her way back into the house, content in the fetching and serving that formed so much of her life, a contentment that Jan disparaged as that of a conscientious maid. It had strained their relations from the beginning. My grandmother had expected Jan to share in her view of life, the word *wife* defining, confining, offering a certainty of action and position; had expected her to be caretaker of son, husband and parents-in-law. Jan was silent, with difficulty, in her refusal. But resentment built on each side, an explosion avoided only by acquisition of our own house.

My grandfather, his words a whisper in the fragile tranquillity, said, "I dreaming your daddy these days."

My *daddy*: a strange word in his mouth, a word never used except in infrequent reference to my father, a word that, forming on my tongue, evoked an excess of saliva, thick, velvety, a froth without flavour.

He said, "He coming to me almost every night. He not saying anything. He just standing there. Looking."

"You've been thinking about him?"

Jan said, "Asha says—"

"Please, Jan."

She glowered fleetingly at me, smiled, brought the glass to her lips and turned away.

"But your mammy not there . . ."

"You talkin' your chupidness again?" My grandmother, irritation and fear braided through her voice, hurried back onto the porch, the water glass half-filled. "Is all he talkin' about these days. Chupidness and *jhunjut*!" She walked over to him, took his hand and wrapped his fingers around the glass; then, agitated, she stepped across the porch to a sofa swathed in red plastic.

My grandfather brought the glass slowly to his mouth, pressed it against his lower lip as if to anchor it, raised it with shaking hand and poured a bit of water onto his tongue. Then he lowered the glass to the arm of the rocking chair, brought his lips together and swallowed. Each action was considered, each movement controlled.

My grandmother, addressing Jan, said, "You know, he ain't even reading the newspaper any more. He does just keep it with him, fold up neat-neat."

Jan said, "Maybe his eyes are tired."

My grandmother pursed her lips, shrugged.

I turned to my grandfather. "Is that right, Pa? Your eyes giving you trouble?"

He turned, eyes misting, towards me. "No-no, the eyesight awright."

"So how come you're not reading the newspaper any more?"

He looked just past me, gaze wavering. "Is just that—" He swallowed again, saliva this time, played his tongue around his mouth. "You see, Son, I been reading the death announcements. Looking for friends. And almos' every week I see one. A friend or a cousin or a—"

"Always looking for dead people," my grandmother snapped.

Jan nodded.

"But now, everybody gone. It ain't have no more names I know. I ain't have no more dead to count."

My grandmother said, "But Pa—" She stopped short, her appeal severed by a crack in her voice.

"That does tell you something, Son. It does tell you—"

My grandmother said, "Pa."

"—that your time coming close."

My grandmother said, "Pa!"

He went silent, slipped into an artless confusion at the sound of my grandmother's voice, at the three pairs of eyes staring, pained, back at him, even at the glass of water gripped in his tensed hand.

My grandmother said, "But why he talking chupidness so?" And she struggled for control.

Jan tinkled the ice in her glass, smiled faintly at me: triumph.

A car flashed by on the road in the rattling rush of roaring engine. I thought I felt the porch tremble.

Rohan, shy in his satiation, stood hesitantly at the door.

I held a hand out to him.

He shrank back into himself, back into the shadow of the living room.

Jan said, "Rohan."

And he ran out, ran across the porch on spattering feet, ran to her and wedged himself into the security between her knees.

My grandmother, voice brittle, said, "You still hungry, Ro? You thirsty?"

He shook his head: no. Inserted the tip of a finger into his mouth, bit lightly down on the nail.

My grandmother sighed.

My grandfather stared at the glass of water, iconic, prognostic.

I looked at Rohan couched between Jan's legs, and I felt the distance of the few cold, shining tiles between us.

Finally, my grandmother said, "How Sagar, Son?"

I thought: Respite. Sat back in the chair, rolled my neck until it cracked, like the snapping of dry bones. "He's fine, Ma. Still taking the pills."

"He not drinking?"

"Can't. Just the smell of alcohol and he'll throw up."

"He watching the office good?"

"Can't complain." There was no point in telling her of Madera's visit. "Nobody's broken in."

It was here, at my grandparents' house, that I first came across Sagar. He was one of the itinerant drunks they had hired to cut the lawn, a man among the many who had come to my grandfather's store asking for alms or knocked at the front gate of the house seeking food. He had begun work late in the morning, around eleven o'clock, when the sun was already high. My grandmother called me in a panic not thirty minutes later: he had passed out. I examined him where he lay, a little old man, short, silver-haired, wiry in an undernourished way. By the time I got there, he had regained consciousness but remained, groggy, where he had fallen. A quick examination revealed no immediate problem beyond the weakness of a lack of food and an overindulgence in alcohol. I helped him to his feet and walked him down the driveway to the back stairs. My grandmother would not have him in the house—he exuded a potent mixture of cheap rum and fermented perspiration—but she busied herself in the kitchen preparing him a plate of food. I sat beside him on the stairs as he wiped at his face, his neck, with a damp white towel that quickly grew dark under his sluggish scrubbing. His breathing was laboured, his skin dark and leathery, pitted beneath the uneven beard by acne scars. He had, it occurred to me, the face of an Australian aborigine, but shy, sly, with the fatal naivety of the deeply subjugated.

I tried talking to him, asking questions. I was curious about who he was, where he had come from, how he had descended into the nightmare of life adrift. But the answers he gave were vague and incomplete, slurred words emerging senseless from hesitant mumbles, sentences that came from nowhere, that led nowhere. Not evasion, I realized, but a kind of mental incontinence. It touched me, flicked at my nocturnal speculation at my grandfather's life spent in the paddies or sugar cane fields, at his energies dissipated over the years into the despair of simple motions endlessly repeated. So sitting there on the stairs beside him as he ripped listlessly at the roti my grandmother had brought, I constructed a biography for him: a vegetable plot, a mud hut, a querulous wife, innumerable children, evenings at the rumshop and, finally, a dazed flight from the predictably uncertain to the perilous predictable. It was a fantasy, but at the time I believed it, seized on it, and then and there offered him a job. I had bought a building for my office, I said, and needed a night watchman, would he be interested? He neither accepted nor refused, but he came along with me.

And so, to my grandmother's consternation, I acquired what Jan, from that evening on, called my pet project. My grandmother said, "But, Raj, he ain't even know how to cut lawn." And she was right. He had wielded the blade inexpertly, had in several places gouged the grass, slashed into the dark, brown earth. I said, "I'm just asking him to keep his eyes open, Ma, that's all." Yet I knew it was not all I would be asking of him, and I was confirmed in the rightness of my action when, not long after, rumours began circulating of a family connection, one claiming him to be my grandmother's brother, another my grandfather's cousin. They were unfounded, mere malicious gossip, my grandparents said; but a part of me never totally discounted the possibility in the byzantine, almost incestuous world of Casaquemadan Indian genealogy.

My grandmother said, "Is a good thing you doing, Son. God go bless you."

"Or at least Sagar will," Jan said.

My grandfather leaned forward in his rocking chair, beckoned with his free hand at Rohan. "Come, Son," he said. "Come to Pa."

Rohan pressed himself more tightly against Jan, stared with suspicion at the old hand clawing feebly at the air.

"Come," my grandfather said. "Come to me, Devin."

And I froze. For in the sway of the images among which my grandfather now often lived, he had called to my son by my father's name.

Rohan sat between us in the front seat of the car, punching the radio buttons. We drove past the Salmonella police station, a huge old building of colonial style, cream walls and wood-brown edging, in front of which grew, as always, a towering mahogany, trunk thick and grizzled, lower branches reaching upward into a profusion of deep-green leaves. Circling its base and lining the driveway, whitewashed rocks ran like a giant string of pitted pearls, clumps of incongruity in the intimidating tranquillity of the station.

Jan said, "And so ends yet another—"

"Pointless visit," I finished the sentence for her. "I know."

"Rohan!" She reached for his fingers, grasped his hands in hers, pulled him away from the radio.

"But it makes them happy."

She put her arm around his shoulder, hugged him close to her. "Prove it."

We drove slowly down the main street, past the old Shell gas station now nationalized into the Casaquemada Petroleum Company, its sign bright and colourful, its concrete paving black with spilled oil and ingrained grease, into the business section of town. The stores and shops were shuttered and barred, the street deserted in the afternoon sun, people dozing at home or watching a movie at the cinema or taking in a cricket match at the playing field on the northern edge of town. The street, much changed in its particulars, was little changed in its character. It had retained, over the years and despite the odd garnish of glitz, the feel of the small market town, the weekday mecca of the fruit and vegetable farmers from the surrounding countryside. Its smells, drifting in through the open window, were familiar to me, calling up flashes of a life long past. I pushed them away, the little scenes of inconsequence—checking books out of the library, drinking chocolate milk from the carton, choosing comic books at the grocery store—that crowded insistently in on me.

I said, "Did you ask her?"

"You've been dying to find out, haven't you."

"Well did you?"

"No."

We went by the ruins of the first store to be fire-bombed. It had been a wholesale food outlet, a cavernous wooden building that smelled of damp flour, its gloomy interior stacked high with boxes and fat jute sacks. Now weeds were pushing up from among its ruins of blackened beams and twisted, rusting metal, the powdery smell of flour replaced by the acrid odour of old ashes.

I said, "Thank you."

"No need. It's not as if I didn't try."

"She wouldn't tell you?"

"She wouldn't let me ask. Soon as I mentioned the little garden she started telling me how to make roti. Again. Like, for the twentieth time, you know?"

I laughed, part relief, part disappointment.

She said, "You don't really like that stuff, do you?"

We came to my grandfather's store, or what was left of it. I braked. A quick look: burnt, broken walls of peeled plaster; jagged shards of smoked glass; snapped poles of charcoal; scatterings of fresh garbage; and, off in a corner, tossed casually onto a heap of brick, the hand-painted sign, one edge eaten by flame, paint bubbled and faded, lettering illegible. My eyes burned. I thought: Save something. I pulled to the side of the road, tire-wall squeaking against the curb, reached to open the door.

Jan said, "No, Raj."

Rohan, clasped against her, blinked quizzically at me.

She said, "Let's go."

I turned away from the ruins, stared ahead for a second or two, stepped hard on the gas pedal. The wheels screeched. We surged ahead down the empty road, away from the stores and skewered memories, past homes small and dark and shuttered, past the house—now obscured by giant bougainvillea—that was to have been mine, past the Salmonella Presbyterian School, down a sudden hill and out of the town into the spreading greenery of uncultivated countryside.

Jan said, "Slow down, Raj."

I eased back on the gas pedal, only then realizing, as control returned, how fine the tire traction had grown, how keen the command of the steering wheel. Driving on a scalpel's edge: the impotence of anger, the danger of fear. I concentrated on the ribbon of road, dark grey and undivided, unrolling and slipping by beneath us. Forest thickened to either side, sometimes coming close to the edge of the asphalt, at times farther away beyond a swatch of grassy verge. Just past a plot of straggling evergreens—an abortive attempt to cultivate Christmas trees locally after a ban on their importation—we went by a red Jaguar, its paint new and shining, crunched deeply into a tree, trunk emerging unscathed from where the driver's seat would have been. It was a recent accident, just a few hours old; the grass on the verge and around the car, flattened by the trampling of many feet, had not yet recovered. Instinctively my eye took in the details, fascinated by the spectacle of destruction, my mind speculating idly at the effect the impact might have had on the driver.

Jan said, "Surein would have loved it."

I nodded. It was how we had come to think of him. But I said nothing of my thoughts; they would have been cause for ridicule, would have occasioned a deserved, undisguised disgust.

We drove on, the trees thinning on the right to afford glimpses of land cleared for agricultural schemes quickly gone bad and now abandoned, machinery rusting and buildings, so recently new, weathering into the denuded landscape. The entrance, a narrow passageway of packed gravel slashed from the road through the trees, was sealed off with a thick, low-slung chain hung from metal poles to either side.

Jan said, "You know, if your parents are really there, it's the perfect set-up. Just think about it, eh? All you'd have to do is weed 'em from time to time."

Not far on, the forest ended abruptly. I grimaced, shook my head at her as we drove between the twin obelisks of riverstone and cement on which were set, low down, deeply tarnished but legible with effort, two brass plaques, which read ROOSEVELT FIELD, U.S. ARMY.

She said, "Wish my parents were that easy to handle." Rohan, asleep in her embrace, threw an arm across her lap.

Roosevelt Field, carved from forest and built into a military base in the throes of World War Two, was now for the most part what its name implied: acres of treeless field covered in high, wild grass. Most of its buildings had been torn down, not in anger but in necessity, a piecemeal dismantling, boards and beams, windows and wiring all carted away and added to countless houses around the island. The only buildings left standing, of reinforced concrete walls four feet thick, had been gutted, the massive two-storey shells abandoned to heat and mildew and the timid scurrying of mice. While its main thoroughfare had become part of the island's road system, its sidewalks and secondary roads had been ripped up or eaten to extinction by the creeping vegetation. The tarmac and airstrip, though, had retained a usefulness; the whine of aircraft taking off in search of patrolling enemy submarines—the middle of the war had seen the sinking of several allied ships off Casaquemada—had been replaced by the whine of racing cars, Hondas and Toyotas with enhanced engines, and bodies plastered in oil-company stickers.

Driving through Roosevelt Field, it was hard to imagine that all of this, fallen so quickly to ruin and frivolity, had acquired by the late fifties a significance both political and emotional in the island. The premier, leading independence negotiations with a Britain eager to divest itself of the remnants of a dying empire, had demanded the end of the U.S. military presence as well. He had headed a march, complete with signs and placards, to the main gate of Roosevelt Field, demanded in a voice of dignified anger, a voice theatrical in its appeal, that the base commander see to the removal of himself and his men and the return of the land to the people of Casaquemada. "We ain't need your damn chewing gum!" he had shouted at the commander, who had come to the gate, and the phrase had become the slogan of the campaign of nationalism the premier was orchestrating. It was painted on walls, printed on posters, turned into a calypso. And it was like a miracle when, not a month later, the announcement was made: the Americans were leaving. A ceremony was held, the Stars and Stripes folded, the gates thrown open. And in the euphoria that followed, in the brave words of challenge and triumph bellowed by the man who would, just months later, become prime minister, few took notice of the revelation that the Americans had decided to give up the base, obsolete in the dawning age of nuclear missiles, six months before, and immediately informed the premier of this and had even arranged the date of the departure ceremony. It had all been a masquerade, a little bit of island theatre, politics as carnival—but the myth had been constructed, and the myth would accompany the premier into his prime ministership, the island into its independence, he the giant-killer, the island his domain. Yet the base had fallen apart, had decayed in the tropical heat and burgeoning vegetation, and with it, unnoticed, had gone the myth. The prime minister's politics had gone from vocation to profession, from vision to manipulation, and Roosevelt Field, conquered, reclaimed, had gone back to what it had been, land useless in its abandonment—an example, Grappler had once said, of independence as the right to do nothing.

Jan yawned, turned on the radio, softly, so as not to wake Rohan. The thin, brassy, bouncy tones of a calypso mingled with the rushing of air and the hissing rumble of the car engine. In the distance, a low bank of forest appeared on the horizon, marking the boundary of the former base.

A car, rapidly approaching us, flashed its headlights twice without slowing.

Jan said, "What's that all about?"

"We'll see. Police are probably timing up ahead."

"Timing?"

"Speed trap."

And it wasn't long before we could see the shadowed figures of men standing singly and in groups around the towering obelisks.

I said, "It's not a speed trap."

Jan shifted in the seat, uneasy. Rohan stirred, stretched, his feet pressing against the side of my thigh. I turned off the radio.

There were about a dozen of them, policemen plainclothed and uniformed, some standing on the roadway with Sten submachine guns, others on the verge with a variety of semiautomatic rifles. We were waved down by a man wearing an untucked white shirt, black pants, running shoes, his only visible sign of authority the Sten he grasped in his right hand. He came to my window, bent over, lay the perforated barrel of the weapon on the sill, peered in at me. "Afternoon." A young face, serious and neutral.

"Good afternoon."

"Your name?"

I told him.

"Address?"

I gave him my driver's licence.

"Where you going, Doctor?"

"Home."

"And you coming from . . . ?"

"Salmonella."

He nodded, passed the plastic licence back to me, eyes moving to Jan, pausing on her strained face, then to Rohan stirring into wakefulness. He said nothing, considered us blankly.

After a moment he straightened up, turned the barrel of the weapon towards my face and ordered me to unlock the trunk.

Looking away from the tiny black hole, feeling the softness, the defencelessness, of flesh, I switched the engine off, got out, opened the trunk. Still grasping the weapon in his right hand, he poked around with his left, shifting the rags and tools, feeling behind the spare tire, digging gingerly into my medical bag. From all around, eyes—casual, bored, sleepy, nervous—focussed in on us. I folded my arms, unfolded them, slipped my hands into my pant pockets, looked around, looked into the trunk.

Finally satisfied, neutral still, performing a function he neither relished nor abhorred, he slammed the trunk shut, walked off towards a patrol car parked at the side of the road, gesturing us away with languid waves of his left hand.

Jan did not look at me, fussed at Rohan as, sleepy still, he sat up in the seat.

I drove off slowly, with an exaggerated leisureliness. The figures at the roadblock grew distant, hazy, blended with the vegetation. The forest petered out on either side, became untended field once more.

Rohan said, "We goin' to the ghost-tree?"

Jan said, "The what?"

"The ghost-tree."

"What d'you mean, Ro?"

"We goin' to buy food?"

"The *grocery*, Ro. And no, it's closed today."

"Why it close?"

"Because it's not open, all right?" She spoke sharply.

Rohan bit at his lower lip, sat back. "Why it not open?"

After the turnoff to the airport—an intestinal road in a constant state of disrepair, crumbling edges hedged by shacks and shops in dilapidation—sugar cane fields rose to either side, stretching away on the right to the base of the mountains, on the left to horizon unbroken but for the distant smokestacks and buildings of the sugar mill, the last operating on the island.

Jan said, "I feel so fucking helpless in this place."

A current of wind rippled across the surface of the sugar cane, its path marked in a wave drifting gently through the mass of congealed green, rising and falling, the fields stirring as if alive. My stomach tightened.

Jan said, "This is *your* place, Raj, these are *your* people. You know how everything works here, you know how to get things done."

It was the kind of vegetation, deceptive in its beauty, that could swallow you whole, a vision of green annihilation into which a man could, unnoticed, disappear without a trace.

Jan said, "Get me the plane ticket, Raj." Her fists clenched on her lap. "D'you hear me, Raj? D'you hear me?"

"I hear you." There was nothing else to say.

All around, the green fields, thick, enveloping, heaved a silent sigh.

8

Small places, places of limited scope, of brutal past, hesitant present and uncertain future, offer but scanty possibility, offer at best a life proscribed.

There was, in the early part of my life, an unspoken assumption that I would inherit my grandfather's store. And at first I acquiesced to it, spending the occasional Saturday morning at the store looking on, wandering around, reading comic books, aware that nothing more was expected of me, that nothing more would be allowed. As I entered my teens, though, more was demanded; my Christmas vacations were given over to the store, working the cash drawer—my grandfather distrusted cash registers, doubted their accracy—in the busiest season of the year. And at first this, too, was acceptable; it seemed a training of a kind for the future that was to be mine.

And then, the summer I was fourteen, Grappler and my Aunt Sylvia took Surein to England for three weeks. A holiday. To show him a bit of the world, my Aunt Sylvia said.

My anger—at Grappler, at Surein, at my Aunt Sylvia—surprised me. It began the moment I heard about the trip, sat burning in my stomach like a voracious acid. I thought: And what about me? I resented what I took for abandonment, but felt, too, a pain too vague to comprehend. It was this pain that steadily grew to touch my grandfather, my grandmother, the store. For it came clear to me that the life to which I was headed was an even further limiting of my possibilities in a land of already diminished possibility. Surein's trip, his glimpse of the world, drew my parameters more tightly around me; the possibilities of his life, suddenly clear, made stark the impossibilities of mine. In the three weeks they were gone, my resentment grew as tight as an angry fist. I ate little, worried my grandmother, enjoyed her worry. And I thought, and thought, and thought. In the coming school year we were to be streamed, into the arts or the sciences, and the choice—French or physics? History or chemistry?—would determine in great part what we would do, and what we would not do, for the rest of our lives. My love of reading and the distinctly unscientific lot that awaited me seemed to preordain the stream into which I would be plunged. But the anger, and the sense of suffocation, engendered by Surein's trip caused me, for the first time, to question the vision of the life that was being created in my name.

The store, with its unpromising beginning and modest expansions, was my grandfather's epic, the satisfying success of a man who had begun life in the rice paddies. But to me, beginning life with the store well established, the thought of remaining tied to it, of continuing without change the life that my grandfather had lived, twisted in little time from unwitting acceptance of the inevitable to the claustrophia of nightmare. I was being used to assure the continuation of my grandfather's success, the store as shrine, I as caretaker. And my opinion had never been sought.

I decided, sometime in those three weeks, that I would not defer either to inevitability or to others, and my thinking went then to what I might do—not an easy task, for Casaquemada, in its smallness, in its simplicity, could offer little. Neither the army nor the police force was socially acceptable; they were the realms of rough men, men of little education, small ambition and dim prospect. Professions that commanded respect, professions that would not cause my grandmother to lose twenty years off her life, were restricted to, in order of acceptability, medicine, law and education, the first because it entailed both title and money, the second because it entailed money and the third because, while neither lucrative nor socially uplifting, it was at least not a disgrace. Dentistry and psychiatry, other possibilities, were suspect, clinging to the edges of respectability by their titles, digging into mouths as shadowy an activity as digging into minds. Beyond this, there was nothing. Nuclear physicists, aeronautical engineers, writers, dancers, painters, tennis players all belonged to another world. In Casaquemada, they were not, could not be, professions; could only be fantasies and hobbies, tolerated and vaguely acknowledged, and to dream of any of them as a life ambition was to be considered, not wrongly in the context, naive at first, odd if it went on for too long, a sign of instability if it failed to wither in the onslaught of social and familial obligation.

So that by their return, I was juggling three choices: medicine, which would stream me into the sciences; law, which would stream me into the arts; and teaching, almost immediately discounted, which would stream me into either. At night, lying awake in bed, I drifted from the first to the second, from the white coat to the black robe and back again. I felt that I had to make a decision, had to be able to say with certainty *This is what I want to do* before approaching my grandparents. It would be a blow to them, I knew; it would put the future of the store into doubt, and it would mean my leaving them to a house they had never inhabited by themselves, having moved here from my grandfather's parents' home with four of their six children already born. And so I juggled at my choices, delaying decision, tending towards law after Perry Mason had muscled his way through yet another successful scenario, medically minded while watching Dr. Kildare stave off illness.

I needed to talk to someone. My grandparents were out of the question, Grappler out of the country. Wayne wouldn't have understood the problem. And so I went to Angela. She and I had grown apart, and not only because we were attending different high schools. Three years before, during the final year of primary school in which we were preparing for the examinations that would qualify us for high school, Angela had been assaulted in a sequence of events that I had inadvertently set in motion. I had been spending much time at the local public library, not studying but simply wandering among the shelves in the small, bright and airy building, fingering the books, flicking through them, sniffing at the sweet, soothing scent of paper. This particular afternoon, setting out for the library on my bicycle, I shouted to Angela that I would be back in half an hour, that we would play then, after I had exchanged my book. In a far corner of the library, though, I came across a small shelf, screwed to the wall, that I hadn't discovered before. Labelled "Reference Only. Not for Loan," it held as if for display a series of books, thick, of large format, the collected tales, folk and fairy, of various lands. The covers, tightly swathed in protective plastic, were elaborately illustrated with smiling Chinamen, leaping leprechauns, smirking samurai, humble Thais, simple Scandinavians: inviting figures, each challenging with the line *Come, let me tell you a story . . .* I succumbed. In the late afternoon sun streaming through the corner window, I sat at a table and went through the books one by one, handling them with care, turning the pages with the tips of my fingers, reading bits and pieces of text, poring over the details and colours of the illustrations, transported, bedazzled in the dense, yellow light. Eventually, regretful at leaving them behind, I left the library, mounted my bicycle and began the ride back to my grandparents' house. As I paused at the corner before turning onto the main road, my grandfather's car flashed by—early, I thought, for the store to have closed—with Angela's mother sitting in the passenger seat beside him. They did not see me, my wave and cry of greeting both freezing in a sudden disquiet.

My disquiet increased a few minutes later as I wheeled my bicycle past my grandfather's car parked at the side of the road in front of the house, past an unknown car parked in front of his, though the front gate, to see Wayne sitting serious-faced in the porch. My breathing tightened, body chilled: there were too many things out of place. I leaned the bicycle against the wall of the house, walked slowly up the stairs to the porch. Wayne looked at me, said nothing. I eased myself into my grandfather's rocking chair, the cushion sighing as usual under me.

After a few minutes, my grandfather came out onto the porch with two men, one the family doctor, a distant relative, the other a policeman in uniform, his white helmet in one hand, his notebook in the other. They conversed briefly, the policeman glancing over at me. He said, "Is the boy?" and my grandfather nodded. The doctor offered a ride to the policeman. My grandfather walked them to the front gate. He came back to the porch after they had driven off, stood with his arms folded looking out at the street, at the forest beyond, and, in a quiet voice, told me what had happened.

When I had not returned from the library after half an hour, Angela, telling no one, had set out on foot in search of me, walking at first down the main road, then turning into the narrow back streets that led, circuitously, to the library. She walked past the fire station with its gleaming trucks; past the undertaker's with its planks of planed wood and unfinished caskets leaning against the wall in the sun; along the edge of the playing field, extensive and erratically grassed, its semicircular perimeter defined by the vegetation from which it had been cleared. As she came to the end of the playing field, a car mechanic called Devil, the character he played in the island's annual carnival, a young man slightly retarded and seemingly always covered in engine grease, came at her out of the tall grass. He seized her arm, began pulling her off the road. She screamed and, as luck would have it, was heard by Wayne, who had just left a shop farther up the street and was on his way to my grandparents' house with a packet of sugar for my grandmother. He shouted, dropped the sugar, sprinted towards her. Devil, alarmed, released her, sprang into the grass and disappeared.

Wayne took Angela to my grandparents' house. She was unharmed, my grandfather said, just frightened, and the police had begun a search for Devil. Then he unfolded his arms, slipped his hands into his pockets and went into the house. I could not look at Wayne for, although my grandfather had said nothing of my involvement, I felt the weight of it; felt the weight of the coincidence of his presence; felt the weight of the responsibility that would have been mine had he not been there.

When Angela and her mother came out of my grandparents' bedroom, I had already secreted myself in my grandfather's prayer room. I have no memory of ever having discussed the attack with Angela. My sense of guilt opened a gulf unacknowledged but palpable. We still spoke, but when we did I was uneasy with the awareness of her guardedness and mine. This self-protection, this acquisition of the private: we had, I realized later, begun to grow up.

Even with the distance between us, immutable after three years, I took my uncertainty, my unaccustomed discomfort, to her, not so much seeking advice as opinion and a safe outlet for frustration. We had both changed, especially physically, in the intervening years, although, to my eyes, she more than I. She had filled out, sprouted breasts, hips, had grown to resemble her mother in manner and facial feature. Sitting beside her in the living room of their little house—her mother had gone to the market in the town—I felt myself less adult than she. There was an assuredness to her, an assertion of womanhood, while I remained uncomfortable with my thickening pubic hair, affected still by the dismay that had seized me at the sprouting of the first strand, a long and fine thread that I had secretly snipped off with scissors. She had begun, too, dressing in closer imitation of her mother, in dresses of conservative cut when in public, in loose blouses and shorts when at home, feet usually bared to reveal neatly painted nails.

We sat on the sofa, on uneven cushions covered in a faded brocade of blue patterned in gold flowers. It was a small living room, a third the size of my grandparents' and crowded with furniture of rounded, polished wood. On the far wall, beside the open windows through which, over the top of the concrete fence, I could see the side of my grandparents' house, stood a bookcase, its shelves stuffed with untidy piles of magazines and books.

Angela, her legs tucked beneath her, held the splayed fingers of her left hand out to me. The nails, cut short, gleamed with fresh red polish. She said, "You like them?"

I saw that her fingers were shaped like her mother's: a ghostly penknife blade flashed, chips of wood flew through the air. I nodded, smiled, wondered what my father's fingers had been like.

"I does do them only on the weekends. They doesn't let us wear nail polish at school."

Exasperated, I said, "You hear anything I tell you, Angela?"

She waved her hand back and forth, to dry the polish. The smell of it, sharp and attractive, filled the air. "I hear everything you say. I think you crazy."

"I ain't come here for you to tell me that."

"So why you come?" She made a face, sucked her teeth in a drawn-out expression of impatience. "Sometimes you does be so intense, Raj. Thinkin' too much. That goin' to get you in trouble one day."

"So what you want? Is my future I thinking about."

"But what it have to think about? You only givin' yourself worries for nothing. You know you goin' to get your grandfather's store when he dead."

"But I already explain. I ain't want my grandfather's store."

"You think you have a choice? You only foolin' yourself, man. You have to carry on, they countin' on you, you's their grandson."

"But—"

"But you hard-headed, eh boy?" She swung her legs out, stood up, stretched her arms overhead, yawned.

"You know what you going to be?"

"Of course." She went over the windows, held her painted fingers up to the light. "A teacher, just like my mother." She turned towards me, pointed at me with her index finger. "Just like you goin' to run your grandfather's store."

It was like a challenge. I stood up, left, my uncertainty gone, my confusion eased. Inexplicably, I felt sorry for Angela, and I knew that I no longer knew her.

The first thing Surein said to me when they visited the following weekend was, "Boy, Raj, them English people ugly for so! They like a tribe o' troglodytes walkin' in the streets."

My Aunt Sylvia, her lips lacquered in a new shade of lipstick the colour of overrripe cherries, said, "Surein decide he going to study law." And she added, with a kind of pride, "In England." She had acquired, in three weeks, a touch of British inflection.

Grappler, relaxed, the lines on his face less prominent, gave me the book they had bought me, *Stories of King Arthur and His Knights*. He said, "You mustn't forget to dream in life, Raj. Nobody goes anywhere without dreaming."

I recognized the opening, seized it: "But is not everybody who allowed to dream." Then I fled with my book to the little prayer room.

Surein wandered in a few minutes later. He stood in the middle of the room, looked aimlessly around, let his eyes rove over our grandfather's altar. His new clothes, freshly unpackaged, smelled of plastic and dry-laundering. He said, "I pick out the book for you myself."

"Thanks. Good choice." But I didn't believe him.

He perched on the edge of the desk in front of the window. After a moment he said, "You want to play cricket?"

"No." I opened the book, let the pages tickle past my thumb; each, of a thick, furry paper, made the sound of a gentle spitting. "I going to study medicine." The words came of themselves, my sudden decision a reaction to his, and even as they formed on my tongue, I grew angry at myself, annoyed at the unplanned divulgence.

His eyebrows raised in skeptical surprise. "Yeah? And what about Granpa's store?"

I shrugged. "I not interested in business."

"That ain't no excuse." He stared at me as if in disbelief. "What Granma and Granpa say?"

"I ain't tell them yet."

He snickered. "But you's a hell of a man, yes, Raj." He got down from the desk. "Come, let's go play some cricket. You bat first."

I refused and he went off whistling. Not long after, through the windows, I saw him wandering around on the lawn, staring up into the mango tree, kicking at the grass. I sat at the desk, opened the book and began reading: *In the old days, as it is told, there was a king in Britain named Uther Pendragon . . .*

A knock at the door aroused me from the magic of the words. Grappler said, "How you doing, Raj?"

I turned around.

He stepped into the room. "You enjoying the book?"

"I just started reading."

He stood in the middle of the room and looked around, as Surein had, but with an air of preoccupation. He stepped closer to the altar, his back to me. "Hanuman," he said. "Lakshmi. Krishna. You know the names of the gods, Raj?"

"Some."

"You know the stories?"

"No."

"You should read them, you'd like them. They're like dreams. Epic dreams. Dreams of battle and flying chariots."

"I tired of dreams," I said, closing the book.

He turned away from the altar, stared intently at me. "Aren't you a little young for that?"

"Surein going to study law."

"Yes. Or so he says now. He might change his mind."

"At least he could do that."

"What's on your mind, Raj?" He sat on the desk, where Surein had sat. "Tell me about it."

I hesitated. Then, clutching the book on my lap, I told him all. As I spoke, my voice began to break, and I thought of the parents I had never known.

When I was through, he ran his fingers through his hair, rubbed the back of his neck, was silent for several minutes. "Your parents," he said finally, "planned to send you to university. Did you know that?"

I shook my head: no.

"Even before you were born they were talkin' about it. They were smart people. Devin felt trapped by the store. The fate o' the eldest son. It bothered him that your grandparents planned to send his younger brothers away for education and keep him here for the store. He felt that you should have a profession you could carry with you. And he was right. He used to say that to be safe here we had to plan our lives like tortoises, ready to move at a second's notice." His voice strained, went brittle. He coughed. "So you want to study medicine. Where? Jamaica?"

"I want to go far away, Grappler."

He nodded. "I understand." He said he would speak to my grandparents for me, got to his feet, walked slowly to the door. Without looking back, he said, "I guess you're your father's son after all, Raj."

I remained in the prayer room for a while, thinking of nothing, feeling the thump of my heart in my chest. Then, after carefully putting the book into a desk drawer, I fetched my cricket bat and ball from my bedroom and went outside, through the back door of the house, to find Surein.

That night I dreamt of a small bright room with low ceiling and uneven walls freshly whitewashed, punctuated all around by countless doorways of varying size, large openings, slender gaps, slim apertures, leading all to destinations unknown. On each hung a door of vertical wooden boards bound together by horizontal wooden slats, each painted a brilliant primary colour; but no door fit its doorway, each either much too large or much too small, and neither doors nor doorways had even lines: nothing fit, everywhere there were cracks and gaps, slices of darkness beyond. But, standing in the middle of the small room, I was comfortable.

And so, just over four years later, Grappler and my grandmother took me to the airport, checked me in, watched me slip into the gloomy chamber of the departure lounge, waved hesitantly as I walked across the short stretch of tarmac to the metal stairs and ascended into the humming metal body of the red and white aircraft. I looked back only once, and then briefly, when I was already at the top of the stairs, in a final twist of vacillation. My emotions were contained: the fear, the excitement, the urge to give up on the entire enterprise and surrender to the undemanding path that could still be mine. Only as the craft, a cool, half-filled tube, moved to the edge of the runway, only as it began sucking the power to hurl itself, screaming, at the sky, did my throat constrict, and when the small terminal building flashed by, I saw it through mist.

In my mind, I followed my grandmother and Grappler through the emptying building, out to the parking lot; was with them as they entered the car, as the engine burst into life; saw the road, smelled the air, felt the sun, all with an intensity greater than reality. The window framed my grandmother's profile, her up-raised chin, the fine nose, the eyes red and watery; her veil, tightly pinned by gold, fluttered in the wind. And contemplating her pro-file, I remembered the only religious concession I made to my grandmother: the date of my departure. My refusal of a good-luck *pooja* had wounded her and made her fearful for my future; so when she asked that the pundit be allowed to pick the most propitious date for my departure, I acceded, stifling my irritation with effort. My mind understood, even if it could never accept, that for the Hindus of Casaquemada, religion was foremost a question of superstition. Marriages were made on the dictates of the stars; houses were built, apartments were inhabited, children were named only after consultation with pundits, unschooled men adept in the arts of mystical public display and charlatanic profundity. My grandmother, raised with unquestioning belief in their sibylline abilities, was no more and no less prey to the im-portunities of magic than any other believer. Reason played little part in many of her decisions, none at all in some. She was of a people who, in the end, respected only their superstitions, lives ruled not by self but by others wielding the paralyzing irra-tionality of the primitive. The flash of my grandmother's face, and the memory of my concession to the fantastical, cooled my emo-tion. My eyes cleared. I undid the seatbelt and settled back into my seat to observe the activity in the airplane.

It was my first flight. I had expected more. After ten minutes, I reached under my seat for the leather briefcase Grappler and my Aunt Sylvia had given me as a farewell present, unsnapped the brass clasps, took out my book—a novel of easy virtue and for-gettable title acquired because undemanding—and slipped into the simpler world of adventure fiction. Only occasionally did a flicker of deeper tension slash from my stomach, disrupting the flow of words and images. Then my hand would reach into the pocket of my jacket, nudge at my wallet, my passport, my return air ticket. It was a little act of comfort, a timid grasping at safety that preserved my play at unstudied ease. It was only when, as lunch was being served and I asked a flight attendant how much it cost, that the mask slipped. I had chosen her because she was Indian and because I had detected, beneath the precision of her Canadian accent, the more languid tones of the Carribean. She smiled knowingly at me. "Don't worry, darlin'," she said. "It's free, just for you." For the rest of the trip, my gratitude to her was boundless. Only later, when I realized my blunder, did I feel embarrassment for myself and anger at her, and acquired in the aftertaste a wariness of racial camaraderie.

It was while walking down the loading ramp from the plane, then through the dimly lit subterranean tunnel of the terminal building, that my head began to spin. Standing a few minutes later in the immigration line, the sensation grew worse, a gentle, irresistible rocking; eased as I sat at the desk of a second immigration officer, a terse young woman who scrutinized my papers, scribbled, stamped; spun again in the bustle and bedlam of the customs hall. My face set itself into a mask of nonchalance, the skin slick with oil, the flesh thickened. My two suitcases, large, of imitation leather, gripped with effort in hands gone frail, the briefcase tucked precariously under my left arm, I exited between sliding doors to the arrivals hall crowded at the door and rippling with subdued conversation.

Grappler had arranged for a friend of his to meet me, mailing to him a copy of my passport photograph, face grim, revealing to the point of distortion. My vision wavered before the myriad of unknown faces staring past me, somehow failed to notice the young man walking out of the crowd towards me.

"Raj Ramsingh?" he said.

I nodded, focussing on his blandly handsome face, his full, carefully groomed hair. I lowered the suitcases.

"Kayso." We shook hands, briefly, his grip firm and studied. Then, taking one of the suitcases, he quickly led the way out of the terminal into the cool, clarified light of an early summer evening.

Despite my suit, still stiff with newness from the made-to-measure Chinese tailor in Lopez City, I shivered, remarked on the cold.

Kayso grinned, said, "This is warm for us, man." There was boast in his voice.

We drove away from the airport at great speed. The highway, wide, of multiple lanes, staggered me, intensified the spinning in my head. My forehead tightened, as if someone were pressing down on my eyebrows. I clasped my hands on my lap, interlacing the fingers, pressed them tightly together.

I said little as we drove, restricting conversation to answering Kayso's questions about Grappler and Casaquemada. He told me that he returned often to the West Indies, usually spending a couple of weeks in Casaquemada visiting family before going off to the carnival in Trinidad. "Is a great life down there, man," he said, his Casaquemadan accent sharpening the more he spoke. "People not too concerned with working all the time. I have friends who does leave work two-three hours before the end o' the workday, and nobody does miss them. Try that here and they on your back before you out the door!"

Distant clusters of buildings drifted by, orderly seams of townhouses, above them a sky of a kind I had never before seen: a fine, high, glazed blue, pure and insubstantial, with the clarity of crystal.

"Don't get me wrong," he continued. "It have nice people here. Is a good place to live. Is just that"—he grimaced, shook his head in disapproval—"it lackin' spiciness. Is a clean place. Too clean. Is as if somebody should sprinkle black pepper all over Toronto. Throw some dirt in the streets. You know, New York is one o' the dirtiest places in the world, but is one o' the most interesting. Paris, same thing. Rome. Venice. A hospital operating room always bright and shining and clean-clean, and it interesting in some ways, but it can't hold you for long. Take a courtroom, though. It clean and bright and impressive—but some o' the stories, the dirt people does fling around! Is a fascinating place, never dull, never boring." With a quick glance backward, he changed lanes, moving to the right. "The *dirt* is the spice."

As I listened to him, to the impassioned, rehearsed description of his curious vision, the spinning in my head abated. I said, "Then Casaquemada should be a world cultural centre."

But he seemed not to hear me, guided the car in a swift, sweeping arc onto an exit ramp, said, "You need the darkness to see the light. Good can't exist without evil. God and the devil live on different sides of the same coin."

I nodded. The words, messianic, were troubling. The light outside had thinned, the colour of the sky deepened. We drove in silence through darkening, deserted streets, the trees and the houses set farther back absorbing the light of the streetlamps, rendering it ineffective.

Soon, after several twists and turns, the neighbourhood changed. The houses were newer, brighter. Fewer trees lined the sidewalk, and those that did were young. Kayso, slowing the car, pulled into the driveway of a house darkened except for a single light above the front door. On the lawn was a realty-company sign with a red SOLD sticker plastered across it.

"Homesweet'ome," Kayso said, triggering the automatic garage door with the push of a button. "For a few more weeks."

"You're moving?"

He switched on the headlights, illuminating the stacks of wooden packing crates that filled the right side of the garage. As he carefully manoeuvred the car into the space on the left, he said, "Well, is supposed to be a secret—I ain't even tell Grappler yet—but we going back home."

"To Casaquemada?"

"In a few weeks, as soon as everything finalize." He switched off the lights, the engine, the descended dusk fusing with the sudden silence into a disquieting inertness. "We selling everything. Taking off."

"How come?" In the darkened garage smelling of spilled oil and straw, my own voice sounded unfamiliar.

"Is time. Life easier down there—"

"You really think so?"

"—and is about time I did something for my people. The island give me an education, it make me what I am today—"

"You didn't put yourself through law school by working as a hospital orderly?" Grappler had told the story in admiration.

"Yeah, but is Casaquemada that start me off, for free. I owe the island—"

"Maybe you owe the hospital for giving you the job."

He undid the seatbelt, opened his door. "You going to understand one day, Raj." A tone of condescension entered his voice. "It have a lot to do in Casequemada, a lot to fix. I want to be part of it." He got out of the car.

We took the suitcases into the house as the garage door powered itself down. Cardboard boxes, some taped shut, others half-packed and open, filled the basement. His wife, he said, had done most of the packing before leaving for New York to visit family; from there she would go to her parents in Casaquemada to await his arrival. "She pregnant, you know," he said, leading the way up the carpeted stairs to the living room. "And we going to be in Casaquemada when the baby come." The living room furniture was swathed into shapelessness by sheets of opaque plastic. He put down the suitcase he was carrying, asked whether I was hungry and ushered me into the kitchen. A warm, webby light flicked on, splattered itself against the windowpanes, stroked along the bars of chrome on the stove and refrigerator, sparkled on the tap and toaster.

We sat at the circular dining table, of glass smoked grey, and ate pieces of cold fried chicken, forkfuls of potato salad and coleslaw, sipped at squat brown bottles of beer.

I asked why he had kept his return to Casaquemada secret.

He held a chicken breast before him as if to examine it, tore a strand off with his teeth. His dark lips shone dully with grease. "Because," he said, taking his time, "because people does always try to discourage you."

"Maybe is because they know Casaquemada better than you." I regretted the words the moment I spoke them.

"I know Casaquemada," he said quickly. "I done tell you, I go back every year."

I nodded, forced myself to remain silent. I had already said too much as it was. Different people had different escapes. I had found mine, and Kayso had found his; and neither of us, it seemed to me, quite knew where it would lead.

He said, after several uncomfortable moments of studious chewing, "You like jazz?"

I knew nothing about it.

"A calypso man, eh?"

I smiled weakly. I knew little about that, too.

He got up, slipped a cassette tape into the player—did they call it a ghetto blaster here?—that sat on top of the refrigerator. A sleepy, atonal, funereal music filled the kitchen. Piano, drums, saxophone, guitar: each instrument seemed to be going its own way, meeting the others only occasionally, as if copulating for a brief moment before running off again into solitary pleasure. It was a difficult music, uneasy on the ears. I smiled nonetheless.

"The best jazzmen," Kayso said, returning to the table, seizing a drumstick and bashing at the air in time with the drummer, "come from poverty. They know what it is to be hungry. They know what it is to be thirsty. They" —the drumstick slashed at cymbals—"pick up their music from the dirt." He bit at the drumstick, sat down. "You have to go to Kensington Market," he declared with a sudden enthusiasm.

"Is a jazz place?" The idea did not thrill me.

He laughed. "No-no, is a market. You know, fruit, vegetables, fish. When it cold-cold and you feelin' the need for some dasheen or some goat meat or some good, hot West Indian pepper sauce, that is the place to go. Things not too clean, and some o' the smells could almost knock you out cold, but that is what does make it *real*. When I down there, is almost as if I back in Central Market in Lopez City. Some o' the signs in Portuguese, but that all right. The dirt is the same. Nothing fake there."

I couldn't separate the humour from the sincerity. I said, "I like cleanliness. Dirt and charm never really mix properly for me."

My remark did not please him: too much sincerity, too little humour. But I was tired.

When the tape came to an end, he waited for the machine to click off. Then, in a silence that amplified sound and with a controlled abruptness, he led me upstairs to my room. In the darkness before sleep overcame me, I thought of the day I had spent, of the morning now so distant and the place now so far away, made an effort not to think of the people. I slept fitfully, twice awakening in a panic of unfamiliar smells and unidentifiable noises. The second time, my head spun. I went to the bathroom and was sick.

"French-Canadians are the nicest people in Canada," Kayso said, wheeling the car onto the wider, busier road. On one side, cramped houses with tiny porches of warped wood painted grey overlooked token patches of lawn; on the other, set back from the sidewalk, squatted an unnerving stretch of miniature mall: a clothes store and a milk store, an appliance outlet and a greasy spoon, a pizza shop and a laundromat, a gas station at the end. "Very open people," he said. "Friendly. And the least racist."

We had just come from rejecting the first of the rooms suggested to us by the university housing office. The woman, big, gruff, of guttural accent, had been less than welcoming, had brusquely escorted us through the cobwebby basement, past the dusty furnace and into the grim chamber for which she was asking forty-five dollars a week, "no food, no vash, no vine, no vimmin." In the deadening light of the single bulb, in the grip of her suspicious glare, my spirits sank. Then Kayso mumbled, "And no vay." We left, studiously ignoring the woman's sneer of displeasure.

The second place—its owner French-Canadian, Kayso informed me—was, from the outside, a little more promising. If the square building of red brick and dulled-aluminum window frames seemed inert and lifeless, we knew at least that the room was on the third floor. "Well, we know you not going to bury yourself before you dead," Kayso said as we trotted up the linoleumed stairs.

When Mrs. Perroquet opened the door, I was appalled. Small and hunched, with yellowed teeth showing from behind her wrinkled, thin-lipped grin, she called to mind childhood visions of fairy-tale witches. She wore furry pink slippers, baggy green shorts and a flowered blouse through which her bloated stomach hung as if in gravitational distress.

But if my first impression of Mrs. Perroquet was less than favourable, the room itself immediately dissipated all objections. Small but tidy, with a bed, a chest of drawers and a desk with a reading lamp mounted on the wall above, it looked out onto the back yard of another, similar building, a neglected garden of junked toys and rusting lawn furniture. But I wasn't looking for a view, and the room had a comfortable feel to it. For twenty-five dollars a week, Mrs. Perroquet said, I would have the room, and free use of the kitchen, the living room, the television, the telephone. For an extra five, she would do my laundry; for an extra ten she would do my laundry and provide breakfast.

When, with a nod to Kayso, I said I would take the room, she smiled her hideous smile and held out a set of the apartment keys, dangling them from the metal ring hooked onto the tip of her crooked index finger. Kayso and I fetched my luggage from the car and he left, with a promise to call soon.

I busied myself for the next few hours, first emptying my suitcases of the carefully packed clothes, breathing deeply—with pleasure, with pain—at their aroma of detergent and sunlight; removing the little packages of homemade sweets my grandmother had tucked into every empty space. Later, as I sat at the desk writing a letter to my grandparents, Mrs. Perroquet knocked at the door with coffee and a saucer of chocolate-chip cookies. I accepted them, with a formality that amused her, made her shy.

The following night, in front of the television, she told me about her family. She and her husband Leonard were from a tiny town in northern Ontario. "Francophone," she said. "You know, French-speaker. And the Anglos had all the job down here in the south. We were young, just married, had big dream. So we moved. Came south. A trade. A language for a job." She screwed up her face, clicked her loose upper denture. "Lousy trade." Leonard, after a lifetime of labour on construction sites, had died five years before. "Smoked himself to death," she said, grimacing and picking up a cigarette box from the coffee table in front of her. "This was his." She tapped at the box, handsome and polished, carved from a single piece of wood and outfitted with brass hinges; weighed it in her hand as if estimating the burden of memory. "Made it himself." She replaced it on the coffee table. "He was good with his hand. If he touched it, it did whatever he wanted. Didn't matter what it was. Plastic. Metal. Wood. Me." She laughed, a hoarse cackle.

I smiled, uneasy with her easy familiarity. My eyes wandered to the television: American troops walking through rice paddies, a village in flames, helicopters whirling above jungle.

My room used to be her younger son's. Joey was married now, lived in Guelph, taught school. Graduation photographs of him and his wife sat on the television: earnest, open faces framed by brown hair, his stylishly long, hers conventionally so. They were neutral portraits, drained of mystery, statements of harmlessness.

"But my first son," she said, her voice falling, her wrinkles digging themselves more deeply into her face. "Andy. He's crazy, full of crazy idea. He—" She paused, gazed across the small living room at me. "You see, Andy, he doesn't— Well, he only like white people." She held me in her gaze, her eyes bright with determination, her lips parted. "You understand?"

I nodded. She seemed to want a reply, a reassurance of some kind. Her embarrassment, like a physical presence, floated over and settled on me. On the television screen, protesters waved placards and brandished banners, mouthed war cries muted under the voice-over of the reporter.

After what seemed a long and difficult silence, she continued in her hoarse voice: "Andy's a fool. Always has been. Since he was a kid. One day we found him trying to pull out his baby teeth. With pliers. He wanted the money from the fairy." She shook her head at the memory. *"Debile."*

"What does Andy do?" I spoke the question, the product of politeness, with feeble conviction.

"He drive a truck. A truck! Imagine! After all his father's hard work. After we gave up a language for a future. A truck! Joey finished university, got his B.A., went to teacher college. But not

Andy. Not Andy. A friend offered him a job driving a truck and the fool quit high school to take it. Wouldn't listen to us. Now that friend drive a big car, and he live in a big house. And Andy doesn't even own his own truck." She leaned forward, elbows on her thighs, hands clasped before her. "Do you know what he did once? Andy? He barge in here one evening, all dirty and drunk and swearing at the top of his voice. I told him to leave if he couldn't behave himself. And he hit me." Her voice did not waver, offered the information without drama. "He hit his father." Her voice cracked, instantly steadied itself. "The neighbour had to call the police."

The television weatherman, pudgy, jolly, gestured with enthusiasm at a display of swirling arrows and sawtoothed lines, mugged at the camera, grimaced, gestured in helplessness, spoke rapidly and faded, with a self-satisfied grin, to a commercial.

"I don't know why he—" she searched again for the delicate words, "—why he only like white people." She opened the little wooden box and, with shaking hands, took out a cigarette. "So different from his brother and his father and me. Mixed with the wrong kind of people, I guess. Or maybe he's just bad, maybe he's got something eating away inside of him." She sat back on the sofa; her right hand fumbled in the pocket of her pink housecoat, emerged with a card of matches. "A woman can't really hate her own son, I don't think." Her worried old woman's eyes gazed at me. "But what I feel for Andy is very close to it." She lit the cigarette, homemade and with a smell so powerful that I wondered what her brew was, and ran her hand, yellowish in the light, through her sparse grey hair.

That night I wrote a letter to Grappler. I wrote about Kayso, but not about his return. I described my room, but omitted the view. I told him of Mrs. Perroquet, but did not mention Andy. It was instinctive. To hold back: it was a kind of respect.

Classes began. I took the bus and the subway, attended the lectures, explored the libraries, took the subway and the bus back again. It was a tentative time, a time when I felt my fragility. My exploration was subdued, curiosity dimmed by the sheer size of the city and by an intimidating lack of knowledge: which streets

were dangerous, which safe? Where were the good neighbour-
hoods, where the bad? I walked often, the legislative buildings at
Queen's Park my focal point, following different streets but never
going too far, my map folded small and secreted in a folder so as
not to expose my ignorance, peeling back the unfamiliarity in
brief, circumspect forays.

Gradually, I came to appreciate that the streets of the city held
little threat. My confidence grew. I worried less about the street
names, began seeing the city with less fearful eyes, noticed now
the different languages, the colours and the dress, the microcosms
of the world that had carved for themselves little neighbourhood
niches in the city. A certain voyeurism came naturally to me—
being in it, but not of it, was how I was most comfortable. Only
occasionally did distress arise: when the observer became the observed, when Indians or blacks sought me out with their eyes,
with nods of invitation. Then I remembered the flight attendant,
and the embarrassment I had opened myself to on the airplane. I
saw myself in these people, saw the admission of weakness and
loss implicit in their stares of racial inclusion, their searching for
comfort in the simplest of ways. I thought their behaviour a form
of racism, not one that rejected but one that claimed, the mirror
reflection of the virulent, this vision of another arising out of the
colour of skin. It was visible minorities who most made me feel a
member of a visible minority, visible minorities who seemed most
to draw the lines of difference. I began avoiding certain areas, or
walked through them with eyes of selective focus.

In this way, slipping smoothly into study, discovering slowly the
joys of anonymity, coveting the lack of community, I created my
own comfort in the bright and bustling city.

Six weeks passed before I heard from Kayso again. He called
late one evening, apologetic, pleading busyness. He had had to
arrange for the shipping of their belongings, see to the selling of
the car, settle various financial obligations. "Tyin' up the loose
ends," he said with a mixture of exasperation and fatigue. "Is like
tryin' to tie several pieces o' spaghetti together into a string."

I commiserated, offered to help; but my words, prompted by

politeness, were hesitant with insincerity. Kayso's tone of condescension, the fragile security of his vision of Casaquemada, had
remained with me, had grown to cover my memory of the evening
at his house. I had little desire to see him.

He said, "I leavin' in a couple o' days."

I said, "Really. Already." His accent, rehearsed, theatrically
heightened, as if he had been practising for his return, irritated
me, was part of the condescension.

He chuckled. "Is about time, man."

I forced a laugh.

He said, "So how things going?"

"Fine. No problem."

"School okay?"

"Fine."

"And the room? How the old lady treatin' you?"

"No problem."

"You gettin' to know the city a little bit?"

"A little bit." His accent had slipped; he had said *siddy*.
"School keeping me busy."

"That's good," he said, noncommittal, drawing the conversation to a close. "You have anything you want me to take back for
you? A letter, or—"

"No-no. Just tell Grappler everything all right." The telephone
receiver was heavy in my hand, the black plastic warm and damp
in the grasp of my fingers.

"Well, good luck, then."

"Yes, good luck." I hung up, took a breath that was like the
first in several long minutes.

The only light in the living room came from the television, a
flickering of bluish white that was like a constant lightning. The
sound was low, barely audible. Mrs. Perroquet, seated on the
sofa, said, "Your friend?"

"Not a friend," I said after a moment. "Just an acquaintance." I
returned to my room and, in the white light of the reading lamp,
finished taping to a sheet of blank paper the small maple leaf,
gone crimson in the cooling air, that I had picked that day from
its tree. Beside it, in black ink and in the neatest hand I could

muster, I wrote "Toronto" and the date, hoping, by capturing a splinter of the beauty, to preserve strokes of the excitement I felt at what was happening around me: at the rapid interplay of cloud, at the freshening of the air, the rustling of the trees, the brittle crinkling of dried leaves underfoot on the sidewalk. At this display of a nature that was not static, of a nature that was spectacle in its inconstancy.

Later, after I had pulled down the window blind and slipped into bed, it occurred to me that I would soon know no one in the city but Mrs. Perroquet. In the darkness, the thought, of a certain defiance, was comforting. I fell asleep happy.

"Smell like snow," Mrs. Perroquet said, closing the window she had opened to let out the gossamer veils of cigarette smoke that had been drifting horizontal throughout the living room. The early winter darkness had already closed in on a day of damp chill and low, heavy cloud. Earlier, when I was returning from the corner store with the can of stew that would be my dinner, there had been a brief flurry, thousands of wet, white petals materializing suddenly out of the frigid air. Mrs. Perroquet slapped her hands together, rubbed them as if for warmth, hugged herself. "Cold." She returned to the sofa. "Do you have snow where you come from?"

"Only in the fridge."

She cackled, coughed. "Imagine that! So you've never seen snow before, eh?"

"Only in pictures."

"It's hot all the time?"

"All the time."

"Even Christmas?"

"Even Christmas."

She frowned, shook her head: unimaginable. Turned her attention back to the television: hockey players scrambled in front of the net, a confusion of arms, legs, sticks. During dinner we had watched "Bowling for Dollars"; Leonard had been an avid bowler, the show reminded Mrs. Perroquet of him. Afterward, while I tried in vain to study—the university had closed for the Christmas vacation, leaving me with a sense of temporary drift—Mrs. Perroquet had watched a French game show, switching to the hockey when that was over.

"You never heard of the *Montréal Canadiens?*"

"Not until I came here."

"The Maple Leaf?"

I shook my head: no.

She reached for a cigarette. "You don't talk too much, you. You don't like to talk?"

"Yes, but—" I made a gesture of helplessness.

"You homesick?"

My throat tightened. "No. Not really."

"Which one? No or not really?"

I smiled. "Not really."

"A little bit, then."

"A little bit." And this was the truth. But it was not the principal reason for my silence. If I said little, it was because I had little to say. I had no desire to speak of Casaquemada. Today and tomorrow were too important to me; dwelling on yesterday could but hinder. If my thoughts went backward at all, it was to my grandparents, to Grappler, to the intensely personal. Instead, I was preoccupied by my studies, undemanding in this first term at least, and by what I was seeing around me, by the television, by the city. Newspaper boxes: it amazed me that people didn't steal from them. The unlittered streets: it amused me to see people stuffing candy wrappers into their pockets or purses, or dropping used tissues to the sidewalk with stiff-armed, secretive flicks of the wrist. Traffic signals: the obedience they commanded from pedestrians was stunning; a clear road crossed against the light brought glares of disapproval from those waiting behind and those waiting ahead. Directions: I took, for amusement, to asking directions of strangers; it was remarkable how people went out of their way to help. It became a game. One man, an expensively dressed businessman of unapproachable demeanour, checked his watch, declared that he had a few minutes, and walked me to the bus terminal. I idled away five minutes after he'd hurried off to his appointment, to make sure he wouldn't see me sneaking out.

And through all this, through my studies and my ventures in exploration, the weather ran like a developing theme. As fall advanced, winter began fighting its way into the city. The temperature fluctuated, winter pushing it down one day, summer, strength diminishing, pushing it back up the next. Sun and wind joined the battle, a heat without bite one day, a wind with icicled teeth the next. At night, though, the field was left to winter as summer withdrew to lick its wounds, gather its weakening forces. It was then that rain would unleash itself, neutral at first, taking no sides, then gently declaring itself for winter with the occasional flurry. I heard about but did not experience the treachery of which it was capable; a girl in one of my classes, driving north of the city one evening, was caught in a sudden downpour of freezing rain; the road turned instantly to ice, the car went off the road, her neck was broken. In this battle, wearying to the city, dampness infused the air like cordite, penetrated walls, turned books, clothes, bedding damp with moisture. The jacket of my suit proved insufficient. I acquired a winter coat, gloves, boots. This small, necessary gesture, the procurement of accoutrements useless in the previous life but vital in the new, helped alleviate my need, slight but potent, for the familiar. I was warm in them, felt protected in their padded clasp. It was like discovering familiarity in the unfamiliar; it was like a step forward.

A flurry of red and blue filled the screen. A stick flashed.

The crowd roared. Red sweaters danced, hugged, clawed at the air in simian celebration.

Mrs. Perroquet murmured her approval, quashed the cigarette with vigour into the ashtray held in her left hand.

There was a knock at the door.

Mrs. Perroquet rose, putting the ashtray onto the coffee table with a dull knock, went to the door in the corridor.

Blue sweaters, drooping in disappointment, skated over to their bench, stepped off the ice, reached for water bottles, drank, spat, doused themselves.

Voices from the darkness: Mrs. Perroquet's thinned in sudden anxiety, a man's of lower register talking over hers with an alcoholic slur.

My body tensed, began to rise out of the chair. And then there he was, I knew instantly, stepping from the darkness of the corridor into the dim light of the living room: this man whose mother feared him. He looked remarkably as I'd pictured him, short and stocky, with soiled, baggy work clothes. His face, like his younger brother's but shorn of innocence, reminded me of an unfinished stone bust, with features distinct but unpolished. His full black hair was streaked with grey. It was impossible to guess his age.

We stared at one another for several seconds, like two suspicious animals meeting unexpectedly in a jungle clearing.

Then he grinned. "Hiya, buddy, what's ya name?"

Mrs. Perroquet hurried past him into the living room, placed herself between him and me. "Leave him alone," she said sharply. "He's busy, he's studying at the university, he have a lot of study to do." In her agitation, her careful grasp of English was crumbling.

Andy grunted, strode over to the sofa, sat down. "Busy watchin' the Canadians, eh? Naw-naw, c'mon, buddy, let me and you have a little chat. Ya wanna beer? Hey, Ma, ya got any beer? My buddy here looks thirsty."

Mrs. Perroquet's wrinkles trembled, her lips tightened with fury. "I don't got no beer, go buy your own."

"Aw, shit." He struggled to his feet, steadied himself, stalked to the kitchen. The refrigerator door swung open, bottles rattling.

His mother seized my arm, whispered, "Quick, go in your room before he come back."

But I stood where I was, caught, unable to leave. I had a vision of his banging on my door, barging in, installing himself on my bed for a little chat.

"Her'yar, buddy, take this." He pressed a beer against my chest with the insistence of a restrained punch, threw himself onto the sofa. "Wha'cha say ya name was? Where ya from? Has the old lady bin sayin' nasty things 'bout me?"

I remained standing, shook my head. "No."

"Y'ain't scared o' me, are ya?"

"No. Why should I be? You seem friendly enough." But my body was light, insubstantial, my mind concentrated on his every word, his every nuance, his every gesture.

He tilted his head back, raised the bottle to his lips, his throat jumping like a pulse under the steady flow of liquid.

Mrs. Perroquet, face crinkling like crushed aluminum foil, swept her hand back and forth as if brushing at flies, motioning me towards my room.

"Friendly? Sure I'm friendly. Ain't I friendly, Ma?" He laughed, eyes absorbed, threw the empty bottle onto the sofa beside him. "Y'know, I like you." He glanced at his mother. "Yeah, I really like him." Then he stood, clapped me on the shoulder. "Well, I'll be seein' ya, buddy. I ain't too welcome here, in my own god-damn mother's house."

"Take care," I said, waiting for him to be gone, for the door to reclaim the darkness of the corridor from the hallway light, before I put down the unsipped beer. I felt relief, touched with a manic exhilaration.

The chainlock rasped into place. Mrs. Perroquet, face set in anger, marched up to me, fixed me with a glare of malevolence. "Why you didn't go in your room?" she demanded.

I shrugged, playing down my unease. "He seemed pleasant enough."

"He was drunk," she snapped. "The next time he come, you go in your room, understand?" She sniffled, looked around. "God know, his father always did." She retrieved the empty bottle from the sofa, searched her pocket for a tissue.

On the television, red and blue sweaters tangled, arms flailing, legs intertwined. Gloves, helmets scattered. The crowd roared its approval. Blood splattered across the pristine ice.

I went, now, to my room, tried again to study, failed, tried to write a letter and found, to my surprise, that my hand shook. I sat at the desk for a long time, disordered thoughts of my hand, of Mrs. Perroquet, of Andy, running through my head. Finally, switching off the light, I got into bed.

Time passed. My mind raced nowhere in the darkness. Faintly from the living room came the sounds of Mrs. Perroquet's reaching for a cigarette: the box snapping shut, its replacement on the table, the repeated scratching of the lighter into flame. They were sounds I had grown accustomed to, sounds that would repeat themselves at regular intervals into the early hours of morning as Mrs. Perroquet smoked away her insomnia before the muted television.

Three sharp bangs.

I sat up, electrified, breath held, ears alert.

Mrs. Perroquet's slippers padded to the door. She said, "Who is it?"

The reply was muffled.

The chainlock rattled as it was opened.

"What are you doing here?" Mrs. Perroquet said in a loud whisper.

"Where's ya nigger?" Andy's voice, resonant in the darkness, crashed down the corridor. "Is'e in bed?" It was as if he were standing just outside my closed door.

I was suddenly covered in perspiration. Should I get out of bed? Should I go out? Hide? Put on the light? Pretend to sleep? The cigarette box: it would have been the perfect weight. But I remained where I was, legs sealed under the blankets, my mind racing like a record at accelerated revolutions.

"Shh," Mrs. Perroquet said. "He's sleeping. You'll wake him. And don't call him that . . ." Her voice fell to an incomprehensible murmur. Not many seconds later the door closed quietly, the chainlock rattled once more, and Mrs. Perroquet's slippers shuffled back into the living room.

He was gone, but this darkness remained. Threat and fear dripped from the ceiling, seeped in under the door. I threw the blankets back, sat on the edge of the bed, my feet on the wooden floor.

The cigarette box banged, the lighter scratched.

I reached out to the window blind, started at the touch of its cold plastic on my fingers, released it. A weak light came in from the frosted windows of the stairwell in the building across the way. Stillness, and a night composed of infinity. I lay back, stretched out on the bed. Then the movement started, dark, lazy flakes floating down in the light. They multiplied quickly, fell more rapidly. The window sill grew higher. I stood up, pressed my face to the freezing glass of the window and watched as enchantment fell out of the night between the buildings and into the small, junked back yards lost in darkness.

The next morning, Mrs. Perroquet said nothing about Andy's visit, and neither did I. But she knew I knew, and I knew she knew: we shared a secret. And in this silence there was bond.

9

At five o'clock in the morning, when the world is
without light and movement is muted, there is no colour. The sky,
a dark grey softened by whispers of translucence, appears stained
with the merged darknesses of trees, houses, lamp-posts.

I had slept badly, mind vigilant but without image, held in subdued awareness by a whistling wind of white mist. Jan, irritated
by my fitfulness, nudged me awake with her elbow, mumbled a
protest. I got out of bed, surprisingly refreshed, checked on
Rohan and, with a cup of instant coffee, sat at my desk in the
study. The room was stuffy, smelled of dust. I opened the window
to the early morning darkness and a cool air came in past the
strands of wrought iron.

In the light of the desk lamp, I began leafing through the medical journals that Jan had stacked neatly in a corner. The wrappers, of a heavy, yellow paper, ripped with a rich and delicious
sound; but the journals themselves, rectangular books bound in
glossy paper, defeated me. They were full of articles dissecting

statistics, discussing possibilities, detailing discoveries, drawing conclusions. There were tales of microsurgery and laser surgery, heart transplants and lung transplants, of the impossible made possible. Machines were mentioned that we would never see, medicines announced that we would never administer. Reading the journals in Casaquemada was like reading science fiction, entertaining, instructive even, but ultimately futile. Their words of promise and hope, their speculation and expertise, were all rendered useless by context. Ours was, by force, a simpler medicine.

I went through them for the form of it—I always had—and stacked them, one on top of the other, in the opposite corner of the desk. The ripped envelopes I left on top of the desk. Jan would throw them out.

The world brightened quickly, but in measured movements. While the trees behind the neighbouring houses remained flat silhouettes, like huge black cardboard cutouts, the lawns began showing their colour: at first, a dark, dank olive; gradually, with imperceptible changes in the light, a less-sombre dead emerald. The sky, bleached, enveloped the few scattered white clouds in its lightness; but soon a soft yellow glow rose from the east, touching the distant trees, deepening them, adding dimension without adding colour, defining with a citron-edged sharpness the galvanized-iron roofs of the houses.

The light in the kitchen of Asha's house across the road flicked on. Her dog, a German shepherd of muscled, graceful dimensions, trotted silent and alert with expectation from the rear of the house, squatted at the gate of the wrought-iron work that enclosed the porch, looked up. A moment later, there was movement in the porch and the gate opened. The hinges rasped with rust, the dog whimpered: in the fresh, clear morning air, the sounds travelled easily.

Asha, a slim figure draped in red from head to foot, showing of herself only face and hands, advancing with the languid movements of the entranced, stepped out onto the lawn, paused to pat the dog. He pushed his head into her hands, his tail whipping, hind legs dancing excitedly from side to side. She rubbed his head, stroked him and sent him off with a sharp pat on his back.

The yellow in the east deepened, cast itself now onto the land, catching on the dew, enriching it, the rest of the sky nudging uneasily from blanched white into a powdery blue.

Asha began a slow walk around the garden, her hands clasped against her stomach. There was something of the sleepwalker to her, the tentativeness of the blind in her steps, as she made her way aimlessly among the plants and the flower beds, the green now lustred bright and crisp, like that of freshly washed vegetables. From time to time she paused to examine a leaf or a stem of the flowerless rose bushes, but in a distracted manner, as if she were not so much looking at them as seeing through them.

Then she turned abruptly and walked with vigorous determination across the lawn directly back onto the porch. The gate squeaked behind her, clicked shut.

I drew closer to the window, watching her through several removes: through the spirals of the burglar-proofing, through the diamond-shaped crosswork of our chain-link fence, through the more distant crosswork of hers, through the vertical iron bars that enclosed her porch. All these fences, all these strands of hardened metal—circles, squares, rectangles, triangles, flowers of iron painted black or white—on windows and doors, around porches, constraining, confining, protecting in frozen profusion: it was like living bunkered in paradise.

In the thinning shadow of the porch, Asha bowed three times in the direction of the rising sun, each bow successively lower, her arms held stiffly at her side. Then she brought her hands together, in a pose of prayer, raised them to her lips, held the position for many minutes. When she was done, she pulled the veil more tightly about her face, bowed three more times, clutched her left fist to her chest and turned towards the open door of the house. At the threshold she paused, turned suddenly, stepped over to the bars and, grasping two of them in her hands, stared towards our house in the same way that she had examined, before, the leaves and the rose bushes: with a penetrating gaze that rendered all transparent.

I pulled back from the window, hid myself in the shadow away from the light of the desk lamp.

She continued to look, for a minute, two, three.

I thought: What is she seeing?

She went inside, closed the door behind her.

I drew closer to the window, rested my fingers lightly on the burglar-proofing. The sky to the east was now a blazing, electric orange painful to the eyes. My gaze shifted to the edges of colour where, with an unseizable subtlety, the orange faded into the powdered blue, neither beginning, neither ending, each simply becoming the other. Little clouds were scattered about, puffs of a dense black against the orange, of a dense white against the blue. But they wouldn't last, I knew. For all their apparent denseness, their ultimate fragility could not be denied.

"I saw Asha at her devotions this morning."

"What devotions?" Jan, hair uncombed, face slack and pasty with sleep, poured steaming water into the cup, stirred the coffee.

"To Baa Baa Black Sheep."

"Jesus. I wish you wouldn't make fun of her, Raj." She splashed milk into the cup, sipped at the coffee, lit a cigarette.

"She bowed, she prayed, she played with the dog—"

"She does what she has to. To survive." She spoke wearily, sat beside me at the kitchen table. "Some play that game better than others."

"I've spoken to the travel agent."

"And?"

"And he'll get back to me."

She shrugged, brushed a strand of hair from her eyes. "What does the road sign say? 'Slow. Men at Work'? Or is it 'Slow Men at Work'?"

"I told him to hurry."

"When was that?"

"Couple o' days ago."

"I'm glad he's hurrying."

I glanced at my watch, stood up. "I'll see you later."

She ignored me, hid her face in the coffee cup.

Rohan was sitting crosslegged in front of the television: "Perspective," a government propaganda program of stilted script and shaky production, was extolling the minor triumphs of a subsidized farm. Rohan absently lifted his cheek for a kiss, never removing his eyes from the cows and the talking head of the terrified farmer.

I unlocked the back gate, reversed the car out onto the road, locked the gate, drove off slowly. It was early still, but from the sky hardened already into a cerulean crucible descended intimations of the great heat to come. The air, moistened, smelled of vapour; the vegetation, dried off, had lost its sheen. The houses of the neighbourhood—single-storeyed, designed for openness, tightened over the years into themselves by metal and the shrubbery of camouflage—appeared deserted behind their gates and fences. Manoeuvring the car carefully around the holes in the road—gouges permanent and expanding that revealed the underlying grid of rusted reinforcing wire—I drove out to the highway. Its double lanes, still fresh with the legacy of oil money, swarmed with the rush of vehicles into Lopez City. The air thickened with exhaust.

My route took me in the opposite direction. This traffic, as tenacious in the evening after work as in the morning before, was one of the reasons I had decided against opening my office in Lopez City; the oil boom had brought with it a tripling of the number of cars on the roads, had turned what had once been a snaking twenty-minute drive into a sixty-minute marathon of stops and starts, fumes and heat, and nerves frayed by the incontinent horns of impatient drivers. The traffic lights flashed green at the traffic circle ahead; with a glance to the right, I drove through the break in the flow of cars, followed the circle around into the eastbound lanes, where the traffic was light. Not much later I turned off the highway into a narrow side road, paved, but crumbling at the edges like dry pie crust into strips of grassed verge, which, after a few inches, tumbled over into mossy drains clogged with all the festering detritus of the street; as the day heated up, as the humidity thickened, imploded, the air would suppurate with the caustic odours of vigorous decay. To either side, the nameless settlement of grey-brick buildings and struggling family enterprise—mechanics' yards, ramshackle shops, vegetable stands—

held back with difficulty the surging vegetation, thick-branched and leafy, of mango, coconut, breadfruit and avocado trees. Few people were about; a mechanic tinkered at the exposed engine of a car, a middle-aged man bathed at a standpipe, a well-dressed woman strode with purpose along the edge of the road towards the highway; occasionally, a stray dog, mangy and emaciated, trotted tremulously across the asphalt.

Up ahead on the left, hugging the roadway, a low white structure the shape of a teardrop turret severed from its tower and lowered to earth came into view. Above it, hanging limp from a spray of dried bamboo stalks, was a collection of faded *jhandi*, little flags of various colours raised by the devout to signal publicly the completion of religious rites, each colour representing a different deity. The profusion above the little temple revealed, then, the obsessions of its builder, the preponderant pinks and blues signalling a longing for wealth, addressed to the goddess Lakshmi, who inhabited a lotus leaf, and repeated appeals to Lord Krishna, Chairman of the God Board. The invocations had so far produced little in the way of tangible result; the builder, a corpulent, taciturn man, still lived after many years of devotion in a shack behind his shrine, still sold newspapers every morning from a chair beside it. It was said that the shrine had been built, was maintained—he whitewashed it twice a year—with the money from this borderline commerce.

Approaching its whiteness, pristine enough to be insubstantial, I slowed the car, sounded the horn once, and, as usual, he came to the edge of the drain, the newspaper folded in his hand. I stopped, nodded in wordless greeting as we exchanged coin and newspaper. He turned back to his chair, glanced at the money. I flicked open the paper, glanced at the headline. Was shaken by the boldness of the type: GUERRILLAS SHOT. Was drawn to the photograph beneath: bereted men tightly uniformed, submachine guns cradled in arms, standing over two shirtless bodies, heads flung back, holes clearly visible in their chests. I noticed, with bittersweet pain, the grass on which the bodies had been stretched out, the river behind, the sunlight cutting with sparkle through the backdrop of trees.

And I wondered then, as I folded the newspaper and drove slowly down the empty road, whether Madera had been involved in this shooting, whether he had pulled the trigger that had released the bullets that had ended two lives on the bright, sunny morning beside the river.

They were days that, even back then, seemed bereft of innocence.

In a small place, I learnt early on, difference was no virtue. Eccentricity was easily qualified as insanity, and the urge to follow one's own path viewed with either suspicion or derision, but rarely with compassion.

Sunil Nadan was, therefore, never considered special, at least not in any positive sense of the word. He would wander into the school each morning as if he had ended up there by pure accident and, placing himself at his desk, would slip quietly into a contemplative absorption. He would maintain this self-contained detachment throughout the day, wandering the corridors at break and at lunch looking, I always thought, like Alice's rabbit in reduced circumstances, scratching at his bristly scalp, wrenching his emaciated face in painful thought.

He said we were friends, and I accepted the label more out of pity than comradeship; for Sunil, always the butt of bemused attention, quite simply had no friends. In the mornings, he would stand waiting outside the classroom, in ambush it seemed at times, pulling nervously with macaroni fingers at the long key-chain looped onto his belt. On seeing me, he would break into a smile, unbrushed teeth, streaked in light hues of yellow and brown, separating upper from lower much like a grinning rabbit. He would hitch up the baggy, pleated trousers that he wore belted an inch below his pectoral muscles and say in his thin, lively voice, "Good morning, mister, all ready for a hard day's work?"

Walking past him, I would nod and smile, say, "Good morning, Nadan, all ready." I could never bring myself to tell him just how much I disliked being called *mister*, how much the word grated on my nerves.

The rest of the day would be spent in trying, with as much

discretion as possible, to avoid him. Success was rare. Sunil was unavoidable, if only because we spent much of the day in the same classroom.

He had all the appearances of the diligent student, sitting at his desk, head lowered over his notebook, pen scribbling furiously. Once in a while he would look up, blank, gnawing at the pen; then he would suddenly resume his scribbling, pen flying back and forth across the page. Observing him, I could almost hear the shouts of That's it! That's it! resounding in his mind.

This pantomime of diligence fooled no one, especially not the teachers. They never asked Sunil a question, wordlessly returned his occasional homework with scrawled, bored Fs, allowed him to sleep during class until his snores, sharp and rhythmic, became disruptive, at which point a piece of chalk aimed with varying degrees of accuracy would be sent whizzing at his head.

If Sunil fooled no one, it was because he tried to fool no one. His diligence was no act. It was simply a question of energy re-directed, of attention channelled into a labour more vital to him, to his sanity, than passing grades in physics or chemistry. He filled several notebooks with his scribbling, but would let no one, not even the few he classified as friends, take a look at the mysterious work. We speculated, in moments of idleness: a novel, short stories, pornography. Missives to the devil, someone once said.

Infrequently, voice barely under control, hands twitching like beached fish, Sunil would feel the urge to speak his thoughts. At such times, he would snare me, usually somewhere along the second-floor corridor that overlooked the parking lot, and declare in a voice of regret: "Life is a hell of a thing, eh, mister?" The sentence was his way of initiating an urgent, ardent harangue.

For Sunil, the world was a mad and dangerous place, man essentially destructive, enjoying nothing more than opportunities to wound. The human race talked about freedom and light but, he insisted, in its confusion, in its fear, in a queer perversion of its vision, welcomed slavery and darkness. He spoke of God as of a neglectful father, and fantasized the delights of escape from the world. He flirted for a time with the idea of Islam—giving fright,

I was delightedly certain, to his very Hindu parents—but his interest had quickly and inexplicably waned. He began dreaming, then, of life in a Tibetan monastery, of meditation and peace, of retreat as tranquillity. His was, it became abundantly clear, a frail soul in a frail frame.

Sunil was insane, or getting there: we all knew it. His need of his psychiatrist, one of only two in the island, was obsessive and overwhelming. And yet, I felt after one of his tirades, there was something essentially accurate in his perceptions, his sense of man as beast restrained, his idea of a human longing for the dictatorial as a kind of coddling, a protection. They were bitter thoughts, and Sunil was easily dismissed, his words, unexamined, taken as ravings. Yet I wondered how many in the class, like myself, were intrigued but would never admit to it, for to do so would have meant claiming for oneself a little bit of Sunil's madness.

Sunil was once away from school for a month and rumours circulated that he had died. Some said he had committed suicide. No one thought of checking—that would have revealed an unseemly concern—but there was a general feeling of guilt in the classroom. I avoided discussion of him, walked away from the speculation struck in a tone of nonchalance, was haunted by a vision of Sunil writhing in fatal pain.

And then, one morning, Sunil reappeared. He said he had been ill, had been unable to leave his bed. When he tried, the room revolved and multicoloured lights flashed searing needles of pain through his eyes and into his brain. For three weeks he had seen everything through a red haze.

Sunil's return, the absence of a suicide attempt, the very fact of his being alive, had an effect on the class. Our sense of guilt turned to an embarrassment at having felt that guilt, and Sunil, unaware, absorbed once more in his intense scribbling, was invested with the blame. He became the butt of our discomfort. Questions, vicious, smirking, were fired at him: Did he play any sports? Could he? Was he interested in girls? Had he ever slept with one? Would he? Did he ever think about sex? If so, what exactly were his thoughts? The questioning, the needling, began at break the morning of his return, continued during the lunch period, resumed the following day before classes.

His response, muted, was devastating in its affability. He would smile, force a laugh, say, "Nah, man." Pushed, he occasionally became irritated, in his fragile way, and gesturing with helplessness pleaded to be left alone. I felt Sunil's distress, refused to join in the hectoring, but could not bring myself to defend him, either. I remained on the sidelines, looking on.

Yet, far from acquitting me from Sunil's coterie of friends, my attitude brought us, in Sunil's mind, closer. At the end of the week, as I was hurrying from the classroom, Sunil stopped me and said, "I know you don't mean it in a bad way, mister." There was a gentleness in his voice, a kind of sympathy, even. I felt chastened.

One morning not long after, while Sunil was off haunting some distant corner of the school, Doug Madera picked the lock on his desk with a pair of dividers. Madera was a minor star on the fringes of high school sports glory, a struggler in the outer regions of academic mediocrity; he wore his khaki pants low on his hips, folded high the short sleeves of his blue school-uniform shirts. He rummaged around for a moment in the exposed desk, burrowing through the jumble of books and crumpled paper; emerged with one of Sunil's notebooks. It was a thin, oversized book bound by a spine of spiralled wire, its blue construction-paper cover soiled at the edges by grease and sweat, by the occasional fingerprint, spidery lines of desperation and tenacity. Madera, with bluster, a piece of exaggerated theatre, began reading from the book. Several boys clustered around him. Unable to restrain curiosity, struggling with a sense of trespass, I joined the group.

Of what we could decipher—the handwriting large, tremulous with a lack of control, like that of a five-year-old in whose grasp the pen was still foreign—we could make little sense. There was talk of cosmic consciousness, ancient Egypt, Buddha, Shiva. Life was linked to the Milky Way, solace sought in the order of the heavens. Thoughts went incomplete as new ones, unrelated to those that had gone before, jumped to the pen. There were ravings about mysticism and religion, superstition and humanity and the United Nations. From each page, in jumbles that wrapped around themselves and more often than not petered out, rose cries of pain and confusion, an internal torture, as if the thoughts were too much of a load, too cumbersome to hold in the mind, and were biting to come out.

Appalled, fascinated, guilty, I understood that here, on these scribbled pages, were glimpses of raw insanity, all the rampant incoherence of a disordered mind. I felt pain for Sunil, pain that, with control, I managed to keep within.

The group around me laughed and snickered, less, I realized, at what they were reading than at merely being able to read. They could not, it seemed, or maybe would not, recognize the enormity of the pain that littered the pages. Theirs was a sense of uneasy triumph and impatience—"Turn the page! Turn the page!"—and a knowledge, satisfying in itself, of violation.

I was enough of a friend to Sunil to suggest, at one point, that we put the book away before Sunil found out; but Madera, the centre of attention, revelling in his boldness, unwilling to acknowledge the criminality of his action, made a show of ignoring me. He licked his thumb, turned the pages, scanned them imperiously in a declaration of bravado: Sunil's feelings, he declared wordlessly, were of no concern to him. And for this he sought and, I knew, received admiration.

Sunil was attracted by the crowd. He always was. He wanted to be, or at least to have the illusion of being, one of the boys, just another student who could laugh and joke along with the others. No one budged when he appeared; it would have been an admission of guilt, a revelation of weakness. We did stop reading, however, and I, in a move that I acknowledged to myself at the time as one of cowardice, slipped to the edge of the group.

Madera, under scrutiny now, prolonged his theatre, extended it even, as his face, pared to the skull by exercise, took on a greater play, eyes narrowing, lips tightening.

"Give the book back to me, please, Madera," Sunil said, his thin voice strained. "I ain't want any trouble."

"Just a minute, man, just a minute." Madera continued turning the pages, his head nodding in mockery.

"Look, Madera, give me the book now." Sunil's voice rose slightly to a tone of untethered absurdity, without even the merest hint of menace or authority. He held out his hand.

"I say, just a minute."

Sunil lunged at him, grabbed the book: it fell rustling to the floor.

Madera held his hands up in mock terror. "Awright, awright, take it easy, partner." He backed away, grinning.

In the silence that settled in the room, Sunil retrieved his notebook, dusted it off with gentle pats of his palm, smoothed the bent pages, put it under his arm and, head bowed, hurried from the classroom.

Madera grinned. The group, uneasy, hands sliding into pant pockets, broke up, boys scattering to desks or into the corridor.

Suddenly a loud, cackling laughter echoed in the room. I looked around in dismay: Surein. He came up to me. I pushed him away, roughly, left the room, went in search of Sunil. But he was nowhere to be found; he had already left the school. He was gone for several days.

Two or three months later, towards the end of the school year, the pressure once more got to Sunil. Final examinations were approaching and the work, to be learned by rote and regurgitated word for word, attitude for attitude, idea for idea, for the pleasure of Mr. Cambridge, the nameless, faceless, unaccountable correctors at Cambridge University, was being piled on by the teachers.

For Sunil, peripheral in every way to the class, it was also an intense period. His parents had promised to send him to a monastery in India if he managed to finish the school year; he didn't have to pass, simply last to the end. No one, it seemed, expected anything of Sunil.

Madera's sporting aspirations had been crushed on the school's sports day by an ankle sprained in warmup sprints. In the approaching examinations, too, he faced failure, a possibility less damaging to job prospects—education beyond high school had never been in his plans—than to family name and reputation. The successes of his scholarshipped sister in Spain were well known, and, if no one expected similar achievement of him, most hoped for at least passable results. Pre-examination tests, however, were not encouraging. Madera, moreover, was smarting still from the abrupt change in status brought about by his sporting failure: the priests of the school had stopped calling him Dougie, had reverted to the more formal, less affectionate surname. For Madera, this was more than simply a public mark of disfavour. It was a fall from grace.

During one particularly blistering lunch period—a day of scorching heat, searing sunlight, the air thick and heavy, as if itself perspiring—Madera found Sunil leaning on the railing of the second-floor balcony, gazing blankly into the swarming courtyard of the girls' school across the street.

"Looking at the girls, eh, Nadan? So, I finally catch you. You can't tell me now that you not interested in girls."

Sunil ignored him, straightened up; but his fingers met behind him, agitated, pummelling at one another.

"Which one you like, Nadan? Eh? Show me which one."

Sitting in the shadowed classroom a few feet behind them, I thought: Pimp.

Sunil said, "Leave me alone, Madera."

"Oh gawd, man, all I want is for you to show me which one you like. What wrong in that?"

Sunil sucked his teeth, turned away.

Madera rushed around, planted himself in front of Sunil as if for confrontation. "Oh gawd, man, Nadan, show me which one. Maybe I could get she for you, I know all o' them. Here, look, lemme show you something." From his rear pant pocket he pulled a clutch of photographs. I knew immediately that they were probably pornographic pictures brought into the island by some sailor. At the time, the fuzzy black-and-white photographs were in vogue at the school; to possess a set was to possess status.

Madera stuck them in front of Sunil's nose, causing him to pull back as if avoiding a blow. Then, innocently, Sunil reached out and took them from Madera's hand, examined them with puzzlement. After a moment, grimacing, he threw them back at Madera.

"But eh-eh, what happened, Nadan? You ain't like them? You know what it is, eh? I could show you more if you want."

"Look, Madera, leave me alone, and take that smut with you."

"Smut?" Madera howled. "Smut?"

Sunil turned, began walking away.

Madera seized his collar, jerked him back. He held the photographs up to Sunil's watering eyes. "Smut? What wrong with that, eh? Tell me, what wrong with that?"

"Leave me alone, boy!" Sunil wagged his emaciated finger at Madera.

I tensed at Sunil's use of the word *boy*. It was a word, unknown to Sunil so lost in his own little world, so unaware of the subtle intricacies that demanded between schoolboys only weeks away from the end of high school the use of the more equitable *man*, a word that would infuriate.

Madera, playing no longer, said, "I ain't leaving you alone till you tell me what wrong with these pictures."

Sunil tried to step past him. "I have to go somewhere, Madera, leave me alone." His hands, hidden in his spacious pant pockets, jerked up and down nervously, rubbing at the sides of his thighs.

A small crowd had gathered around them. I stood up, walked slowly into the corridor.

Madera was planted firmly in front of Sunil, legs splayed in a fighting stance. "I say you not going anywhere till I finish with you." His right hand reached towards Sunil.

Suddenly Sunil's placid face filled with fury. His teeth clenched and his tiny hand flew to the pencil in his shirt pocket. With a groan of protest, a savage, throaty grunt, he buried the pencil in the back of Madera's hand.

Madera lashed out, sending the pencil clattering to the floor. Blood dripped from the wound. He snatched at Sunil, twisted his arm behind his back. The arm, pared of flesh, bones held in place by skin frightening in its translucence, threatened to come apart. Tears streamed down Sunil's unshaved cheeks.

Hands rushed to separate them.

Sunil, wiping the tears on his sleeve, quietly picked up his pencil and walked away.

Madera, wild-eyed, held up his bloody hand. "All-you see that! All-you see that! He stab me in my hand, he *stab* me! He mad no-ass!" He brought the hand to me.

I looked at the wound, said, "Is a bad cut you have there, Madera, how it happen?"

He glanced wildly around, seeking support. Drops of blood soundlessly hit the wooden flooring. The gathered boys turned away, or stared back at him, unconcerned. I returned to the classroom. Sunil never mentioned the incident.

Several months after graduation, in the final days before my departure from the island, I received a letter from Sunil. In the same crabbed handwriting that had scrawled its way across the notebook pages, he wrote that he would be leaving for India in a few weeks. He hoped that I would write to him. He ended the letter with "Good luck, mister." Strangely embarrassed by the letter and thankful that Sunil, distrustful of machines, hadn't simply telephoned, I put it away, out of mind. I knew I would never write to him.

I saw Madera only once, by accident, on the eve of my departure. He was dressed in a suit, carrying a briefcase, was about to open the door to an obviously new car. I averted my eyes, attempted to slip away into the crowds on the busy sidewalk, but he spotted me, called out. We shook hands, and I saw the scar, small and round, a shiny brown. He was working for an insurance company, he said, "an agent," a job his father had found for him. He announced, casually, that he planned to marry soon, car keys jingling as he tossed them up and down with a satisfied confidence.

I said little, grunted, nodded.

He said we should get together for a drink. It sounded like recently acquired insurance agent talk, the invitation strange from someone I still associated with school and uniforms. He said it would be nice to talk over old times.

"Old times?" I said. "But they not so old." And I realized that Madera was well into his role. Then I added, "Sure, man, give me a ring some time." I decided not to tell him that I was leaving; it felt cleaner leaving Madera, with his suit and his briefcase and his new car, uninformed. Our days were over.

Over. Yet years later, Madera had reappeared, once more uniformed, a revolver hanging from his belt, a bolt of silver lightning glistening on his beret.

Sunil, I knew, had died, expiring quietly in his monastery, the rigours of which he had failed to anticipate.

Madera. Madera with a gun. The thought would not leave me. And blood. Blood on his hand, blood in my office, blood in the photographs. It seemed the theme of his life.

I left the newspaper in the car, fighting the voyeurism that wished to examine the photograph more closely, to enter into its intensity. The building, decrepit in the sunlight, its whitewash faded and peeling in spots, droned with the effort of the air conditioner. My medical bag hung heavy in my hand.

The gas station across the street was busy with taxis getting their morning fill-up. Many of them had already made multiple runs into Lopez City, transporting office workers and store clerks, shoppers and students. But the drivers were quiet in the slackening of the early-morning rush; no fingers drummed, no horns sounded impatience. The service bays to the right sat inanimate in their darkness.

Shirley had already opened up the office. I stepped into the waiting room, into its aquatic light, into its silence that was still that of the night. Shirley was not at her desk, but three women, sitting uneasily on the plastic orange chairs, nodded tersely as I walked past them towards the door of my office. A stalk of green bananas leant against the front of Shirley's desk: payment. It was how far we had gone, increasingly back to the days of barter.

The office was cool, comforting in its isolation. I clicked on the light in the examination room; the overhead bulb flickered, spat, burst into whiteness. I opened the medical bag, hung the stethoscope around my neck. My energy was low, from the restless night, from the draining of memory that, returning in a rush, remained powerful.

"Mornin', Doctor," Shirley called from the other room.

"In here, Shirley."

She brought me the files of the waiting patients: high blood pressure, tension headaches, rheumatism. Tinkering and fine-tuning. I felt myself a mechanic of the human body.

Shirley followed me to my desk, said, "Doctor, it have something you should see." She was hesitant, apprehensive.

I waited for her to go on.

"Is Sagar."

"What's he done?"

"You have to see for yourself, Doctor."

"Can it wait?"

"I don't think so, Doctor."

I rose wearily from my chair, followed her out through the waiting room, out through the front door to the rear of the building to the open door of Sagar's quarters. The grounds at the back of the building were extensive, shadowed by closely grouped orange and mango trees through which the sun barely penetrated. The lawn here rarely dried out, and a fine, damp moss grew at the base of the building walls.

Shirley paused at the door. "I not going in again. No way."

I opened the door all the way—the light was on—and stepped inside to the bitter, biting stench of stale vomit. Pools and puddles of it sat thick and crusting on the unmade bed, were splattered across the floor, dripped in thin strings down the walls. Sagar's clothes were strewn about the room, garbage piled in the corners, beside the closet a cracked mickey of rum, uncapped, contents pooled like pee around it. And sprinkled all around the room like confetti thrown in anger were the tiny white pills that represented his hope, the tiny white pills become now his hopelessness.

My stomach heaved. My hands reached for the scattered clothes, gathered them up in frenzy, flung them past Shirley standing steeled in the doorway onto the dank lawn outside; ripped the mattress off its iron frame, dragged it out, dumped it on the clothes; seized the garden hose, played its scalpel of white water on the walls, on the windows, on the floor, on the furniture. It was like spitting out my fury.

Shirley said, "Doctor."

I heard her anxiety, ignored it.

The walls darkened, furniture glistened, the floor swam with water.

I shut off the hose with a twist of the brass nozzle, let it fall with a splash to the floor. "Where is he?"

"I think he gone, Doctor."

Saliva thickened in my mouth. "You haven't seen him?"

"No, Doctor, I look all around."

The saliva bubbled, turned bitter. I spat, onto the floor, onto the bedframe, onto a wall. Wiped my lips with the back of my hand, turned, my shoes soaked through, the hems of my pants heavy with water, and left the room, strode back to the office.

Shirley followed slowly behind me.

I sat at my desk, glanced through the first file: high blood pressure. I thought: Why not? Picked up the phone, asked Shirley to send her in.

That evening after dinner, while Jan gave Rohan his bath, I sat on the porch with the newspaper. The story was sketchy on details. Two men, of unknown identity, armed with revolvers and Molotov cocktails, intercepted by the police, pursued, cornered, shot: drama of death reduced to its basics. I returned to the photograph, aged in the yellow light, but it had lost its power, was beyond me, engendered now only a sadness that was not of itself.

Jan came to the door, said, "Thinking about Sagar?"

"No." But maybe I was, without knowing it.

She said, "I'm sorry, Raj."

"What about? He was just my pet project."

She sighed, sat down. "I don't like prisons. I'm not sorry for him. I'm sorry for you. He's probably lying dead somewhere. At least he's escaped."

"You're not making any sense."

"Aren't I?"

I said nothing.

She chuckled. "But I wouldn't be, not to you."

"To Asha, maybe."

"Right." Her voice had hardened.

Later that night, as I walked through the house checking the doors and windows, turning off the lights, an explosion rocked the neighbourhood, and the house shook, echoed with its blast. The sky to the east was ripped by a distant, towering flame. Soon, sirens of varying pitch filled the darkness; the flame died to a pulsing glow.

Rohan stumbled from his room: his entire body trembled. Jan picked him up, hugged him.

The phone rang. I answered, apprehensive.

Asha, giggling with a touch of hysteria, said, "The lightning, Raj, the lightning hit something."

I said, with impatience, "Asha, the skies are clear."

But she just giggled.

I hung up.

The next morning, the radio told us that a propane-gas dealership had been firebombed. A family of five living above the store had been incinerated alive.

10

Surein pushed his glasses higher onto the bridge of his nose, exhaled raspily, as if squeezing the air from his lungs through narrowed passages.

Lenny, standing behind Surein's chair, half of his face cast in shadow by the yellow light, hopped uneasily from foot to foot.

Jan said, "So you were in town yesterday."

Grappler lumbered to our corner, filled Jan's glass with white from the bottle in his right hand, filled mine with red from the bottle in his left. His shadow fell on us, a caricatured silhouette.

Surein said, "Yeah, Lenny and me. And Lenny still shakin', right, Lens?"

Grappler cast a baleful glance at Surein, turned abruptly and lumbered back to the group—grandmother, grandfather, aunts, uncles, cousins: the family bush—clustered around the dining table that had been dragged out onto the porch.

Lenny said, "Right, Mr. Surein." His eyes, restless, flickered along the floor.

Surein leaned forward, elbows on his thighs, both hands gripping his beer bottle. "It was terrible, *gheeul*. Terrible. Hundreds o' nigs in front o' one o' your banks"—*your* meaning *Canadian*—"wavin' black and red flags and shoutin' for the white man to go home. The police line up in front o' them, the riot squad, nuh, with sticks and wicker shields. A inspector with a megaphone call to the crowd to disperse, but not a man budge, more and more people was coming all the time. Lenny and me was standin' in the square at the foot o' Raleigh Street, watchin', watchin', wonderin' what going to happen. It was like if the air itself was hottin' up, right, Lenny?"

"Right, Mr. Surein."

"The flags wavin', the crowd chantin', the inspector shoutin' through the megaphone. Then bam! Somebody throw a stone through the window o' the bank. Bacchanal! The police move in like waves from three sides, sticks high, tear-gas guns poppin'. People screamin', fellas scatterin' like chickenfeed, the police chasin' them up and down, sticks landin' bam! bam! bam! on heads, on shoulders, on backs. The air in front o' the bank was t'ick with tear gas. Fellas runnin' past us, heads drippin' blood, eyes bust up. The tear gas start to hit us, eyes and nose start to burn. Right, Lenny?"

"Right, Mr. Surein."

"So we take off, up Raleigh Street, run into Woolworth just before they close the door. And we watch from there, the police chasin' fellas up the street, down the street, across the street. Fun for so! I tellin' you, you never see nigger move so fast! Right, Len—"

"Watch your language, Surein." My Aunt Sylvia, passing with a platter, shook her head in admonition.

Surein, taken by surprise, looked sharply at her, withheld comment.

She smiled at us with teeth of unnatural white, a smile that included only Jan and me, pointedly excluded Lenny; asked if everything was all right, if we needed anything. Her hair, freshly dyed, was like flame in the light. Assured of our comfort, she stepped into the house, leaving me with a tincture of regret that our conversation never amounted to much more than this: an offer of refreshment, an asking after comfort.

Surein brought the beer bottle to his lips, filled his mouth so that his cheeks puffed, swallowed slowly, in measured gulps, Adam's apple leaping in time.

I thought, unexpectedly, of a ravenous squirrel.

Jan smirked, smothered it in a cough.

At the dining table, Uncle Shashi, my Aunt Indira's husband, was finishing a story: "So he went to pick up the boy at the karate place, and is then that he meet the karate teacher, one big, black, nigger-man. That was it, right then and there. You don't want your son associatin' with that type, you know what I mean." Heads nodded in assent around the table. "The boy was out o' the class in two-twos."

Surein listened with interest, turned back to us with a shrug. "Call a cockaroach a cockatoo if you want, is still a cockaroach." He sipped at the beer, belched. "Right, Lenny?"

"Right, Mr. Surein."

"Anyway, we stay in Woolworth for a while until things cool down, then we slip out the front door and head straight up the street to the carpark. All the stores were shut up tight-tight, a couple o' windows was broken, a Mercedes was smash up, and here and there on the pavement we had to walk around pools o' blood. A lot o' the fellas was hangin' around still, not a police in sight, eyein' us but keepin' their distance. Then—"

"Were there only blacks?" Jan asked.

Surein grinned. "Only cockaroaches? No, it did have some Indians, too, but you know the type, cane cutters, *ganja*-pushers."

I said, in a low voice, "Granpa used to cut cane when he was young."

"So? He did use his cutlass against cane and grass. These fellas does swing the blade against anything and anyone. You not tryin' to compare Granpa with them, eh, Raj?"

"Don't be ridiculous." I knew what he meant; we had grown up with this feeling that some of us, our families, had progressed in the world, while others, through laziness, through lack of initiative, had remained behind, condemned to labour still in the same fields as their grandparents had. They lived in little towns and villages, mean and crumbling, scattered throughout the quilt of the cane belt. Their men dressed sombrely, drank cheap rum, kept their machetes close at hand; their women were overworked, overbeaten, overreligious; their children overdressed, overgreased and undereducated. Their speech, in voices invariably high and thin, marked them; they drank *urange* juice, awoke before dawn to early-morning *fug*, dreamt of being *muddles* in fashion shows. We recognized a racial brotherhood, but we saw too in them a version of ourselves as we might have been, and this vision, frightening, earned them our distrust and our contempt. It was a vision, a reminder, we could not forgive, from which we sought to distance ourselves: to marry from among them was to invite silent ridicule. Yet, to hear Surein dismiss cane cutters and drug pushers in the same breath disturbed me. It made stark the thought: But for the drive and luck of our grandfather . . . Even with my discomfort, though, my protest remained feeble. Like Surein, I had been shaped in certain ways, given certain fears. To defend the dog was to become the dog. Despite my grandmother's approval, my attempt to aid Sagar had become a bit of a family joke, a nervous joke, for in helping Sagar I ran the risk of becoming Sagar. It was the only point on which Jan and Surein ever found themselves in agreement, and there passed briefly between them a complicity of relief at my failure. Only Grappler had expressed real regret. Lenny, of course, was of these people, but he had been domesticated, was of use in ways that Sagar could never have been.

Lenny said, "Don't forget the nuns, Mr. Surein."

"I gettin' to that, Lenny." He held the empty beer bottle up to him, sent him to get another. With a flourish of his arm, he cleared the air back to the story. "So we walkin' up Raleigh Street, me and Lenny, quiet-quiet, huggin' the walls, avoidin' eye contact, when what the ass I see comin' down the road but two old Hail Marys from the convent school. And a whole group o' them fellas followin' them. Right away I smell trouble. Me and Lenny duck in a doorway. Suddenly the fellas surround them, shoutin' at them, pullin' their robes this way and that way. One fella drop his pants and wave it around in front o' them. It was gettin' real ugly, I tell you, the nuns frighten-frighten, holdin' on to each other, confuse. What the hell they was doin' there, you could tell me? But it was too late now, they was caught. The crowd around them get bigger, nastier. I decide is time to get out o' there. So I whip off the glasses, open up the shirt, tie Lenny's red jersey 'round my head, and the two o' we head out bold-bold, walkin' like a couple o' Sylvesterstallonies. Straight through the crowd, straight past the nuns. Me pushin' Lenny, Lenny shoutin' at me—the boy have a mouth, I tell you!—as if we havin' a big quarrel. Not a man look at us, not a man moles' us. We was lookin' just like them, we was gettin' on just like them."

Lenny returned with the fresh beer.

Surein took the bottle, sipped, ran his tongue along his lips. "We hit the parking lot practically runnin', jump into the car, and in two seconds the rubber was burnin' on the pitch. Just as we shoot across Raleigh Street the police was movin' in on the crowd, sticks swingin', blows fallin' like rain. Licks for so, man! I almost hit two fellas but—I tellin' you!—we ain't stop to look, the gas pedal suck the floor all the way home." He looked up at Lenny, standing once more behind him. "Right, Lenny?"

"Right, Mr. Surein."

Jan said, "You make it sound very exciting, Surein." Her voice was flat with skepticism.

"You could call it that."

I said, "There wasn't much about it on the news."

He feigned surprise. "You sayin' I lyin'?"

"No, but TV had no film, it was on the third page of the newspaper this morning—"

"So they want to keep it quiet. Nothing new in that."

Jan said, "Casaquemada isn't the world's largest island, Surein. Everybody knows everybody else's business, it's a big small-town."

He shrugged. "And because of that, the government own the TV station and they does tell the newspapers what not to print."

He waved his index finger in an act of remembrance. "A few years ago, a couple o' years before you come back, the *Casaquemada Times* had a columnist by the name of—what it was?—somethin' Latin, Caesar or Hercules or somethin' like that. He lace into the government, this fella, twice a week. Inside information. Language like a knife. Everybody was talkin' about it, everybody was waitin' for the next revelation. It last for five, maybe six weeks. Then the word come down from the government. The *Times* print a short note on the front page sayin' that Caesar or Hercules gone into retirement. End o' story. Is what they does call freedom o' the press here. The press free to print what the government want." He looked up at us. "And they ain't want people to know 'bout what really goin' on in this island."

Jan said, "So what's not to know?"

"Easy. People gettin' killed left, right and centre."

"Maybe that's because other people are bringing too many guns into the island."

He half-smiled. "I like the American approach. Everybody have a gun, everybody safe."

"Or dead."

He chuckled, shrugged. "Look, a place like Casaquemada, life is a lottery. The more tickets you have, the better, but there still ain't no guarantee. Nobody know if they comin' or goin'. Who does take on the *Times* or the *Guardian* these days? People buyin' the weekly scandal sheets, they think they goin' to find truth between the gossip and the UFOs. And maybe they right. This is Casaquemada, after all. I used to know a Mr. White who was black and a Mr. Black who was white."

I leaned closer to him. "Things have settled down now, haven't they? Fun's over?" It was what I wanted to believe.

"If you say so, Raj. Right, Lenny? Things settle down?"

Lenny said nothing.

I reached, surprising even myself, for Jan's hand, seeking reassurance, for her, for myself. She moved it away.

Surein sniffled, rubbed his chin. "Listen to me, Raj, and listen to me good. When they start cuttin' off heads, is not only mine they goin' after, is yours, too." He turned to Jan. "And yours." He looked towards the living room, where the children were gathered in front of the television. "And Rohan's."

I snickered. "This sounds like a sales pitch, Surein. For the little item you brought by the other day."

He sucked his teeth, pulled back. "You think I was doin' you a favour? Eh-eh, well I never! Listen, mister, the favour was for me." His eyes hardened; he spoke lowly, between clenched teeth. "My father does talk endlessly 'bout you. Is as if you's his son. And somehow, in his mind, my destiny get link up with yours, like he can't separate us. If anything happen to you, he goin' to become more obsessed, and he goin' to forget me—"

"Surein—"

"I have to make sure you all right. Somehow I end up responsible for you, in a way that I ain't even understand. You see, Raj? You see? That gun wasn't for you, it was for *me*, all right?"

I was disconcerted. I didn't know what to say.

He swallowed hard, as if to control emotion, said, "Fuck." Relished the word.

At the table, Uncle Shashi was making a point. "They want it all. And they ain't want to work for it, they want to take it. This place goin' west, I tell you, and if we ain't watch out people like us goin' to be the Jews of the Caribbean. Yessir"—he slapped the table— "the Jews of the Caribbean."

Surein said, "Sorry, Raj."

But I didn't know what he meant, what he was apologizing for. I said, "Surein." The words stopped; no thought came, only a confusion, for a part of me wished, too, to have been Grappler's son. I looked out between the bars into the dark night.

Jan's hand came onto mine, grasped, squeezed. And I wondered why the gesture seemed to come too late.

Surein said, still in a voice of apology, "Don't worry about the guns, man. It's just that, you know Casaquemadans. They want to be Cubans now."

Suddenly, I feared for him.

·   ·   ·

The dense yellow light of the single bulb failed to reach beyond the vertical iron bars enclosing the porch. These iron bars, recently installed, were like manifestations of Grappler's growing despair, his concession to change, his accession to the fears of my Aunt Sylvia. The night that began just beyond seemed a rigid mass pressing in on our bunkered gathering.

Family. A big word in a small place, a word that went beyond mere legality, mere blood relationship, to a kind of claiming, a cocoon that comforted and confined at the same time. We sat apart, Jan and I, quite without design; it was usually like this, a corner somewhere not far off from which participation was possible but not obligatory, from which observation came more easily. And so we found ourselves watching them talk and drink; watching them shake heads in intemperate disagreement, nod gently in sage agreement; watching them empty enough bottles of wine, whiskey and rum to convince themselves and each other that, yes, indeed, they fully grasped their situation, knew the rot of the politics, saw the desperation of the economics and, more than this, could, given the opportunity, fix it all, make the island the paradise that it could, that it should have been.

All the coulds, all the shoulds, all the might-have-beens: they were conversations I could no longer really listen to, had heard too often, had come eventually to see not as expressions of concern but as declarations of fear. Life in Casaquemada was too fluid, made of certainty a fantasy. There was no sense beyond the chimeric of what would come next; events and incidents popped from the right, from the left, from within the bowels of the earth. If no personal secret could remain so for any length of time, secrets of every other kind abounded; and to have no secrets—no British bank account, no American visa, no Canadian investment—was to indulge in a perilous naivety, to slip from the optimistic to the foolish. And to pretend to authority, to claim for oneself the necessary clear-sightedness, the indispensable logic, was to play a game of vanity with oneself and with others. Besides, all of those people around the table, all of my relatives—except for my grandfather, absorbed to the point of absence, and my grandmother, chipper and nervous, with eyes confused to brilliance—had their foreign nest eggs; all had prepared their ways out, all would be running to something. So their prescriptions for the island were so much fluff in the air. They were the thinkers, others the doers, and they felt no commitment beyond this.

From the living room, in an irritating cacophony of stereoed percussion, came the sounds of a calypso with Hindi lyrics, a bizarre combination, I thought, a hybrid on par with reggae in Russian or flamenco in Finnish. But it had achieved popularity, despite, or maybe because of, the incongruity of its sound. More distressingly, though, it had acquired, too, the mantle of cultural triumph. Few in Casaquemada's Indian population understood more than a word or two of Hindi—the rhythms and idioms of black America were more familiar from movies, music and television—but they had welcomed the song with a chauvinistic enthusiasm, claiming it for the game of racial and cultural identity through which differences were marked from the black population. It was a song impossible to ignore, the nasality of the singing as shrill as that of an ill-humoured mosquito.

From the table, Ram, a cousin from a distant corner in the labyrinth of family, was speculating on the health of the prime minister. "But he not dead yet? They sure he still breathin'? How they could tell?" He spoke in a shout, in the tone of alarm that was his normal speaking voice. Partially deaf from childhood, he had early assumed that everyone spoke too softly and had decided to compensate, taking his voice to a low shout. When he whispered, heads turned. With Ram, there was no such thing as a private matter; no one ever dared confide in him for fear of having it quite unintentionally broadcast. "They say he have a PhD"— the prime minister, long reclusive, had become an almost mythical figure in Casaquemada, to some an object of awe, to others a distrusted object of ridicule—"but, eh-eh, since when PhD mean positively hard-head an' deaf?"

Grappler appeared in the doorway, holding now a bottle of rum in one hand, a bottle of whiskey in the other. In the yellow light he looked older, less robust than usual, as if labouring under a deep fatigue. The streaks in his wavy, swept-back hair seemed more prominent, the lines on his forehead thicker and more deeply etched, the bags under his eyes more puffed. He stood for a moment in the doorway peering from glass to glass, searching for emptiness to fill.

Surein stood up, walked past Grappler into the house, his cowboy boots sounding sharp on the tiled floor. Lenny followed in his wake, padding painfully along on the soles of a new pair of boots.

Grappler came over to us, sat with a sigh in Surein's chair, balanced the bottles on his thighs. "How you doin' there, Jan?"

"Just fine, thanks." She let go of my hand, hot and sticky, sipped at her wine.

I said, "You look tired, Grappler."

"Tired?" He smiled slightly, was as if considering the implications of the word. "Yes, I suppose. I suppose I am tired." He put the bottles on the floor, sat back, crossed his legs. His eyes were hooded.

"You know, your granpa and me, we used to argue a lot about politics. He was against independence, didn't believe in it. He used to drive me crazy. His generation thought—feared—that it would lead to a republic, no more queen, no more royal family. And as far as they were concerned, republic was a synonym for anarchy. So he was afraid of independence. Most of them were. We had long arguments about it. In the end I would give up, would say, 'The future will tell, Pa. One way or another, independence coming.' Well, I was right. The future has told. And I'm afraid that maybe your granpa was right, maybe independence for us just meant the right to loot ourselves.

"I feel I'm being left behind, Raj. I grew up in a different time, we could afford optimism then. Britain was in retreat and we knew it. We, my generation, we were over there at the time, after all, getting our 'higher educations.' We saw the empire putting on the brakes, getting out before the going got worse. And we knew our time was coming, it was unavoidable, it was frightening, it was exciting.

"You know, a child doesn't really see himself growing up. He doesn't see himself acquiring strength and knowledge, he doesn't realize he's accepting little responsibilities, beginning to take his life in his own hands. And suddenly one day, when it's already a fact, there it is: he's his own man, making his own decisions. And if he's lucky enough to have been well prepared, by the time he realizes it there's no problem. Not only is the awesome responsibility in his hands but it's been there for a while, unperceived.

"But we didn't have that privilege, we weren't trusted enough. And suddenly, there it all was, all this power, all this privilege. My God, Raj, it was electrifying. We were sure we could do it, though. You wouldn't believe the optimism of the time. We had no idea we could screw up so badly, no idea that so many of us would learn other, darker lessons. We assumed, naively, that everybody, even the worst among us, simply wanted to do his best for the country. And later on, when the dark lessons surged in us, we didn't question them. We jockeyed for position, didn't want to expose them for fear of tainting us all. So we let them take over, let them rule us in the end. And who were they, these men? They were all those who had led us into independence, black, Indian and white, men with bigger dreams than we knew. Brilliant people, people of education. But people who saw in politics the soundest refuge of the scoundrel.

"The rest seemed to come quickly. In reaction. A radicalization. Imported ideologies. People building their personalities on other people's ideas, other people's experiences. The kind o' people who are continually quoting someone else, people who never more dishonest than when they say 'I think,' never more honest than when they say A said, B wrote, C held and D believed. People who react predictably to any given situation, intellects tied up in intellectual straightjackets, never allowing reality to interfere with their vision of the world because if their ideology is challenged so is their sense of self.

"Trust no one who claims to speak for the people, Raj. He almost never knows what the people want, but what they should want. And he will make sure they get it, even if he has to batter them into accepting it.

"Who would've thought back then, in the excitement of the

flag, the anthem, the hope and the promise, that we would devolve to this mishmash of race, religion and politics, this carnival of intolerance? Christ!

"It was what your granpa was afraid of. I felt he didn't have enough confidence in us, didn't trust us to run our own affairs. I don't want to believe he was right, but I wouldn't want to have that conversation with him today."

Ram spotted Grappler sitting with us in the corner, shouted, "So the old man, he dead yet or what?"

Grappler, not looking at him, eyes squinting through the bars at the night, said, "And how I going to know?"

"But you does work for him, not so?" He sounded aggressive, but it was just his attempt at humour. "You doesn't see him in cabinet meetings?"

"Boy, you know as much as me, yes." Grappler's jaw tightened, a sign of his irritation, but he was a man slow to anger.

The simple diplomacy pacified Ram. "Well," he shouted, "it ain't matter anyhow. You hear the latest, Grappler? Now they sayin' that PhD mean 'Parently here but Dead." He broke into a laugh that was like a scream, became all mouth, all teeth, all tongue.

Grappler smiled faintly, shrugged his eyebrows.

At one end of the table, my Aunt Emma was in avid conversation with my cousins Sandra and Sara, two of my Aunt Indira's daughters.

Sandra said, "Is a problem, awright." She was heavy with her third child, mopped constantly at her full, perspiring face.

My Aunt Emma said, "I don't know what I goin' to do, eh, girls." She was a carefully put together woman, everything in its place, even the streak of grey retained through dye like a feather plastered to her hair.

Sara said, "The way the economy goin', who knows? Buy, sell, hold on . . ." She was the prettiest of the four, small-boned, fine-featured, but was aware of it, was tainted by the knowledge.

My Aunt Emma said, "I only usin' one, after all, the other one just sittin' there all day, all week, all month, doin' nothing."

Sandra said, "Might as well sell one, then. If you could get a good price these days."

Sara said, "It always have somebody lookin' out for a Mercedes."

"Get the money."

"Send it out."

My Aunt Emma patted at her upswept hair, her face suddenly enigmatic.

Grappler observed the gesture, seemed regretful of it, turned back to the night.

"Is like growing up. Even if you had the worst parents imaginable, even if they neglected you, abused you, exploited you, once you're an adult and free of them—although you might still have psychic damage—there comes a time when you have to take a look at where you are and, despite the past, decide where you want to go and how you going to get there. You've got to realize that you're your own worst enemy, and then work hard at it.

"This is where our intellectuals have failed us, Raj. They've been so busy looking backwards, so busy shouting the simple politics of blame, so busy throwing barbs at the British, the Americans, the first world, the second world and any other world that presented itself, that they forgot to help prepare us for our chance. And when that chance came thanks to the Arabs, when through pure luck oil became like liquid gold flowing into our coffers, we blew it. We stole it, we gave it away in bribes, we squandered it on useless projects, we exchanged it for imported everything. Even with all the development expertise available here or abroad, we acted like a nouveau-riche nation. Economics as buying spree. All the money did was sharpen our evils. It did nothing to soothe them. It meant little more than theft on a grander scale. If before you could steal ten thousand dollars, then after you could steal ten million.

"Our leaders taught us how to blame, but not how to help ourselves. They gave us the psychology of the victim. So that when the money came we practised the politics of greed. We acted like those who had ruled us before. As they exploited us, so we exploited each other. As they raped our land, so we raped our land. As they took, so we took. We had absorbed the attitudes of the colonizer, and we mimicked the worst in him. We learnt none of his virtues, grasped at all of his vices. That is what people don't understand. And now it have only one question left, and I wonder if it's even worth asking: When will we grow up? We're a failed experiment in nationhood, Raj, one among many. We haven't matured, we still view criticism as attack. A first step would be recognizing the difference between the two. But even then, considering how far we've come, if we manage to grow up one day, won't it be too late? Will it even matter?"

"Jan." My Aunt Emma, her voice touched by a controlled stridency, called across the porch. "Jan, you're from Canada, you've been to art galleries, you know what portraits are like." She had black, bulging eyes, the skin beneath each lightly greyed in semicircles, like faint birthmarks. "They're paintings, not photographs, you can't stand too close to them, you have to look at them from a distance." Her cheeks were narrow, sloping into a tiny mouth of thin, pinched lips: the face, I'd always thought, of a mongoose. "A painter can't make an exact copy of another painting, it's always a little different, and is the same thing from a photograph, you always find little differences . . ."

The story was well known, had with so many others made the rounds of the parties and the weekly scandal sheets. Aunt Emma, wealthily widowed early in life and quite lost with her money and her time, had taken to having portraits painted of relatives and friends, portraits that were then presented with a ceremonious solemnity and always with surprise, for they were portraits done, secretly, from purloined photographs. The photographs were sent to a Toronto painter— "And the man's a genius, I tell you, especially with the eyes, they look as if they following you when you walk past the portrait"—who sent back the completed paintings, unsigned, with the airline pilots Aunt Emma used to smuggle her nest-egg money out of the island.

When, a few months before, her lawyer's wife died of a sudden heart attack, Aunt Emma, well-meaning, wishing to add a certain classical touch to her memory, had secretly commissioned a por-trait. The lawyer's reaction at the unveiling was less than enthusi-astic. The face staring blankly back at him from the canvas was that of a stranger with a crooked mouth who bore only slight resemblance to his departed wife, and the painter had decided quite on his own to fill in the fairly prominent gap between her two front teeth.

Aunt Emma, accustomed to a gushing gratitude, was wounded by the lawyer's reticence, his visible hesitation between humour and despair. She left his home quickly, angered at the discomfort he had caused in her, later declared him too emotional, clearly unappreciative of art, and she hadn't yet stopped telling the tale of his ingratitude. She especially had not forgiven him for his final remark: "But, Emma, you know you right. The man's one hell of a painter. God and the dentist couldn't fix that gap in her front teeth . . ." Stung by the appearance of the story in the scandal sheets only weeks later, Aunt Emma changed lawyers, but still sought succour and support from family and friends.

There was something silly about Aunt Emma. She seemed, like her mother, my grandmother, to hunger after the status of icon. Childless, she dispensed unsought advice to her brothers and sis-ters on the rearing of their children; Surein, resentful, had once likened her interference to that of the pope's in matters sexual: neither spoke from experience, both counselled from fantasy. Yet she had paid little attention to me when I was growing up, maybe because not even she would have presumed to counsel her own parents on child-rearing, or maybe because I alone had chal-lenged her early, at the age of nine or ten when, one day at the beach, I had obeyed with obvious anger her order to move into shallower water. I had been made to apologize, and I had done so, but briefly, with a minimum of sincerity; she accepted, then kept her distance from me.

Perhaps because of this distance, though, perhaps because I did not afterward, like Surein, have to put up with unwanted discus-sion of my present and my future, I came to feel a certain sympa-thy—or was it pity?—for my Aunt Emma. She was a woman who had fallen in love once and who, too early in life, before building a bank of sustaining memory and haunted by the mystery of possibility lost, had found herself confronting an unfillable gap. The highlight of her life now was being asked to lead in the winning horse of the feature race at the Christmas races; it assured her photograph in the newspapers, pictures that she clipped and pasted into a leatherbound scrapbook: a curious collection, page after page of my Aunt Emma, looking each year a little older, with grinning horse and smiling jockey.

My Aunt Emma said, "You know what I'm talking about, right, Jan?"

Jan, accustomed to the game, said, "Yes, Emma, of course, you're damned right."

The gentle expletive amused my Aunt Emma. She pulled out a chair, tapped its leatherette seat. "Come by me, Jan," she said. "Leave your husband side for a little while, he not going to run away, right, Raj?"

But as always with my Aunt Emma, I was being included only peripherally. I said nothing, smiled, nodded.

Jan set her face in a smile, stood with her wine glass, made her way over to the table. To be called by Aunt Emma was a sign of favour, a privilege rejected with scandal in a tight family in a small place. Obedience, at least on the surface: it was a constant of life in Casaquemada.

"When we were moneyless, there was hope. Once there was money, we were hopeless.

"I know a lawyer, a highly successful lawyer, who was charged with wholesale bribery of judges, juries and witnesses to win his cases. So he bribed the judge, jury and witnesses in his own case, and won. Then he boasted about it, openly. His practice boomed. He knows the island. We admire the successful scam, resent the successful worker. Stolen money is more glamorous to us than hard-earned money. Where can a society like this go? Tell me.

"Abroad, of course. Like the businessmen. They're all packing up and running. Some aren't even packing up, just transferring money out, getting ready to abandon everything that can't be transported—houses, cars, land. I could tell you about businessmen who own apartment buildings in Miami, about former government ministers who own malls in Toronto. So they're running, leaving their dead behind, two or three generations of bone and ashes. This little Casaquemada of ours has become the kind of place people run from. Flight, and preparation for it, is the necessary condition of life.

"People say life unfair, Raj, but that's not so. Is very fair, too fair, but fair in a different way. Is fair in that things tend to even out, the accounts balance themselves. For every little joy, there's a little sadness. For every moment of ecstasy, there's a moment of despair. This is how life is fair: it gives equally of the good and the bad. For every birth, a death, every win, a loss. Life guarantees nothing. We've been through our orgy of wealth, Raj. Now comes the reckoning."

A child screamed from the living room, alerting every parent in the porch. Seconds later, the voice of my cousin Shanti, Sandra and Sara's elder sister, cut through the sudden silence in loud amusement: "But honey, is only a fly. The way you scream, I thought it was a nigger-man."

Surein, standing in the doorway, emitted a high-pitched cackle. Titters and chuckles filled the air. Conversations resumed.

Uncle Shashi said, "What I really don't like about the Russians is that they're crude. They have no class, man, no class at all."

Surein said, "But Uncle, is supposed to be a classless society, not so?"

But Uncle Shashi was in no mood for frivolity. "That's not what I mean and you know it."

Surein sipped at his beer. "Yes, Uncle." Uncle Shashi's obsessions—with class ("He's a low-class son-of-a-bitch" was one of his favourite insults), with brahminism (he took great pride in being of the highest caste), with the purity of his racial ancestry (anyone of mixed race was a mongrel)—were well known.

Grappler got wearily to his feet, clapped me on the thigh. "Let's go for a little walk, Raj. I need air."

I put the wine glass on the floor and, treading past relatives, walked to the gate in the wrought iron. Surein's eyes sat heavy on me as Grappler slipped the lock, a formidable block of brass and steel, from its slot, rasped back the bolt and swung the gate open. I could not look back at him, could not face directly the pain that I now knew to be his, felt my breathing constrict at my discomfort.

Grappler put his arm around my shoulders—an embrace undecipherable in its give and take—and, together, we stepped out into the night.

The air held a chill. Soon after the sun had gone, leaving the sky a greyish blue, night had descended in swift, dramatic fashion, like a clinging soot materializing suddenly out of nowhere, coating trees, houses, cars, defied only by the bulk of mountain, murky and one-dimensional, folds flattened, edges blunted, against the sky of a lighter shade. Way up above, the distant lights of the fort hung forlorn in the darkness.

We walked across the grass into the middle of the lawn. From the porch came the sounds of another calypso, its gaiety, jaunty and rhythmic, disguising at this distance the political bitterness of the lyrics. Above the clanking beat, the cassette player rang with a metallic hollowness. The voices of the others, talking, laughing, wrapped themselves around the music, soared above it, swept beneath it as if in an intricate, oral dance. And for a brief moment a sadness came to me, a taste of the nostalgic, the music, the voices, the distant, familiar faces—this animation of warmth and comfort—become a vision of a distant yesterday, as if the present, occurring at that very moment, instantly acquired the atmosphere of good times past. I inhaled deeply, felt the air rush into my lungs, press tightly against the wall of my chest.

Grappler removed his arm from my shoulders, moved ahead with quick strides farther into the night to the fence, whitewashed and only waist-high, paused there, legs apart, and looked up at the sky in attitude of prayer.

I remained where I was, respectful of his absorption, uncertain of what was expected of me. Surein's cackle rose above the music and a confusion of excited voices surged as if in pursuit.

"Evenin', suh." The silhouetted form of a policeman, helmet

heavy on his head, emerged from the shadows. "Everything awright, suh?" Grappler had hired him to protect the parked cars from the casual vandalism that struck with increasing frequency.

"Evening, everything's fine. You need anything? Something to eat? A drink?" He spoke conversationally, with familiarity, the night swallowing his words. This ease with people: it was one of Grappler's talents.

"No, thank you, suh, jus' checkin'." He tipped his helmet, moved slowly back into the darkness of the street.

Grappler turned, leant against the wall, eyes, reflecting the light from the porch, glittering in disquiet at me.

I approached the fence slowly, hands in my pant pockets. Mosquitoes buzzed about my head, tickled at my ears.

"It's all screwed, Raj." Grappler spoke quietly. "All screwed. From beginning to end. Twenty years of work, and nothing left, nothing to show." He slapped at a mosquito on his neck, flicked it away from his fingers. "This place, this island, this Casaquemada of ours. Is crashing."

From the darkened garage off to the side, the dogs, a pair of German shepherds locked in their cage, whimpered hopefully at the sound of his voice.

"It's crashing right now, and there's nothing anyone can do. The cupboard's bare, Raj, the pennies are rattling around in the piggy-bank. God knows, I've done everything I could, but the old man's not listening to anyone these days. Not that he ever really has, though. He's always done his own thing. Runs cabinet like a high school class. A major problem, that. Is something to see, I tell you. Ministers left and right going yes-sir no-sir, and so long as they follow orders, he doesn't give a damn whether they stuff their pockets or not."

The dogs began whining, pacing back and forth on the newspaper that lined the cage.

"Twenty years in one damned ministry or another. Twenty years of effort. And now my son and your son don't have a future here. None."

"And what about you and me?" I could not bring myself to reassure him about Surein.

"Ditto."

"But Grappler, before oil there was sugar, and the place—"

"And the place was always one step away from bankruptcy. But you see, Raj, everybody knew there was no free lunch then. Now they're used to it, to the do-nothing jobs, the free school books, the free shoes." He looked around at the night, as if surveying the entire island in his mind. "You have to understand the point we're at now, Raj. We're not really feeling the pinch yet, but a lot of those people out there are. The ones living in the shacks. The young fellas who spend all day hanging out on Raleigh Street. The students coming home to no jobs from university in Trinidad or Jamaica. And what you have to understand, too, is that in my office, and in probably just about every government and business office in the island, we have less discourse than intercourse. The time for talking and planning and worrying is long gone, it's too late. So now everybody's running around trying to screw everybody else for every last cent. No discourse, just intercourse." He chuckled, but without sincerity.

"So what am I doing here, then, Grappler?" My legs were as if hollowed.

"You tell me, Raj. What the hell *are* you doing here? Why the hell did you come back? Didn't anyone ever tell you the new motto of this place—If you're out, stay out; if you're in, get out?" There was anger in his voice.

"And why didn't you tell me all this before I sold everything in Toronto?" I couldn't restrain my own anger.

He folded his arms on his chest, pursed his lips in thought. In the faint light, he looked suddenly old, his face softened into a middle-aged sponginess. "Selfishness," he said finally.

My breath seized. My mind struggled with the simple word, with its complex implications. But I realized at the same time that this could go no further, that I could let it go no further. I thought of Surein, of his face as we had been speaking, as Grappler and I had left the porch together.

The dogs, whining still, pawed at the door of the cage. Grappler said, "So just why did you come back Raj?"

"Kayso—"

"Kayso?" He laughed, genuinely this time, but with an edge of bitterness. "Look, Raj, nobody wants a reformer here. Not all those people who attack banks and burn stores. They want power. Not all those people who talk about change and complain every waking minute about corruption. They want money. No, Raj. You see, real reform would touch too many people. Everybody. Real reform calls for sacrifice. And none of these complainers, none of these would-be reformers, is prepared to pay a price, no matter how small. Real reform would take away the possibility of power from the first and take away money from the second. So there we are, caught between greed for power and greed for money. All ideas of selflessness and service took a plane out of Casaquemada years ago. It's one of our diseases. You're a doctor. Got a cure?"

A tiny star slipped out of its orbit and streaked to extinction behind the shadow of the mountains.

I shook my head: no. "How about you?"

He rubbed the back of his neck with his left hand, ran his tongue along his lips, exhaled an alcoholic vapour in a sigh. "Poverty brutalizes, Raj. There are no saints among the poor."

In the garage, the dogs whined. In the porch, another calypso whirled from the tape.

"Cures. Answers. Solutions. Maybe we should start by acknowledging a reality we've never liked, maybe we should admit that we're *payols*, too."

"*Payols?*" It was our name for Latin Americans, our island corruption of *espanol*. "I don't follow you."

"We started off as part of the Spanish empire, after all. Then the British made us think of ourselves as off-colour Englishmen. Then the old man came along with his vision of us as Casaquemadans. Casaquemadans: we haven't quite worked out what that means yet beyond the silly tourist nonsense of fun-in-the-sun islanders, but I think it's beginning to go full circle, I think we're beginning to define ourselves as truly part of the remnants of the Spanish empire. As *payols*."

Mosquitoes buzzed at my ears, tickled at my eyelashes. My skin itched at their touch, real and imagined.

"And if we're *payols*, with *payol* problems, then maybe we need *payol* solutions."

"*Payol* solutions? What solutions?"

"Like Argentina. Like Chile. Guatemala. El Salvador."

A mosquito bit at my cheek, squashed wet at my slap, crumbled under the tips of fingers.

"You're a doctor, you know sometimes you have no choice, you have to cut out the cancer."

"I also know that sometimes you have to cut out healthy tissue, too."

"That's part of the price, for life."

"And sometimes you incapacitate the patient, sometimes you take away all quality of life. Sometimes you even kill him, in trying to save him."

"I've told you, life guarantees nothing. There are risks. As a doctor, you should know that."

"There's acceptable risk and there's unacceptable risk—"

"And what about your Hippocratic Oath? You're sworn to save life, sometimes you have no choice—"

"Sometimes the only choice is no choice."

"And sometimes the only choice is full of risks. You can't do nothing."

"Even if the life you save ends up crippled? Men who can't get erections? Women with mutilated chests? People with bags attached to them? I've had patients scream for treatments that don't exist and I've had patients turn down treatments that do. Because sometimes the life saved is hardly a life at all, and the treatment to get there is like a road through hell."

"Sometimes you have to travel that road, Raj, whether you want to or not."

"But I can't make that decision for my patients."

"And sometimes the patient can't make a decision. Someone has to."

"You can't be serious, Grappler."

"I'm dead serious."

And I began to see the son in the father, the father in the son. "So what's your answer? Death squads?"

He unfolded his arms, stuck his hands into his pockets, looked away towards the porch. "You know the two men the police killed recently?"

I nodded, thought once more of the newspaper photograph: of the sparkle of sunlight cutting through the trees.

"That was no shoot-out. That was an execution. And it's not the first time it's happened. You think we don't know about it? And you think there's anything we can do about it? Once something like this starts . . ."

"That's no answer, Grappler. That's surrender." But a shiver tickled down my back.

He turned, faced the shadow of mountain, said quietly, "It's the times we live in."

And what, then, was there left to say? What words of comfort to offer a man seeing his life's work come to nothing? What argument against his sense of futility, against his rage? And what to say through my own fear? It seemed not a moment for intellectual jousting, not a moment for greeting-card sentiment; seemed a moment for mourning.

The calypso faded, abandoning the voices in high suspension. They continued, impassioned and unintelligible, for several seconds before eroding of their own accord into a lower register. The silence surged, reasserted itself.

In the garage the dogs yelped in restrained excitement. Grappler twisted his head in their direction, clicked twice with his tongue, hissed soothingly. The dogs quieted down, fell silent. Grappler stepped away from the fence, sniffed, turned to me with a look of defiance.

And once more I saw the son in the father: saw Surein challenge me with boxing gloves, saw him dare me to shoot, saw him place a revolver in my hand. Saw, too, Surein's nocturnal terror, the vibrant impotence of a boy with a kitchen knife.

But the son had gone beyond the father, had acquired strength of a different kind. What for the father was acknowledgement of helplessness was for the son declaration of determination. One's disillusion was the other's occasion, one's ending the other's beginning. And in neither could I find myself; in this link between them, this link that went beyond words, beyond blood itself, I had no place. I said, "Grappler, no."

But I spoke to his back. He was already trudging across the lawn towards the porch, bearlike, his thick-set body become a burden, revealing that Grappler, a steady drinker, had this evening consumed more than usual.

The policeman strolled past along the road, paused at the locked gate farther on. The dogs in the garage growled, erupted in ferocious barking. The policeman moved on.

I felt suddenly isolated in the darkness. My senses sharpened: the lawn went spongy under my shoes, the air brushed like cattails against my skin; above the renewed music and the tightened voices, a constant buzz filled the night; my fingernails lengthened, skin tightened, my hair rustled in growth. Somewhere in the distance another dog barked, then another and another, growls of alarm telegraphing across the neighbourhood and into the next, each restless and nervous creature, jealous of role and terrain, staking out its territory of sound.

I turned, walked slowly back towards the porch, towards the light that glowed a dead yellow behind the vertical stripes of black metal, towards the people, my relatives, whose voices, in the silence between songs, grew sharp and loud with an animation that struck me as forced and overdone in the night that inflated everything but a sense of safety. And as I walked I wondered about Grappler's question: Why had I returned? Yes, Kayso had something to do with it, but these people—these people whom I didn't particularly like or admire but to whom I felt myself bound—these people, too, had played a role. For I had told myself, had told Jan, that I wanted my son to grow up knowing his family, wanted him to be at ease with them in a way that I never had: it seemed a strength that I was offering him. Yet that was only part of the truth. I had come back, too, for myself. I had enjoyed my life alone, a life that was busy, serious, a life of purpose; but finding myself with a family, finding myself responsible for three lives, I grew to need the security of being surrounded by those who would support me without question. I came to seek a safety net.

Approaching the gate left open by Grappler, approaching the voices and the music and the light, I suddenly saw the absurdity of my position: I was seeking protection from people who themselves needed protection, seeking comfort from people whose own comfort was being slowly, steadily shredded. I understood now my sense of the present shifting swiftly to the past. The hole was beginning to gape, and in the widening aperture the viper couched in the heart of comfort was coming clear.

I entered the porch, stepping into the light, pulled the gate shut behind me, made my way past legs and shoes to the chair in the corner. Jan glanced noncommittally at me. Surein, sitting next to her in the seat vacated by my Aunt Emma, caught my eye, immediately looked away. I picked up my wine, sipped at it, watched my family talk and drink, watched the sepia-photograph images of actions that belonged already to a past growing steadfastly more remote.

A moth flew in between the bars, began dancing circles around the single lightbulb, its shadow, enlarged and grotesque, flitting on the walls. Then, in an intemperate movement, one of inadvertence, its wing struck the bulb. It fluttered out of control, fell to the floor. Surein, quick, jumped from his seat and brought his boot down on it, the leather a sharp clap of thunder on the tiled floor.

Voices gasped. Uncle Shashi said, "Shit."

My grandmother clutched at her heart, and my grandfather stared glassy-eyed up at the light.

Not long after, as we drove home through the quiet night along the narrow mountain road, unlit and winding, I reached to the glove compartment and removed the three airline tickets, each in its own glossed cardboard folder, that the travel agent had sent to me at the office. Held them up in my left hand as if to display them for a television commercial.

Jan, sitting in the back seat, Rohan stretched out asleep, his head on her lap, seized them avidly, pulled them from my grasp.

Below us, through the dizzying swirl of empty darkness, the

lights of Lopez City, avoided by this route, shone in regular rows of yellow and bluish white, dollops of glowing egg yolk and smoky crystal that petered out in the foothills to the right, in mangrove marsh and rice paddies to the left, that marked with a certain abruptness the unseen blending of land and sea at the coast straight ahead.

Jan said, "But there's no dates. When's the reservations for? Raj?"

In the centre of the town, in, as best as I could judge, the grid of streets where many of the government buildings constructed during the boom were clustered, a fire burned angry and orange, tongues of flame licking greedily out from the centre, smoke disappearing into the nocturnal void.

"Raj?" she said, insistent.

"It won't be long, Jan. I need some time to arrange things at the office."

"So you're coming, too." It was less a question than a statement of dissatisfaction.

I did not reply. The headlights of the car picked out the narrow road ahead, the crags of rough-hewn and dynamited rock on one side, the land falling off into nothingness on the other. The route was picturesque during the day, perilous at night. You never knew what lay around the next corner.

The pigeons strutted stiffly, collapsed in cluck-
ing confusion in their confining wire cages stacked one on the
other at the edge of the sidewalk, their acrid excrement spilling
and dripping like a thin grey gruel into the drain. The cheese
stores, narrow, crowded, brash with blaring radios, emitted the
rankness of age and curdle. Outside the vegetable shops, quan-
tities of discarded fruits and greens suppurated in the heat like
miniature heaps of compost. Before the seafood stores swarmed
the biting freshness of fish on ice, while the meat stores, windows
hung with plucked chickens and slabs of red beef, oozed sliced
flesh and the peculiar heaviness of congealing blood.

Kensington Market, with its air of international peasantry,
with its hand-painted signs in Portuguese, Hindi, Italian, with its
promise of French pastries, Jamaican meat patties, Jewish bagels,
with its intestinal streets clogged by cars and vans, with its im-
plosive hothouse atmosphere, was a disappointment, an expan-

sive version of the Salmonella market where, every Saturday morning, my grandmother did her shopping.

My wanderings in the city, before winter closed in and the winds made impossible my errant rambling, had not brought me there. I had, without quite deciding to do so, avoided the area. Kayso's description, his projection of it as balm for homesickness, had disturbed me; it seemed an admission of psychic frailty, of an inability to secure himself. My own struggle with this longing for the safe and the familiar had been surprisingly brief. Mrs. Perroquet had, as was her custom, gone to spend the Christmas holidays with Joey and his wife in Guelph. I was left alone in the apartment, for the first time truly on my own, and I delighted in it: in this air that was only mine to breathe, in this silence that was only mine to disturb. On Christmas Eve, though, my thoughts returned to Casaquemada, to Salmonella, to my grandfather's store, to its busyness and its bustling commerce, to the cash drawer and the calendars and pens that were slipped as "free gifts"—Were there any other kind?—into any bag containing a purchase over five dollars. I saw my grandfather too busy to drum his fingers, my grandmother, veil tightly in place, fussing and fretting as customers fingered merchandise and mussed the displays. And I was with them as, at eight at night, seven Toronto time, my grandfather counted up the day's receipts, usually the most lucrative of the year, stuffed the cash into little cloth sacks then into an innocuous paper bag, tied the account books together with the same string, spectacularly knotted, that he'd used for years, locked the metal gates that Wayne had already drawn across the glass doors, and set off, driving slowly through the emptied, darkened streets, for home. I entered the house with them, felt its silence weigh on me, heard the drumming of the water from the kitchen tap as my grandmother set about preparing dinner, saw my grandfather, fastidious as ever, slowly removing his tie and hanging it, carefully undoing his shirt—first the right cuff, then the left, then the neck, then the rest—and folding it into the wicker hamper that sat just beside the sink in a corner of their bedroom.

All of this—the feel of the air, the smell of the dust, the creaking of the floorboards underfoot—I lived, sitting on my bed in the unlit silence of my room. The apartment was chilly that evening, and outside a steady rain washed away the crusted snow. The radio had spoken of a green Christmas, but the theme, from what I could see, was one of grey. And I wondered what I was doing in this place where there was no one to ensure my warmth, where it was so easy to lose oneself in anonymity. But at the same time I thought: There is always a price to pay. Anonymity and its joys, anonymity and its price. I was, in small but significant measure, comforted.

When eventually, shivering, with muscles stiffened, I made my way to the bathroom, held my hands and wrists under flowing hot water, I could barely recognize myself in the mirror, and after a moment of staring, the misery and fatigue of my unshaven face struck me as comic. I laughed and laughed and laughed, appreciating the touch of the manic, treasuring it, recognizing in it a kind of salvation. I showered, shaved, dressed as if to go out and helped myself to the Jamaican rum—a gift brought back by Joey and his wife from their honeymoon trip—that Mrs. Perroquet had offered to me before leaving.

Just before midnight, the telephone rang. Grappler, in high spirits, wished me a happy Christmas, asked how I was doing. My grandfather, sounding tired, told me the store had done well over the Christmas season. My grandmother said, "Son—" and sobbed, blubbering incomprehensibly until, without warning, the line clicked and went dead.

But it was enough. A new picture came to me, of my grandparents, Grappler, my Aunt Sylvia sitting together in the living room of my grandparents' home, sipping from water glasses the Gilbey's sherry that was the only liquor in the house. The dusty bottle, retrieved from a high kitchen shelf for tiny servings at times of celebration, was a bit of a family joke. It seemed to embody the essence of my grandmother's sense of style, but it served in the inebriated aftermath of the telephone call as a kind of central image around which the new and gayer vision could coalesce. By the time I went to bed much later that night, the rum bottle half empty, my mind had arrived at a hazy comprehension of the tricks it was capable of playing on itself. Here, then, my homesickness, my urge to slip into fantasies of today fashioned by memories of yesterday: maudlin machinations of the mind, intrinsically futile, perilous with their power to blind. It was a knowledge I would foster in the coming years, even with a certain aggression. When, once, a philosophy student ventured that the table in front of us might not be real, might be but a figment of our imagination, I offered to smash his head onto it, so that he could experience a figment of pain. But even this faith, this insistence on the rational, kept hidden its hazards, revealing them only when it was already too late, after I had returned to Casaquemada.

It was soon after this, my first Christmas in Toronto, that I received, to my surprise, the first of many letters from Kayso. I had not thought of him after his departure for the island, had heard of him only once, from my grandfather, after he and his wife had been to Sunday lunch—stewed chicken, white rice, sliced tomatoes, grated carrots in mayonnaise, soft drinks—at my grandparents' in appreciation of his having met me at the airport. My grandfather, though, in his usual way, had offered no assessment, no news of Kayso's progress or his prospects.

Kayso's letter, several neatly penned pages, each carefully numbered in the top right-hand corner, was contemplative in tone, as if written in the silence of late night. The first, like the others that were to follow, said little of the island or of his life there, revelled instead in the musings of a man longing for that which he had recently left behind. He wrote often of Kensington Market, as if anxious that it not change, as if the reality of which it had once reminded him was more precious than that reality itself, the dream more valuable than the fact. They were curious letters in this way, letters that led nowhere in particular, that wandered over Kayso's psychic landscape but reached always backward, into the past, with an airy, dreamy quality. I got the sense, after several letters, that they were not so much attempts at communication as efforts at maintaining a link, however tenuous, with a place and a life that he had only latterly learnt to appreciate. It was not to me that he wrote, but to himself.

Spring arrived, struggling its way through the weakening ravages of winter. Final examinations came, went, with comparative ease. The route to a medical degree, as I had come to understand the process, was less daunting than popularly perceived, the intellectual effort being, in the main, one of memorization and not of originality, a process rendered less demanding by tricks and endless repetition, the exams exercises, admittedly exhausting, in information retrieval.

In the frequent rain and dampness, Mrs. Perroquet complained of pains in her joints, walked with a greater difficulty, sighed as she looked through the living room window at the glistening street, at the hurrying umbrellas and children hooded in yellow raincoats: "Hanother spring! Maybe the last one I see, eh?" But as the clouds thinned, retreated, as the warmth took hold, she gained strength, took delight in pointing out to me the little changes to which, unaccustomed, I remained blind: the fragile buds, the deepening greenery, the subtle shifts in the light.

It was on one of these days of shredding cloud and receding tensions that another of Kayso's rambling letters reached me. He began, as he often did, by admonishing me for my infrequent replies—I had little to tell him, even less that I *wished* to tell him—but quickly went on to relate, in words that waxed expansive one moment, that cringed into near incoherence the next, various aspects of his life, sequences connected only by the unchannelled flow of his mind. He wrote of the bars where he'd drunk, the restaurants where he'd eaten, the apartments where he'd lived. He wrote, in a hand that slurred in the way of a voice warped by alcohol, of the women he'd picked up, the prostitutes he'd bought, none of it a boast, though, but a record of a curious dispassion. It was like reading of a life picked to pieces, shards and slivers held up for fleeting scrutiny. He ended the letter unusually, slipping out of reverie to a request that struck me as not so much odd as onerous. "I want you," he wrote with the slightly offensive directness of an order, "to send me photographs of Kensington. Take thirty-six. Mail the negatives. Keep the prints." Into a separate sheet of paper he had folded a Canadian twenty-dollar bill, and on yet another he had listed the various shots he wanted: the stores, the corners, the angles of vision.

My initial reaction was one of despair, not at the request but at his making it, the staccato phrases more revealing, more afflicted, than all the gushes of autobiography. The picture formed in my mind of a man treading water, the surface choppy, spraying and splashing into his face.

I put his request out of my mind, took refuge in my not owning a camera. The money I folded small and tight, as if to make it disappear, and concealed in a corner of my wallet. And when I wrote, it was about spring and exams and Mrs. Perroquet's pains.

His next letter, however, repeated the request, in terms no less direct: "Where are my pictures? I am still waiting."

I felt myself obliged. It could be put off no longer. Mrs. Perroquet—speaking of the market as a place of charm, although she hadn't been there in years, not since before the death of Leonard—lent me her Instamatic.

My disappointment was keen. Kayso had mentioned the stench, but even his vivid description of its effect seemed muted in the vibrant reality. The charm of the market escaped me, and I recalled with puzzlement another of Kayso's declarations that, while much of the city slumbered in a scrubbed sterility, Kensington Market brimmed with the vitality of real people, as if, somehow, cracked accents and brusque manners were of greater value, were more human, than self-discipline and a sense of propriety. Kayso's was a comfort, it seemed to me, that required a touch of the unclean. And this market, the object of his longings, caused me to see him as a man undefined and incomplete, as a man struggling with his dissatisfactions.

I took his pictures, quickly, following his written instructions, barely seeing the scenes framed in the lens. After the last shot, I walked away from the market, my pace rapid, driven by a wish to breathe a purer air. I had not come to Toronto to find Casaquemada, or to play the role of ethnic, deracinated and costumed, drawing around himself the defensive postures of the land left behind. And this display of the rakish, this attempt at Third

World exoticism, seemed to me a trap, a way of sealing the personality, of rendering it harmless to all but the individual. The life implied by Kensington Market gave me nightmares for weeks to come, of heat, of suffocation.

But it was not so for Kayso. I had the film developed, mailed him the negatives. And when Mrs. Perroquet asked me what I had thought of the market, I was at a loss for words, said simply, after a moment, "I don't need it." I gave her the prints as a gift.

It was August. Mrs. Perroquet had gone "up north," to a cottage Joey and his wife had rented for the month to sweat out in comfort, beside a lake, the days of a heat sufficiently intense to put me in mind of Casaquemada: a hardened sunshine pounding through air glutinous with moisture, shadows merely illusions of shade.

I sat on a chair, a textbook on my lap, my feet propped up on the sill of the bedroom window opened wide but useless in the molten stillness. Outside, in the junked back yard of the neighbouring building, a woman of fading youth, reddening skin and lifeless hair spilled and bulged from a black bikini. Occasionally, without looking away from her magazine, she reached down from her rusted lounge chair into the uncut grass for her bottle of beer. From the road beyond came the sounds of impatient traffic: horns, brakes, screeching tires.

Concentration on my textbook did not come easily. My mind wandered to the somnolent gestures of the woman in the bikini, to the perspiration that seeped effortlessly from my pores, to the hush of heat that sat like a light blanket on the distant noise, blunting it, cutting its resonance. And I was glad, then, of my grandparents' obstinacy; they had rejected without compromise my plan to get a summer job, had written with what seemed to me a touch of tempered anger: "Your job is to study. Your job is to become a doctor." There had been a time, money scarce and life a struggle, when the children of the family too had had to work, when education had to be seen, for survival's sake, as a luxury ill afforded. This was no longer so, they reminded me, and it was a point of my grandfather's pride, a sign of his success, that he had educated two sons into professions and would do the same for a grandson. So study, they had written, learn, do well. In the great heat, in as great a comfort as could be mustered, I attempted with difficulty to do just that. The days, dawned from sultry nights, passed slowly by. I went out little, only when I needed exercise to clear my head, or a book from the library, or a beer at the bar. Most of the time I spent in the quiet of the apartment, sitting with a book before the open window or in front of the television watching tightly groomed men give away cars, stoves, refrigerators—all the dazzling produce of the American dream— to hyperactive men and women hysterical with the urge to acquire.

I was at the window in my bedroom, watching the listlessness of the woman in the bikini, attempting with difficulty to find co- herence in my textbook, when the knock at the front door re- sounded loud and insistent throughout the apartment. My instinct was to remain seated, silent, to pretend no one was in; we had few unexpected callers, and they were usually ragged chil- dren selling chocolate bars at exorbitant prices. The knock sounded again, more urgent this time, and muffled voices con- versed in the corridor. I lay the book on the bed, got to my feet, carefully, so that the floorboards would not creak. Just at that moment, a key scratched in the lock. I hurried out as the front door swung open.

Joey stood in the doorway, a bunch of keys in his hand, looking in. Peering over his shoulder, face going furious at me, Andy said, "What've you been up to? You deaf or somethin'? We've been knockin'—"

"Cool it, Andy." Joey stepped into the apartment, his face tense, his eyes assessing. "Didn't you hear us knocking?"

"I was asleep, I didn't know who it was." The lie was uncon- vincing to my own ears.

Andy said, "Or maybe you were goin' through my goddamn mother's things, eh? Is that it? Eh?"

He pushed past Joey, crowded me against the wall. My arms raised, stiffened in anticipation of attack.

"Andy!" Joey pushed him aside, laid a restraining arm across his chest. "Look, cool down. Just go start puttin' the things to-gether, okay?"

Andy nodded, thrust himself between us into Mrs. Perroquet's room.

Joey, gently grasping my arm, led me into the living room. "Look, Raj—that's your name, eh?—you're gonna have to find another place to live."

"How come?" I thought: You can't throw me out, this is your mother's place.

"My mom's in the hospital," he said. "She had a stroke last night."

In my shock, I saw Mrs. Perroquet's face, saw the pain and distress gouge themselves into her collapsing features. "A stroke." Repeat the words, it was all I could do.

Joey, looking boyish still, as in his graduation picture, wan-dered slowly around the room, picking up this object or that, examining one as he would a relic, blowing dust from the other with an archeological care. "Yes," he said. "And it doesn't look too good." He spoke with conviction, his voice whole, but with an undertone of sorrowed regret.

I pictured Mrs. Perroquet lying in a hospital bed, a figure turn-ing blue under white sheets, linked to machines and monitors by the plastic umbilical cords of a technology I did not yet under-stand. And in the horror of the picture, the question slipped out without examination: "Are you saying she's dying?"

"No. Probably not." He ran both hands through his brown hair, styled, carefully cut, parted down the middle. "But, well, she won't be back here, I don't think." He looked uneasily at me. "You see."

I nodded, saw spittle bubble at the corner of Mrs. Perroquet's mouth, saw it draw a line like liquid plastic down her cheek. "She'll be living with you?"

He shook his head slightly from side to side. "We live in an apartment, there's no room, she needs care round the clock . . ." His voice petered out, defensive, and his hands splayed in a gesture of helplessness. "We'll find her a place. A home. An institution."

222 **N**eil **B**issoondath

"In Guelph? Near you?"

"Somewhere. Here, there, it won't make much difference. Not to her. Now."

He was beginning to lose his composure, and I was glad of Andy's reappearance at that moment. "What's it to you where she ends up anyways?" he said, coming into the living room. "You're just the fuckin' boarder, after all." In one hand he carried a small suitcase, in the other the battered cardboard file in which Mrs. Perroquet kept what she called her documents.

Joey said, "Got everything?"

Andy nodded, tossed a glance in my direction. "We gonna leave him here?"

"What d'you wanna do? Toss his stuff out on the sidewalk?"

Andy shrugged. "That's an idea."

"Don't be stupid, Andy."

Andy reddened, acquired what I thought a murderous look.

Joey stalked across the living room towards the front door. "Let's go, Andy."

Andy hesitated, seemed to consider flinging the cardboard file at me.

"Andy."

"I'm comin', I'm comin'," he said impatiently, not taking his eyes from me. He turned away, walked towards the door, paused, spun around, his chipped face inflamed. "I want you outta here in a week, you un'erstand me?"

I did not respond, knew there was no choice now.

His eyes darted around the living room, came to rest on the coffee table beside him, on the wooden cigarette box. He slipped the file under his arm, bent over, picked up the box, nodded once to himself. Then, with face set and work boots pounding on the floor, he stalked past Joey out of the apartment.

It was this theft, this casual looting, that gave an unexpected focus to the confusion of sorrow, fear and anger surging through me. I stepped forward as if to follow him, with the single thought of putting the cigarette box back where it belonged.

Joey quickly stepped between me and the door. "Let him be," he said. "She doesn't need it any more."

"Then you should have it, not him."

"He smokes. I don't."

"But—" But what? A little injustice? They were her sons, after all.

Joey said, "It's just a cigarette box." As he pulled the door in behind him, he added, "And between you and me, be gone in a week. I know him, he's gonna check."

I waited, watching from the living room window, until they had driven away before going back to my room. Andy had left the door to his mother's bedroom open. I had never seen Mrs. Perroquet's room, had no desire to now, there had been enough violation for one day. But as I reached in to pull the door shut, my eyes fell on the far wall where, just below a framed and fading pastoral print, hung a cross of straw, a colour photograph of the pope pinned to it by a tack through the holy neck.

It was, for several moments, as if my fragile world of comfort, of security, had collapsed in on itself, burying me under its disarray of rubble.

I moved out six days later to a house that, for much of the day, smelled like a Chinese restaurant during the dinner shift.

Mine was the third-floor flat: living room, bedroom, bathroom, kitchen, whitewashed walls patterned with hairline cracks, ceiling falling and cutting at odd angles after the contours of the roof. In the living room, a disused fireplace held an electric heater disguised as a stack of logs, flickering red light and backdrop of wrinkled aluminum paper doubling for flame. In the bathroom, the tub, showerless, sat off the floor on four lion's paws of blemished brass. In the bedroom was a large bed, in the kitchen a small table with one workable chair. At the back, through a screened door beside the kitchen sink, stretched an expansive sundeck, recently installed, its wood fresh and fragrant, from which a narrow metal fire escape of treacherous footing led precipitously down to the disordered vegetable garden in the back yard. After my room in Mrs. Perroquet's apartment, in the sparseness of the furnishings to which I had added only a few boxes of books and two suitcases, the flat seemed vast, and even its dark-

ness—the windows, small, had been designed in an age distrustful of sunlight and envious of milky skin—even this darkness
did not deter my enthusiasm.

The second floor was divided into two flats, one to either side
of the stairwell. To the left lived an old Indian man, unsettling in
his resemblance to my grandfather, and whom I met the afternoon I moved in. He came out of his flat as I was trudging upstairs with one of the boxes of books. We nodded to each other,
and he watched me, wordless, climb the final flight to the third
floor. I met him on the way back down: he was coming up with
one of my boxes. "You take it from here," he said in the accent of
Guyana. "Is a long way up for a ol' fella like me." He brought
each of the remaining boxes to the tiny second-floor landing,
pausing only at the end to introduce himself: "Harbans," he said
with formality, offering his hand.

"Thanks for the help, Mr. Harbans." His hand was smooth
and fine in mine, the hand, I thought, of an office worker, a hand
unfamiliar with the implements of his generation: the hoe, the
fork, the machete.

"Not *mister*," he said. "Just Harbans."

"All right, Harbans." But I was uncomfortable with the un-
titled name; it was like calling my grandfather by his first name.
"Thank you."

"Is awright, man."

I wanted to offer something, refreshment of some kind, but I
had nothing, not even a cup or a glass to pour some water into.

"Is awright," he said. "I have to get to wo'k anyway."

I had noticed his blue jacket, several sizes too large, with secu-
rity-guard patches sewn onto the shoulders. He took his hat,
peaked, with a similar patch sewn onto the front, from the doorknob where he had hung it and made his slow way down the
stairs. The hat, when he placed it on his head before leaving the
house, proved also to have been made for a bigger man, seemed to
swallow him. I wondered, unkindly, what he could possibly be
guarding.

In the other flat, to the right, lived two black women, sisters, I
guessed from their resemblance, in their late thirties or early for-

ties. We never spoke, passed each other on the stairs with murmurs of politeness. One, from her uniform, was a nurse; the other, always well if sombrely dressed, gave no hint of vocation. I sensed in them a tale of personal tragedy, one tightly retained, an unfulfilled femininity moving inexorably into middle age. Occasionally, on the sundeck, I would hear the faint strains of religious music, rarely merry, floating from their flat.

On the first floor lived my landlords, a voluminous Chinese family whose kitchen seemed continually to be boiling and bubbling with cauldrons of food, the vapours seeping into the stairwell and up the floors, all the way to the third. I saw little of them, only occasionally glimpsing the husband, a slim man with a shock of black, flaccid hair falling across his forehead into his glasses; speaking with the wife on the first of every month when I handed over my rent in the cash they insisted on. I most often came across the grandmother, a dour, wiry old woman who moved at her chores—mopping the stairs, washing the windows, clipping the front hedges—with a vigour that belied her age; an uncommunicative woman, but maybe her English wasn't up to it. I had the feeling walking past her that all her senses were concentrated on me, aware of my every step, my every gesture. The children I saw rarely, heard them at vociferous play on my way out; at my return, as I stood fumbling with keys at the front door, several pairs of almond-shaped eyes would peer over the window sill at me, remaining distant, neither friendly nor unfriendly, responding to neither smile nor teasing grimace. But once, when my tongue wagged at a single pair of eyes, the almonds widened and bulged into marbles, rose slowly to reveal the grandmother's face twisted into a scowl, her thin arms bared to the elbow, hands encased in pink rubber gloves and clutching the rags with which she had been washing the floor. I thought myself lucky, after this, to still have a place to live, and limited my acknowledgement of the staring almond eyes to brief and noncommittal smiles.

Over the next days and weeks I furnished the flat with the castoffs of others: boards and bricks and a ripped-up armchair rescued from piles of discards awaiting the garbage truck; a small desk, a chair and a brass floor lamp, shadeless and in need of new wiring, purchased for pennies from neighbourhood lawn sales. From the Bloor Street stores just two blocks away, I acquired plates, cups, cutlery, towels and bedsheets, all the quotidian provisions that I had always taken for granted—they were always there, pulled from crowded cupboards and closets; their need I realized only in their absence, perceived suddenly with an astonished amusement. The walls I left bare; their clean expansiveness pleased me, and there was nothing that I wished to hang on them, nothing I could think of that would not tarnish them.

On a day that looked more beautiful than it felt, a day of great sunshine and greater humidity, I watched, secreted behind the window in the back door, as the grandmother, intense and businesslike, smeared a black protective paint over the planks of the sundeck; stared in disbelief and silent hilarity as she painted herself into a corner then, dropping the brush in horrified realization of her predicament, hopped, skipped and jumped her way across the painted surface to the fire escape, like an aged ballerina dancing on a pit of hot coals. The pathetic element did not escape me, but I would not dwell on it, only reflected later on how easily enemies were made: I could have rescued her simply by opening the back door.

One evening, as I put my latest acquisitions—a secondhand rug and a sidetable for my armchair in the living room—into place, Harbans knocked at the door. He said, "You have glasses now?" In his hand, he held two new glasses still in their cardboard package.

I wasn't in the mood for conversation, was nervous of his company. We had passed each other several times on the stairs, and each time he had greeted me with an increasing friendliness. I had grown wary in the weeks in my new flat; the house, not far from Bloor and Bathurst, within easy walking distance of the university—that had been one of its attractions—was in the midst of one of the city's many multicultural enclaves. Eastern European delicatessens jostled with Korean convenience stores, Latin American bookstores, West Indian fruit markets, all huddled in the shadow of the monolithic emporium that catered—low prices, low quality, bazaar atmosphere—to immigrant needs and greeds.

It was the kind of area in which ethnic eyes sought other, similar ethnic eyes: blacks would nod at me, Indians of west or east would smile, all seeking contact and comfort in a brotherhood of skin and race. They were entreaties that I resisted with harsh glares or with gaze calculated in its unfriendliness, for in their search for easy contact I sniffed a defensive racism, the threat of mental ghetto. So, through no fault of his own, I had grown suspicious of Harbans, wary of his motives, of his geniality. I tried pleading the demands of my studies.

He held the two glasses up. "A present," he said, pressing them into my hands.

I accepted, helpless, and invited him in.

When he saw my living room, he said, "Well, it ain't hard to see you poorer than me, man."

I took offence. He had wounded my pride in my efforts to furnish the flat.

"Never mind," he said, looking around at the bare walls, "most o' the people in the world poor, it ain't have no shame in that."

I offered what I had, coffee or orange juice.

"Gimme some orange juice, man." He took a mickey of vodka from his back pocket. "I bring my own fuel for it, I done figure you ain't have none."

He accompanied me to the kitchen, washed the glasses as I shook the container of juice and told him of my grandfather's department store, of his several dozen employees, of the grand house in which he and my grandmother regularly held community prayer meetings with several pundits in attendance.

As we made our way back to the living room, the glasses brimming with juice and healthy doses of vodka, he said, "Still, it ain't no shame to be poor."

I had failed to convince him even with the lie that had grown beyond me, my grandmother's lesson—poverty was not a state of pride—having taken root and suddenly sprouted in me before this old man's assumption of my penury. My being poor: it seemed at the time like an accusation.

He sat in the armchair, crossed his legs, right calf on left knee, at ease in this environment suddenly grown shabby. "So you from Casaquemada," he said.

I sat in the chair that I had dragged over from the desk. "Have you been there?"

"No, man." He drained half his glass. "I pass through Trinidad on my way up here, is the only other Wes' Indian place I ever see, but only from the airplane."

"You've been here long?" The drink—it was my first experience with the peculiar bite of vodka—was not to my tastes; I thought, at my first sip, of turpentine.

"A while. A few years. You know."

The vagueness of the answer intrigued me, but I had no wish to push, wished instead to shorten the visit as much as possible. "You like it?"

"Well, boy, what I go say?" He twisted the glass between his two hands. "Is not really a life up here. Long days. Long nights. I does work shift, you know. And the lifestyle—" He broke off to sip his drink, smack his lips. "The lifestyle ain't like home, things easier down there."

"How?"

"Well, the lifestyle, you know. People. After wo'k, people does visit each other. On the weekend. Always somewhere to go, somebody to see. Family. Friends." He paused, looked squarely at me. "You know, I know some other Wes' Indians up here, and everybody always saying life was better back home, but nobody ever going back, 'cept for holidays. But is the first time somebody ask me how it better." He rubbed at the side of his nose, thoughtful. "How it better."

I waited, took a second sip of the drink, better this time if not yet enjoyable.

"It better because it have to be better," he said finally. "Just like back home, it did have to be better up here." He tipped some more vodka into his glass. "Understand?"

I nodded. "The grass is always greener."

He uncrossed his legs, sat forward, wagged a finger at me. "You think it so easy? Grass? Back home we have more grass, and it greener, than they have in this whole damn country. Nah-nah, me boy, it ain't just that the grass greener. Is more—how to say?—is more complicated than that. You have to remember is a whole life you dealin' with." He reached a finger into the glass, stirred the drink around.

I offered more orange juice—the liquid in his glass now barely yellow—but it was as if I hadn't spoken. In the light of the floor lamp, he appeared even older than in the leavening light of day. His scupltured hair, thinning eyebrows, light stubble sat silvered on him; his skin, rough, tightened on the sharpness of his cheekbones; his eyes swam in a watery fatigue.

"You see me, boy," he said. "You see this old man sitting here? You see this fella who dressing up every day in security guard clothes and guarding people gate? Well, this old fella, me, I was a somebody back home, I was a headmaster in a primary school, people use to say good mornin', suh, good afternoon, suh, to me. Suh! I was a man with respect, I was a man with . . . with . . ." He emptied his glass. "And then I decide to come here. They close down my school, you see. No more respect, suh. No more job, suh. So I come here, thinking maybe I could find it again, maybe I could find a school or a classroom or a little bit o' respect." He snickered. "I find a room and a security guard uniform." He tapped the vodka bottle with a fingernail. "And this." He considered the bottle for a moment, shook the transparent liquid, examined it as if seeking something more. "So you see, boy, you dealin' with a whole life in another place. It have to be better back home, it just have to be."

"You couldn't get a job teaching? With the experience you must have—"

"Thirty years' experience in a little country school in B.G.—"

BeeGee. British Guiana. A term curious because archaic in the prideful glow of independence. A term that I had heard only my grandmother still use, when talking of family over there. *BeeGee.* It had always seemed to me the name of an Indian town, its flavour conveying visions of heat and dust and a genteel poverty.

"—with only blackboards and chalk for equipment to teach hundreds o' barefeet chil'ren. That ain't count for too much up here where they only want to see paper and certificate. The machines they does use, the subjects they does teach. Is like going from the Stone Age to the Space Age. It ain't have no room for a caveman in the schools up here."

"You can't go back?"

"Go back?"

"Home."

"Home?" He said it as if it were a word alien to him, a word without meaning.

I thought: His eyes are melting.

When he left a few minutes later, he was staggering.

But I thought I knew why he had come, was ashamed of my reticence. I poured the rest of my drink down the drain, washed the glasses, dried them and put them away. For the rest of the evening, my grandfather would not leave my thoughts, informed my fleeting speculations on fate and fortune, and the playing out of lives cut hopelessly adrift.

A cold rain drummed steadily on the roof, fell like slivers of glass through the light of the streetlamp outside. Leaves dead and discoloured clung to the sidewalk, plastered themselves against the wet asphalt.

Static filled the phone line, popping and crackling like a steady log fire, and it may have been this, the effort of speaking around it, that added hesitation, a suspicion, to Joey's voice. Guelph was far, sounded even farther.

A car drove slowly by, windshield wipers measured and frantic, pausing at each house as if to examine it. Raindrops burst like bubbles of spit on its slick red roof, on its rear windshield and trunk as it drove on out of the light farther down the street, leaving behind only the dimming glow of its rear lights.

He didn't recognize my name, had forgotten me, had to be reminded. And how had I got his phone number, he didn't recall having given it to me: suspicion made explicit.

My own voice was unsure, quivered, trembled, thinned with uncertainty. Before leaving Mrs. Perroquet's apartment for the last time, before locking the door and slipping the key through the mail slot, I had noted down his number from the list his mother kept beside the telephone, noticing as I did so—but I did not tell him this—that Andy's number had been scratched out with a pen that bit deep and hard.

And why? What did I want?

I wanted to visit her, if I could.

But why now? It had been months.

I had thought of her often, but had not wished to trouble anyone. This weather, though, had put me in mind of her. This dampness. Her arthritis.

Arthritis? He seemed surprised, as if he had not heard of it before. But that was the least of her problems now. She wouldn't recognize me, it would be a waste of time.

Still.

And it was to get rid of me that he rattled out the address, downtown, east of Yonge, but not so far south, not close enough to the lake, to be encouraging. He hung up abruptly, without a further word.

A handful of raindrops flung themselves frenzied against the windowpanes. The light dissolved, rain blended into a curtain of quicksilver. I thought of winter licking lightly at the land with a salivating tongue.

The bad weather lasted for several days, and it wasn't until the sun came out in a day that dawned clear and crisp that I set off, after an afternoon class, for the Pleasure Dome, the private nursing facility—it was Joey's phrase—that had become Mrs. Perroquet's home.

The address took me into a section of town I had not visited before. Away from the bustle and hustle of Yonge. Away from the brightness and sparkle of glass and steel, from the towers of black and white and gold. To single- or double-storeyed buildings of brick peeling where painted, weathered where not. Faded signs, hand-painted or of broken neon, hung like forgotten decorations, functions receding, marking in their forlorn way barber shop and burger pit, fish 'n' chips and shoe repair. At one corner squatted a billiard hall with its air of glamour scuffed and down but not out;

at another a tavern, doors of mock oak losing their varnish, the Riviera Nightclub and Tavern offering Girls!Girls!Girls! and table dancing for five dollars. Men and women walking by on the sidewalk—boys arrogant with the trumped-up manner of men, girls cocksure with the abrasive self-absorption of runaways— were like members of an army: hair long, faces gaunt, T-shirts black and jeans tight on bodies bony and undernourished.

An old man lounging in a bus shelter asked for a cigarette, was chagrined that I had none. On the ground beside him lay a pink plastic prosthesis, the lower half of a leg, the foot socked and shod. He asked for money— "Some loose change, then, eh?" — and fingered the empty lower half of his left trouser leg. His was the face of a trustworthy rogue, a face that suggested he was doing me a favour in helping me lighten my load. I gave him what change I had. He took the coins matter-of-factly, with an almost calculated insouciance, as if they were his due, a man still, his manner seemed to say, with dignity and an idea of his worth. "The Pleasure Dome?" he answered. "Just a little ways further on. Can't miss it. But what's a young feller like you want with that place? Try the Riviera, it'll be more to your likin', I should think." I assured him I would, later, when my visit was over. He sniffed, palmed the coins, turned his attention to the street as if offended. "Have it your way, then."

I continued past a little park deserted but for pigeons scratching and picking in the grass. At the corners now, standing or pacing restlessly in the shadows of the trees that lined the cross streets, were women, young, old, fat, thin. Most of them brought to mind the word *used*. They stared intently, hopefully, at each approaching car, flashed lengths of thigh, smiled crooked smiles. They ignored me as I walked past them, their commerce vehicular, their talents movable. Few cars came by; business was slow. Even so, I was surprised when a woman, wrapped in a light coat, smiled shyly at me, said, "Hi, there, want to go out?" She must have been forty, or maybe a used thirty-five, and the dark circles under her eyes made her look ill. Simply ignoring her, or a blunt refusal, seemed cruel. I shrugged as if in regret, pointed out that I didn't have a car. "I have a place near here," she said. "It won't take long." I demurred, a question of an appointment, was late already, in fact. "Okay then," she said. "I'm always here. Anytime." And I knew, leaving her behind, not looking back, that she was.

And then, at the next corner, there it was. The home. The facility. The Pleasure Dome. A new building, of grey brick, box-shaped, that proclaimed its name in large letters of orange plastic. I thought: There's no dome. I saw, on the small patch of lawn, a clutch of old people, bundled in coats and blankets, sitting in wheelchairs. No one spoke, no one smiled, each hunched into his or her own world, each a separate reflection of misery or fatigue. Two nurses, one black, the other Filipino, gossiped together in low voices, paid no attention as I walked up the short concrete path to the door and went in. I thought: There's no pleasure, either.

"Second floor, rec area," said the woman at the reception desk, waving me towards the elevators in the wall just past a waiting area—brown carpet, orange armchairs, violets wilting in a pot. No one else was around, and the silence, greater than the shapeless piano music that whispered from speakers hidden in the ceiling, sat as inert as dust.

The elevator, chromed and silent, opened to a corridor of white tile and varnished doors, the ammonia smell of industrial cleanser thick in the air. One of the doors opened and a young man, dressed in white, came out pushing a laundry cart with one hand, carrying a mop and pail in the other. I asked where the rec room was. He flicked his long blond hair from his eyes with a sharp twist of his head, glanced quickly at me with pale blue eyes. "Dong de corridor, bredda. Torn right."

I said, "Jamaican?"

"Dahmn right, mon."

Around the corner, double doors opened to the rec room, large, with picture windows that looked out to the red-brick wall of the neighbouring building. In the fluorescent lighting, sharpness absorbed by an expanse of brown carpeting, sat groups of residents, some in wheelchairs, others in armchairs or on sofas, some watching television, others leafing desultorily through magazines and newspapers, most simply dozing or staring through bleary eyes at the carpet. Over in a corner, two men, one tall and thin, ostrich-like, the other his opposite, excessive bulk on a small frame, each peering through glasses perched low on his nose, hunched unmoving over a chess board. In another, an old woman slept in her wheelchair, head thrown way back, snores sputtering uneasily from her open mouth. Scattered around the room, reading or chatting quietly with one another, were white-uniformed attendants, men and women of varied age and race who seemed, themselves, in worlds other than the actual.

I did not see Mrs. Perroquet, could not pick her out of the crowd. The age, the infirmities, were like visions of an inevitable future; they clouded my sight, scrambled my thoughts, made me fearful of them.

An attendant, a middle-aged Indian woman, asked if I was looking for someone.

"Yes," I replied, "a woman—" Only then did I realize that I didn't know her first name. "Mrs. Perroquet," I said.

"You from Trinidad?" she asked.

"No. Casaquemada."

"So, we almost neighbours." She seemed delighted by the discovery.

"Is Mrs. Perroquet here?" I pressed.

"Yeah, man, just over here." She led me to the group at the television, pointed, beaming as if in triumph, to a shrivelled figure wrapped in a blue housecoat and slumped in a wheelchair.

I squatted before her, said, "Mrs. Perroquet?"

The attendant said, "You does speak French?"

Mrs. Perroquet shifted her eyes from the television to me, but in their frightened squint there was no recognition.

"No, why?"

"She only speakin' French, she don't speak English."

"Yes, she does. With an accent, but—" I leaned closer to her. "Mrs. Perroquet? It's me, Raj."

Her hair, white, thinner, was dishevelled. At the sound of my voice, she pulled back, eyes watering, face crumpling into the aspect of witch that had been my first impression of her.

The attendant said, "She have a son, not so?"

"Two."

Mrs. Perroquet worked her lips, with difficulty, as if trying to get control of them. She was not wearing her dentures, and her mouth, when she opened it to rasp guttural sounds, was a cavity of pink, wet flesh.

The attendant said, "Two sons. They must think they orphans a'ready. We doesn't see their face 'round here, I tell you."

I said, "Pardon me, Mrs. Perroquet?"

Saliva bubbled and popped at the corners of her mouth; her sounds were those of strangulation.

The attendant said, "She not understandin' you, you know."

Suddenly, Mrs. Perroquet's neighbour, a woman as old as she but more alert, who had been avidly following our attempts at communication, hissed in fury: "Go away, leave her alone, she doesn't want you, she doesn't need you. Go away, I tell you." And her frail right hand clenched into a fist, lashed out at me, grazed my cheek. I fell back onto the floor as she fell out of her wheelchair, arms flailing, onto me. The attendant—"But eh-eh!"— grasped roughly at her, pulled her up. I scrambled to my feet, the room abuzz with consternation, glanced at Mrs. Perroquet. She was grinning, toothless and grotesque.

I fled, running down the corridor—the Jamaican cleaner looking up at me in surprise—to the stairs, down and out through the reception area to the street.

Already the light was dying, thinning shadows, giving way to the chill of evening. I walked quickly away from the Pleasure Dome, past the multiplying prostitutes—the one who had propositioned me was getting into a red sports car, didn't see me avert my eyes—past the donut shops and convenience stores, the greasy spoons and parking lots. My mind raced, would not be slowed.

"So you're back, eh?" The voice, calling from the bus shelter, brought me up short. "But you've walked past it, don't you know?" And the old man gestured with the plastic leg he held in his hand to the Riviera Nightclub and Tavern behind me, to its sign—Girls!Girls!Girls!—flashing red and yellow in the surging darkness.

I said, "Yes, I know," turned around, entered its interior of pulsating vibration and searing strobes to watch, through several hours and several beers, perfect female bodies writhing and gyrating in gynecological dance.

When I got home later that night, I ripped to shreds Joey's number and sought in sleep to forget the lessons of the Pleasure Dome.

My landlady said, "Harbans? Who Harbans?"

"The old man, from the second floor. You know."

"Harbans? You mean Ali. Salim Ali. He gone. Not coming back."

I had found his door open, the flat stripped of everything but the furniture. "But where's he gone? Has he—"

"Immigration come. This morning. They take him away. He not coming back. False paypa. Visa not good—"

"His stuff—"

"I throw 'way. Not good. Old stuff."

"His friends—"

"No friends. Nobody visit. He alone. Gone now. Not come back."

And it was true. Harbans, or Salim Ali, never came back, disappeared as if he had never existed, returned unceremoniously to the BeeGee he thought he had fled forever.

Two nights later, the first snow of winter fell.

I thought: There's no escape.

I pulled my life in around me, made of study a protective shell of self-absorption. People came and went from Harbans' flat—an encyclopedia salesman, a young woman who may or may not have been a prostitute, a Latin American man of aboriginal features who hugged the wall when we passed on the stairs—but they remained distant, people marked by transience and the aftermath of promise unfulfilled.

At school, I made acquaintances, as was inevitable, but even as the years went along, even as we all donned white coats and draped stethoscopes around our necks, as we tramped the corridors of hospitals acquiring knowledge and experience with aches, pains and disease, I learnt nothing of these people, revealed nothing of myself. They would remain faces to me, features without names, without backgrounds. I went to the occasional party, arriving late, leaving quickly; they made me uneasy, were breeding grounds for a familiarity I wished to avoid. I preferred, when I needed to relax, a few hours at the Riviera. It was in the anonymity of its darknesses that I felt safest.

12

His *finger circled the small round scar on the* back of his hand, rubbed gently at it as if to summon a genie. He said, "It burnin', man, Ramsingh. It burnin'."

A solitary frog croaked in the darkness, the call clear and content.

He said, "I'll take a orange juice."

Shadow sat on his shoulders. Seeped like octopus ink from his uniform. Clustered around his chair like mendicant children.

"I have beer, wine."

His face wouldn't come clear, was as if obscured in some way by the weapon—two lengths of black metal, one tubular, and the other long and rectangular, meeting at right angles—that lay on his lap.

"No. Orange juice."

"On duty?"

"No."

His boots, matte black and tightly laced, sat flat on the floor, stark against the whiteness of the porch tiles.

I went to the kitchen, nervously prepared the glass of juice. A jeep had pulled up to the front gate, let him off.

Jan, tense, said, "What's he want with us?"

"I don't know."

Wayne padded in behind her. He had turned up, unexpected, that afternoon, a canvas bag slung casually over his right shoulder, declaring his intention to stay with us until, as he put it, "things quiet down." Voice low, he said, "Them fellas is trouble, boss." He was careful to stay away from the kitchen window.

"I went to school with him."

Jan said, "You're friends?" There was hope in her voice.

"I wouldn't exactly say that."

Wayne said, "Nobody's friends with them fellas. He here because he want something."

"He's not on duty."

"They does take their guns home with them. They always on duty. They not ordinary policemen, boss. Is the army that train them. They does think like soldiers."

Rohan wandered in from the television room, said, "I want to see the policeman gun."

Jan, feigning annoyance, shushed him, ushered him back to the television.

I took the two glasses of orange juice to the porch, held one out to Madera. He did not take it immediately, waited until I brought it close to his hands before accepting it. I thought: A game's being played, but no one's told me the rules. Or the object.

He sipped his juice, a shadow of minimal movement, said nothing.

Finally, when it became clear he would not initiate conversation, would just sit there waiting—for what?—I said, "It's strange."

"What?"

"You in uniform."

"What so strange 'bout that?"

"Last time I saw you, you were wearing a tie. And you were carrying around a briefcase."

"When was that?"

"Lopez City. Just before I left for Canada. You were going to get married soon."

"I don't remember. What was I doing?"

"You were selling insurance—"

"Stop playin' the fool, man, I know that."

"You were about to get into your car."

"I don't remember."

"It was just for a few minutes, nothing special."

He grunted, noncommittal, rattled the ice in his glass.

"You still married?"

"That's a hell of a question."

"These days you never know."

"Still married. Three children. Two boys and a girl."

It was difficult to picture. Madera. Uniformed. Armed. With a wife. Three children. Details of domesticity that would not coalesce, that offered only their parts without a sum. "I have a son—"

"Rohan Devin. Three years old. And a wife. Janet Linda. Twenty-nine."

Anger, sudden and irrepressible. "All right, Madera, what's up? What have I done?"

"Who say you do anything? I done tell you, I not on duty."

"So why did you check up—"

"I just want to know what happenin' with my old friends." He chuckled, but without amusement. "I guess you could say I learn the value of homework. You probably remember. I wasn't too good at that in school."

I relaxed. Self-assessment, especially of the negative kind, had not been part of the younger Madera's personality. "I didn't think you'd end up a policeman," I ventured.

"And I didn't think you'd end up a doctor," he replied. "Thought you'd end up in a Tibetan monastery with your friend Nadan."

"He's dead, you know."

"Best thing that coulda happen."

"Come on, Madera, he was harmless. Frail as spaghetti."

He fingered the scar, pulled the mantle of shadow more tightly around his face. I had said the wrong thing.

"And the insurance job?" I said too quickly. "Didn't work out?"

"Yeah, it work out. For a couple o' years. Hell of a job though, convincin' people to be afraid of things they never thought about before. Fire. Flood. Tree fallin' on your house."

"That's why you gave it up?"

"But you ain't understand, Ramsingh. I still in insurance, but not the after-the-fact kind." He patted the submachine gun lightly. "The before-the-fact kind. I've become an insurance policy for people like you."

A police siren wailed on the highway, faded rapidly into the night.

He drained the juice from his glass.

I offered more.

"No," he said. "Just one." He tilted the glass, rolled the ice cubes into his palm, flung them without preamble at the wall behind me. The first shattered, showering me with splinters of frozen fire. The second bounced off the wall into the lawn. The third, too, shattered, hit my skin like a dead man's spit. The fourth remained whole, landed at my feet, slithered along the tiles to the edge of the porch, fell over.

The game, I thought, but what are the rules? I didn't move, didn't speak, waited for the demonstration—of supremacy? of invulnerability?—to end.

He placed the empty glass on the floor, leaned back in his chair so that his face became featureless with shadow. "The Argentines," he said, "pitched people out of helicopters. The Chileans burnt them. The Guatemalans cut their heads off. But the Venezuelans! Ah, the Venezuelans! Masters, I tell you, masters. They understand is all a question o' balls. The side that have more is the side that goin' to win. So they come up with a unique way of dealin' with the problems they had back in the sixties and early seventies. Cut-or-bu'n. Ever hear 'bout it?"

I shook my head: no. But I thought of Grappler, thought of *payol* solutions.

"They catch a fella, right? A real bad-john. They question him. Maybe they get information, maybe not. But then, is what to do with him. Court? Maybe. If they have evidence. But they's fellas with experience. They know that more often than not evidence don't mean too much in a court system where everybody up for sale. But somebody had to do something 'bout these bad-johns, somebody had to take them off the street. And send a message to all the other bad-johns out there.

"So they'd pick up a fella and, when they finish with him, head out to a field somewhere. Cut down a tree, nail a chain to the stump. Build a little hut around it with dry branches and grass, nothing fancy, just big enough to hold a man, it don't take long. They strip the fella naked, wrap the other end o' the chain around his balls and lock it. Then they put a razor blade on the stump in front o' him and set the hut on fire. You want to live? Cut it off." He paused, his words resonant still in the darkness, contemplating the scene he had conjured.

Or possibly giving me the time to contemplate it, to feel the bite of the chain, the lick of the flame, time to finger the glistening blade and wonder what I, caught in this circumstance of nightmare, would do. But I would deny him the pleasure of my discomfort. I said, "The Venezuelans did this? You're sure?"

"So they say. Maybe it true, maybe it not true, you never know with them fellas. But that ain't the important thing, man, Ramsingh. So what if it have a few *payols* walkin' around talkin' in soprano? You want to play bad, then people go play bad with you."

I thought it an old lesson, one that he had learnt from Sunil Nadan. But I simply nodded, wondered where all of this was leading.

"Balls," he said. "That's the whole story right there, Ramsingh. You have to have the balls to do whatever necessary. And you have to cut off theirs before they cut off yours."

"Who's they, Madera?"

"Whoever."

It was the answer I feared. "And the law? You're a policeman—"

"I'm an insurance policy. I do what I have to, to insure." His right hand slowly caressed the ammunition magazine of the submachine gun. "The only thing is, it not like TV. You remember 'Combat'?"

The series, like television, had come late to Casaquemada, had seized, like Humphreybogart before and Brucelee after, the popular imagination, the cherished fusion of style and violence, implicit or explicit, growing raw with the years.

"How many Germans Sergeant Saunders shoot every show? Five? Six? And how much blood you remember seein'? But you must know what I talkin' about. You see any blood when Dr. Kildare operate?"

"I didn't have to see it. I always knew it was there."

"And the first time you see an operation? How you felt?"

"I threw up."

"And that is why I don't watch TV no more. Everything clean. Everything heroic—"

"But I didn't throw up the second time. And by the third time I wasn't even noticing the blood."

"The job does take over. I know. It have nothing neat, nothing clean when you shoot a man, either. But the job does take over, and experience brings finesse."

Experience brings finesse: a wonderful phrase, I thought, and one that made me shudder at its implications.

Madera shifted the weapon on his lap, leaned forward, bringing his face into the light, as if seeking a greater intimacy, but shifted his gaze away, at the unseen lot, at the croaking of the frog that continued steady and unperturbed. And in that face, semi-profiled, dimly lit, the schoolboy who had dreamt of athletic glory was not to be found. It was a face handsome but coarsened, not on the surface but beneath the skin, a face utterly devoid of delusion.

He licked his lips, swallowed, said, "We had to kill him, you know."

We had arrived, I knew, at the point of the visit. "Kill who, Madera?" I asked quietly.

"Espinet."

"Who's Espinet?"

"Don't play with me, man, Ramsingh." His voice, for the first time, took on an edge of menace. "You does read the newspaper, not so?"

But the name meant nothing to me. Every day offered published summaries of theft, rape, murder. What had begun as a Crime Corner had become a Crime Page, Crime Pages and, finally, Crime Corners scattered throughout the paper. The reports, vivid, often tripping over the border between journalism and sensationalism, were too numerous, too repetitious in their detailing of mayhem. They could not all be read, could not be retained except in image. Two young sisters are hacked to death in a cane field, a man is decapitated and dumped into a cesspit, a family of three is slaughtered during a robbery. One imagines the scenes, ignores the names—they are meaningless, without context—and moves on to Dagwood and Andy Capp.

"Raymond Espinet," he said. "They had a picture in the paper. Front page."

"Trees," I said, remembering. "And sunlight beside a river."

"Right."

"You were there? I wondered."

"I pulled the trigger."

"Jesus, Madera."

He looked slowly, grimly, at me. "Balls," he said, and I couldn't tell whether it was a comment on his courage or a rejection, albeit gentle, of my reaction.

"But why are you telling me all this, Madera? It must have been hard, I understand that—"

"Cut the bullshit, Ramsingh. What I tryin' to tell you is, we had to execute him. Them."

"But it was either them or you." Only after I had spoken the words, the cliché of Hollywood westerns, did his verb—*execute*—impress itself on me. I thought of Grappler, of his despair.

His face took on a look of puzzled suspicion. "You mean you ain't recognize him?"

"Who? Raymond Espinet?"

"Shit."

Now I leaned forward, towards his eyes glittering under crumpling composure. "Who's Raymond Espinet, Madera?"

It was the student holding his hand dripping blood that replied, "You know him. You fixed him up for me. In your office."

"The mechanic."

"Don't tell me you ain't recognize him."

"In that picture?"

"It was him plain-plain."

But I had examined the picture, had seen only two bodies with holes in their chests. "So that's why you're here."

"It was him plain-plain, I tell you." His voice was brittle with disbelief.

I repeated his words: "It was him plain-plain." Paused. Added, after a moment of silence: "Only if you see him everywhere, Madera."

I felt for him, felt for his victim. Felt for me. Felt for the distance we had travelled since the days of high school and for the place in which we found ourselves. Thought: *Payol* solutions.

Before I left to drive Madera home—he had insisted on it, was even challenging in his insistence: Did I have the balls to be alone with him? he seemed to say, now that I shared his knowledge of bloodletting—Wayne offered to come with me, mumbled unhappily at my refusal.

Jan, resentful, said, "Just get him out of here, Raj." Added, as an afterthought, "Be careful."

But I had seen the schoolboy in Madera, had found an element with which to identify, was certain there was nothing to fear. His face had come clear, the weapon diminished, extraneous even.

Traffic was light on the highway into town, the dark road animated only occasionally by a passing car or truck. I drove quickly, headlights picking out from time to time stacks of building materials—piles of gravel, bags of cement, rolls of rusting wire—abandoned at the side of the road. The mountains, as if cuddling the town in a towering embrace, twinkled in the distance with the lights of hundreds, maybe thousands of shacks.

"Why'd you bring him to me, Madera? You knew what was going to happen."

"They needed him clean. For an example."

"Who's they?"

"You ain't want to know."

"The old man?"

"Don't push, Ramsingh." He spoke easily, quietly, but with determination.

He was right, too. I didn't really want to know, feared the futility of dangerous knowledge in a place like Casaquemada. "So what happened?" I asked finally, unable to restrain my curiosity, pretending at placidity.

"It ain't work out."

"So you shot him." There was no way to say it without judgement; such words could never be neutral.

"Don't say it like that, man. You have to understand."

"I know. The courts don't work."

"But is more than that. This fella, everybody in the force knew him. He was a harden little son-of-a-bitch. Young. With more offences than years. We knew. We were sure. No doubt. But we never able to get enough evidence."

"What did he do?"

"Theft, most o' the time. One rape we know of. And a couple o' murders."

"And you couldn't bring him up on charges?"

"Fellas like that does laugh at charges, man, Ramsingh. All that ain't mean nothin' to them." He rubbed the fingers of his right hand together: money.

"But you arrested him."

"We thought we had evidence. Then a judge order us to release him."

Arguments, neat and philosophical, crowded into my brain, about fairness and justice and the rule of law. But as I sat next to him in the car hurtling into the city, his weapon resting heavily on his lap, they seemed inconsequential, would, I thought, be dangerously insulting to him.

We drove past the garbage dump, recently enclosed in a barbed wire fence and lit at regular intervals by large spotlights, the air above it smoky and unreal, solid with the smells of suppuration. At the locked gate, a lone policeman cradled a rifle, watched the cars go by, his only company fat vultures, as black as chips of the night sky, sleeping on the fence posts or hopping gracelessly around on the ground of packed earth.

"Guarding garbage," Madera said. "You think is a job for a man?" He sucked his teeth in disgust.

A little farther on, the lights of the shantytown glimmered from the other side of the highway. They were like those of any other suburban housing development, the houses maybe a little smaller, a little closer together, of recent construction, perhaps, given the stripped, untended earth and piles of unidentifiable material scattered around. But it was all an illusion of the night and of electric light without reach. The shacks of wood and metal debris—rusted soft-drink advertisements, bits of galvanized iron—had been bulldozed away in the wake of riots, brick houses erected, electricity lines strung, water mains installed. But the grounds had been left denuded—dust in the dry season, mud in the wet—with not even a modest pretence at adornment, the people left unemployed with not even a modest attempt at employment. So they'd continued as before, men, women and children, barefoot, scantily dressed, picking in the smouldering garbage dump. It wasn't long before they had once more accumulated outside their houses the collections of retrieved refuse from which they somehow eked out a living. Within weeks, the blue and pink paint of the houses had faded, windows had been smashed, lean-tos erected. The shantytown, in short, had returned, more solid than ever. At the razing of the old shantytown, the government had surrounded the garbage dump with barbed wire—a question of sanitation, they had said—posted a guard, established hours for scavenging. And so this, too, had been institutionalized.

"Did it bother you, Madera? Killing him?"

He felt the scar on his hand, rubbed it, circled it.

"No."

"Nothing?"

"Wasn't the first time."

"Just how often—"

"Only once before. Me, I mean. We chase down five fellas from a store they break into on Raleigh Street. About two o' clock in the mornin'. Finally catch them. We line them up against a wall and turn the guns on them. The bodies turn up one by one. Over time. In different parts o' the island. Nobody ask questions. Them fellas wasn't a loss to nobody."

The road narrowed, skirted close to the water's edge, where the land had not been filled in. Rotting jetties reached out to the dark water dangerous with half-sunken boats and anchored fishing pirogues. Farther out, a few ships' lights bobbed disconsolately in air that smelled of decaying fish. I turned right at the old lighthouse, long unused, on a weakening foundation, inclining towards the sea, and I headed away from the water, past the bus terminal, through the square surrounded by "Jan's" banks— places that bustled during the day, eerie now in their nighttime desertion—into Raleigh Street.

The street, narrow, had changed in character over the years. Shopping centres had sprung up in various parts of the island, servicing suburbs and outlying areas, each becoming a little focus of economic and social activity, drawing the moneyed from the larger, more traditional stores of Raleigh Street to their boutiques overwrought and overpriced with Italian crystal, Brazilian leather, Chinese silk, Indian brass, American toys, Swiss watches, and enough designer clothes, bags and shoes to turn the entire population into walking billboards. So, steadily, Raleigh Street lost its most lucrative customers, was largely abandoned to the unemployed and the beggars, became, in Jan's word, scuzzy. Then, with the fall in the oil fortunes, came bankruptcies, closures, the burgeoning of the unemployed. Anger, frustration: firebombings had left blackened gaps on either side of the street, the remaining stores sealed behind bars or metal gates. Over there, on the right, there had once been a jewellery store; a block farther up, on the left, that had once been a secondhand bookstore specializing in creased paperbacks and cheap American war magazines; just beyond that, blackened walls, charred timbers and twisted metal were all that remained of the cinema, recently firebombed, where occasional Friday afternoons were enlivened by the mild titillation of jumpy, roughly sliced films offering quick glimpses of bared breasts and lengthy displays of febrile acting. Madera, following my gaze, said, "Is not as bad as it looks. A lot of it is insure-an'-bu'n."

But it still seemed to me evidence of a terrible, indiscriminate anger, a despair that sought redemption in fire and devastation.

There were few people on the sidewalks, solitary young men furtive with a studied nonchalance, hands hidden in pockets or arms swinging loosely at their sides. They strode rapidly, though, eyes lowered or averted, as they shuffled past the not infrequent police patrols, groups of three or four men, uniformed, armed, gas-mask containers strapped to their waists. Our car, the only one on the street, attracted their nervous attention.

Madera slipped his beret onto his head, pulling the right side low, peaking the lightning bolt; leant closer to the window.

Halfway up the street, a legless man, perched on a four-wheeled trolley, his hands wrapped in greyed rags, screamed religion into the empty streets, called out threats of extinction, promises of salvation.

Madera said, "Just like the pope. Only louder." He chuckled.

He was Catholic. I'd forgotten that. He'd been an altar boy, a member of the Virgin Mary Society. "Still go to church?"

"Religiously."

The question came naturally, irresistibly: "Do you ever pray for him? For them?"

"Why you keep on talkin' about them so much?"

"You came to see me, Madera."

He had no reply.

At the Freedom Park two blocks farther on, a large fire, fed and tended by figures silhouetted against its flame, illuminated the central bandstand, a circular dais pillared and roofed in metal wrought into intricacies of solidified lace. Madera pointed out the people before I saw them, clusters of men and women standing around in the darkened reaches of the park, sullen and casual, as if awaiting something unpleasant but essential. "Look there," he said. "And there. And there." Following the sweep of his finger, I saw that across from each entrance to the park stood groups of policemen, all helmeted, some with rifles slung on their shoulders, others bearing riot sticks and wicker shields. "All they have to do is lock the gates," he said. "Sitting ducks."

"They wouldn't dare."

"Whatever necessary," he said languidly.

Freedom Park, an expanse of patchy lawn crisscrossed by paths of cracked concrete and crowded with shade trees, was the most recent name conferred on the square of land in the middle of the town. Plaza de la Virgen, Place Bellefontaine, Victoria Square. But there had been no virgin, no fountain, and the fat queen had never visited. It became Freedom Park on the day of the island's independence, name changing, as did so many other titles and labels, with the midnight raising of the new flag. It was surrounded by a fence of thick metal bars painted wine red, entrances at each corner and at the midway point of every side. At independence, the heavy gates had been removed, hung with pride and explanatory plaques in the museum, where I first saw them during a school visit, a wall of gates explained by a teacher as a symbol of our new freedom. Before independence, he said, the park had been the private reserve of lords and ladies out for their Sunday afternoon strolls; their dogs were allowed in, he continued with rising passion, but not ordinary Casaquemadans. Now there were no more lords and ladies, only misters and missusses: the park was for everyone.

Everyone. But it was soon taken over by the unemployed and the unemployable, the young men—rarely women, I had noticed, wondering where they were: labouring in kitchens not their own? labouring in beds not their own?—who spent their days wandering the narrow streets, lounging at the corners, languishing against the walls, demanding in extortionate tones a dollar, two, ten, twenty, from scowling passersby.

The gates remained in the museum for over a generation, until the days that the unemployed and the unemployable began realizing that the misters and the missusses had metamorphosed into less-obvious but equally potent lords and ladies, as wealthy, as dominant, as arrogant. As the park became the focal point for political unrest, a cauldron of discontent, the gates were quietly remounted on their hinges, chains welded to them, used at times to deny entry, at times to deny exit, depending on the purposes of the police.

Madera said, "Is a stupid duty. Just standin' around and waiting for people to make trouble instead o' movin' in on them before things get out o' hand."

"But they're not doing anything wrong."

"They going to. Look, if I see a drunk fella getting behind the wheel of a car, I not going to wait till he kill somebody to arres' him, I going to try to stop him before he turn the key."

Past the square, Raleigh Street became quieter, changed suddenly in character. The buildings, recently constructed, were of concrete and glass stacked in multiple, self-effacing storeys. Office buildings: medical suites, insurance companies, computer companies, the headquarters of one association or another. On the front wall of each, large signs offered commercial space for rent. In days past, all of this had been a row of one-storey buildings, some of rutted concrete, others of plain wood greyed by age. Houses, front doors giving directly onto the sidewalk, windows hung with discoloured lace; tiny, unlit shops selling everything in general and nothing in particular: habitation and commerce perched together in precarious subsistence, swept away in the onslaught of dollars and untenanted offices.

Up ahead, the cream walls of the school clung dully to the night. The grey gates, massive metal sheets pinned to poles of ornate iron, were locked, the buildings glimpsed above the wall shuttered, the dim lights of the outside corridors casting a pall of desolation. We had never used these corridors—the one where Sunil Nadan had marked Madera was on the other side of the school—and I wondered if this was because from here we could see the shacks of the poor climbing the hills around the town, shacks that were reminders of failure in a land that pretended at hope. I put the speculation to Madera, asked his opinion.

"Because o' the shacks? But you must be jokin', man. The girls' school on the other side, it ain't have no better reason than that. And besides, the sun was always hot-hot on the Raleigh Street side."

He was probably right, had managed to sum up in his riposte so much of our schooldays: standing in the shadows looking at the girls, while our teachers, men of erudition, priests and laymen alike, lectured us in vain on our responsibilities, to the past, to the present, to the future. Men of Grappler's generation, in the end theirs was the fantasy, ours the failure. I wondered whether Madera would have seen it that way, but dared not ask.

At a corner across from the school, yet another new building, monolithic only in the narrow street, had replaced a little shop of dubious salubrity—the sinister gaps grinning between the floorboards seemed the passageways of rats—where a Chinese couple of indeterminate age and uncertain English sold soft drinks, candies, cookies and bits of preserved mango, dyed red, that set the teeth deliciously on edge. I wondered what had become of those Chinese people, and whether the stories about them—that they were secretly wealthy, with cookie cans of dollar bills crowding closets, and energetically fertile, with countless children cached in gloomy back rooms—had any basis in fact or were the slightly fearful fancies of young minds in search of mystification.

"Yes," Madera said. "I does pray for them."

It seemed a good thing to know. "So you believe in God."

"Always." He swept the beret from his head, crumpled it on his lap. The Sten showed like a metallic shadow in the passing light of a streetlamp. "I ain't have no choice in that."

The school fence ended at a side street, unlit and claustrophobic; on the other side rose the intimidating walls of the Lopez City Prison. Immense and solid, of stone painted cream, it dominated this part of the street with sheer massiveness. No sign indicated its function, yet everyone knew what it was. Behind these walls were housed the island's most dangerous criminals; somewhere in its labyrinth stood the scaffold on which were performed the predawn executions of convicted murderers. Save for the madhouse, the prison, more than the law courts, more than the morgue, was the most feared building in the island. If the one inspired invariable shivers of horror and distaste, the other imposed the silence—as if sound itself were cowering—of a funeral procession.

"Why'd you really come to see me, Madera? I don't know what game we're playing, I can't figure out the rules."

"Game? Rules? I was sure you recognize Espinet in the newspaper. I just wanted to make sure you understand—"

"You mean, that I don't say anything."

"Same difference."

At the top of Raleigh Street, the land opened out to the park where the horse races were held at Christmas and Easter. The darkness hid the grandstand, gave the impression of open sea at night. Up above, sitting at the top of the unseen mountain, the old fort glowed like a fallen star. We followed the road around the park. Grappler lived just west of here, Madera a bit farther east, but they inhabited worlds hermetic in their dissimilarity.

We drove by the president's stone palace floodlit behind hedges and a high iron fence. The soldiers on guard at the gate no longer wore dress whites, were dressed as if for combat. Madera stared at them as we passed, studying them as if they were a sight unknown to him, said, "Monkeys."

"Pardon?"

"Monkeys. Them soldier-boys. Lef'-right, lef'-right. Marching up and down in their pretty uniforms. We been on operations with them. Drug raids. Arms smugglers. I tell you, I wouldn't want none o' them behind me. My little son know how to use his fork better than them fellas know how to use their rifles."

"Incompetent?"

"From the brigadier on down and with a capital I."

"But you know what you're doing, right?"

"Always."

I had no doubt of that, but was uncertain which I preferred, which I feared more: the incompetence of the soldiers or the assuredness of Madera.

After the botanical gardens that adjoined the presidential grounds came the zoo, a place I had visited only once, in childhood, possibly on the same school trip that took me to the museum and the wall of gates. My memories had remained vivid: of smells that burned the nostrils, urine and excrement mingled with food decayed in the heat; of malodorous animals trapped in cages only slightly larger than themselves, misery on public display; of outdoors that seemed, to my young nostrils, airless. There were lions, snakes, monkeys, crocodiles: all the usual fauna fit to be imprisoned. Most striking of all to me, though, was a big black bear, an animal that seemed more alien to the island than the rest. It lay listless on the damp concrete floor of its cage, gazing through the bars with sad and teary eyes. Disturbed by the group of children tossing pebbles, peanuts and balled candy-wrappers at it, the bear finally stirred itself, moving its bulk with effort, rising on four legs shaggy and unsteady, its mucinous snout bumping into the bars. It took a step backward, into more bars, growled in ineffectual frustration and slowly, painfully, squeezed its huge body around in the tiny space, lumbered to the rear wall and settled into a dank corner. Its motions released pugencies of wet fur and mildew, elicited titters of derision from the children. I felt myself stifling with the bear, felt its confinement; my skin went damp with a cold sweat. I claimed a headache and spent the final hour of the tour in the botanical gardens, sitting at the base of a tree watching the race horses, shining, well-muscled animals, exercising on the grassy fields of the park across the road.

Madera said, "And you? You know what you doing?"

"I like to think so."

"So how come you come back to Casaquemada?"

"You saying I shouldn't have come back?"

"Is not for me to say. Is just strange to me, how a fella—and it have a lot like you—how a fella could leave the place where he born, where he grow up, where he get educated, then come back a few years later after the place suddenly get rich." The idea was simplistic, the words those of accusation, but his tone reflected genuine puzzlement. "I ain't know, man. Like, is a question o' gratitude, you know?"

"Your sister left, too, didn't she? Went to Spain?"

"And she still there. Don't like to come home too often."

"What does she do?"

"Translating for a insurance company, but don't ask me how. She forgettin' her English, she soundin' like a Spaniard who learn English in Casaquemada. With our accent, but their accent, too. And when she vex, is a whole string o' Spanish cuss-words that comin' out."

"You ever thought of leaving?"

"Never. Not once. I ain't even like to go too far. Went to Trinidad once for a police training course. And once to Barbados, business again. Our own beaches good enough for me, man, why I should go someplace else?"

"To learn relativity," I said.

"Everything I want to learn, it have here. Even my passport expire."

I didn't bother to pursue the point.

Ahead, at the side of the road, the oily flame of a torch lit up the donkey-cart on which it was mounted. A man was standing in silhouette on the cart, a cascade of coconut halves—convexities of dull green, concavities of creamy white—forming a pyramidal backdrop to him in the flickering yellow light.

"My sister still Casaquemadan," Madera said. "Even if she not livin' here no more, even if she don't want to live here no more."

The coconut vendor, a middle-aged Indian of meagre build, was chipping with his machete at the head of a fresh coconut, opening it for a lone customer. The blade in his right hand flicked effortlessly at the nut swivelling with precision in his left; white tongues of coconut husk spun into the air, fell to his feet; with a flash of the machete, he opened a hole in the exposed kernel, handed over the nut as we went by. The entire operation, the sureness of its execution, reminded me of an autopsy swiftly and skillfully prepared: the peeling forward of the scalp, the removal of the cranium in a quick baring of the essential.

"I hear you come in on a Canadian passport," Madera said. "It didn't feel funny askin' for a residence permit in your own country?"

"No. It's just paper."

"And the Canadian passport? Is just paper, too?"

"Yes."

"Don't give me that, man, Ramsingh."

"So what is it then?"

"Two things. First, extra insurance—"

"Extra?"

"Your wife is a Canadian, after all. All-you could get back in whenever you want."

"And second?"

"Second, we could call it lack of commitment."

"To?"

"To here. To your home. Casaquemada."

"Or maybe it's a different commitment. To my wife and my son. To myself."

"You not going to throw Canada in there, too? Stop bullshittin' me, man." He seized the Sten in his right hand, held it up to me, said with anger, "You want to see commitment? This is commitment."

"Yes, but to what?" The words came out flat, without inflection, sounded more caustic than I'd intended. For running through my mind was the coconut vendor we had just passed, the old man who would soon put out the torch, pick up his reins of rope, snap his whip once or twice at the tired donkey and trundle slowly along the deserted streets, along the deserted highway, to a home, hours away, of earth walls and coconut-branch roof and stagnant rainwater collected in a rusting oil drum. The eighteenth century moving through the twentieth, reality crawling along the frayed illusion that was this sad playing out of a dying dream. "To what, Madera?"

"I am," he said with difficulty, "a policeman."

Suddenly, from the darkness ahead, came the shrill of a whistle and barked orders mechanically amplified: "One-two, one-two! Come on, come on, keep it goin', keep it movin'." At first we saw nothing, the sounds, like the lights on the unseen mountain, fragments of detritus discarded into the night. "Let's go, let's go, one-two, one-two!" Then, along the sidewalk, as the whistle shrilled staccato once more, two lines of men and women in white T-shirts and red shorts jogged smartly into sight. Beside them, the instructor, similarly dressed, megaphone in hand, large silver whistle jumping and bobbing on a string around his neck, buzzed around like a dog herding sheep, barking, cajoling, encouraging. Their running shoes tramped in unison on the concrete, the self-containment of serious runners covering the group like a mass trance. As the last of them ran past, the stragglers showing the strain, the instructor dropping back to urge them on, I could see sweat gleaming on their faces and thighs in the gluey light of a streetlamp.

"Running," Madera said. "Around and around and around." He laughed quietly. "And goin' nowhere. Sometimes I think people in this place crazy."

The road branched right, heading down the other side of the park past the general hospital, massive, drab, of unreliable efficacy and care, through a street-warren of prostitutes and drug dealers, back to the water.

"Take the next left," Madera said, directing me into a section of the town, Lavender Hill, that I knew only by its reputation of a glowering shadiness and easy violence. An area that reached back to the early days of Lopez City, it consisted of a maze of narrow streets hedged by small, single-storeyed dwellings packed tightly together in replication of European density. The beams of my headlights laid the street bare, revealed crooked houses stripped of paint to concrete cracked and mildewed, a roadway gouged and rutted, asphalt peeled back in places to the original cobblestones, and these ripped out in places to the underlying gravel. An old man clung to the wall as we drove by, screamed an obscenity.

"Watch it," Madera said with a grin. "In this area, you hit somebody, they out for your blood. I'd have to arrest you to save you."

It was curious that he lived here, in this area where, it seemed to me, policemen would enjoy little popularity. Wasn't it dangerous, I asked, for him and his family?

"You take a look at house prices recently? Or even rents? What you think a policeman could afford?"

House prices had quadrupled, quintupled even, during the

short years of the oil boom, had decreased little in the swift economic slide. The island was rife with tales of homeowners defaulting on mortgage payments and of banks, already burdened with unsalable properties seized from bankrupt clients, agreeing to indefinite suspension of payments. What, indeed, could a policeman afford?

"But is not just that, you know," he continued. "Even if I could afford it, I not sure I'd live up by you."

"It's safer."

"Yeah, but is not just a question o' security. Is a question o' respect. Down here, people know me, they respect me even if they ain't like me. Up by you, surrounded by all them doctors and lawyers and businessmen, nobody going to like me, either, I know that. But one thing for sure, nobody going to respect me. You ever notice how people does talk to policemen up by you? Like servants. Like people beneath them. Well, I prefer it down here. I know where I stand."

The street widened, climbed gently into the foothills, the houses larger, of weathered wood, the poverty less desperate. Little stores appeared—rumshops, food shops, a tiny bakery—hugging the sidewalk obstructed by piles of garbage, discarded boxes, sleeping strays. Young men in wool caps or with cascading dreadlocks, shirtless or draped in smocks of African prints, were gathered in drowsy groups, hands in pant pockets, smoking, talking desultorily, squinted eyes restless and wandering. The car attracted attention.

Madera said, "You should go back where you come from, Ramsingh. You not even Casaquemadan no more. No point in stayin'. Everything it have to take already taken."

The street grew quiet again. Houses, shuttered and dimly lit, front porches deserted save for the occasional grandmother, head swathed in cloth for protection from the cool evening air, following us with gaze distant and intangible. "You have no idea why I came back, Madera."

"That one," Madera said, pointing to a house indistinguishable from the others, as weatherworn, as closed in on itself.

I pulled to the side of the road, stopped, the house strangely familiar until I realized it had brought to mind Wayne's parents' house, not so much physically as in my sense of its impenetrability: it was not a place I could enter in my imagination.

Madera said, "Blow your horn."

I sounded the horn, once.

He looked towards the house, said, "Blow it again."

I did as he asked.

A light went on in the porch, the door opened, and a woman in a white dress came hesitantly out, stood at the railing looking down at the car. She was a slim, pretty woman, hair short and tightly patted down, the suspicion that tightened her face into severity unnatural to her.

"Your wife?" I said.

He nodded. "Sandra."

Then three children came out, two boys and a girl in mid-adolescence, stood beside their mother looking like little replicas of her.

I felt Madera watching me watch them, knew that he had wanted me to see this, the vision of domesticity that he had created. And I understood, watching them, that in a curious way Madera was Grappler pushed further, given opportunity, each seeing his duty, each executing it, each believing he was building a better world.

Madera said, "Tell me something, Ramsingh. You remember Jimi's Juice Bar? On Raleigh Street?"

My face went warm. I knew where he was leading. "Yes."

"And you remember the day you were thirsty?"

"I remember." It was not long after the incident with Sunil Nadan. I had gone into Lopez City one Saturday morning to pick up a box of goods for my grandfather. It was hot, I grew thirsty, stopped in at Jimi's for a drink. And there, to my surprise, working at the counter, was Madera. He wore a white uniform, had a cap on his head, a bandage still around his wounded hand. He spotted me the moment I walked in—I would have immediately turned around and left had he not—and called me over to the counter. Embarrassed, I sat on a stool, asked for an orange juice. He tried to make conversation, but we had nothing to talk about:

Sunil Nadan and his pencil stood between us. I finished the juice quickly, paid the thirty-cent bill with a dollar and, waiting for my change, wondered in confusion about the tip. On thirty cents? Nothing? But that wouldn't do. Ten cents? That was absurd, insulting even. So I left the change, seventy cents, and fled before he found the coins. Humiliation there, for both of us.

"So you remember. Good." He reached into his pant pocket, withdrew a dollar bill, crumpled it. "Here," he said, tossing it against my chest. "Thanks for the orange juice." He got out of the car, slammed the door shut and, without looking back, walked towards his house and family.

I picked up the balled dollar bill from the seat beside me, tossed it out the window.

On the way home along the mountain road, I thought of the mechanic, this Espinet whose name was meaningless to me, whose face was already fading in my memory, and recalled the afternoon of heat when he had delivered to me his promise of a casual brutality.

I decided to call the travel agent the next day. We would choose a departure date.

The wall had been ripped away, but the rest of the building had remained intact. In the distance, on the horizon, great fires burned the sky orange. I stood in the darkened street among rubble, listening with wonder as a man in coattails sat at a grand piano in the wreckage of the second storey and played Chopin . . .

The telephone woke me early the following morning. Grappler said, "Don't go in to work today. They going to declare a state of emergency."

The young men of Freedom Park had taken to the streets. Buildings had been incinerated, a fireman killed by a grenade tossed onto a firetruck. The government had called out the army into a Lopez City in flames, its streets a battleground.

Jan and I got out of bed, turned the air conditioner off and stood at the bedroom window, looking out at the dawning day, listening to the silence uncanny in the sunlight.

13

Slim and well-proportioned, with full brown hair falling halfway down her neck, she looked taller than she was, moving with the uneasy agility of the loose-limbed on high heels, balance precarious on the small wooden box. Her clothing, scanty, of black lace, was draped on the backs of chairs to either side of her, brassiere on the right, panties on the left. On her left hip, precisely on the ridge where the pelvis poked startlingly at the skin, a blue and pink tattooed butterfly bobbed with a circumscribed grace.

The man, young, plump, tie loosened at the neck, leaned back in his chair, let his eyes roam unabashed over the body not two feet in front of him.

She squatted onto her haunches, leaned back onto a chair she had placed behind her so that she was on supine display, opened her thighs and ran her right hand through the trimmed thicket of light-brown pubic hair down to the flesh, fingers parting the folds, eyes and lips doing a brief parody of ecstasy.

The man smiled, but shyly, as if he knew it was expected of him and he had no wish to disappoint. But his eyes, intent, followed her hand, missing nothing, recording the gesture, storing it.

She pulled herself forward, onto her knees, grasped both breasts in her hands, kneaded at their fleshiness, pulled them outward until the tips of her fingers had circled the orange nipples, tweaked them, rubbed them, made them erect.

The man stared, smile forgotten in the growing intensity of the public display of private acts.

She propped her right knee onto the seat of his chair, leaned in close to him, swept the nipples one by one lightly along his lips.

His chest heaved, fell, head enveloped in the enfoldment of arms and breasts.

She pulled away with an insistent grace, a smile twisting her lips, but eyes frowning with a controlled panic: he had taken a liberty.

The man, breath short, sat back unwillingly.

She pouted, shook her head fleetingly at him.

He stared back, serious and unflinching.

Her eyes locked onto his as she raised the right breast, brought the nipple to her lips, kissed it, circled it with her tongue, planted the lips around it and for one second, two, three, sucked at it.

His lips parted, eyes mesmerized.

The music dwindled, faded. A smattering of applause.

She stepped down from the box, unsteady in her high heels.

The man reached two fingers into his shirt pocket, extracted a folded bill, slipped it onto the table and flicked it towards her change purse.

She ignored the money as she dressed, staring at herself in the mirror behind him.

He followed her every movement, staring between her legs as she pulled the panties up, at her breasts as she strapped the brassiere into place. Sought, finally, her gaze.

But she was distant, already forgetting him. She picked up the bill and squashed it into the change purse, winked at him. Picked up the box, swung it overhead and treaded her way through drums crashing from the speakers to a man two tables away who had nodded an invitation to her.

The room, murky, lit by multicoloured flashes that concealed as much as they illuminated, seemed bigger than it was, illusion created by the large mirrors covering every inch of every wall.

The man reached for his beer, sipped, belched lightly, turned his attention to the stage straight ahead where a woman, as fully dressed as women ever were in this place, was strutting and leaping her way through the opening steps of her routine.

The waitress came by, switched my empty beer bottle for a full, said, "Hi, there, how're ya doin'?" She was plump in her outfit of black tights, had features round and unremarkable, wore her long hair twirled up and pinned. She was pleasant, at first in a professional way, but as she saw me more often, in a more personal way, for it was here, to this carnival of cheap thrill and fleeting fantasy that was the Riviera Nightclub and Tavern, that I went to relax, to have two beers and empty my mind of disease and diagnosis, patients and textbooks. I no longer had to order the second bottle; she kept her eye on the first, replaced it when the time came.

"Can I ask you something?" she said.

"Go ahead."

"How come you never buy a table dance? Most of the guys usually get around to it."

"I come here for the beer." I didn't want to explain, had no wish to reveal that I sought a thoughtless solitude, that I used the noise and the spectacle as defence against the volume of work that occupied my mind the rest of the time.

"You can get beer anywhere, probably more cheap, too. What is it? You don't know what you want?"

"Just the opposite. I know what I don't want."

She nodded, disbelieving. "You gotta be in law or meds," she said. "All you guys are the same."

"What d'you mean?"

"You always know what you don't want, not don't know what you want."

"Pardon?"

"You figure it out." She gave me an all-knowing smile, turned to take the order of the man behind her.

"By the way," I said when she returned with his beer. "What's your name?"

She hesitated, said, "Janet."

It was only when I was leaving twenty minutes later that she came to ask my name.

Night, touching everything into a nothingness of darkness, effacing context.

Crash: the violent crunching of metal, the twisting of steel into sharpened ribbons. Glass shattering, tinkling slowly like a line of periods into the hushed aftermath.

It was like running on firm cotton, movement swift and sure-footed, guided only by a fading memory of sound.

A lone car, crumpled into abstraction, sitting inert in the nothingness. I approached it slowly, gingerly even, but with determination: my role, this. I could not turn away.

The metal, a shining black where not abraded, was warm to the touch, the splintered glass pulpy underfoot. My eyes, unwilling, travelled downward: not glass, then, but swatches of scalp roughly ripped, flesh fresh, clutches of hair black and lustrous.

My fingers grasped at the crushed and flattened roof of the car, peeled it back without effort to the interior of chaotic shadow, to the two figures slumped in the front seats, leaden shades cadaverous in their stillness. My mouth opened to speak, to call out, but no sound came, my vocal cords as if cut.

I thought: Their faces, must see their faces.

My fingers reached out through the febrile air towards the silhouette, male, I could tell, scrunched into the steering wheel. But there was no solidity to his form, my hand moving through him as through liquid, emerging wet and warm and sticky. No, not blood. Earth, liquefied and odorous.

Suddenly, without reason, the car began to vanish, evaporating in chunks as if chewed at by the darkness.

My arms lunged in, seeking the silhouettes, wanting to rescue them from the coming oblivion.

And they were gone. Just like that. Shadows and car thinned to infinity.

My hands grasped at the emptiness, fingers tightened, cringed. My throat constricted. Darkness surged.

The night was without air . . .

The impossibility of possibility.

The dream began halfway through my third year of medical school, continued with intermittent regularity through internship, mocking the knowledge I was acquiring, dampening into a private circumspection the enthusiasm, the optimism, of professional indoctrination. It came and went without variation, leaving me in a fevered sweat, sleep distant, mind a confusion of images, the only disquiet in this period of my life governed by the contentment of routine, a time that would remain in my memory as one of ease—even with the tensions of volume, the draining fervour of exams—focussed on the essentially simple responsibility of study and of patients, guinea pigs of symptom and treatment and experimentation, not our own. Coffee, classes, books and journals. Meals, quick and meagre, prompted not by clock but by appetite, consumed at odd hours in the haze of a pleasant fatigue.

And yet.

And yet it is neither a time nor an enterprise that I would seek to mythologize. There is, already, enough of this in the world, this elevation of medicine, the acquisition of its knowledge, the wonderment at its practice, to a status so rarefied that no medical practitioner, even of superior ability and remarkable fortune, could possibly fulfil its expectations.

I learnt, as unspoken corollary to the certainties of medical delivery, the greater uncertainties underlying the bravado.

And yet.

And yet there was, there could be, no total immunity from bravado.

The white coats studiously shapeless; the stethoscopes casually stuffed into pockets or draped around the neck; the understanding acquired of the intimate, subtle and brutal ways of the body; the secrets of defence, attack and counterattack; this sense, around nurses and with families, of being in the know: it was a heady combination, offering seductive illusions of dominance.

The popular, modern imagination makes much of medical school, more, probably, than there is to it: any place that fashions from the prosaic paragons of principle and protection is a place that would inspire awe. Until, that is, something goes wrong or fails to conclude as planned, as not infrequently happens.

But the starry-eyed vision of my profession is not discouraged. As students we complained of fatigue, of endless hours trudging the shining halls in our running shoes, of insufficient time for overabundant work. We offered our puffed and reddened eyes as proof of superhuman effort, revelling in the joke that had us on the go twenty-three hours a day, with the twenty-fourth to reflect on it.

There was, in all of this, only a little exaggeration, just a touch of the play-acting that had us a little more frazzled, a little more hustling than we actually were. But there was, too, another element, one acknowledged only in brief moments of respite and reverie when, alone in the silence, hunched into a corner of the library or dreaming at our desks in our flat, we awed ourselves with visions, embarrassingly heroic, of the enterprise in which we were engaged, our own, quiet machismo.

We were not a quixotic bunch. Motivations ranged from the monetary to the altruistic, with most falling somewhere in between, in an uneasy balance of self-service and self-sacrifice. I remember Dimitrios—or was it Kostas? I knew no one well enough, was acquainted with too many, to keep their names tied to them after so many years. Burly and vociferous, with thick, nimble fingers that he attributed to lifting boxes of fruit and vegetables in his father's neighbourhood market, he spoke of serving the Greek enclave on Danforth Avenue with an eagerness matched only by that with which he described the red Corvette he would one day buy. And I remember Kathy—or was it Wendy? Elizabeth?—with her look best described as utilitarian, who fancied a life of frontier medicine on a remote Indian reserve only to have her ambition crumble bit by bit over the years before her, in the end, undeniable attraction to the glitter and flash of the city.

When asked—and I sought to avoid situations where I would be—why I had decided on medicine, I at first found myself at a loss for words. I had no particular ambition to which I could point, could claim no wish for wealth, no desire to serve, could not explain that my calling had come from escape and safety and the portability of profession. So I concocted an answer: "It's a steady job." I would say it cavalierly, dismissively, provoking inevitable laughter, satisfying curiosity. Saying the words—and listening to the conversation move on through the laughter to other people, other topics—Grappler's voice, or rather the tone of it, would run through my head, seizing the words, moulding them, lending them a flavour not my own. Protecting me.

So it remained a comfortable world, I content in it, living quietly in my flat. Downstairs, life went on as before. The two sisters maintained their customary silence broken only by their music of exaltation. Harbans' room continued to provide temporary shelter for transients, its smallness discouraging to the anonymous dishwashers and waitresses and store clerks; there seemed always to be a new face entering or exiting from the room. On the first floor, the almond eyes, freed from behind the glass as they grew, slashed slapshots on the sidewalk, remained as distant as at the beginning but more egocentric, with eyes for nothing but themselves and their concerns. Their shouts followed me as I took my mail from the brass box at the entrance, trotted up the stairs to the flat and sat in the living room to read my letters.

They came most frequently from my grandfather, flimsy air-letter forms carefully penned in a script concise and gentlemanly. He wrote of the store and its business blossoming in the oil boom, of my grandmother and her various, never serious, always discomforting illnesses, of neighbours I knew—Wayne's father died, Wayne quit the store, Angela's mother remarried, Angela moved to Lopez City trailing rumours of pregnancy—and of distant family I didn't. Grappler, too, wrote occasionally, but usually of others, rarely of himself, and then always of the inconsequential: he had taken up jogging, then given it up because of sore knees; he had acquired a dog, then, quickly, another, to keep the first company; Kayso he mentioned only once, noting without explanation that his wife had left him, had returned to Canada with the baby. Kayso himself, after the letters he had sent me at Mrs. Perroquet's, never wrote, the photographs of the market having apparently satisfied his urgent and enigmatic need. It was my grandfather who, as the years went along, would send the occasional newspaper clipping of Kayso's legal activism; the descriptions of him, eventually accompanied by the same serious, studio-posed portrait, went from, at first, "Lopez City lawyer" to, later on, "Lopez City civil-rights lawyer." It was an indication of the progress of his dream: he was serving his people, repaying his island.

My replies were brief, scribbled between classes or in the late night when my brain could absorb no more information and the printed word sat tenuous before my eyes. They were boring letters, I knew; it was not one of my strengths, this recitation of the simple details of daily life, but it was all that was required and I complied as best I could. I wrote of the weight I had put on—my grandmother was delighted with the news—and of my attendance, on a whim, at the National Ballet's *Nutcracker*, and of how halfway through it, despite the music and the spectacle and because of the music and the warmth, I fell into a fitful doze, roused only at the end by the explosion of applause. I described the flat, detailed my courses, wrote in all probability too— because my grandmother worried about my being alone—of the people I knew, of the Kathys and the Wendys and the Elizabeths, of the Kens and the Williams and the Edwards, wrote undoubtedly, too, of Dimitrios-Kostas.

Dimitrios-Kostas was my closest acquaintance, not by my choice but by his. Short and heavily built, he invariably displayed a sharp-edge jolliness that assumed the entire world to be friendly and everyone to be accessible. He would have been irritating were it not for his humour, intrusive were it not for his frankness. The corpse we shared, anatomically sliced, he dubbed Henrietta, slapping her heartily every morning before peeling back another part of her. Noting her large feet, he decided Henrietta was probably

Greek: "Between you and me," he said in a voice that boomed in theatrical whisper, "Greek women have feet like ducks. Large ducks."

We often haunted together the narrow and gloomy aisles of the bookstacks in the science and medicine library, treading with care its floors of opaque plastic. Dimitrios-Kostas would peer up through the gapped edges to glimpse under skirts and dresses. "I hate bluejeans," he said more than once. "Mini-skirts! That's what I need, and pretty damned soon, too." Those voyeuristic gaps in the floor were, he claimed, the only reason he spent as much time in the library as he did; they triggered his adrenalin, got his blood moving. We would clamber down the narrow, grey metal stairs to low-ceilinged rooms crammed with books on metal shelving, the light thin and indefinite; it was like descending into the claustrophobic bowels of a submarine. Moving quickly, we would select the books we needed and flee up the stairs, he to the bright reading lounge, to its sofas and armchairs and windows that looked out onto slivers of greenery, I to a corner in the quieter recesses of the library, to a tiny carrel with its blinders on three sides and its illusion of privacy.

One blustery Friday afternoon, in January or February, the air cold and damp, the sky spitting intermittent flurries, a group of us left the MedSci building together, Dimitrios-Kostas as usual regaling us with a story. I was looking forward to my Friday afternoon ritual of a hot beef submarine, Coca-Cola and the newspaper, followed by the only nap of the week from which I was not awoken by my alarm clock; during this tranquil and delicious time, like the almond eyes slashing slapshots outside, my mind relaxed its intensity and lapsed into a self-protective, self-contained self-indulgence. Dimitrios-Kostas kept us standing on the iced and snowy stairs as he finished his story, yet another amusing tale of his rambunctious childhood, the expanse of King's College Circle—Convocation Hall, Knox College, University College and the snow-wasted field before them—wet and uninviting in the gloomy afternoon. He brought the story to its conclusion, his voice warping into a laughter that evoked a greater reaction than the punch line. We trotted down the stairs, each heading in a different direction, Dimitrios-Kostas falling into step with me as I set off past the library, heading up through the campus to Bloor Street.

He said, "You busy tomorrow?"

"Studying."

"Tomorrow evening, I mean."

"Morning, afternoon, evening. There's a difference?"

"Cool it, smart ass, my mama has a word for people like you."

"Good thing your mama doesn't know me."

"But she could. Look, I'm havin' a few people over for dinner tomorrow." He named several people from the class. "Souvlaki. Moussaka. As much as you can eat and, knowin' my mama, more. Hot, fresh, homemade bread. Wine like you've never had before, like you've never dreamt of before! Wine of the gods! Wine—"

"Wine from Zeus' cellar itself."

"You got it! So. Can you join us?"

"No."

"No? What no?"

"I can't make it."

"And why not?"

"Look, I'm sorry, I just can't make it, all right?"

"What is it? You don't like Greek food? Okay, so we'll get you a Big Mac."

"Look, I'm just busy, okay? Nothing personal, but I just can't make it tomorrow night. Maybe some other time." And I walked away, leaving him behind. The invitation had thrown me. I hadn't expected it, saw it at that moment as an intrusion on the weekend I had planned, of quiet study, of a bit of television, of maybe a trip to the Riviera.

The following week, Dimitrios-Kostas was just as funny and as friendly as ever. But he never again repeated the invitation, accepted as marked the boundaries of our acquaintanceship.

I did apologize to him for the abruptness of my refusal. He brushed it off, understood. As Jan had noticed that evening at the Riviera, the subtle arrogance they called confidence was beginning to show through in many of us.

"So where're you from, Jar?"

"Jar?"

"Shit, it's the other way around, isn't it?"

"The other way around? Yeah, right."

"Sorry. Memory trick. Forgot a step."

I chuckled, paid for the beer, added a tip.

"So what kind o' name's that, anyways?"

"Indian."

"Red or East?"

"West."

"I don't follow."

"I'm from Casaquemada."

"That in Mexico? You speak pretty good English."

"The West Indies. You know, the Caribbean."

"You're from Jamaica?"

"Casaquemada. It's a different island."

"You don't look like a black guy."

"There are Indians in the West Indies, too."

"Neat. I'm part Indian, or so my granny says, anyways."

"East?"

"Red. My dad says she's crazy."

My anonymity at the Riviera eroded slowly. Janet—I short-ened her name, grew accustomed to it, only much later—con-tinued to bring my beer as before, without my having to ask, with a pleasantness balanced between the professional and the per-sonal. Conversation came in spurts, quick exchanges of question and answer circumscribed by the thirst of clients and the impa-tient urgings of Frankie, the owner of the Riviera and a man iras-cible in his perpetual unhappiness.

"So how come you moved here, eh?"

"Why not? It's as good a place as any, better than most."

"But it's cold."

"And it's hot in Casaquemada."

"I'll take the heat any day."

"You can have it."

"You don't like summer?"

"Sure I do, but I like winter, too."

"You're kidding."

"When you grow up with heat, it's no big deal—"

"See, I don't understand that."

"You grew up with winter."

"S'not the same thing."

"Sure it is."

"One's hot, one's cold. That's like good and bad."

"There's no good or bad in the weather, Janet. But you're right, there is a difference."

"Between hot and cold? Come on, you're makin' it up, right?"

"It's a very practical difference. It's cold outside, you put on a coat, you go out. It's hot and humid outside, you stay inside and sweat. Heat limits me, winter doesn't. It's a question of having choices, you see."

"I see. Smart kid. Choices, eh?"

"Choices."

"Yeah, right."

It was a reticent crowd at the Riviera, intent on its voyeurism, niggardly with its applause. Young toughs in black leather shared tables with middle-aged men in jackets and loosened ties; young businessmen growing flabby let down their dignity, mimed heartiness and a sporting camaraderie with each other, eyes darting towards the anatomical action on the stage, settling there finally in acknowledgement of fantasies far removed from home. Clustered around the edge of the stage, intent eyes—black, blue, brown, young, old, slanted, straight, squinted, staring—sought the slightest flutter and spasm of the Sherry or the Candy or the Foxy convulsing in the feverish lights. Frankie, short, closely shaven, dark hair swept back by the compulsive stroking of his right hand, wandered constantly through the room, eyes darting here and there, surveying, monitoring, directing waitresses with impatient stabs of his index finger towards empty bottles, drained glasses, congested ashtrays. He grew over time to recognize me— he acknowledged all the regulars with a perfunctory nod—but we never spoke. When he opened his mouth, it was to admonish a waitress or to call crude encouragement— "Come on, come on, move that ass!"—to a listless dancer. His restlessness, the fussy vigilance were familiar. I recognized in them my grandfather's anxiety, another, more profound symptom of the dictatorship of small business.

"So you like T'ron'o, eh?"

"You say that as if you don't."

"What's to like?"

"What's not?"

"Playing smart again, eh?"

"Simple question. Simpler than yours."

"You think so."

"What's not to like?" I asked.

"I asked first: What's to like?"

"All right, I'll tell you. The smell."

"The what?"

"The smell."

"Shit. And I thought I could spot the weirdos a mile off."

"I'm sure you can."

"I know I can." She smiled. "So what's this about the smell?"

"This is in general, right? There are exceptions, like Kensington Market, but the city has its own peculiar smell—"

"We call it pollution."

"No, it's a fresh, clean smell—"

"Sure, maybe in spring."

"That's the smell, of spring, as if everything's just been scrubbed and washed."

"Yeah, but that hangs around for what? One week? Two?"

"No, it's always there, you just have to be aware of it. Even in the humidity, in July or August, you can sniff it just under the heaviness. Like a new piece of furniture you've had in your apartment for a couple of months: even if it's covered in dust, it's still there, that smell of newness. Know what I mean?"

"Not really. I buy all my furniture at Goodwill."

I usually sat in one of the three darkened corners—the fourth was dimly lit by a fake Tiffany lamp—or, if they were already taken, found a seat against a wall, positioning myself so that the room was always before me, from one angle or another; I shunned the middle, avoiding as best I could its openness that was like exposure. There were times when the Riviera, revelling in the illusion of grandeur conjured by its mirrors, in the shimmer and flare of the strobe lights, brought to mind a bubbling bordello. Heads and shoulders shadowed the flickering brilliance, and all around bodies black and white bared themselves with the sinuosity of snakes, miming eroticism, parting their legs for the clamouring gaze of visual philanderers. Men came and went, circled unsteadily around the tables, darted in and out through the washroom door, brushed past waitresses bustling by writhing bodies and inert eyes. At times like these, when the Riviera was full of men with too much time and too much money, of women with too little hope and too little money, it took on aspects of a surrealism engendered in male imagination, the last bastion, as the disc jockey exuberantly announced between sets, of male domination.

"So how come you don't dance? I hear there's more money in it than waitressing."

"I have my licence."

"You need a licence?"

"Sure, they regulate everything in this place, don't you know that yet? You get it down at City Hall, just costs a few bucks."

"So how come you don't dance, then?"

"What? And waste a good degree from the famous U. of T.?"

"You went to U. of T.?"

"Four years. French."

"So what're you doing waitressing?"

"What good's a French degree? Teaching? I can't stand kids."

"So why'd you study French, then?"

"I liked the language, the sound of it. And I couldn't think of anything else. So, why not?"

"Maybe because you're here now, waitressing."

"Smart ass."

"Maybe you should've majored in something else, something more useful."

"You sound like my father."

"Your father wouldn't have asked you why you don't dance."

"You don't know my father."

"So how come you don't dance?"

"I do dance, but I always keep my clothes on."

"And what about your licence? Why'd you get it?"

"Ever heard of a contingency plan? See, I like having choices, too."

"And stripping would be a choice?"

"Better than the street corners, eh, wouldn't you say? *Salut*, Jar."

Jan was not particularly good-looking. Her face, formless in its plainness, was unarresting; her hair, twirled up and pinned, sat lifeless on her head; her body, of average height but large-boned, showed evidence through her black tights of negligence and a fondness for carbohydrates. I attempted, in the idle wanderings of my mind, to picture her unclothed. It was not difficult. The tights revealed all her contours, the ample breasts, the flaccid stomach, the heavy hips and thighs flowing into flared calves. The picture—I completed it with large, dark nipples and pubic hair—pleased me, not because it was in itself a pleasing picture but because she worked at the Riviera, keeping to herself what other women here minutely revealed.

"Those all your own teeth?" she asked.

"Pardon?"

"They're all so perfect, they don't look real."

"Of course they're all mine, what d'you think?"

"They look too good to be true."

"Thanks. And how many tissues did you stuff down your bra today?" Arrogance: my own words surprised me. They came of themselves, from the special male freedoms of the Riviera, this atmosphere in which inhibitions gave easy way to caprice.

"That's the real stuff, buster."

"Oh yeah? Prove it."

"Not on your life."

"Maybe that's why you don't dance. Under-qualified." My words had a life, a logic, of their own.

"You'll never know, eh?"

"Guess not."

Floating above my words, like a snippet of wayward awareness, was the thought that this was not me, this was another man. But the pleasure was in ignoring it, in playing, for a while at best, an unaccustomed role.

"You comin' here Saturday night?"

"Saturday night? Probably not. Got work to do. Studying. Preparing for rounds."

"Sounds important."

"Takes time."

"My, my, such discipline."

"No choice."

"I'll give you one. I'm havin' a party at my place Saturday night. Here's the address if you feel like comin'."

"Thanks, but—"

"Hey, if you feel like takin' a break, you know. Bring something to drink if you come, beer, wine, whatever."

"And if I come, how should I dress?"

"Dress? You can come naked as far as I'm concerned."

"Sorry. Don't have a licence."

"Don't need one *chez moi*. See you Saturday?"

"Sorry, too much work. But thanks anyway."

"Well, at least you have a choice now. *Au revoir*."

The difference between Jan's invitation and Dimitrios-Kostas' was this: it was safe. School was inevitable; the Riviera was one of many such places, easily replaceable. I suppose that, in the end, it was curiosity that drove me to take the subway from Bathurst to Dundas West on that Saturday evening in January, curiosity about why she had invited me, about Jan herself, her home and her friends, even about my own curiosity itself. And it was caution, sudden and unexpected, that caused me to ignore her instructions, written in a bold and flowing hand, to take the streetcar to the eighth stop on its route. I wanted the time to test the strength of my curiosity, to preserve for a few minutes more my freedom to turn back.

The night was cold and windy. The radio had predicted snow, and the smell of it, a fresh moistness, was in the air. The sidewalks were deserted. Few cars passed. The occasional streetcar rattled by in a rush of metal and light, pausing at stops ahead to let off or take on passengers. Lights, of stores, of streetlamps, of a shut shopping centre across the street, were without reach, brilliance cut by a thin gruel of greyness hanging in the air. As I walked along, my boots silent on the sidewalk, warm in my parka as the wind whipped at my hair, and fanned at my face, my apprehension eased, altered to an unaccustomed boldness. I wondered only briefly at why I had rushed out just before the liquor store closed to buy a six-pack of beer, why I had searched with a certain frenzy for the note Jan had given me at the Riviera.

As I turned the corner onto her street, as the first snippets of snow stung into my eyes, slapped themselves with a cold bite against my skin, it was her voice, teasing, challenging, suddenly shy and resolutely nonchalant with the invitation, that came to mind, that pushed away the questions, dampened the last dregs of discomfort, that brought me at last to the house at the end of the cul-de-sac. I paused briefly on the sidewalk, looked up at the bared windows of the second floor where she lived. Shadows and silhouettes crowded the yellow light, like suggestions of animation. My apprehension returned. By the time I rang the bell at the front door, thin drifts of fresh snow were swirling lightly on the road, and the night air was a confusion of wind and frenzied flakes.

He was tall, slim, round-faced, with lank brown hair parted in the middle, and if I remember his name, it is because he was, or had been until recently, Jan's boyfriend. He had come in not long after me, and in the few minutes between my arrival and his, several people had needled her about his absence: Where was Jim? Had she invited him? Was he coming? She had replied to each with what struck me as an amalgam of testiness and indifference: probably still at work; yes; she didn't know.

When he walked in, shaking snow from his shoulders and hair, kicking off his work boots into a corner, she greeted him with pronounced diffidence, taking his coat into the bedroom and sending him into the crowded kitchen with his twelve-pack of beer. When he emerged a few minutes later, a silvered Crusader fading on the front of his black T-shirt, he had a beer in each hand. He made his way through the crowd, groups of men and women in worn jeans and lumberjack shirts, responding with a forced heartiness to their greetings, ignoring the tone of raillery that seemed to underly their every word. He looked around, nodding here, smiling there, sipping first from one bottle, then from the other. His eyes lighted on me where I stood in the living room, a beer in my hand, sorting through the welter of names Jan had run past me and wondering, perplexed, what to do next, how to join one of the groups that sat or stood around in conversation hectic and hermetic. His eyes paused, moved on, returned. He was, I thought, avoiding the familiar turned vengeful, seeking haven in the certain uncertainties of the unknown. He came over to me, nodded, introduced himself, and through the babble of voices, above the wail of an electric guitar streaming from the stereo, asked who the hell I was.

"So where'd you meet Janet?"

"Well—"

"Robarts Library." Jan was suddenly beside us. "Come on, Jim, you giving him the third degree?"

"Curious, Janet, that's all. It's just weird, eh? I mean, you've known this guy since university, you tell me you met on one of your few trips to the library, and you've never mentioned him. How come?"

"I don't have to tell you everything, do I?"

"It might help."

"Give it a rest, Jim."

"Sorry, just tryin' to make conversation, that's all."

"So why don't you ask him what he's studyin'?"

"You still at U. of T.?"

"I'm in meds."

"Amin' for the bucks, eh?"

I shrugged. Why disabuse him? "You were at U. of T., too?"

"Been workin' since I was seventeen. Never had time for school."

"What do you do?"

"Little bit o' this, little bit o' that. I've been steady at a storage warehouse out in Scarborough for the last coupla months. I'm hopin' it lasts."

"Sounds like hard work."

"S'not too bad. Pays the bills, buys the gas."

"Right." I didn't know what to say next, was defeated by the meagreness of his satisfaction. "That's important." I was out of conversational gambits, took a long draw of my beer.

Jan turned away to greet with restrained enthusiasm a group of new arrivals.

Jim said, "So what's it like cuttin' into a body?"

"You mean surgery?"

"No, don't you guys slice up dead winos to study the parts?"

"We slice up any body, not just winos."

"So what's that like? Diggin' out some guy's heart or liver and stickin' your nose in it?"

"You wouldn't believe the smell—"

He grinned widely. "Fuckin' sick, man, fuckin' sick."

A young couple approached, the woman leading the reluctant man by the hand. She was short, thick-set, of a rough attractiveness. "Hey, Jim," she said. "How ya doin'?"

"Sandi." *Sandi with an i*: it was how Jan had introduced her.

Her boyfriend, tall, thin, of a tremulous indoor paleness, smoothed his sparse moustache as if willing it to greater stature.

"You got any stuff, Jim?" Sandi said.

"What d'you have in mind?"

"Whatever you've got."

"Hash okay?"

"Good stuff?"

"The best."

"You bet."

Jan, coming up behind me, said, "You into smokin' up, Raj?"

"Sure," I lied, without knowing why. "Sometimes. But I'm not in the mood tonight."

Jim said, "No charge. Great stuff."

"Thanks, but I think I'll pass."

"Your loss."

Sandi said, "Okay if we use your bedroom, Jan?"

"Yeah, sure. Just open the window, okay? I hate sleepin' in an ashtray."

"Yeah, yeah. Let's go, guys." Impatient, Sandi led Jim and her boyfriend to the bedroom.

Jan said, "You're not really into smokin' up, eh, Raj?"

"How could you tell?"

"Wasn't hard. Nothing's more transparent than a guy playin' cool. Why'd you do it?"

I shrugged. "I don't know."

"That's a switch."

"What?"

"There's something you don't know."

"But I know that I don't know."

"Naturally."

"I've got a question for you."

"Shoot."

"Why'd you invite me here tonight?"

"I wanted to see if you'd come."

"And how many other guys did you invite from the Ri—"

"You're my first. And only."

"So what's the real reason?"

"You do get to the point, don't you?"

I said nothing.

"All right, I'll tell you why." She took me by the arm, led me to a pile of cushions in a corner, made seats for both of us, said, "Because I need someone I can talk to."

It started that night, I think, curiously at that very moment: this inability of Jan to hold my full attention. Part of my mind seemed to go wayward, to reach out to details, of place, of people, of conversations, around us. It was not rudeness, not boredom—I heard every word she said, reacted, responded, questioned—but it was as if, in her plea to be heard, some part of my unconscious could no longer take her seriously.

"Ever tried to run away from home? I did. When I was fourteen. Didn't get very far. We'd just moved here from Calgary. A step up for sure. Calgary—you ever been there?—it's gotta be one of the ugliest places on earth. I mean, at least we've got trees in this city, right? Out there, even the flowers are concrete. But we hadn't been here long, I didn't know the city, just slipped out one night, must o' been around ten or eleven, and started walking."

"Why?"

"Why? Don't know. Just had to. Anyways, started walking. And this was out in the 'burbs, right. Late at night, middle o' the week, so it's deserted, all the good little lawyers and doctors and accountants and middle-management types—you know the kind, you've seen them on the subway wearing five-year-old suits and reading the business section of the *Globe*—all already in bed jerking off or humping their wives and thinkin' o' the secretary. The road ran through a stretch of golf course, the darkest part, right, streetlights all along but the golf course was just drinkin' up the light. Just as I'm about halfway through, this guy appears up ahead walking towards me. Tall, curly hair, blond or light brown, I dunno. As he gets close to me, he asks if I've got the time, and before I can even look at my watch he opens up his coat and flashes me. Man, was he ever excited. I was fourteen, right? So what does a fourteen-year-old do? Scream. Soooo innocent. Made the guy's night. He took off into the golf course, hand between his legs. And I turned right around and headed home. My parents were watching TV. The news. They've always been big on that. Never even noticed I was gone."

She was dressed differently that night, in black slacks and a roomy blouse that shimmered in the light; dressed as if to camouflage the weight I knew to be there. She had let her hair down, parted it in the middle, pinned it to either side just above her ears. I complimented her—it seemed the thing to do—and she acknowledged my words, quickly offered, with a perfunctory smile.

"My folks aren't rich, you know. Comfortable. Well off. Something like that. They paid my university tuition, but I had to work—switchboard, waitressing, supermarket cashier—to earn money for food and books and clothes. My dad's chief actuary at Luminal Life, you know, the insurance company? He's been with 'em, like, forever. Spends more time downtown than at home, like he's more comfortable down there? Makes sense, I suppose. You should see him. Ruddy. Well built, works out every morning. Hair, silver for as long as I can remember, so crew-cut you can see his skull. Really piercing eyes, blue-grey, but you never get the feeling he's seeing you. Always in a three-piece suit, blue or grey, white shirt, wine-coloured tie. Even on weekends, watching TV, reading the paper, barbecuing. Always in this fucking suit, like it's his second skin or something. I used to fantasize that he had a mistress downtown, that's why he spent so little time at home. Seemed more exciting than actuarial tables. I mean, statistics! How can you devote your life to statistics? Well, fat chance. Over-active teenage imagination. He just isn't the type. You should see him at the office. He's like a little king. Gets in early, usually before Mrs. Micawber, his secretary. Sits at his desk, takes out a file. When Mrs. Mic arrives, she prepares coffee and serves it to him in a silver setting on a silver platter. And the way he pours it! Just so much coffee, just so much cream, not a drop spilled, every movement neat and precise. Like it's fucking Buckingham Palace or something."

She saw that my beer bottle was empty, took it from my hand, went to the kitchen, brought me another, said, "On the house."

"And the tip?"

"We'll talk about that later."

"Sounds ominous."

But she made no reply, merely smoothed the back of her blouse with her left hand and lowered herself to the cushions. The sharp scent of fresh perfume rose in her wake.

"Would you believe my folks sleep in separate bedrooms? Have for years. My dad used to disturb my mum when he went to bed after working late in his study downstairs, so when I moved out, my mum moved into my bedroom. Don't think it's affected their sex life any. Sometimes I wonder how they managed to come up with me. My dad must've worked out the probability on his cal-culator, you know, so many screws over so many weeks equal so many—"

I laughed.

"Hey, this is no joke, my dad's capable of that, you don't know him. And my mum probably helped him plan it. Way I see their marriage, she was lookin' for a husband and security and an out from her dead-end sales job at Eaton's. He was lookin' for a way to impress the higher-ups with his stability and trustworthiness— this was back in the fifties, right? In Calgary, yet—and what better way than a wife and kid? Guess it worked. He started climbin' in the company—his office just got bigger and bigger over the years—and then they finally moved him, moved all of us, out here. And we've been here ever since, one not-so-big, not-so-happy family, but reasonable, as my dad would say. So how's the weather, Dad? Reasonable. So how's work goin', Dad? Reasonable. My dad's the most reasonable person I know, as far as he's concerned."

"And your mother?"

"My mum? God knows. I was her fair-haired little girl. Trouble is, fair-haired little girls grow up and leave home. She didn't know that. Still doesn't. Hey, my folks are typical Canadians, man. You know, do not do unto others as you would not have them do unto you. My mum and I once went to get tickets to a show at the O'Keefe. Two windows were open. There was nobody at one, and a line of about thirty people at the other. Mum joined the line. I couldn't believe it, she joined the fucking line. I grabbed the money from her, went up to the other window. Had the tickets in a minute. You should've seen the dirty looks I got from the people in the line. And not one of 'em moved, all stayed there like a line of ants. My mum still hasn't forgiven me for that. And you know what my dad said? Because my mum told him, of course, she was furious, eh. He said, 'Janet, you must be more reasonable in the future. You embarrassed your mother terribly today.' So what do I say? 'Yes, Dad, all right, Dad.' I mean, these are people who apologize when somebody steps on their foot. What d'you do, you know?"

"What do they think of your working at the Riviera?"

"Who says I've told them? Shit, they'd die. Probably disinherit me or something like that. Not that they'd have anything to complain about, if only they'd think back to when I was born. D'you know that they were so poor when they had me, I spent the first year of my life sleeping on my mum's fresh bed linen in the top drawer of a dresser. My dad was drinkin' pretty heavy at the time, eh. Gin, mostly, my mum says. Pressure of work. One night he got out of bed to go to the bathroom, still under the influence, eh. Bumped into the open drawer, forgot I was there, shut it. My mum found me the next morning sleeping like, well, like a baby. I guess I was already going solo even then."

"You think it marked you?"

"No, no way. I just think it says a lot about my personality, that's all."

"You're comfortable in drawers?"

"In a way."

She had spoken as of a memory, and an embittered one at that. It produced in me a wrinkle of unease, my hands fussing at the bottle, index finger shaving at the film of moisture on its surface. My eyes, my mind, wandered, reached out from our claustrophobic corner to the living room languid with circled heads and lounging bodies, conversation muffled through thin smoke and a boisterous, blanketing music.

It was a room of ample size lit by an old floor lamp, a pole of tarnished brass topped by a homemade shade. The green walls, lined at the base by boards of scratched wood, were roughly patched in white here and there where nails or picture hooks had ravaged the plaster. On the wall straight ahead was pinned the only decoration in the room, a print, edges curled, of Magritte's *The Conqueror*, a plank of wood emerging, headlike, from a tuxedo while, in the background, an uprooted tree flew over a white wasteland into a sky blood-red at the horizon, solid black higher up. "Family portrait," she'd said when I'd noticed it soon after my arrival. Below the print, a single-sized bed doubled as a sofa. To its left and below the windows, a brown armchair, its fabric frayed at the seams and corners, squatted like a declaration of discomfort on the green carpet that stretched wall to wall except in the places where it had worn away to a shredded colourlessness. The room, in its reduction of comfort to the essential, had a remarkably familiar feel to it.

She said, "You know, I can remember being in bed with my

parents only once. Must've been five or six. My grandmother, my mum's mum, had just died. Somehow I caught a chill at the funeral. My mum took me into bed, put me between them. My dad was reading. Mum sniffled from time to time into a Kleenex, mumbled this or that about her mum, about the funeral. You know how people get. 'She looked beautiful, didn't she?' 'It was a wonderful service, the minister did such a good job.' She went on and on. Don't think my dad heard a word she said. Par for the course, I suppose. Then, without even lookin' up from his book, my dad said, 'Everybody's got to die sometime. Just look at the statistics. One hundred per cent certainty.' Today, I think he was tryin' to be funny, to cheer her up a bit, eh? But I was scared shitless. I asked if I was going to die, too. He said in his reasonable voice, 'Of course, Janet. Don't you know that yet? Everybody's born to die.' Sensitive guy, eh? I mean, he might as well have told me I was gonna die in a day or two. That's what I thought, anyways. I broke out in tears like you wouldn't believe, like somebody'd turned on a tap. Couldn't stop for the life of me. And didn't, till my mum took me back to my own room. Didn't want to be in the same bed as him, and I remember resenting her for not staying with me, or rather for going back to him. Strange, eh? I remember that as if it happened yesterday, the fear's still fresh."

"Of death or your dad?"

"Both. You followin' this? Any o' this make sense to you?"

"Sure, it makes sense. Almost everybody's afraid of death."

"Are you?"

"I don't know."

"But what about your parents? D'you like them?"

"My parents were killed in a car accident when I was a baby."

"You an orphan?"

"Well, I was brought up by my grandparents. Does that make me an orphan?"

"Don't know. But seems to me life would be easier that way."

"Think so?"

"Expect so."

A couple walked in from the kitchen, the floorboards under the carpet squeaking a symphony of wooden protest as they made their way in stockinged feet to the group clustered on and around the sofa.

I said, "Are we being antisocial? Shouldn't you be talking to your other guests, too?"

"They can talk to each other. Besides, they're not guests, they're friends. They know how to take care of themselves. They come, they stay as long as they want, they go. We like keeping things simple, you know?"

"Sounds a bit like the Riviera."

"Fuck off." She laughed, handed me her empty bottle. "You get the next round."

I'd had enough—my head was beginning to nod with an alcoholic heaviness—but offered to get one for her.

"Shit, Raj, loosen up. Another beer won't kill you. Besides, it's on the house, remember?" She got unsteadily to her feet, grasped my arm, pulled me up and propelled me ahead of her into the corridor that led to the kitchen. The crowd in the apartment had diminished; the kitchen ahead was deserted, the Formica table littered with glasses, bottles, cans and the spilled detritus of half-eaten snack food. At the closed bedroom door, Jan came to a sudden halt, sniffed the air, frowned at the bite of cigarette smoke that seeped from between its loosely set edges. "Shit," she said. "I'll bet that bitch didn't open the window." Still grasping my arm, she opened the door, looked in. Froze.

I followed her gaze, to the coats flung in disorder to the floor, to the bed lit by the headboard reading lamp, to the three bodies stripped of clothes and actively engrossed in the middle of the mattress. She stared for a moment, as if impressing the scene on her mind. Drugged, absorbed in their activity, they remained oblivious to us. Then she closed the door, led me to the kitchen and, over the next two beers fitfully consumed, told me of university and the growth of her uncertainty over the meaning of life.

"Hey, Jan?" The voice, male, husky, called softly from the kitchen door.

It was late. The music had ended some time before and no one had bothered to put it back on. A quiet had settled on the flat.

Three men, walking gingerly on the cold plastic tile, came into the kitchen. Their eyes blinked, squinted, in the brightness, harsh and incongruous, of the fluorescent light.

Jan said, "You guys leaving?"

"Well, we wanted to talk to you about that." A young blond man advanced to the table.

"What's up?"

"You looked outside recently? It's wild out there."

We trooped into the living room. The bedroom door was still closed—Jan didn't even glance at it—but the smell of smoke had dissipated.

The young man—Dave? Colin?—switched off the brass lamp. The sudden darkness brought, through the window panes turned transparent, the spectacle of night ferocious with wind and snow. In the light of the streetlamps, stripped trees flailed wildly at the maddened flakes and the road lay submerged, curbs and paving engulfed in sparkling white. The houses across the street, as solid and as imposing as the one we were in, were effaced by the swirling storm.

"Well," Jan said after a moment, "guess you guys won't be driving out to Scarborough tonight."

"That," said the young man, "was what we wanted to talk to you about. Can you put us up for the night, or what's left of it?"

"I'm not going to send you out in that weather, that's for sure."

A panic rose in me. "I'd better get going," I said. "Before it gets too bad."

"Got news for you, friend," the young man said. "It already is."

"I don't live far away. Bloor and Bathurst."

"And how're you gonna get there, Sergeant Preston? Dogsled?"

Jan said, "In this weather, even the streetcars call it quits."

"I can walk to the subway."

"Subway's closed. You're spending the night here." She turned to me, grinned. "Even if we have to tie you down."

Outside, a tree branch snapped, fell heavily to the snow.

I felt choice slip from me.

Jan gave a sleeping bag and two summer blankets to her friends, turned to me and announced there were no more, someone would have to share the bed with her. "And you're it, Raj."

Her friends stripped to their underpants, spread their covers on the floor and rolled themselves into cocoons of warmth. Jan went to the bathroom, returned in a white flannel nightshirt that reached to her knees. She got into bed, pulled the blanket over her. "Get the light, will ya, Raj?"

I snapped off the light and once more the storm raged in the windows.

Jan said, "I've got the wall. I'm not gonna be the one that falls off."

I sat on the edge of the bed, hestitated, finally stretched out.

Jan said, "You're not plannin' to sleep in your jeans, are you?"

"It'll be warmer."

"Don't be ridiculous. It's too uncomfortable. Take 'em off."

"No-no, I'll be fine, really."

"Raj, nobody sleeps in jeans."

"For Christsake," a drowsy voice said from the darkness. "Take your jeans off. I'm tryin' to get some sleep here."

Reluctantly, I slipped off my sweater, undid my shirt, removed my jeans and socks.

"There, that's better," Jan whispered as I pulled the blanket over me, felt the warmth of her thigh pressing against mine.

I lay awake for a long time, sleep distant, mind emptied of thought, listening to the contented breathing of the others in the room, to their snores and coughs, to the wheezing whistle of the wind outside.

Jan turned onto her side, nestled her head against my arm. And her hand began travelling steadily up my thigh to my underpants, caressing, gently squeezing; freed me from the strain of the clinging cotton and brought the game to fruition with firm and precise strokes. She held me until I had softened, released me, turned onto her back, slightly parted her legs and began an unabashed stroking of herself. When she was done, she gasped as if she were choking on a small bone.

Twice more that night she reached for me, fingers manipulating me into helplessness, urging me both times onto her, into her, pressing me each time to a deeper spending of self. And after my final sighs, when I had rolled off her, she returned with her hand to the certainty of self-satisfaction.

When, finally, I fell asleep, my thoughts roamed through the snowstorm outside and saw again and again the tree branch snapping and falling helpless to the snow.

The next morning I was awoken by the hoarse and urgent whisper of the young man, Colin or Dave. "Get out o' bed," he said. "Jim's up." I threw the blanket off, reached for my clothes.

Outside, the sun was shining.

A Friday afternoon, just over a month later. I had just come in, exhausted, with the newspaper, a hot beef submarine and a can of Coca-Cola. I settled crosslegged on the bed, into this position that pulled me back to childhood and playing *pooja* with Angela, spread the newspaper out, unwrapped the sandwich.

The telephone rang in the living room.

I swore, went to it unwillingly.

"Raj," Jan said. "I've been trying to reach you for days."

"I've been busy." I regretted having given her my telephone number.

"You haven't been to the Riviera recently." She spoke with an edge of accusation.

"I told you, I've been very busy. Very tired."

"Look, Raj, I have to talk to you."

"Can we leave it for another time? I'm—"

"This can't wait."

My stomach tightened, resolution hardened as she tugged at my choice.

"Raj, I'm pregnant."

"You're what." The words came out flattened by the tension that shot through me in a cold shiver.

"You heard me."

"And." My mind raced, saw once more the night of storm and the snapping tree branch.

"It's yours."

"Maybe it's Jim's."

"I haven't slept with Jim in months."

"So how come he was at the party?"

"We tried to be friends, it didn't work out. I don't see him anymore."

"And have you . . . ? I mean, is there anybody . . . ?"

"Anybody else? In a word, no. You're it, Raj."

"I'm it." The words, so innocent, words of childhood games, acquired menace. "So what now?"

"Well, I'm not going to get rid of it, if that's what you're thinking."

"I'll pay for it."

"That's not the point. I don't want to get rid of it."

"So where does that leave me?"

"It's your child."

"But a child, now—"

"D'you want your child growing up without a father?"

She had, inadvertently, hit on the crux of it. My Aunt Sylvia came to me, and again I was lost in the colour and texture of her skin, the unreadability of her gestures. In a few seconds of silence, I confronted as I hadn't since childhood the impenetrability of my own void.

A few weeks later we were wed at City Hall in a ceremony so rapid that when it concluded I asked the judge, "Is that it?" He nodded, in vague surprise. In all, it had taken less time than to prepare a syringe.

Jan's mother, red-eyed, distant, arrived at the last minute, a bouquet of wilting roses clasped in her hand. Her father did not attend. My grandparents I informed only days later, in a telephone call during which I pretended that the interference on the line was worse than it actually was; I was brief, to the point, presented them with a fact, but not all the facts. I promised a letter with pictures and more information. It was a letter I never wrote.

The following week, Jan's parents took us out to dinner. They gave us a choice between Swiss Chalet and Ponderosa. We chose

Ponderosa. It was an uncomfortable evening. Her father, severely suited, ruminated actuarially on life. Her mother, silent most of the time, sniffled pointedly into an endless stream of paper tissues, her eyes heavy on me as I pretended to listen to her father and make sense of his statistical statements. The evening ended early.

Two weeks later, while I was at work, Janet miscarried. A taxi took her to the hospital, I was paged to Emergency, but there was nothing to be done.

There was nothing to be done about anything.

Jan quit the Riviera, got a sales job at Eaton's, in the shoe department.

We moved into a house her parents owned on a quiet street at Yonge and Eglinton. They kept the rent low. "We'll make no money on this," her father said, with only a tincture of regret.

Curiously, the conversation Jan and I had at the party was the first time and the last that we spoke with any intimacy. All that came after was like a barrier. And for this reason, perhaps, Jan never really came into focus for me, remained a person, mysterious, amorphous, that I never grasped.

14

Asha said, *"I have been getting flashes."*

Jan said, "Flashes."

Raffique said, "You hear the latest rumour? They say the British sending two warships." He had returned, unexpectedly, the day before, possessions piled in the car; had been greeted by Asha with her usual tranquillity, unloaded the car, resumed his place as if there had been no interval.

Asha said, "Yes, pictures. You know."

Jan said, "What of?"

"Yeah," I said. "Heard it on the BBC this morning. Our news had nothing about it. 'The situation is under control.'" We were sitting in our living room. Asha had called, needed, she said, to speak to Jan. Seeking to leave them alone in the living room, I led Raffique to the porch, but he would not have it, insisted on joining them.

Raffique said, "So what new in that? Remember when the army revolted—what, ten, twelve years ago? Is the BBC that told us, and is *Time* that fill in the details afterwards. The old man never bother to tell us that he had American soldiers sitting in the airport and Venezuelan navy ships off the coast."

Asha said, "You have been running through my mind all day."

Jan said, "How? What d'you mean?"

Raffique turned his attention to them. His drinking habits hadn't changed: in his left hand he held a bottle of beer, in his right a glass of whiskey.

Asha said, "Two things, Jan. First, you will not be living much longer here in Casaquemada—"

"It's just a holiday, for God's sake, Asha," I snapped, irritated by her tone of reverential certainty.

My words seemed to perplex her. She cocked her head, as if listening to a voice that spoke only to her. "You are going on a holiday?"

"Come on, Asha, stop pretending. Jan must have talked to you about this—"

"When? Soon?"

"We haven't decided yet."

Jan said, "*You* haven't decided yet."

"And I suppose you haven't said a thing to her about leaving."

"Not a word."

Asha said, "But it is not long from now. A matter of days, maybe."

I feigned surprise. "Is that right? And does that go for me—"

Jan said, "And the second thing?"

Asha touched a finger to her lips, her eyes large, and the gesture, an unusual uncertainty, heightened the silence of the house. "I am not sure," she said. "It is . . . it is not very clear."

Raffique said, "But Asha, they can't leave now, the airport close down, remember? Nothing coming, nothing going."

"No," she said, speaking hesitantly. "It is a car I see." She turned in growing animation towards Jan. "Yes, a car. A big car. Someone will offer it to you. And there will be a chauffeur, with a uniform and a cap. But the strange thing is that you will not want this gift, you will resist it. But you will have no choice, you will have to accept it. I see you entering the car, but unwillingly. You feel a mistake has been made and the car is for someone else."

Jan laughed, "Fat chance!"

Asha smiled, but with her lips alone, stretching them into thin ribbons of red.

I said, "And does she get this limo before or after leaving?"

Asha looked seriously at me. "I do not know," she answered with a studious sincerity.

"And where am I in all this? And Rohan, for that matter?"

Raffique chuckled. "You're probably the chauffeur. You'd look good in a uniform and a cap."

Asha said, "Rohan goes with Jan."

I said, "We're all going, for a few weeks."

"No," she said quickly, paused, then added, "But you will be travelling, too."

"Someone's going to give me a yacht?"

"Is that your dream?"

But I had never thought of sailing. It held no attraction for me. "No, just thought, maybe . . ."

"I can tell you no more than I already have," she said.

"So we're all travelling."

She nodded, thoughtfully.

"But not together."

"That is correct."

Jan said, "That was the original plan."

Asha turned once more to Jan. "I see you happy, Jan. You are wearing a red dress, dancing in a beautiful garden. You are carefree and light on your feet."

"That's you," I said. "Ol' Carefree Lightfoot."

Jan said, "And where is this garden, Asha?"

"I do not know, but it is not here. Maybe it is in Canada. The garden is well taken care of, everything is clean and trimmed and swept."

"Clean? Swept?" Jan's eyes twinkled. "Sure as hell ain't here, then."

Asha glanced towards Raffique. "Are you ready?"

And Raffique, to my surprise, put both beer and whiskey on the sidetable and stood up, almost meekly, like a middle-aged schoolboy rising to attention.

Asha gathered her veil around her, clutched at it, rose and, in her mincing steps, glided from the living room. Jan followed.

Seizing the opportunity, I asked Raffique why he had come back.

His age, and a disturbing fatigue, showed when he replied, "A man can only take so much whorin', Raj."

"And she accepts that?" I had never understood Asha's reaction to her abandonment, had seen her religion as retreat, understood even less her acceptance of his return.

"She never caused any trouble, Raj. She knew all along I was coming back, says it all had to happen. Astrology or something. I don't know. Maybe it have something to it after all."

"Astrology?" And I felt at that moment as I'd felt the night the young girl had slipped onto the sofa next to him: dismay, and a sense of sanity slipping. "But Raffique, astrology, that's just superstition dressed up as knowledge, and superstition is nothing more than socially acceptable stupidity, you know that."

"But she knew, Raj." And his eyes glittered. "It's as if I never left home."

It was like talking to a man who, having just watched a magician saw a woman in half then put her together again, believes in the reality of the illusion.

I picked up his bottle and glass, put them on the kitchen counter, walked him out to the back gate, to Jan and Asha. Just before they left, Asha, on impulse, leaned close to Jan and kissed her on the cheek. An unexpected gesture, a disturbing one: Asha had always been leery of touch. We watched them go, waited until they had entered the house.

It was a clear night, a night nervous with the clicking of crickets, the croaking of frogs, the greater silence beyond.

As we walked back in, Jan said, "You were a pain in the ass tonight."

"Me?" Her words had stung. "The fucking island's falling apart and she wants to talk about limousines and dancing in a garden? And now she's got Raffique believing in astrology." I pulled the door in behind us, began slipping the bolts, snapping the locks.

"And what's wrong with that? Christ, Raj, the guy's business is going down the drain, he can't even afford his apartment any more. He's gotta have something to believe in, right?"

"How'd you find out all this?"

"Asha. They're just about living on their savings now."

"When'd she tell you?"

"At the gate."

"And how come you're telling me? This is a first."

She pushed the bedroom door open. A draft of cool air drifted out on the hum of the air conditioner. "The word," she said, "is compassion."

"For them or for me?"

But she had already closed the door.

From the little room beyond the kitchen, Rohan shrieked in excitement as the television crackled with gunfire.

It measured about six inches by four inches, had a soft navy blue cover and twenty-four white pages intricately webbed by pink, wavy lines. The inside of the cover, overrun by flying maple leaves fading into a light blue background, was vaguely reminiscent of a bank note, and I wasn't surprised to see in fine print at the bottom "Canadian Bank Note Company, Limited." Beneath the dark blue coat of arms—the lion, the unicorn, *A mari usque ad mare*—a cursive script, beautiful and mechanical, read: *The Secretary of State for External Affairs of Canada requests, in the name of Her Majesty the Queen*— And, just to the right: *Le Secrétaire d'Etat aux Affaires extérieures du Canada, au nom de Sa Majesté la Reine*—

Bold black print at the bottom of page one declared the passport bearer a Canadian citizen. Page two defined the bearer in broad strokes. Name: Rajnath Ramsingh. Birthdate: 1953-06-06. Birthplace: Salmonella Casaquemada. Sex: M. Height: 175 cm. Hair: Black. Eyes: Black. Passport issued at: Toronto. Page three offered, on the left, the bearer's signature, an illegible flour-

ish in black ink that I once spent an evening developing and practising after Surein had demonstrated his facility with forgery; on
the right, the bearer himself in unflattering pose: full hair slightly
tousled—that had been deliberate—above a face rounder than
now, eyes slightly startled by the photographer's flash, lips dark in
the photograph, not quite meeting. An unsatisfactory photograph: I hadn't been ready. Pages four, five and six were un-
marked, but page seven had been stamped twice in messy blue
ink; the first, askew, authorized my entry into Casaquemada; the
second, more carefully placed, gave me the right of residence in
the island.

The rest of the passport was also blank except for the last page,
number twenty-four, where I had printed in the requested information. In case of accident or death notify: Janet Ramsingh. Relationship: Wife. But the address given, in Toronto, was no longer
valid, and I was unsure of how to go about changing it. Simply
scratch the old address out, insert the new? But would that deface
the passport, render it invalid? Page one had warned, "This passport is the property of the Government of Canada. It must not be
altered—" So I dared not alter it; it was a measure of my fear, my
unwillingness to jeopardize, in even the most minimal way, the
one document that, come what may, was a guarantee of
tomorrow.

I closed the passport, lay it on the desk in the direct light of the
lamp. Lying there, a navy blue rectangle stamped in gold, it
seemed a fragile security.

Two sharp raps at the window startled me.

A hoarse whisper: "Boss?"

I parted the curtains to the ribs of burglar-proofing that hung
between me and the night. "Everything okay, Wayne?"

"Everything quiet, boss." His right hand, long, thick fingers
with nails square and hard, like chips of ivory on his dark skin,
clung to a strand of the metal. "You have the time?" His face
pressed between two black swirls: soft, widely spaced eyes, well-
defined cheekbones flowing down into dimples that framed a
strong, wide mouth. He hadn't aged as I would have thought. His
features had thickened into a resemblance of his father. But he

remained a handsome man, waist still trim, arms veiny and muscular.

"Getting sleepy, Wayne?" It was just after two.

"Nah, man, nothing to worry about, I not going to fall asleep on you."

I offered coffee.

"Thank you, boss."

"Raj, Wayne."

But he would not have it, had arrived with this title on his lips, as if he had long been practising it. As, indeed, he probably had.

I told him to meet me on the porch, and I wondered why it was that, in memory as now, there seemed so often to be a window between Wayne and me, but a window of inaccessibility.

He moved onto the lawn, invisible in the darkness. His flash-light clicked; the beam cut through the night: slices of grass, chain-link, road flew in its path. And the brashness of the light, its furtive probing, caused my heart to pound. I pulled the curtains together, waited for my tension to subside before unzipping my pants and inserting the passport into the largest pocket of the moneybelt strapped around my waist. Into the others, in my own play at furtiveness, I had already put Jan's passport, a thousand dollars in U.S. cash and five thousand in traveller's cheques, emergency funds—such is the nature of life in Casaquemada—secreted for just such a moment in the freezing compartment of the refrigerator. I had had, earlier in the day, to chip the packet out; ice and frost had grown thick over it.

Few lights were on in the house. Faintly, through the closed bedroom door, I could hear the hum of the air conditioner. Jan had insisted on taking Rohan to bed with her. He was afraid, she'd said. But Rohan was too young to understand what was happening. The fear was hers. Wayne's arrival—she did not know him—had unsettled her; he seemed to bring uncomfortably close events that had so far remained remote, rumours and radio re-ports, words rather than fact of emergency.

The kitchen light, a pair of fluorescent tubes, caused my eyes to ache, to feel the fatigue that had settled in them. I filled the kettle, plugged it in, got out two coffee mugs, spooned in the instant coffee. In the silence, weighty, almost measurable, every sound—the swirl of the cap on the coffee bottle, the clink of the spoon on the cups—amplified itself into approximation of alarm. My movements slowed, grew tentative. My ears strained, not at the silence but beyond it, to the almost active absence of sound, to the menace that would not be heard.

The kettle boiled, and it was with relief that I busied myself preparing the coffees.

"You better take off the lights, boss," Wayne said when, after unlocking and unbolting the living room door, I stepped out into the porch. "The police passing about every half an hour. They going to wonder if they see a light on at this hour."

I gave him the cups, stepped back into the house, snapped off the lights. Darkness fell in a sudden descent of shadow and sparkling lights. It was several moments before my eyes accustomed themselves to the rectangle of open door, to the silhouette of mountain on sky.

Wayne gave me my coffee and, holding it with both hands, I sat down. He put the flashlight on the floor, withdrew his machete from the leather sheath strapped to his waist, sat down on the chair next to mine, the machete on his lap. For several minutes neither of us spoke, just sipped at the coffee, sighed without meaning. From time to time, Wayne would blow into the cup, cooling the steaming liquid with his breath.

As I sat there listening to his hiss and staring, sightless, into the yard, I wondered, not for the first time, why Wayne had come, machete and flashlight hidden under clothes in the canvas bag. Suspicion did not come easily to me. More than once, I had been told that I trusted too easily, took with insufficient guile the stated intentions of others. It was not that I believed in their goodness; it was simply—and this was probably more naive in the end—that my mind could not twist automatically into the byzantine. My logic, facile, told me that if I did A, B would result. I could not accustom myself to the way of the island: A was followed not by B, but more usually by X or W or T, and getting back to B required time, patience, obsequiousness and—the key, this—a touch of the underhanded, a clutch of dollars here, a bottle of whiskey there. It was life in, as I had come to think of it, the light-bulb society: just as contact had to be made with a switch to get a light bulb to work, so contact had to be made in the island to get anything done. Applications, for a building permit, for a telephone, were viewed not with an eye to merit but with an eye to acquisition.

Yet Wayne had asked for nothing. He had simply arrived, formal and diffident, shyly polite with Jan, quietly declaring his intention to stay. I showed him, under Jan's suspicious gaze, to the spare room at the back, a room originally intended as maid's quarters but turned gradually into a storage and laundry room; watched, with Rohan standing wide-eyed between my knees, as he cleared himself a space on the floor, spread out an old mattress that I had never gotten around to throwing out, and removed from the depths of his bag the flashlight and the sheathed machete.

I offered a beer, and we sat on the porch, struggling through stilted conversation while Rohan rode his tricycle up and down the lawn beside us. It was a while before I realized that Rohan, not an extroverted child, a child who took with difficulty to strangers, was showing off, and not for me.

Wayne, grown reticent with age, as if the years had somehow deprived him of words, or shown him their capacity for deceit, only gradually drew for me the grand lines of his life. I understood, as he spoke, that he had left my grandparents' employ sometime after my departure from the island. His father had been killed in a car accident, and his mother's meagre income had to be supplemented somehow. Work with meaningful remuneration had been impossible to find in Salmonella, so he had left for Lopez City, living at first with his older sister and drifting from odd job to odd job; he had done many things, he said, some legal, some less so; he had lifted everything that had to be lifted, had scrubbed everything that had to be scrubbed, had swept more floors than he cared to remember. Eventually, after moving in with the woman—it was how he referred to her, as "the woman"—he had made pregnant, he had joined the police force in his search for steady employment and income. That, however, had not lasted long. Life in the service had not suited him. "Is not everybody could be Clinteas'wood," he said with a kind of sadness.

He resigned from the police force just after the birth of his son—"The woman wasn't too happy, I tell you"—but just at the time when the new wealth was beginning to assert itself in the island. Jobs were more plentiful, money easier to come by. He signed up for a government work program and soon found himself labouring—although that wasn't quite the right word; he'd worked harder cutting my grandparents' lawn—on a road repair crew and taking home a monthly salary that rivalled his mother's annual income. Bliss: "I never see so much money in my life." Almost: "The woman wasn't workin', she stay home takin' care o' the baby, and the money, all that money, was goin' faster than water. You name it, she buy it. TV. Radio. Stereo. And I ain't got to tell you what was happenin' to prices in them days." The woman wasn't happy; nothing he did satisfied her; and one day he returned to a house deserted and emptied. The neighbours told him that a truck had pulled up to the house just after he'd left for work that morning; that the woman and a man they'd noticed hanging around for several weeks had loaded everything onto the truck and driven off, the baby between them. Who the man was, no one could say. One girl said that the woman had told her he was her cousin, that Wayne didn't like him and so he visited only when Wayne was not at home. "But she tell me she ain't have no family in Casaquemada, she from Grenada."

He'd gone crazy for a couple of weeks—"You could a build a house with the bottles I empty"—but, with the help of his sister, managed eventually to pull himself together and return to work. "Things was okay after that. No big thing." Until the money began running out. He was not among the first to be laid off, but his turn soon came—"Is all the big boys they keep"—and he found himself once more drifting from odd job to odd job, once more lifting and scrubbing and sweeping for pennies. He had no idea where his wife and son were now, could only guess at what his son might look like.

As we spoke, Rohan's tricycle wheel hit a bump in the lawn; he tumbled with a cry.

Wayne was beside him in a flash.

He put the empty coffee cup on the floor, carefully, as if searching for bottom through the darkness, grasped the machete in his right hand and raised the blade.

Neither of us had spoken, each lost in thought, each possibly wondering what he was doing here.

I said, "You ever used it?"

"This, boss? For cutting cane."

"I mean, against a man."

He took a deep breath, exhaled with a sound like that of a light cough. "Once."

"Hurt him bad?"

"You could say so."

"What happened?"

He lowered the blade, laid it once more flat on his lap. "I was workin' at the Crest in Salmonella. Pit doorman. Before I went down to Lopez City. A Brucelee film was showin' and, you know what is like, the fellas get all hot-up. When the show get out, some young fellas was tryin' out their kicks against the wall, it couldn't kick back, and others was choppin' up the air with their hands. Anyway, two fellas really start gettin' into it with each other and I tell them to stop, go do it outside. Next thing I know, one o' these bad-johns pull a *poignard*"—he raised the blade— "this *poignard*, on me. No big thing. I take it away from him easy-easy. But he an' his friend was thinkin' Brucelee. Both o' them come for me. I swing the *poignard*, just to warn them. But, well"—his voice fell, slowed further—"the fella hand just come off. The right hand. From the elbow. Just like that. The blade was sharp-sharp, you coulda shave with it. Went through flesh and bone like it was cuttin' through butter."

And I could see the details of it: the flash of the steel, the meaty glitter of the stump, the arm soaring in brief, awkward flight.

"They save the fella, he ain't dead."

"Were you arrested?"

"No, man. Is the fella they lock up. I was a auxiliary."

"A what?"

"A auxiliary police. Them police fellas ain't like it when one o' their own get attack."

"But the guys didn't know you were a—"

"That ain't make no difference." He scraped his thumb across the edge of the machete: the dispassionate shaving of dry skin. "When you have the power, right and wrong don't come into it."

"That's what frightens me."

"Only because you ain't have the power." He chuckled. "They give me the *poignard* after the trial. They say it go through the arm so fast, it ain't even get a drop o' blood on the blade."

I nodded, let the lukewarm coffee lap at my upper lip. How far, I wondered, did I trust Wayne? And it occurred to me that, in a bad movie, something with the word *massacre* in the title, this would be the moment for the machete to swish through the air, in close-up, cleaving through my neck with a dramatic gush of dark liquid.

"A funny thing 'bout the cut-off arm," Wayne continued. "The fella's friends squeeze it into a shoe box and hold a wake. I hear they was drinkin' an' eatin' an' playin' cards all night. The next mornin' they dig a hole in the playing field by the north end o' the cricket pitch—the fella was a fast bowler, nuh—and bury it. They even say prayers." He paused, exhaled, expelling tension. "I don't mind telling you, boss, I dream 'bout that hand every night for two months."

The confession was heartening, a reassurance of virtue. I said, "And if something happens, tonight or tomorrow night? If you have to use the *poignard* again?"

"No problem, boss." He spoke quietly, without hestitation. "Nobody going to hurt you or your family."

"But if you have to use it?" I pressed.

"Then they lucky if all they lose is their hand."

And I heard, with the clarity of memory quickened, the clang of cutlass on hardened concrete; saw blood arch through the air, felt its sticky warmth splatter onto my skin. The night seemed to stand still in a darkness that coursed back through the years to Angela's face frozen in horror and the ruins of our *pooja* scattered at our feet.

Wayne rose, sheathed the machete, snatched up the flashlight. "Time for a rounds. You comin'?"

My muscles were beginning to stiffen; a shiver of fatigue ran down my spine. The late hour and my anxiety were telling on me.

"Come on, boss, stretch your legs. Take some fresh air. Then you could go to bed and sleep like a baby." He giggled, pleased with his words, and stepped from the porch into the greater darkness of the lawn.

Moving with effort, I pushed the doors in, locked them, pocketed the keys.

Wayne was at the fence, running the beam of the flashlight through the chain-link at the grass that grew wild and thick in the lot beyond.

"You think they're going to come through the grass, Wayne?" It was an attempt at humour.

"You never know, boss. Better not take a chance." He played the light deep into the lot. "If them fellas coming, they not driving up in a car." He switched off the light, walked slowly up the lawn.

I followed, wondering where caution ended and paranoia began.

The beam of light sliced on again, slashed along the length of fence.

I froze: a pair of eyes sparkled from the bush.

The light held for an eternity of seconds. Then Wayne, with a low curse, scratched the blade of the machete along the chain-link. The dog, taut with fear, retreated into the grass. He re-sheathed the machete as I walked up to him grateful for the darkness in which he could not see my grin, one not of humour but of fright made foolish.

We followed the fence to where it met the road. Wayne paused, leaned his shoulder in against the chain-link, played the beam along the deep drain: cracks in the cement, stagnant water, moss of a virulent green, a faint odour of putrefaction. Wayne said, "They could crawl through the drains. Like that, the police ain't able to see them from the jeeps."

"Well . . ." I thought it unlikely.

He switched off the flashlight, turned slowly towards me. "You want to take the chance, boss?" He spoke matter-of-factly, as if what he offered were really a choice. "I could go and sleep this minute, you know, I tired too." He did not wait for an answer, resumed his walk along the fence.

Neither of us spoke. The air, cool for the island, held the peculiar freshness of late-night, early-morning, a nethertime when the world seemed on the verge of evaporation, as if fearful of facing the firestorm of dawn. Walking on the soft lawn, the fantasy came to me of a world suddenly cleansed, a world scrubbed of ugliness, a fantasy which, for a few delicious moments, I caressed with my mind.

"I know them fellas, boss," Wayne said finally. His voice, softer, seemed to belie the title that slipped so easily from his lips. "They not stupid, and they not just playin', either. I use to be a police, and I tellin' you I ain't sure the police know how to handle them." He walked on. "T'ings could get very bad, boss. Very bad." The flashlight clicked on, and the beam played ineffectually on the grass: a patch of phosphorescent green flitted nervously on the field of black. "You know, boss, I here now with you and your family, is where I want to be, but part o' me sayin' I should be out there, too, with the boys and them."

"The police, you mean?"

"No, boss. The others. Is time black people have power in this country—"

"But Wayne, the government's black, the prime minister's black."

"The old man? Kind o', I suppose. The others, yeah, sure, but only on the outside."

"And inside? They're white?"

"No, boss. Green. The colour o' the Yankee dollar. They not interested in helpin' people, just in buyin' them. Like the last time, after the riots twelve years ago, they build house for the people in the shantytown, but in truth nothing change if you look at it. The people still unemploy, they still diggin' in the rubbish dump day and night, the chil'ren still runnin' around barefoot and not eatin' enough." He tapped the flashlight gently against his thigh. "They say it have Cubans in the hills."

"They're saying a lot of things these days."

"The only fellas gettin' their regular pay these days is the police and the army. I think we have the government runnin' scared."

"So what are you doing here, then, Wayne? They blame people like me, people with some money."

"My quarrel ain't with you, boss. I know you does work hard for your money, I know you does help a lot o' people."

I thought of Mrs. Lal, thought of Sagar, said nothing.

"And I like you, we go back a long way."

And Rohan, I thought, doesn't he play a role in this, too? "That was childhood. Long time ago."

"You ain't know this, but remember when you was young you use to watch me from the window early every mornin' when I was cuttin' the grass—"

"You knew I was there? I didn't think you ever saw me."

"Is only one time you ain't come, you was sick, a cold or something."

I remembered. A high fever had gripped me for the greater part of a week. Hawks and eagles had swooped through my bedroom, shadows and light had danced together on the ceiling, and in the far corner often stood a man, tall, shadowed, wearing a hat, who said nothing, did nothing, just looked on with a gaze I felt to be benign. In my delirium, I asked my grandmother who he was; she shushed me, told me not to look, and spoke my father's name in a voice tremulous with fear. My memory garbled her words, made them irretrievable, but the tone, of prayer, of entreaty, remained with me as a token of my resentment; for her words had driven away an apparition that I would have wished to examine further.

"Is why I here now," he continued. "Because o' those mornings."

"I see." It was inadequate as explanation, but I would get no more from him. If, young, I had seen Wayne as employee in relation to myself, I was uncertain now of how to view him; our relationship was of a complexity that I could not penetrate. I thought, briefly, of Surein and Lenny.

"It have some people to kill," he said. "But it have some people not to kill, too."

In the distance, a dog barked. Wayne looked up, alert. Soon another dog picked up where the first had begun, and then another, closer now.

"Let we head for the porch," he said, switching off the flashlight.

We walked quickly, Wayne hurrying along on the balls of his feet, his urgency communicating itself as through electrified filament, with a directness that stung, that declared its predominance. We sat on the porch, in the darkness. Waited.

The dogs barked. Closer now, so that they were sounds not just of warning but of menace.

Still, I could hear nothing else. "Maybe they're taking another street."

"No. Listen. They comin'."

Presently the low moan of a vehicle slowly driven built itself behind the canine outcry.

Wayne sat quietly, eyes on the road.

My body tensed.

Wayne said, "They comin'."

And slowly, a sight unreal: a jeep appeared, headlights extinguished, a frieze of shadows—the driver, an officer beside him, four or five men in the tray behind—pointing rifles at every direction, thrusting threat at the unseen. I could feel their eyes, and their ears, and the rawness of their nerves; could sense their unease and smell their fear. Only my eyes moved, following them, as they glided by on the road.

In seconds they were gone, a fleeting apparition that had squeezed a chilling sweat from my pores. The barking all around subsided, first the more distant dogs, then those at closer quarters. My mouth had dried.

"Why aren't their headlights on?" I asked.

Wayne chuckled. "Harder to shoot at." He stood up, hefted the flashlight in his hand. "Time to finish the rounds. You coming, boss?"

I remained where I was, needing suddenly the security of walls and locked doors.

Wayne chuckled once more. "Is awright, boss. You go on inside now. You ain't have nothing to worry 'bout, not so long as I out here making my rounds."

Only after he had gone off into the lawn and I was locking the door behind me did I understand why his words of reassurance had struck me as peculiar. It was that I was unaccustomed to having them said to me. *You ain't have nothing to worry 'bout, not so long as I out here making my rounds.* Here, in words almost identical, was the sentiment I expressed daily to worried patients, words I always managed to pronounce with a greater confidence than I actually felt, with a greater assuredness than I knew, often, to be justified. So that his words, intended to reassure, had proved unsettling. But that, I recognized, was because of myself, because of my own bravado, because I had caught in Wayne's words a glimpse of my own comfortable and flippant game.

So, sleepless, I returned to my study and trained the beam of the desk lamp on Rohan's maps.

The world spoke to me of scale. There was Canada, there Casaquemada, the one unseizably massive, the other unseizably minute.

My eyes travelled east, across Africa, through the Middle East, past the Arabian Sea to the cone of the Indian subcontinent. Then, searching, the way back by sea: south through the Indian Ocean past Madagascar, around the Cape of Good Hope into the South Atlantic; north—cutting a path between South America and the west coast of Africa—up to the Caribbean, past Trinidad up the chain to the wobbly red circle that marked Casaquemada.

Was this the route they had taken? I could see no other. The journey, epic by air, had been undertaken a century and a half before in ships that I imagined to have been a step or two above slavers in comfort. They had arrived, after untold weeks of misery, to a life of uncertainty in an island that was, in terms of empire, superfluous, in terms of the world, trivial. What had driven them, these faceless ancestors of mine, to undertake a journey that, for them, must have been courageous in the way of Columbus? For they could have known nothing of Casaquemada beyond what the British colonial officers, indenture papers in hand and promises of land and money in mouth, had been willing or able to tell them. What irreparable poverty had they fled? What desperation had driven them? What ignominy? What fear? What hope?

I had none of the answers, and those who could tell me without frill or fantasy were long dead. There was, in our family, no myth of nobility: no maharajahs, no palaces. Ours was a background of grinding poverty alleviated only by claims to the sagacity of brahminism; we were of the intellectuals, the learned men; we could read the holy books, penetrate their mysteries. Yet, this being so, why had they gone to an island, if an island it had to be, no bigger than the head of a pin? Had they had a choice? I suspected not, suspected them to have been a people without choice, that even their immigration here had been less of a choice than they realized at the time.

And that journey, the length of it, the unimaginable horrors of it, seemed to me a melancholy epic. For they had come bearing within them the twin seeds of achievement and unravelment. The urge to work, to education, to wealth, came couched beside notions of race, of hierarchy, of caste, that would colour more and more over the years our view of ourselves and of those around us. Blacks we wrote off as lazy, Chinese dirty, Moslems malicious, mulattoes impure. We retained an idea of ourselves as racially superior, an arrogance reinforced by the success of our efforts, proof presenting itself in every new lawyer, every new doctor, every burgeoning business. Surein, with his ready antagonisms, was but the logical distillation of generations. I, on the other hand, with my taste for words, with my belief in their power, took seriously the pious invocations of our independence, our anthem of equality and harmony, our motto of united achievement. And it was a shock to me, in my late teens, to see as myth the easy diversity of which we so fervently boasted. Yes, every race was in the streets during our carnival, but whites were with whites, blacks with blacks, Indians with Indians. Only the tourists mixed; only they, ignorant of our estrangements, brought truth to our pieties.

So there we were, African and Indian, a curious hybrid living in Spanish Casaquemada, using French *poignards*, dealing in offices with English *clarks*, driving along American highways.

As the island filled in, developed activity in economy, in politics, it failed to solidify into a recognizable entity. We were formed of too many bits and pieces. There were too many things that we were not, too few things that we were. If we could claim identity, it was only in the travel posters that had been done up by a New York advertising agency to promote the island's minimal tourist industry. Only here was there uniformity of vision. Only here was there a sense of stability and calm. Only here were the beaches swept of debris, only here did the sand shine with a pristine brilliance.

On the day that Marilyn Monroe died and Nelson Mandela was arrested, Casaquemada received its independence. The events, linked only by date and discovered years later in a newspaper article, stuck in my head as a fateful Trinity of our own.

There we were, then, free to make our decisions, free to make our mistakes, free to take the path that led eventually to nocturnal patrols of policemen clutching rifles.

I turned off the desk lamp.

A dull ache pressed at my skull. Oil and sharp stubble covered my cheeks. I thought, my hand rubbing at my face, of Sunil Nadan, understood in sudden intuition the sadness of his life.

Wayne had made his last round some time before, had stopped at the window to let me know he would soon be heading to bed. "Nobody comin' now," he'd said. "Is too late." Then, with a laugh, "Or too early, I ain't too sure at this point."

I tugged the curtains apart, just a few inches. The sky was beginning to brighten, a cool light, fragile blue growing in the east. The air coming in past the burglar-proofing was cool on the skin, put me briefly in mind of early summer mornings on the large sundeck of my Toronto flat, looking out over the city bright and clean and shining, the sun holding the promise of a summer heat. I'd enjoyed Toronto most then, in those mornings infused with hope.

The telephone rang. I hurried to answer it. Raffique, excited, said, "Ey, Raj, boy, I hear the army revolt again. They say the whole cabinet up at the airport, it have a 707 waiting all gas-up." He had had a call from a friend in Lopez City, who claimed to have got the news from a relative in the Coast Guard.

I thanked him, hung up. There was nothing more to say, nothing more to ask. I went outside to tell Wayne of the new rumour, but he was already asleep on his mattress. Beside him, within easy reach, were two beer bottles with lengths of cloth stuck into their throats. Wisps of fading gasoline fumes hung in the musty air. I went back inside, sat close to the radio.

At seven o'clock, the local news asked tersely that the population of the island stay at home. It did not explain why.

At eight o'clock, the BBC World Service calmly confirmed Raffique's rumour of an army revolt. It did not say where the cabinet was.

Jan, sipping her first coffee, tried to telephone the Canadian High Commission. There was no answer.

When Wayne awoke, he amused himself teaching Rohan techniques of self-defence.

15

Jan's parents' house, the house in which we settled into a semblance of domesticity, stood atop a ridge that folded gently east from Yonge Street, petering out several blocks farther on into a flatness of small shops—antiques, used books, militaria—crouched between high rises and low rises of unremarkable composition. The house, acquired by Jan's parents as an investment for their retirement, was not unlike others of its age, of a vintage a decade or two more recent than the one I had lived in for so long. The narrow front lawn sloped sharply up from the sidewalk; a stairway of concrete cracked and askew led to a short path, itself chipped and tilted, to wooden steps painted an unappealing grey, to the wide porch, exposed and, so, unused except at night, with the light off.

Viewed from the sidewalk, the house looked larger than it actually was, the attic—access difficult through a trap door, the room itself airless, musty with dust and cobweb and bat dropping—looming with an illusory majesty against the sky. The basement, approached from the kitchen by a narrow stairwell, had never been finished; its low ceiling made it impracticable as a playroom, and spring flooding made it unreliable as a storeroom. So we were left with the main floor, sandwiched between a useless room above and an uninhabitable one below.

The living area, a large square, had been divided up with a chaotic simplicity. A corridor, running from the front door all the way to the kitchen at the back, split the house in two. Off the corridor to the right were the main bedroom, its windows looking out onto the street on one side and onto the neighbour's driveway on the other, and the cramped bathroom, with space enough for a bath of elbow-bruising dimensions, a toilet bowl, a sink and one careful adult. On the left of the corridor lay the living room, perpetually sombre despite the large, sealed, steel-framed window that had been installed in its southern wall. Through its glass, beyond the porch-railing and above the roofs of the houses opposite, the downtown office buildings soared by day, twinkled darkly at night. But the sun, slicing into the edges of the porch, could come no farther. Even in the glow of the floorlamps, the living room retained a gloomy air, not from a lack of light but from a surfeit of shadow. With our various pieces of furniture tossed together, with a worn sofa left behind by the previous tenants, with Jan's family-portrait poster pinned to the wall across from the fireplace, the living room gathered itself into a forlorn comfort.

The kitchen at the back, brightened by cupboards painted white and trimmed in red, large enough to accommodate the dining table from Jan's flat, was the warmest room in the house. It became, quickly, the centre of our daily activities. It was here, at the table, that we ate, drank, exchanged details of the day; here that Janet read her romance novels, leafed through magazines of sweater patterns, taught herself—with frequent calls to her mother—to manipulate wool and knitting needles; here that I read the newspaper, opened the mail, wrote letters. Yet the kitchen was also the most idiosyncratic room in the house. The floor, covered in red rubber tiles, sloped appreciably, so that walking across it to the stove, we had the sense of trudging uphill, while turning around to go to the fridge created a dizzying sense of descent; in this room, standing or sitting, we felt always slightly off balance.

Three doors led from the kitchen, one to the basement, one to the second bedroom—eventually, as our arrangements fell into place, my study—and the last to the back yard, a long and narrow strip of land, grassed, unrolled, an overgrown compost heap rising into a mound against the fence at the far end.

The house, even as it filled in with furniture and knicknacks— Jan developed a passion for little boxes, amassed a collection of tiny containers of wood, brass, acrylic—retained a feeling of hollowness, as if despite our presence, despite our attempts to impose ourselves on their emptiness, the rooms resisted being peopled. Here, cocooned in a reigning silence that established itself despite constant chatter and music from the radio or television, Jan and I lived our individual obsessions.

She cooked, she cleaned, she sold shoes. She engaged in brief enthusiasms, picking up one little craft—needlepoint, rug-hooking, egg-painting—after another, completing no project, stuffing the tools and unused materials into the linen closet in my study. In the second or third year, spurred by a record she'd heard on the radio, she dipped into her savings and bought a piano, an old upright painted dirt brown, claimed her childhood piano books from her mother and spent evenings, entire weekends, working through the well-thumbed repertoire, from the lilting simplicities of lullabies to energetic passages of Chopin. But she could not go beyond the books, beyond the retrieved routines of childhood training. After a few months, the piano lost much of its allure, became a display stand for her collection of little boxes.

I cooked, I cleaned, I studied. Haunted the hospital halls. Received, eventually, the title so long sought, set about establishing a practice—early mornings, long days, late evenings—in a seventh-floor suite of a building on Cumberland Avenue, on the edges of Yorkville, surrounded by surgeons, obstetricians, pediatricians, dietitians, dentists, psychologists, gynecologists, cardiologists, almost the entire specialist panoply of modern health care. So that Jan and I moved forward, more by event and the passage of time than by decision and the exercise of choice, less in a life together than in lives parallel.

How easily, in how unmeasured a manner the years slipped by, without rhythm, without crackle, inert in their sameness. Years that sit amoebic in my memory, edges fluctuating, the centre indefinite and ductile. Years without flow, composed of individual scenes—Jan playing the piano, the view from the living room window, the belly of the bedroom ceiling, the back yard emerging in spring from under the snow—that add up to a kind of mental photo album, images frozen without context, without energy, without a connecting theme.

Jan in this period: She stands wrapped in her winter coat, in the middle of the street outside. It is a Christmas morning, after a night of heavy and unexpected snowfall. Fresh snow, white and powdery, lines every twig of every branch of every tree. The sidewalk is smothered, the street, yet unploughed, impassable to cars. The sky glows a dull grey overhead, but the air, stilled, is soft and without bite. Jan, the centrepiece of the picture, stands impassive, looking at me, her boots sunk to the ankles in the snow. Her gloved right hand holds a large shopping bag, gifts for her parents with whom we will, as usual, be spending the day; her gloved left hand, unburdened, is clenched into a fist.

Of myself in this period I have no picture.

"But you gettin' old fast, man, Raj." Kayso's fingers flicked at my hair, at the strands of premature grey that flecked the black. "He should dye it, you don't think so, Janet?"

She smiled, uninterested. "I think he looks fine."

"Besides," I said as she took to the kitchen the bottle of wine he had brought, "it's good for business. A doctor shouldn't look too young."

He laughed. "I guess you could say the same thing for a lawyer"—he ran his hand through his thick black hair— "but I ain't never let that stop me."

He had phoned the office the day before, an unfamiliar voice using words of enthusiasm— "But is Kayso, man, you forget me a'ready?"—though speaking them dully, as if unable to summon up the appropriate energy. He was in Toronto on a short holiday, he said, had brought a letter for me from my grandparents. Curious to see what he had made of himself, what had become of him beyond the newspaper clippings my grandfather still occasionally sent me, I invited him to dinner.

Physically, he surprised me. I remembered a certain litheness, a certain fleetness of foot. But he had grown heavier, into a fleshy thickness that filled out to the edges of comfort his sheenless black suit cut with a severity that offered no concession to style. When we sat, he on the sofa, I in an armchair, he did not undo the jacket buttons, tucked the tie of black silk flat against his white shirt. It was, I thought, like sitting down with an undertaker, an impression in no way relieved by his stern, even mournful demeanour.

"So, Kayso, how are things?"

"Things are fine, man." He spoke slowly, his eyes darting around the room, examining every chair, every vase, every carefully placed container, for no more than a second but with an intense suspicion. "So you're a doctor now. Dr. Ramsingh."

"That was the object."

"I knew you'd make it. You were young, but you knew your mind."

"I wasn't the only one. My grandfather's been sending me newspaper clippings about you."

Jan came back in carrying drinks, wine for Kayso and me, beer for herself. "You don't look like your picture, though."

"Is an old one, I was younger then. And for some reason, they don't want to use the newer ones I send them." He took his wine, nodded in thanks.

Jan gave me mine, took her beer, sat beside him.

I raised my glass to him, said, "The picture must be wearing out by now, they've used it so much. Looks like you're doing great things down there."

"Chickenfeed, man, Raj, chickenfeed." He sipped the wine, smacked his lips. "I not even scratchin' the surface. We just don't have the people down there, you know. The expertise. And sometimes you just can't tell who is your enemy and who is your friend."

"Do you regret having gone back?"

"No way, man. Is a hell of a lot better than writing wills and drawing up deeds and shufflin' around paper like I was doin' up here. Driftin', you know. No purpose to my profession. And is a lot more excitin', let me tell you. Nobody ever threaten to kill me up here."

"Somebody's threatened to kill you?"

"At least once a day."

Jan said, "You don't take it seriously?"

"Of course I do. I have a Smith and Wesson. Powerful little thing. Never leave home without it."

"And the police?" I said.

"They doin' fine." He chuckled.

"I mean, you report the threats."

"Used to. I figure there's no point now, though. I filed suit against them for police brutality a few months ago. I hear they not too happy 'bout that."

Jan said, "But that happens here, too. The police don't stop doing their job."

Kayso looked at her for a moment, smiled, shook his head. "Ah, the happy Canadians! So innocent. You know, Janet—and I don't mean this personally—Canada has got to be one o' the most naive countries in the world. I mean, you people just have no idea, no idea at all, what the word corruption means. Where I come from, people don't steal thousands, you know, they steal millions. And is a small place, everybody knows everybody else. Everything is personal, it have no such thing as a dispassionate system of law. You attack an individual, you attack the group. And is the group that turnin' on you, every man jack, because everybody's part o' the system, you have to be if you goin' to survive."

"You, too?" Jan said.

"In a way. But on the opposite side."

"That first night," I said, "after the airport, you said something about good and evil being on the same coin—"

"God and the devil live on different sides of the same coin."

"Is that what you mean?"

"More or less."

"But you're not alone. The island has other honest men."

"Depends on how you define honest. Sure, we have lots o' honest fellas. They always talkin' about the stealin' and the incompetence and all the rest of it. But most o' them have spent years hungerin' after power, just waitin' for the old man to die."

"But no matter how you define it, there's still, say, Grappler, labouring away, doing his job. He's never wanted to be P.M."

"Grappler. Yes." He sat forward, his grip tightened around the stem of the wine glass, stood up with a deep and audible sigh, walked slowly over to the piano. "Afraid I not seein' Grappler too much any more." His fingers reached out to the keys, back unbending, punched out a plaintive jazz melody.

Janet said, "You a jazz fan?"

He said, "Oscar Peterson came to Casaquemada once. A few years ago. Gave a great concert. Somehow he made me feel homesick, even though I was home."

I waited, impatiently, for an explanation of his relations with Grappler, finally had to ask.

He remained where he was, eyes averted. "Listen, Raj, I know you close to Grappler, but there's something you have to understand." He paused, sipped his wine. "You and I know Grappler's clean, no doubt 'bout that. I willing to bet my life he's never taken a cent that wasn't his. But, you know, he's been workin' for the government for so long—"

"But he's a civil servant, he has nothing to do with politics."

"You've been livin' here too long, Raj, you're becomin' as naive as these Canadians." He smiled at Jan.

"I know," she said. "I won't take it personally."

"Look, Raj, the Casaquemada civil service, or most of it, is as political as a party, or at least that's how people see it. I think is more than just a problem of perception myself, but that's another

story. The point is, that even Grappler, just by workin' for them
. . . Even Grappler, well, people think of him as a party man, the
old man's man. He's tainted, you see. He's been around too much
bad meat for too long. The rotten smell hanging on him, too."

"That's a hell of a thing to say about an old friend."

"Is the straight goods I givin' you here, Raj. Professionally
speakin', I cannot afford to be seen too close to Grappler. If people see me with him, all credibility gone out the window."

It was all I could do to nod, for while I recognized the truth of
what he was saying, to acknowledge it felt like a betrayal of
Grappler.

Jan stepped into the silence to offer more wine, and I seized the
opportunity to end the conversation by fetching the bottle myself
from the kitchen. When I came back in, Kayso was explaining to
Jan who Don Quixote was. "It's how I see myself sometimes," he
said.

At dinner he told her of Casaquemada, of the mountains and
the beaches and the look of the sky at sunset. He grew expansive
by the second bottle of wine, unbuttoned his jacket, loosened his
tie. I remained silent much of the time, letting her ask questions,
letting him answer them, envying his tone of a man content with
life and self, feeling my own drift, my own lack of purpose. I
wondered, with a kind of fear, if this was what he had felt before
returning to Casaquemada.

It grew late. I called a taxi, and when it came we walked him
out.

He said, "You ever think about comin' back home, Raj?"

"Never."

"You should. There's a lot to be done, and, frankly, there's a lot
of money to be made. Not as much as a couple of years ago, but
there's still a lot floatin' around. Besides, I think you and me'd
make a good team. The hospitals are a scandal, there's brand-new
medical equipment, millions o' dollars, just rustin' away on the
docks because somebody didn't pay somebody else off. It's a
whole field, Raj, medical incompetence. But the expertise, I
mean, I don't have it. Think about it, you and me, you in white,
me in black. A team."

"Yin and yang," Jan said with a laugh.

"And those beaches," he said to her. "Nothing else like it in the world."

"Cool it with the propaganda, Kayso," I said, irritation showing.

"But you going to think about it, right?"

"I'll think about it." I spoke dismissively, could hear my own insincerity.

Jan said, "I'll make sure he does."

He kissed her lightly on the cheek, shook my hand, said as he entered the taxi, "And the Grappler business, Raj. Understand, okay?"

The taxi drove off, sparing me the necessity of an answer.

Jan said, "Nice guy."

"You liked him."

"Well, he's a man with a purpose, eh. He has a reason for living that's not just for himself, even if he sees himself as a donkey."

"Not a donkey. Don Quixote." There were times when the gaps in her knowledge astonished me.

"Whatever, eh? I like what he's doing. You know, his wanting to help. I respect that."

"He's a little dramatic, though, don't you think? That suit. His Smith and Wesson. Kayso Paladin. Have gun, will travel."

"At least he's doing something. You, you never even mention Casaquemada. As if you're not from anywhere. Or as if you're running away from it. Christ, you never even told me there were beaches there."

"You never asked. Besides, sometimes running away's the only thing to do."

"Horseshit. I know, I've tried it, remember?"

"For self-preservation. His marriage broke up when he went back to Casaquemada. He's here visiting his kid."

"So he's willing to pay a price."

"And what about you? What would you say if I said I wanted to go back to Casaquemada?"

"You saying you want to go back?"

"I just want to know what you'd say."

"I'd say I could use some adventure in my life."

"Meaning?"

"Meaning anything you want it to mean, Raj." There was a sarcastic challenge in her voice; my stomach tightened at its bite.

It was a chilly evening, cloudless, stars distant and defiant in the relentless sky. We went inside, piled the dirty dishes into the sink, got into bed, tossing, turning with restlessness. My irritation, after a while, took a curious turn, manifested itself in physical arousal. Jan, as usual, in the pattern that had long established itself, was compliant, opened herself to me. She was unprepared, grunted in discomfort as I probed with an unaccustomed brutality at her dryness. When I was done, with a cry more angry than sexual, she sighed, pushed me off, curled away to the edge of the bed. It was, I believe, in this way, on this night, that Rohan was conceived.

Confirmation of her pregnancy a few weeks later—by her regular G.P., to whom she still went for any problem more serious than a cold—erased all thoughts of Casaquemada. Jan had spoken only rarely of her miscarriage, and then with a dismissive reluctance. The first pregnancy—the result, she once confessed in a fit of anger, of an impulsive urge to vengeance on Jim—had left behind, in both of us, a caustic residue; we had never even broached the subject of having a family.

The child might have offered a purpose, might have formed a focus for effort that slipped daily into a greater absurdity. But my dissatisfactions ran too deep, had mined themselves into too many pores. As I pondered the news, as I sought with difficulty to make room in my mind for a child, questions left unspoken presented themselves to me: Where was all this going? What in the long run, or the short for that matter, was the point of it all? Where did it come from, and why, this sense of life as running water, turbulent and beyond control?

I avoided the questions as best I could, for I could provide no answers to them.

But when they came, unbidden, disconcerting, I recognized in them the catalytic effect of Kayso's visit and acknowledged privately—as I attended to an endless flow of flus and hangnails and ears blocked solid with wax—my envy of him.

It may be that events conspire. Or it may be that, seeking signposts, wishing them into being, the mind consolidates coincidences into oracular significance.

In the following four months, three letters arrived at the house.

The first, mailed from Casaquemada but on the stationery and in the envelope of a Miami hotel, the address crossed out, was from Surein. He had never written to me before, and, on seeing the envelope on my desk, I wondered at the unknown handwriting, tiny and cramped, the final letters of every word melting into illegible lines. I ripped it open with a pen, read, with as much accuracy as the scribbled and slanting lines would allow, the letter that began "Surprise! Surprise!"

The excuse for, but not the object of, the letter was that Surein had run into a friend of mine from high school. Did I remember . . . ? Surein's concept of friendship had always been freer than mine. He mentioned a name I only vaguely recognized then, have forgotten since. But this friend had got him thinking about me, his weird cousin, and he'd decided on a whim to write. He covered, in stilted, notelike language, the state of health of various members of the family: his parents, our grandparents, a smattering of aunts and uncles—he was worrying here about filling the entire page—were all reported as "doing fine." He wrote of a boy he'd hired, Lenny—he was fast losing his literary enthusiasm at this point, was clearly on the verge of crumpling up the paper—a "stupid coolie" from the country who would be of use to him in his burgeoning business. "You know these people," the scribble continued, "they too frighten to disobey and too stupid to steal. The perfect employees." With the mention of his business, though, a renewed vigour infused his writing. It was the word *bacchanal* that he used to describe what was happening in the island. Why, he knew of a computer engineer who had quit his job to open a trucking company, of a teacher who'd abandoned her classroom for the lucrative lure of imported luxuries, of a doctor who spent as much time supervising his construction projects as treating his patients. There were shortages, supply could not meet demand. His car, for instance, a little Toyota he'd bought a couple of years before to use while awaiting delivery of his Corvette; he'd recently sold it, in so-so condition after the pounding it had taken on the roads, at a profit of twenty per cent. Everybody in Casaquemada owned a car, or wanted one. Cars didn't depreciate here, they appreciated; they had become an investment.

So what the hell, he wanted to know, was I still doing in Toronto?

It seemed that everyone who had ever left the island was returning. Planes daily disgorged Casaquemadans outlandishly dressed and speaking in American or British or Canadian accents, all returning for their share of the key lime pie, key lime, he explained, because it was green and sweet, like the U.S. dollars that were drawing them back. Law was far behind him now, he wrote, there was too much money to be made in importing anything, everything. There was nothing foreign that Casaquemadans would not buy. He had made a killing on Hong Kong watches, Taiwanese radios, Chinese wool caps—the Rastafarians had snapped them up and Surein figured that, in providing the means to hide so many heads of dreadlocks, he had performed a public service. His biggest seller to date, though, was American-made bathmat sets. He had imported thousands of them, of every colour and pattern imaginable, the boxes filling an entire room in his house from floor to ceiling. Not a single one remained, save the one in his own bathroom, and he'd estimated that almost a quarter of the bathrooms in the island were adorned with his sets. He claimed to have seen one even in a latrine. And on and on it went. He'd just received a large shipment of cowboy boots, which he expected would do almost as well as the bathmat sets.

With all this going on, with the making of money having become as simple as slicing salami, he wanted to know how come I hadn't yet joined the flood of returnees. Or did I still think that I was too good for the island?

This final line scribbled above the swirl of his name—a giant, confident *S* flowing into an indecipherable wave—was irritating in its dismissive simplemindedness, but his letter had evoked other, more distressing visions, of a desperate, acquisitive scramble, of the island awash in tin and plastic and multicoloured acrylic.

The letter depressed me. I folded it into the envelope, put it into the top drawer of my desk and forgot about it as best I could.

The second letter, on an air-letter sheet carefully folded and sealed with extra glue that had seeped hard and translucent from under the flaps, was from my grandfather. He had written, as usual, with his old, wide-nibbed fountain pen, the ink a rich royal-blue on the lighter sky-blue of the paper. His handwriting, grown larger through the years under his failing eyesight, was methodical and judicious, showing still the meticulous economy of childhood classes in penmanship.

He began, as he always did, by asking how Jan and I were and assuring us that "we"—I was never quite sure to whom this "we" referred; it seemed to encompass more than just my grandmother and him, to extend to the family, to friends, to the island itself— that "we" were fine. Then in his ordered way, as if he had made a list beforehand of the points he wished to cover, he brought me up to date on the minutiae of family matters. On my grandmother's ailments, as numerous and as life-threatening as ever. On Grappler, about whom they were concerned, for he seemed to be overworking. On Surein, whom they rarely saw but who was said to have lost a substantial amount of money on cowboy boots. On Kayso, whom they saw rather more frequently and who was now an almost daily feature of the news in a public fight with the police. "We are not sure about what he is doing. Casaquemada is becoming a dangerous place these days. The money is new but the temptation and the layzyness is old. The police must deal with some very violent people. Kayso talks about human right all the time so the police and many people are not happy with him. But he is famous in Casaquemada now. Even the Trinidad and Jamaica papers wrote about him. His Mercedes was delevered last week. He came to show it to us on the weekend and he took us for a drive to the beach. The road is very bad these days, potholes

A **C**asual **B**rutality **325**

everywhere and the pitch very bumpy, but riding in the car was like riding in a airplane. Your granma said we should get one but she changed her mind when Kayso said he paid almost a quarter million dollars (C) for it. Kayso has worked hard. He is a big man in Casaquemada now. Your granma like him very much. She says when he is here it is like having you back."

Only at the very end, after stating that he was feeling well, did he mention that he had developed a "little heart problem."

A *little heart problem*: I knew my grandfather, distrusted his understatement.

Jan read the letter—prompted probably by my sudden concern—while I telephoned my grandparents, for the first time experiencing the island's new money by being able to dial direct. My grandfather answered, his voice, filtered through technology, diminished and tentative.

I asked how he was, told him of my worry about his little heart problem, asked for details.

He was fine, he said, nothing to worry about. He'd had tests, the doctor had him on medication, was keeping a close eye on him.

Then my grandmother took the phone. Or, rather, my grandfather passed it hurriedly to her. She was sobbing already, her voice high and cracking. "Son," she said, "Son, how you?"

"Just fine," I said. "No problem." Tried to ask her about my grandfather's condition.

"How Jan? She awright? Nobody sick?"

"We're both fine. How's Granpa?"

"He workin' too hard, Son. He harden-harden. He goin' to kill heself one day." Her voice dissolved. "Son, Son."

"Granma. Granma, let me talk with Granpa again."

"Son, Son."

My grandfather returned to the telephone. "You mustn't worry yourself too much, Raj," he said. "Everything under control. You know how your granma like to fret. The match have a long way to go still and I battin' strong. Beside, the umpire on my side, he makin' sure I don't get bowled out."

"Yeah, Granpa, just make sure you don't step back onto the stumps."

"Never," he laughed, before saying goodbye and hanging up.

Jan, sitting at the dining table, held the letter up in her left hand, snapped the middle finger of her right at it, said, "And I thought my mum was the champ of guilt trips."

"What d'you mean?" I remained where I was, at the telephone mounted on the wall beside the fridge. Looked at her as from a great distance.

"This Surein's making money. Down there. Kayso's a star, with a Mercedes no less. Down there. And poor old grandad's got problems with his ticker. So what d'you call that, eh?"

"News?" But my sarcasm, unintended, was revealing.

"You know exactly what it is. Quit foolin' yourself, Raj."

"Surein's a piranha. Kayso, that's just a question of small pond, big fish."

"And the phone call? That made you happy, eh? I can tell." She folded the letter, tossed it onto the table. "Now," she said, hands descending in uneasy caress onto her distended belly, "let's talk about little fish in big oceans and kids as investment for the future."

The third letter, in a business envelope with the return address embossed in black, was waiting in a stack of bills and junk mail just over a month later. Kayso, in hasty hand, had written on a sheet of his letterhead, the paper thick and silky to the touch. The first sentence, the only complete one, the only one that conceded to formality before the text dissolved into a string of simple staccato phrases, thanked us for the evening at our place four months before. "Been very busy," he wrote. "Casa. continues usual way. Which means worse. Or maybe just learning more. Just perception worse, who knows? Not worse—clearer. Through the smog of Tropical Paradise. Police case getting nowhere. One witness killed. By thieves they say. Client's memory going hazy. Well . . . What to say? Move on. Little things. Some union work. Infamy grows. Smith, Wesson and me. Going to change the letterhead. Two new partners. Real hot shots. Ha ha. But in truth, onto something new. Maybe big. Medical story, possible malpractice, maybe bigger. Hope to toss the net wide (should have been a fisherman, easier to catch sharks in the sea). But just beginning. Fact: one dead baby. Fact: one frighten couple. Fact: four dumb doctors. Fact: two frighten nurses who ready to whisper but not to talk. Rumour: hospital machines that nobody knows how to operate but they try anyway. No case there. Yet. Reading books on medical procedure (had to order them from the States). Feeling like a fisherman at sea, no compass, cloudy sky. Be a while before I find my way. Frankly: weather stormy, but still wish you were here. Any chance? Thought about it at all? Questions? Doubts? Hesitation? Drop a line or give a call." He signed it, simply, K.

Janet read the letter with an unrestrained avidity, her fingernails tapping at her empty water glass. I sat across the table from her with my glass of wine—in her abstinence, she came to develop a fixation on my drink, drummed with an itchy longing as I sipped at it, so that by the time she could consume alcohol once more it was wine that she longed for and not beer—thinking about Kayso, of his evident weariness and the hints of faltering courage.

When she was done, she looked up at me, said, "So." But her tone was not neutral; it matched in its quiet fervour the unanticipated glint in her eyes.

And on impulse—words and images and uncertainties telescoping into incognizant resolution, so that, as so often before, it was as if we simply fell into it—I said, "After the baby."

She nodded, bit at her upper lip. Such was our moment of decision.

Outside, a wet December snow quietly drifted down.

The next day, in a move of caution, I applied for Canadian citizenship, and a few weeks later, sitting in a spare, tiny office, I assured a vigorous and self-satisfied old man that Canada had ten provinces and two territories, that the national capital was Ottawa and that British Columbia was on the west coast; agreed with him that we spent far too much on defence, not enough on health and education, and that, yes, the NDP deserved a chance to try its brand of socialism in government. He shook my hand warmly, informed me that I had displayed sufficient knowledge of the country to qualify for citizenship. A few weeks after this, in a large room with fifty or sixty other people of varied colour and accent, I sat and listened with impatience to a platitudinous lecture on the rights and duties of the Canadian citizen. The judge, a tall, bony man with hair, unnaturally black, parted down the middle and plastered to the sides with generous pastings of gel, relished his role and the splendour of his robes, delivering the speech with an enthusiasm that compensated for the occasional impenetrability of his heavy Italian accent; the word *multicultural*, which occurred often in the text, he read with a special care, with a reverence usually reserved for religion. Afterward, having chorussed the citizenship oath, we sang the national anthem as the resident Mountie, spectacularly stiff-backed in full scarlet-and-brown regalia, solemnly saluted a colour photograph of the queen mounted on the wall beside the judge's towering bench.

That very afternoon, armed with my brand-new citizenship card, I applied for a passport and called the Casaquemadan consulate about residency permits.

Jan had a normal pregnancy, was in labour for just under ten hours. When, finally, she held the baby in her arms, she examined him as she would a curio of passing interest, looked up at me with exhaustion, said, "So what d'you wanna call him?"

We hadn't talked about it, hadn't even thought about it in the bustle of the preceding months. I was at a loss, felt nudged by the half-smile and expectant gaze of the nurse beside her. "How about Devin?" I said finally.

"You've got to be kidding," Jan said. "Devil?"

"No, Devin, my father's name."

The nurse said, "It's a fine name."

Jan said, "Other kids'll call him Devil anyways. No way."

"How about Rohan, then? Rohan Devin."

"What's that?" Jan said. "Your mother's name?"

"No, Jan. The first name of a famous cricketer. Guyanese. A childhood hero of mine."

"Beats Devil. It'll do, I guess."

The nurse lifted the baby from Jan. "Fits like a glove," she said.

"It'll do," Jan repeated sleepily. "Better than 'Hey, you,' eh?"

I left the hospital a couple of hours later feeling curiously satisfied. Even pleased.

These last weeks in Toronto were hectic with departure arrangements, too much to do in too little time. I spent hours bustling around downtown, seeing to the shipment of our belongings, selling off what we would not be taking, buying what we would be needing, anticipating as best we could the contingencies of the island: the shortages of disposable diapers and sanitary napkins, the prohibitive price of shampoo and deodorant.

Late one afternoon a few days before we left, I went to an army surplus store downtown to buy a moneybelt. My sense of caution was growing as the day of departure approached, and my tension was soothed by such little gestures of self-protection. I found myself not far from the Riviera, in an area little changed over the years: the same dry cleaners, the same convenience stores, the same billiards hall, the same burger pits and barber shops. The old man, prosthesis propped beside him, still inhabited the bus shelter; and the Riviera, its doors recently revarnished into a bad imitation of oak, still offered Girls!Girls!Girls! and table dancing for five dollars. I continued walking, past prostitutes gathering at corners and cars cruising slowly by, wading unseen through the pantomimed interplay of bodily suggestion and wary inspection. Kept on walking until I arrived at the Pleasure Dome.

I hesitated only briefly before going in, the waiting room unchanged except for the addition of a few plants in the corners. The woman at the reception desk was puzzled at Mrs. Perroquet's name, said, "Doesn't ring a bell." Checked her files, said, "Not here, I'm afraid."

"You sure? Perroquet." I spelt the name.

The elevator opened and a nurse, the Trinidadian I had met on my first visit, emerged.

The receptionist said, with irritation, "I'm sure, sir. We have no Perroquet staying with us."

The nurse paused on her way past. "Mrs. Parakeet? I remember her. She long dead, man. About a year, a year an' a half ago."

"Do you remember me?" I asked. "I visited once, several years ago."

She examined me, shrugged. "Sorry."

"Would you know what happened to her body?"

"Lemme see. If I rememberin' right, her family take her away. A son or a daughter. She didn't have no husband, I don't think."

"You wouldn't know where—"

"If you ask me, she sleepin' dead to the worl' in Mount Pleasant right now." She chuckled at her own witticism and headed off down the corridor.

On my way back, I stopped in at the Riviera and had a beer. For old time's sake.

As we waited for the flight to be announced, Jan turned suddenly to me, said with a touch of panic, "Why are we doing this?"

"For us," I said without hesitation.

"You mean, for you."

"And for you. And for Rohan. He should know his family as he grows up."

"He'll have mine here."

"*The Conqueror?*" I said. "It's too late now. Besides, we can leave any time we want to."

"Can we?" And her voice was plaintive.

Like stepping into a still-smouldering fireplace: a boiled heat capable of crisping the skin on your flesh, a burnt, vapid air holding out threat of strangulation. Breath seized, air gone molten searing its way through the nostrils and sticking there, at the top of the throat, as if solidified.

We paused briefly at the top of the metal ladder, exposed, bewildered, the tarmac, oily and wet-looking, spread before us in the dusk. Faces obscured by shadow gazed up towards us from blue overalls and uniforms of crisp white shirts tucked into dark trousers. In the near distance, the terminal building shone dully, its light damp and insubstantial, the waving gallery dense with figures indistinct and tentative in their expectation.

Jan's balance wavered. She turned abruptly, as if to seek the confines of the airplane. I steadied her with my right arm—Rohan, asleep, was in my left—and guided her down, step by step, to the concrete. Held her arm as we walked across the tarmac through air acrid with gasoline fumes and the hot breath of machines. Released her as we joined the line—long and unruly, bulging and bubbling with the contained excitement of an impeded stream—to the distant immigration booths. The room, high and narrow and bright, buzzed with subdued conversation. On the ceiling, large fans spun with a lazy inefficacy in the hot, heavy air.

The line moved slowly. Rohan, tight in his blue jumper, grew fretful, stirred and kicked in my arms. Jan, flushed, reached over and unzipped the jumper. A tear of perspiration crept from her hairline, trickled unsteadily down her temple.

Ten minutes went by, fifteen, twenty. I grew lightheaded in the exhausted air. Jan's eyes, skittish, glittered with apprehension in the searing light, their squint wrung with wordless accusation. Hand-painted in red on the far wall were the words WELCOME TO CASAQUEMADA. I was grateful that her back was to what seemed, in that moment, a sneer of artless sarcasm. Rohan kicked, gurgled, whimpered in discomfort. Jan reached into the travel bag at her feet, took out his bottle, inserted the nipple into his mouth. He sucked greedily at it, settled down.

An immigration officer, a young man with sleepy eyes and a languid manner, walked slowly alongside the line, lips pursed in a soundless whistle, eyes playing casually on the impatient faces and glares of misery. He paused beside us, looked briefly at Rohan, at Jan, at me, said quietly, "Dr. Ramsingh?"

"Yes?"

"The whole family. Come with me." He gestured with a flick of his head.

Jan said, "Raj—"

He was already walking away. I turned to her, shrugged in

puzzlement, said, "Come," hurried after him past the curious stares of those in the line.

The young man led us past an unoccupied immigration booth, pulled up suddenly and signalled us to stop. There was a commotion up ahead. A policeman, right hand resting lightly on the butt of his holstered revolver, was escorting a frightened Indian man from the customs area back to immigration. The man, young, long-haired, emaciated, wearing a mismatched suit long unwashed and several sizes too large, cringed in the policeman's grip, looked around with blinking, unseeing eyes, as if the event were overtaking his ability to comprehend it. An immigration officer, a small, battered suitcase in one hand, led the way to an open door. The policeman pushed the man roughly into the room. The immigration officer followed him in, slammed the door shut. The policeman clipped the holster flap over the revolver, took up his position in front of the door.

Only then, in the echoing click of the policeman's holster flap, did I notice that the crowded room, transfixed by the little drama, had gone silent. It was a breathless minute before the buzz of muted speech rose once more, like a loud, indefinable whisper.

The immigration officer led us to a table at the side, half-turned, mumbled, "Passports."

I fished them from my coat pocket, said, "What was that all about? Drugs?"

"Fuckin' Guyanese," he said without passion. "All o' them comin' here for the money."

"I hear life's difficult in Guyana these days."

"So they say." He examined my passport, stamped it, removed the landing card I'd filled out on the plane.

"How come we're getting special treatment?"

He sniffled, ignoring my question, stamped Jan's passport, handed them to me and dismissed us with a wave of his hand.

"Thanks," I said. He walked off without looking back at us.

Jan said, "Is something wrong? What's—"

"No, no," I reassured her. "Everything's fine. We just went through immigration."

"How—"

"Welcome to Casaquemada. Somebody's got a friend. Grappler. My grandfather. They're making things easier for us."

We walked to the customs area. It seemed less hot here despite the crowd, people milling around waiting for luggage that was being tossed with little regard for fragility through an open door at the far end of the hall. The door gave directly onto the tarmac; beyond the men working at the luggage cart, the aircraft we had just come from sat clean and white in the glare of powerful spotlights. As I stared at it pushing at the darkness, holding it off yet deepening it, too, a sense of loss came to me, a mixture of fear and love, for it seemed the only link between the known and the unknown, and soon that, too, would be gone.

Jan said, "Give Rohan to me. I'll wait here while you get the suitcases." She had calmed down, grown listless with fatigue, eyes losing that look of dancing lights.

I moved hesitantly through the crowd to the mounds of stacked luggage. And it was there, at the very front, that I saw my grandfather. He was in deep conversation with a man I did not know, did not see me in the crowd, and I hung back instinctively, seeing him with what I thought to be new eyes, with what I gradually understood to be Jan's eyes.

He was shorter and trimmer than I'd remembered, his grey hair swept back neatly. His face, grave, had the look of leather softened and darkened through use. Most surprising to me, though, were his shoulders, in my memory squared, muscled through his vigorous gardening. But under his white shirt—open at the collar and tucked neatly past a small paunch into pleated grey pants—his shoulders sloped precipitously, as if collapsed, enhancing his look of physical diminishment.

At last he looked up, caught sight of me, squinted and smiled in muted pleasure.

I pushed my way past people and luggage to him. He took my arms, large hands clasping my elbows, reached up—when had he grown so very short?—to plant a light kiss on my cheek. He smelled of aftershave lotion, unsubtle and antiseptic. "Raj," he said. "Son." And his eyes watered, but whether from age or emotion I could not tell.

His friend—the chief immigration officer, my grandfather whispered during an opportune moment—helped us locate our four suitcases and lug them over to Jan and Rohan. I introduced my grandfather, stood back to watch what would happen. Saw Jan force a smile, clasp Rohan more closely to her. Saw my grandfather, eyes quickly assessing, become correct, offer a formal kiss; saw him soften at the sight of his great-grandson, but maintain a physical distance: my grandfather's essential shyness, a curious sight in a man who had reached an age of implicit dignity.

His friend, a man filled with the solemnity of self-importance, led us towards the exit, past the lines of people waiting with burdened luggage carts at long, low wooden counters. The amount of baggage was staggering. Many people had two, even three carts, piled high with bags and suitcases and boxes, radios, stereos, televisions, video recorders. The customs officers, surly with indifference, dug through every box, every bag, every spilling suitcase, held up exotic toys for inspection, shook every bottle, examined every can. From somewhere in the hall a baby's wail sliced sharp and clear above the din. At one counter, a man haggled heatedly with a bored-looking customs officer over a stack of four car tires. At another, a woman hid her face in embarrassment as an officer pulled from her suitcase an endless string of multihued panties. At a third, an officer shook his head in rejection of a man's protests over the confiscation of two copies of *Playboy*.

At the exit, the customs guard nodded in recognition at my grandfather's friend, said to me, "This all you have?"

"Yes." I reached into my pocket for the suitcase keys.

But he, too, like the immigration officer before him, paid no attention to me, bent over and rapidly slashed chalk Xs on the suitcases.

Outside, to the molten light of a single bulb and the crush of a grinning, chattering crowd, their earnest, sweating faces almost aboriginal in the light. Jan seized my coat, crushed against me in sudden fright. My grandfather's friend cleared a path for us with the suitcase he was carrying, led us through the crowd to my grandmother.

She had dressed for the occasion, a diaphanous white veil,

pinned to her hair by a golden butterfly, draped stylishly over her right shoulder and held in place on her salmon-coloured dress by yet another golden pin, this one an extravagant flower. She flung her arms around my neck, the slash of golden bracelets on each forearm tinkling like wind charms, kissed me repeatedly on the cheeks and the lips, chanted my name as if in disbelief, large tears rolling from her eyes. She smelled of powder, a scent as familiar to me as the press of her wet lips. I saw, absurdly, the powder puff she'd always used, saw it lying in its compact on the dressing table; felt at my fingertips the silkiness of it, and the tremor of electricity that ran up my forearm at the touch of it. I knew, then, that were it not for Jan and Rohan, a part of me would be a child once more, revelling in the snug comfort of the familiar.

It was with difficulty that I pulled myself from her grasp, brought Jan and Rohan forward. Watched my grandmother manufacture a ribbon of a smile, lips tautening into compressed strips of flesh. Watched, with incredulity, as my grandmother extended her hand—a calculated distancing, I thought unkindly, forgetting for a moment the Hindu tradition that denied warmth between mother and daughter-in-law—leaving to Jan the stiff and automatic offering of a cheek. It was Rohan who took her attention, who received a caress once more genuine. "Raj," she said, "he lookin' just like you, just like you."

I smiled, as was expected. Caught Jan's fleeting grimace. For it was not true, my grandmother was seeing what she wanted to see, was flirting, I thought, with a Machiavellian manipulation. Rohan was too young, had not yet developed identifiable features. The game lacked subtlety. I squeezed Jan's shoulder, and her frown of response as my grandfather ushered us on towards the carpark, aqueous and surreal in the distance, told me of her tightly held displeasure.

We drove out of the airport compound hurried on by an impatient policeman armed with a small black submachine gun. It was, to me, a new sight. Security, my grandfather explained, nobody quite knew why. The new security director, a former police chief, had suddenly and without explanation flooded the airport and the Lopez City docks with heavily armed policemen. There were rumours, of course: drug smugglers, arms smugglers, Cuban infiltrators. But the government would confirm nothing, and the few protests were muted. The security director had been appointed by the old man himself; no one wanted to press too much for fear of giving offence.

"So the old man still pulls all the strings."

"He goin' to pull the strings even when he dead."

The road was narrow, unlit, hedged on the right by the chain-link fence surrounding the airport, fell off on the left to the stifling, moss-green density of sugar cane fields. My grandfather drove slowly, peering ahead through the windscreen at the ribbon of road revealed by the headlights. From time to time, the crumpled and rusted hulks of crashed cars glinted in the light, monuments and warnings eloquent in their disintegration.

At my grandmother's insistence—it had something to do with her understanding of male and female roles, of one's place in the world—I sat in the front seat with my grandfather. She had relieved Jan of Rohan, heaved herself into the back seat behind my grandfather. Jan had pointedly placed the travel bag on the seat between them. Their conversation, halting, uneasy, was about Rohan, my grandmother asking the questions— "He eatin' good? He does sleep a lot?"—and Jan, deciphering the language, replying carefully, as if speaking to someone unsure of English.

My grandfather, never taking his eyes from the road, never taking his hands from the steering wheel, spoke slowly, in a reflective voice, in response to my questions.

Business? Business wasn't bad, wasn't what it had been, people had less money now, fewer and fewer people came into the store with inch-thick wads of hundred-dollar bills, but still it wasn't bad, he wasn't about to complain, he'd done well during the boom years and you had to expect that, with the fall in world oil prices, things would tighten up a bit, but there was still a lot of money floating around the island, nobody was hurting, yet. The problem, though, was that incomes were falling, but the high prices that had come with the boom were not, and he wondered how it would all end up as the money shrank even more and prices continued to rise; he saw the effects in the store every day, the inflation that the government called ten per cent but that affected new goods by twenty and thirty per cent. If this continued, how were people going to afford food, clothes? "I think maybe we headin' for some *jhunjut*," he said quietly.

Jhunjut. It was a reassuring word, a word my grandmother would use when the rice spilled over on the stove or the roof leaked, a word I associated with childhood scrapes and tumbles.

Grappler, what about him, and my Aunt Sylvia, of course, how was she?

"Who?" he said.

"Grappler and Aunt Sylvia—"

"Kenny, nuh, Pa," my grandmother called from the back seat.

Kenny: Grappler's real name, but no one ever used it now, no one had for years. It was too fragile, too timid a name for the man.

My grandmother said, with an undercurrent of fear, "Your granpa gettin' dotish in his old age, Son. He does forget things sometimes." She gave a nervous little laugh.

"Is that right, Granpa?" I said.

Peering at the road ahead, deserted, a ribbon of grey in the darkness, he raised his chin a little higher, as if resentful of my question. "Little things. Nothing important. A name, nuh. Phone numbers. Nothing to worry 'bout. You know your granma, she like to worry."

"I like to worry? Eh? An' who forget the keys for the store the other mornin'? Me?"

My grandfather's face, lit by the dashboard lights, remained impassive.

Rohan hacked drily, whimpered.

"Shh, Son, quiet," my grandmother whispered.

Rohan whimpered again, uttered a low wail.

I turned around, reached my arm out to him. Jan touched my hand, stopped me. "I'll take him," she said, reaching over the travel bag and lifting Rohan from the cradle of my grandmother's embrace. He quieted down. She zipped the jumper up, and even in the darkness I thought I could see her smile, her turn to score a point. My grandmother sniffed, straightened the veil on her shoulder.

I turned back to grandfather, said, "So. Grappler, and Aunt Sylvia."

But it was my grandmother who spoke first. "Son," she said, "your Uncle Grappler hard-head just like your granpa. He workin' too hard, night and day, he never slowin' down—"

"Grappler have a job to do," my grandfather said.

"But he goin' to kill himself if he ain't watch out. Jus' like you. Is that you want?"

"What you frettin' so far, Ma? Nobody goin' to kill himself. And they gone to England for holiday."

"They're in England?" I said.

"A short holiday," my grandfather said.

"Too short," my grandmother said.

"Two weeks," my grandfather said.

"They comin' back next week," my grandmother said.

"Better than nothing," my grandfather said.

"Sylvia had to drag him," my grandmother said.

"Is the economy," my grandfather said. "The downturn, nuh. The government goin' to have to retrench some workers—"

"Retrench?" I said.

"Is the word they usin'. I suppose they afraid to say fire, nuh. So it keepin' Grappler busy. He overwork himself in the last few months, is good he get away for a little rest."

"You listenin' to yourself?" my grandmother said. "Is good advice, not so, Raj?"

"Very good advice, Granma." The headlights picked out the stone pillars that marked the beginning of Roosevelt Field. As we passed them, the feel and sound of the tires on the road changed, from a rippling rattle to the fluent hiss of flowing water. I told Jan where we were, briefly explained its history.

She peered for a moment through the window, said, "It's too dark to see anything."

My grandmother said, "It ain't have anything to see, anyway. Just some old break-down buildings."

We drove on in silence for a few minutes, the headlights peeling back bits and pieces of the night: the wide roadway, the long and tapering grasses at the verge, the decaying carcass of a dog.

"And Kayso," I said. "What's he up to these days?"

Silence suddenly charged. The tires seemed to grind more heavily on the road.

My grandmother said, "Son—"

"Ma." My grandfather cut her off, his tone less one of severity than of caution.

I waited for a moment before asking what was the matter, had they quarrelled with him?

And it was another moment before my grandfather said, "Open the glove compartment, Raj. It have a newspaper in there. Take it out."

I removed the folded tabloid.

"Today's," my grandfather said.

"Son," my grandmother said, anguished.

I reached above my head, switched on the interior light, unfolded the newspaper. Saw Kayso's picture, a more recent one. Read the headline without grasping it, had to go over it again, slowly, letter by letter, putting them together one by one and extracting meaning: CIVIL RIGHTS LAWYER DEAD. I skimmed the story, badly printed, cheap ink on cheap paper. It told of a suit he had filed the week before against several doctors, against a hospital, the Ministry of Health, and the minister himself. It told of his parents finding the body in the bedroom of his apartment; he was lying on the bed, naked, beside a life-sized electric sex-doll. The doll was still plugged in. Kayso had been electrocuted. The walls of the room, the reporter had added at the end, were covered in blown-up photographs of a market, tentatively identified as Kensington Market in Toronto.

Jan said, "What is it, Raj?"

But I could not reply, simply passed her the newspaper.

As we drove on through the darkness, my grandmother sobbed in the back seat.

Jan and I, of course, talked that very night about not staying. She said only, "We can go back any time, right?" I assured her of it, even if I was no longer so certain. In the smells and creaks of my grandparents' house, all so familiar to me, all so alien to her, the very air of the island seemed to crystallize around my body. We would be here, I felt, for a long time.

Grappler and my Aunt Sylvia returned the following week. We spoke only once of Kayso, and he was dismissive. "Kayso didn't know what he was doing," he said. "No idea at all what he was gettin' himself into. He was jugglin' fire, and eventually it consumed him. That's all there is to it." And he was right. It wasn't long before the words *civil rights lawyer* became a term of derision in the island, and whatever reputation Kayso had enjoyed, a source of ridicule. His lawsuit died with him, and the rumour mills held, with conviction, that he'd never really had a case anyway, that it had all been a grotesque quest for publicity. His death was seen not as a loss but as the revelation of a man, grown too big for his boots, brought down by secret perversion. It was, in Casaquemada, the most appreciated kind of scandal. When Surein visited, he said with a laugh, "But your friend Kayso really fuck up there, man, Raj." I told him that I did not believe the story, was suspicious of it. He rejected out of hand my hesitations. The story was simply too good, he said. Truth was completely irrelevant. The man was dead, and the manner of his death had importance now only in its entertainment value.

Jan, stunned, said, "What kind of a place is this, anyways?" We had been, once, to Lopez City, had seen the many homeless, of every age, wandering ragged through the streets, begging at the corners, expiring, somnolent, on the sidewalks. It had been a shock to Jan, even to me, for their numbers had multiplied in the midst of wealth. But I was able to put it into perspective, even if not to Jan's satisfaction, for Casaquemada had never been a place that looked after its unfortunate and its handicapped. That was left to families, and when they couldn't or wouldn't cope, those incapable of fending for themselves were abandoned to the lottery of the streets, a game of chance that had no winners, only varieties of losers. "It's scandalous," Jan said. "How do you people think?"

"Us?" Surein said. "Don't give me that, *gheeul*. Up there where you come from, people does care more about their dogs than about other people. Is a billion-dollar industry. Dog food, dog clothes, dog houses, dog toys, dog medicine, dog barbers, dog psychiatrists. And don't tell me you ain't have poor people up there in Toronto."

His vehemence silenced her, and I let the conversation die there—it had already set the tone, between Jan and Surein, of a mutual dislike—deciding there was no point in mentioning the soup kitchens, hostels and subsidized housing with which Toronto was at least attempting to deal, however inadequately, with similar problems. And I remember thinking that here, in Casaquemada, people didn't care even for their dogs unless they performed a function; useless, they were abandoned and, like people helpless in the demands of life, set loose to scavenge. In the island of Casaquemada, life was worth less than a house or a car; it could not be bartered for anything; it could not be graced with monetary value. It was, I thought, the final blow of colonial heritage: life as financial transaction. It was why Kayso, speaking of human rights, of life as having an intrinsic value of its own by the mere fact of its existence, was seen at best as odd, at worst as a publicity seeker. It was why, too, in the end, a man such as he had to be ridiculed, his legacy vilified. He had come demanding competence and honesty and effort in an island that no longer, if it ever had, cared about such things. He had challenged too many deeply held prejudices. He had challenged a rape of the land colonial in its actions and attitudes. He had, in the end, challenged history, and in this he could not be the winner.

So we were here, and there was money still to be had in this island that understood best the mercenary motive. We were here, with my grandfather growing forgetful, his heart inefficient, my grandmother growing fretful, her nerves unstable. I had packed in a suitcase the three letters that had come to me months before; now I took out Kayso's, ripped it up, threw it out.

We sold the little house I had never inhabited, the little house that had helped put me through university: I had no wish to live in Salmonella, and Jan wanted distance between my grandparents and us. For several weeks we visited houses for sale in different parts of the island, seeing many that were new, few that were attractive. A peculiar, distressing architecture outrageous with the frivolity of excess: massive structures of mismatched corners and jutting edges, juggernauts of concrete and steel; and everywhere iron bars standing at rigid attention, on windows, on doors, around porches. It was architecture, Jan said, out of a Crackerjack box.

We finally found our house in a middle-class development halfway between Salmonella and Lopez City. There was a sense of openness to it, even with the burglar-proofing on the doors and windows. The porch, at least, had not been barred.

The night we moved in, Jan and I, Rohan in her arms, stood on the front lawn and gazed at the sky.

"Look," I said, "how much more clearly you can see the stars here."

"Yes," she replied. "But that only means that the night is darker."

It was a few weeks later that she took up smoking. In defiance of me.

16

Life in an ethereal zone.

A world without information. No newspapers. No magazines. No mail. Radio newscasts, every hour on the hour between fifty-five minutes of commercials, weather forecasts and songs of the American Top Forty, that offered without details reassurance that the situation—but what situation?—was under control. Television newscasts, thirty minutes every evening of bombs in the Middle East, assassinations in Central America, cricket matches in Australia, slipped between the machinations of the Ewings, the whining of the Ropers, the plotting of the Carringtons, that offered without details reassurance that the situation—but what situation?—was under control.

Life in a vacuum, reality assailable, solidity sucked out of it.

The emergency had closed down the island, blocked BBC broadcasts, left us with only local telephone service and the rumours that it brought, from Surein, from Raffique.

"I hear Cubans floodin' onto the beaches from a submarine."

"A friend o' mine call me from Lopez City, she say she hearin' sirens and gunfire all night."

"Lopez City done, boy, finish. A police friend tell me it scarcely have a buildin' that ain't get a firebomb. The firemen and them can't cope."

"They say it have dead bodies lyin' all over Raleigh Street, fellas with head and legs blow off."

"The Americans comin', boy. I hear some o' them already land at the airport. Tanks and t'ing."

Each a little alarming, each a little disarming, each diluting the situation—but what situation?—into a thinner tangibility.

An embattled sky, storm clouds boiling and thickening, hardening into matted steel. The afternoon sunlight, filtered and uncertain, as if liquefied in the air humid and pungent with the sweet decay of awakened vegetation. A ragged cable of lightning shimmered purple across the sky, and seconds later thunder rumbled in the distance like a reticent lament. Mist filmed the mountain tops grey, swirled thickly against the lower viridescence. The rain came slowly at first, in a pregnant pitter-patter; quickened perceptibly, darkening the lawn and the concrete skirt of the porch, drumming like a multitude of fingers on the galvanized-iron roof of the house; intensified into a deluge of effacement, crashing now onto the roof in continuous explosion so that it, and no longer the landscape, was the only spectacle through the metal rectangles of the small kitchen window.

In the porch, Wayne sat somnolent in a chair, hands crossed on his lap, legs splayed, on the floor beside him a three-sided file and the machete, the cutting edge freshly silvered. Rohan, shirtless, stood before him, flexing his biceps.

Jan said, "Stop dreaming, Raj. The toast."

"Sorry. Didn't hear it." I took the slice from the toaster, buttered it.

"Where's your mind, anyways?" She salted the egg, whipped it with milk into foam.

"Out there."

"The 'situation'?"

"The weather."

"You not worried?"

"What d'you think?"

"Nothing's easy with you, is it, Raj?"

"Remember why we came here? You wanted adventure in your life?"

"Don't give me that. We didn't come here for me. Or for us."

The toast, overdone, cracked into three pieces under the pressure of the knife. "I know."

"He's not going to eat that now. He likes them whole."

"He'll eat it."

"You don't know your son. He won't eat it."

In the porch, Wayne reached out to squeeze Rohan's biceps, contrived a look of admiration.

"Just put in another toast, Raj. I can't take his screaming this afternoon."

I did as ordered, while she sliced off a wedge of butter and plopped it, sizzling, into the hot frying pan, swirled it around with a spatula, poured in the egg.

The rain lessened, settled into a steady downpour. Already the sky had lightened.

"Rohan," she called, stirring at the congealing egg. "Almost time to eat. Come inside."

But he paid no attention to her, struck a karate pose.

"Rohan!"

His little hands chopped at the air, eyes glancing at Wayne for approval.

"Yeah, man, yeah." Wayne winked, smiled. "You doin' it good."

"Rohan," I said quietly, and his hands, flitting through the air like a hurried Hindu dancer's, shredded my call.

"Rohan!" Jan spooned the scrambled egg onto a plate. "Get in here, your egg's ready."

Rohan straightened up, glared towards the window, wavered at the sight of me, focussed on the strands of white metal between us. "I not hungry," he said.

"Rohan," I replied, using his name as an instrument of terror, "you were hungry ten minutes ago."

"I not hungry now," he pleaded.

"I *am* not hungry."

"Me too." And he grinned, aware he had made a joke.

Wayne gazed out at the rain, fought a grin of his own. "Go inside now, boy," he said. "Your mammy callin' you."

"But I not hungry," Rohan said more softly.

"You have to eat, boy. Your muscles need protein to grow, otherwise they goin' to stay small-small, jus' like a girl."

"Egg have proteem?"

"Egg have plenty protein. And milk, too."

Rohan turned without another word and ran into the house, climbed onto a chair at the kitchen table and turned expectantly towards us.

I carefully buttered the new slice of toast, placed it on the plate beside the egg. Jan took it to him, put a fork in his hand. "D'you need help?"

"Nope." He began to eat, inexpertly scooping the egg towards his mouth, spoonfuls overflowing and furious. Bits of yellow littered the table, flecked his chin and cheeks.

"Christ, Rohan." Jan bent over, picked up pieces of egg from the floor. "Slow down, the food's not going anywhere. And eat your toast."

"Toast have proteem in it?"

The explosion on the roof abated into a soft drumming as the rain eased. Outside, Wayne dozed in his chair. The landscape, grey, green, black, as if somehow thickened by the rain, reasserted itself.

"Yes. And it's pro*tein*."

Rohan picked up the slice of toast, delicately, pinching it between the thumb and index finger of each hand, opened his mouth wide, inserted the bread and bit sharply down, severing a corner. He chewed vigorously, mouth flapping open like a horse snapping at hay. "Proteem," he said.

Jan went to the sink, washed the egg off her fingers.

"What's the use?" she said wearily to herself.

I offered coffee, plugged in the kettle. Jan, weary, sat beside Rohan, watched him finish off the toast.

Wayne sat up in his chair, yawned, rubbed his face. Had a moment of panic until he saw the machete lying beside him, close at hand.

"Coffee, Wayne?"

"Thank you, boss."

"Not boss. Raj."

He picked up the machete and the file, stood, stretched.

"It's sharp enough?" I said. "The cutlass?"

"You could shave with this *poignard*, boss." He inserted it into the sheath, slipped the file into the pocket of his shorts.

Jan said, "You liked the egg, Rohan?"

"Yes."

She brushed the yellow flecks from his chin and cheeks. "So what d'you say?"

"Yes."

"C'mon, Rohan, what d'you say?"

"Thank you."

"You're welcome. And what about Daddy? He buttered the toast."

Rohan turned to me, wiping the grease from his lips with the back of his hand, grinned, said, "Thank you, boss."

Jan chuckled, said, "Smarta—" Stopped herself. "Aleck."

Rohan slid from his chair, ran, bare feet slapping on the tiled floor, back out to the porch. Presented himself to Wayne, flexed his biceps, said, "Proteem."

Jan picked his plate up from the table, put it into the sink.

The drumming on the roof eased, fell to a low rumble.

The kettle boiled, steam pouring from the spout. Jan unplugged it while I got the mugs, the coffee, a spoon. She looked at the steam, said, "Three wishes, genie. Get me out of this place. Make me rich. Give me three more wishes."

"Greedy, greedy," I said.

But she ignored me, turned back to the sink.

The rumble on the roof ceased.

I said, "It's stopped raining."

She washed the plate, turned off the tap. Said, after a moment, "Yes. But listen to the silence."

Waiting. But for what?

For the radio and the television to announce, in Oxbridge-tinted English, that the situation—but what situation? The one that was under control?—had returned to, for want of a better word, normal.

And this was one of the problems, one of the welter of confusions: first, to imagine with accuracy the reality of *out there*, to conjure up in detail the convulsions in Lopez City, and then—the greater difficulty, this—to decide what it would, what it could, all return to, if indeed it were to return to anything.

And waiting, too, through days indistinguishable in their sameness, daylight and darkness now nominally named, for the telephone to ring not with rumour, not with gossip, but with fact and the reassurance of certainty. Another of the confusions: to listen to the rumours, to wonder at the facts. At the best of times, a difficult task in Casaquemada; in a time of upheaval, an impossible one. We were a people who preferred fiction. Witness the thrills of political melodrama we have embraced throughout our history, the smoke and mirrors of manipulated truths. Witness the backlit signs at local Kentucky Fried Chicken outlets, the goateed colonel negrified for the profit of politics and the politics of profit. A people, in the end, conditioned to concoct fables and fantasies. It is why the masquerade of our carnival is so good, why it rivals Trinidad's in vision if not in volume. We, like them, spend the year dreaming.

The television had nothing to offer; we had already seen the film, on the mating habits of insects, five times. "What's going on at that TV station?" Jan said, incredulous. "They're either a bunch of entomologists or dirty old men. Real sickos. Either way!" She fetched a stack of old fashion magazines from the bedroom, began impatiently flicking through them, the pages snapping drily in the silence.

I went to my study, looked through a medical journal, lost interest. Rummaged in the middle drawer of the desk, pulled out pens, pencils, paper, Canadian coins and, from the very back, the letters I had brought with me, from Surein and my grandfather. I read through Surein's, read about Lenny and the boots and the money, remembered with a curious fondness the little house in which we had lived, with a sudden yearning for the view from its living room window.

The telephone rang, once, twice, three times. I went out. Jan, still flicking through her magazines, pretended not to hear it, wished, she said, to hear no more rumours.

Raffique said, "Raj, boy, better start prayin'."

"What's it this time, Raffique?"

"I hear things really out o' control in town. They killin' people like wildfire."

"They who, Raffique?"

"I hear some o' the police gettin' in on it now. Way I understand it, they gettin' rid o' people they ain't like, trouble-makers, nuh. Jus' wipin' them out. Goin' in their house and openin' fire."

"And where are the Americans and their tanks you heard about, Raffique?"

"Well, I ain't know for sure—"

"And the Cubans?"

"Maybe is them who—"

"Tell you what, Raffique, you pray. You and Asha. You have more experience. We really wouldn't know what to say."

"You should try it anyway, Raj. It ain't have nothing to it, all you have to do is ask for what you want."

"That's all?"

"Nothing more. You want me to come over? I could show you—"

"No, no, never mind. We can handle it. Just ask for what we want, right?"

"Right."

I hung up. Jan said, "So what's it this time? Russians?" She sucked anxiously at her cigarette.

"The usual. The sky's falling."

"Chunk of it must've hit him on the head, eh?" She laughed, smoke streaming from her mouth.

"Right between the eyes."

The telephone rang again.

Without even looking up she said, "For you. Surein. Wants to tell you about this hole he just noticed in the sky."

But it wasn't Surein, it was my Aunt Sylvia. "Raj," she said in a voice breathless with anxiety. "Is Surein by you?"

"No, he's not here."

"Have you heard from him today?"

"This morning. He called."

"What time?"

"Around eleven or so. What's up?"

"I've been trying to ring him for the last two hours and no-body's answerin'."

"Maybe he's gone out."

"Raj, he's livin' in the middle o' Lopez City. Now is not the time to go out. I hope he not crazy enough to do that."

Grappler took the phone from her. "Raj," he said, "how all-you doin' up there?"

"Fine."

"Everything quiet?" I could hear fatigue in his voice.

"Everything's quiet."

"Boy, you know your aunt just like your grandmother. Like mother, like daughter. Worryin' for nothing. I tell her so many times, the boy probably sleepin'. And you know Surein, earth-quake not wakin' him up."

My Aunt Sylvia, close to the phone, said, "But Lenny should be there, why he not answerin' the phone?"

"He's probably in the garage," I said. "Cleaning the car."

Grappler repeated my words to my Aunt Sylvia. "What I tell you?" I heard him say. "Didn't I tell you the same thing five min-utes ago?"

"Two hours to clean the car?" my Aunt Sylvia said.

"He probably fell asleep in the back seat," Grappler said. Then to me: "You wouldn't say so, Raj?"

"It's possible. Especially if Surein himself's asleep."

"Well, your aunt will probably keep callin' anyway until they get up. It ain't have nothing else to do, I suppose."

"Grappler, do you have any idea exactly what's going on?"

"Only rumours," he said. "Rumours, rumours everywhere, and not a word to believe. Sit tight. Don't worry too much. Watch some TV—"

"You've got to be kidding."

"You know how prayin' mantis does mate?"

"So you've seen it, too, huh?"

He laughed. "How Jan and the boy doin'?"

"Fine."

"Tell Jan not to worry too much. Is jus' a little bit of adventure in her life."

"I'll tell her," I said.

Back in my study a minute later—Jan had grimaced at Grappler's encouragement, sneered "Whoopee"—I looked out the window at the dripping world: at the slicked lawn, the darkened road, the greyed sky surging above Asha and Raffique's house. Saw again, with marvel, the layers of fence and barrier behind which we had had to barricade ourselves, behind which we were now caught, cornered in the ignorance we had willed on ourselves by those we had for so long discounted.

Wayne walked by, unarmed, hands clasped behind his back, bared feet sinking deep into the grass. And behind him, in miniature imitation, came Rohan, as intent as Wayne was thoughtful, his legs moving with a stiff rapidity to keep pace. I hung back, deep in the shadows of the darkening study. Held my breath. Waited for him to go by, absorption intact.

Clouds drifted, shredded, eddied in viscous swirls. I thought: An ominous peace.

Minutes later, a police patrol drove past, four men crouched in a jeep, one behind the wheel, three clutching rifles, each looking off in a different direction.

And then—or so, at least, it seems to me now—they turned as one and, for an eternity of seconds, stared at our house as though through walls transparent.

It was Jan who answered the phone the third time it rang that afternoon. I had fallen into a doze, was startled awake by her bustling into the study, calling me with urgency. My eyes opened to the window, to the burglar-proofing solid as night against a sky of burnt orange.

"Raj," she said, "quick, it's your grandmother. She's upset, I don't understand a word she's saying. Something about your grandfather."

I have no memory of getting to the telephone, recall only a flurry of words: of shouting at my grandmother, of understanding through her stammering panic that my grandfather had a bad pain in his chest, was lying in bed moaning and unable to speak. "Granma!" I shouted, cutting off her confusion of words. "Hang up. Hang up now!" And to my surprise, she did. I called the Salmonella District Hospital, asked them to send an ambulance. Called Grappler, but got only a busy signal. Thrust the phone at Jan, told her to keep trying to reach Grappler.

I dressed quickly in my medical whites—as a doctor on an emergency call, I would have reason enough to satisfy police questions about my being on the roads—while Wayne, offering to accompany me, unhappy at my refusal but soothed by my greater need of him at home with Jan and Rohan, unlocked the back gates, opened them wide.

Jan was on the phone, dialling, a butt burning acrid between her fingers, as I hurried out to the car.

Just before I drove off, as I shifted the gear from reverse to drive, I glanced through the window at Wayne locking the gate. He held Rohan in his left arm. Rohan, for some reason, was crying.

I drove fast along the roads deserted as never before. No cars, not even police patrols. No bending bodies labouring in the fields. No cows, no goats grazing. The vegetable and fish stalls abandoned. Through Roosevelt Field, sprawling shadow already in the day slipping quickly into night. Through the shuttered main street of Salmonella, past the unlit stores and inert ruins and the police station brilliant in its lights behind locked gates.

It was dark by the time I got to the house. The ambulance was there, parked at the side of the road. I pulled up behind it, got my bag out of the trunk, ran past the open gate, up the stairs, through the porch—there were people sitting, standing, neighbours, I assumed—into my grandparents' bedroom.

An ambulance attendant, hands in his pockets. A white-coated intern—a distant cousin several years my junior—slipping the stethoscope from his neck, a gesture of helpless finality so familiar to me. And my grandmother, kneeling beside the bed, head bowed, right arm crashing, as if in slow motion, bit by steady bit, onto my grandfather's chest. She groaned, a sharp, ripping sound, as her fist thumped against him. Screamed: "Gawd, oh Gawd, no! Pa, come back, don't leave me, don't go."

The intern looked up at me, shook his head. The attendant, uneasy, looked around the little room.

The bag in my right hand seemed to evaporate. A heaviness filled my head.

"Gawd," my grandmother pleaded, "Gawd, listen to me. Send him back, send him back and I give you anything you want. Gawd, we does pray every day, why you doin' this to me? Send him back, Gawd. Jus' tell me what you want. Don't do this to me, Gawd. Anything, anything you want." She fell forward onto his chest, here her greatest betrayal. All those *poojas*, all that spectacle, *her* spectacle, and now, before my grandfather's lifeless body, her religion deserted her, collapsing into the final superstition. The gods offered no deal.

Neighbours gathered, old men and old women subdued and regretful falling into silence only as we carried my grandfather's body, shrouded on a stretcher, out to the ambulance.

When I came back in, several old women had soothed my grandmother onto the bed, were rubbing her arms, her legs, her head with coconut oil and bay rum; others, making themselves at home, were preparing for a long night of vigil by brewing coffee in the kitchen, while the men, settling into their chairs in the porch, lit up cigarettes and uncorked rum bottles. They were all strangers to me, people whose faces I recognized from the religious gatherings of my childhood. They smiled at me, shook my hand, embraced me, kissed me. I was grateful for their presence, their bustle, the assurance with which they took charge of a situation that more and more baffled me. It was at this point, the death certified, my responsibility over, that I had always withdrawn, retreating to the maps and my contemplation of their arterial mazes. But I wished, too, to escape these people, to flee the expectations of me—of ceremony, perhaps, of ritual and religion—that they would harbour; wished to secrete myself in a corner not far from them, within reach of their voices but beyond reach of their arms. There, but not there, secure on the periphery.

I broke away from them, made my way to the bedroom, long unused, known for simplicity's sake as the telephone room, shut the door behind me. Breathed deeply of its settled dust, felt the inanimation, the dislocation of its barrenness. The telephone, old-fashioned, bulky, of a black plastic that had long lost its sheen, sat in a corner on the little wooden shelf my grandfather had mounted for it. I picked up the receiver, called Jan, gave her the news, my words direct, dispassionate.

She was silent for a moment, said, "I thought so." Was silent again, added, "But I've been expecting it, eh, Raj. I mean, weren't you? Let's face it, he's been dying for a long time."

I knew what she meant, but could only grunt in reply. To acknowledge this, at that moment, seemed somehow wrong. "How's Rohan?" I said.

"Asleep."

"And Wayne?"

"He's patrolling, I guess."

"Did you get Grappler?"

"No. Their phone's been busy, they must've taken it off the hook or something."

"No, that's not possible. Sylvia must still be trying to reach Surein. I'm going to call Indira and Emma now. Keep on trying Grappler, okay?"

"Well, all right."

"Look, if you don't want to—"

"No, no, I'll do it. I just have a hard time giving people bad news. I mean, what d'you say?"

"Just tell him Granpa's dead and he can call me here."

"When are you coming home?"

"Well, I think I'd better spend the night here. The family can't come till tomorrow morning now, and I don't want to leave Granma with just the neighbours."

"Not to mention being on the roads at night these days."

"Will you be all right?"

"Sure. No problem. I'll bring Rohan to bed with me."

"And let Wayne know I won't be in, all right?"

"I'll tell him."

"I'll call you tomorrow morning."

"Raj—"

"What?"

"Never mind. Sleep well."

I then called, in quick succession, my aunts Indira and Emma. Indira screamed, dropped the phone. Emma took the news well, asked if, by chance, I might have a picture of my grandfather— "Not too recent, eh. From before he get sick, nuh." I promised I would look. They asked about their mother, my grandmother, were pleased at the intervention of the neighbours, urged me to "give her something, a shot or a tablet" to help her sleep. Emma offered to call my uncles, but I reminded her that the island was still cut off from the world by the emergency. "Oh, yes," she said. "The emergency. What a bother. But these people chupid, eh, boy, Raj?" There was nothing to do but agree.

My duties over, I sat on the bed, wide and soft and like everything in this house old-fashioned, listening through the wooden walls to the low conversations of the neighbours, hearing their muffled laughter, the clinking of their cups and glasses, the raucous scratching of their matches. A great, draining weariness took hold of me, and a growing sense of the enormity of the evening's events, the word *death* itself suddenly so full of impalpable implication: a dance of chimera, a grasping at shadow. The emergency, and the events out there, the rumour and the reality of Lopez City: how unreal it all seemed at that moment, how insignificant and fanciful, its threat a triviality in my growing grief.

I stood up, shook myself, walked slowly into the adjoining room, to the smells of burnt oil and cheap perfume of my grandfather's prayer room. Stood at the window looking out into the darkness of the yard, realized with sadness that the burglar-proofing, installed just two years before, permitted a view of only bits and pieces of the mango tree. I turned away, switched on the light. Stood before his altar, this confusion of brass plates and vases, of gods physically deformed, of *deeyas* and wilting flowers, and thought that here, in this spot so quintessentially him, I could smell something of my grandfather. I took a match from a box lying beside a brass plate, struck it, held the flame to the burnt cotton wick of a *deeya*. But it would not catch. The oil had all burnt off.

The telephone rang. I hurried to answer it. Grappler, hoarse-voiced, said Jan had just got through to them. He had been on the phone all evening, trying, in vain, to reach someone, anyone of authority. For he had given in to my Aunt Sylvia's entreaties, driven into the city to Surein's house, had found it open, deserted, furniture overturned, floor ripped up, ceiling ripped down. Neighbours, fearful behind their barred doors, had shouted to him that the new policemen, the ones who dressed like soldiers—Madera flashed into my mind—had raided the house, taken Surein away in the back of a Black Maria. Grappler had called everywhere, everyone he could think of, but no one could give him any information. No one knew what was happening; no one knew who had been arrested, why, or where prisoners were being held; no one seemed to know even who was in charge.

I could offer no reassurance. I knew too much about Surein, and I knew too much about Madera and his kind. "Grappler," I said. "Granpa's dead." For the first time that evening, tears filled my eyes.

"I know," he said softly. "I know. You managin' to handle things up there all right?"

"Yes." But my voice was tentative.

"Try to get some sleep, Raj, you sound tired. Either your Aunt Sylvia or me will come up tomorrow morning. Lopez City too dangerous to drive through at night. It have police everywhere, and they not in a friendly mood. One of us will be there first thing in the morning. Promise, okay?" And his voice, tender, was like it had been the day we had spoken in my grandfather's prayer room of my hopes for the future and my father's dreams for me.

I hung up, stretched out on the bed and, after a while, fell into a fitful sleep, dreaming again and again that my grandfather had returned incorporeal from the dead to pull my toes, just as he had once laughingly promised when I was a child.

When, the next morning, my aunts Sylvia and Emma arrived, I had already been up for several hours. The old ladies had made coffee, fried thick slices of bread. My grandmother, weakened, frail in her grief, had been taken into the kitchen, forced to eat some of the bread, swallow some of the coffee. In her stupor, she seemed hardly to recognize me as I awkwardly hugged her, kissed her on the cheek, gagged at the fetid odour of bay rum and coconut oil. She had just been helped back to her bed when Sylvia and Emma arrived. They still had no news of Surein, my Aunt Sylvia said, and Grappler had decided to drive to police headquarters in the city to see what he could find out. He would be calling here the moment he knew something. My Aunt Emma kissed me on the cheek, whispered a reminder about the photograph. Then, together, they entered my grandmother's bedroom. After a moment, a shrill wail pierced the wooden walls and sobbing filled the house.

I went to the telephone to call Jan. It was time for me to leave. The house had become airless, and the smell of bay rum and coconut oil would not leave my nostrils. My finger shook as I dialled the number, suddenly in need of hearing Jan's voice. The phone rang, once, twice, three times. Rang again and again. Thirteen, fourteen, fifteen. I hung up, dialled again. It rang and rang. Eighteen, nineteen, twenty. Hung up again, dialled again. After the seventh ring, I was crashing through the living room, out the door, through the porch, past the gate, into the car.

I have no recollection of the drive home.

The first thing I noticed as I drove past the front gate, still chained, was that the doors to the porch were open, but that there was—curiously—no one on the porch.

Around the corner. And the back gates were open.

I left the car in the middle of the street. Stepped, suddenly cold, freezing in the morning sun, towards the open gate.

"Raj!" A woman's voice.

I turned around, the sun dazzling. Asha, and behind her Raffique.

"Raj! No!" Asha, sheathed in red, running towards me.

"Raj!" Raffique, dishevelled, unshaven.

"Good morning," I said, and the words seemed the utterance of an idiot.

Raffique placed his arms on my shoulders.

Asha, eyes like shattered mirrors. "Your nigger, Raj, your Wayne. He tried to stop them. With the cutlass. But they had guns, Raj, the fellas with the lightning on their head, I tried to warn you. I told you, watch out for the lightning."

The world spun, slowly.

Raffique, eyes blinking out of control. "That boy, your cousin's yardboy, he was with them, he was laughing, he was pointing—"

Nausea. "Jan?"

What was this? A white blouse? Why was Asha holding up a white blouse? And what was that hole in it?

"They rip it off her before they throw her in the van, Raj—"

"Like a sack o' rice, man."

"We pick it up from the road afterwards, after they left."

Somewhere, a dog barked.

"Rohan?"

Raffique, fingers digging into my shoulder blades. "He was with Jan when they drag her out, man. He was right there, in the line o' fire."

Asha, with tears in her eyes. "She didn't want to get in the van, Raj. Is why they shoot her, she was fightin' them. And Rohan, little Rohan, he was cryin'—"

My hands around her throat, her thin, bony throat. Gurgling.

A roaring in my head, the world spinning faster and faster and faster.

An arm around my neck. A hand punching at my side.

Nausea. My stomach rising to my throat.

Relaxation.
Exhaustion.
Raffique helping Asha to her feet.
The blouse in my hand.
And, finally, alone.

17

The only sound was from the car radio: the hiss of empty air, broken from time to time by the excited chatter of a triumphant voice. I turned the volume down, but could not bring myself to turn it off: I needed it as a reminder. Here, surrounded by hills, rounded peaks rising, unchanged, exactly as they had when Columbus first spotted them from the deck of his ship almost five hundred years ago; here, drowning in the deception of greenery and congealing sunlight, it would have been too tempting to pretend, if only for a second or two, that nothing had happened, that all was right with the world, that, indeed, all that I called my world existed still.

I let my eyes rest on the upper half of the steering wheel, so that the hairline cracks that had developed in the black plastic beneath the transparent coating took on the acuteness of lines on a road map. It caused the rest of my vision to blur and for one minute, two, three, until the moment the pain sharpened itself in my eyes, the world was effaced and my brain registered nothing but that grey road map on a field of black.

The pain, lancing from within, pulled my eyes shut, to a darkness behind the lids that was peopled: faces I did not wish to see, expressions known too well contorted now, by imagination, by experience, into expositions of pain all the more powerful for not having been witnessed. My eyes forced themselves open.

The windshield was coated with dust, tanned, so that all before me appeared varnished: the cream hood of the car sweeping forward to the winged figurine gilded by the sun; the green of the lawn reaching, twenty feet further on, to the low stone parapet; two black cannon, muzzles reaching over the lip of the parapet and pointing down into the valley that fell away to the plain, populated and dissected, then harbour, then sea, water and sky dripping gold from the setting sun, grey cloud stretched parallel to the horizon resisting the tint but for edges frayed flaxen.

I leaned back in the seat, let my eyes drop to my hands resting on my lap. Fine hands, fingers slim and strong, network of veins showing faintly blue beneath the light-brown skin. I liked my hands, had always liked them; they were not weak, were hands of finesse, formed for fine work. One of my professors, watching me carve my cadaver, had called them the hands of a surgeon. "Or of a pianist," he had said, walking away, dissatisfied with my wielding of the scalpel. But now, looking at them lying palm downward, I thought them absurd, ineffectual. They had helped save no one, had soothed much simple distress, had prolonged the inevitable with some, had gestured feebly or sat helpless before others. My wife, my son, my grandfather, even my pet project: they had all proved, in the end, to have been beyond my reach. And these hands, instruments of apparent possibility, had shown themselves in the end to be finely wrought trappings fashioned solely for display, like handsome theatrical props of papier-mâché. I turned the left hand over, examined the palm: lines and creases, curving thumb, band of gold ringing the fourth finger. It was familiar, yet not; seemed almost alien to me. Then I looked at the car seat, white leather artificially creased, and I didn't know that, either.

From the radio came once more the murmur of triumphant voice: a momentary distraction, words indistinct, sound going somehow to the base of my skull, wrapping itself around the strands of muscle and registering there as physical irritation.

My right hand moved to the door handle, tugged at it. The latch clicked open and the door moved an inch outward, settled there, heavily, as if the air beyond the glass of the window were pressing in on it. The hand settled on the armrest, fingers spread in pause on the white leather: the hand of a stranger, a limb acting with independence. Then the fingers clenched and hit abruptly at the door. It swung weightily open, hesitated, caught finally on the other side of the balance and settled out, extended on its hinges. The car rocked once.

I looked forward again, through the windshield, and the sun glinting off the winged figurine stabbed at me. My eyes lowered themselves to see fingers, my fingers, curling around the steering wheel, grasping, clenching, veins growing bluer and more rigid, knuckles revealing the ridges of bone, skin bronzing with blood. Finally, losing strength, they relaxed, clung to the plastic circle by their curled tips. I sucked through parted lips at the hot, exhausted air.

From the radio came the hiss of emptiness, like the lazy whistle of young men in the streets of Lopez City calling in admiration to passing women. Like the hiss, I imagined, of the Hydra. I stared at the radio for long seconds, at the silver knobs, at the vertical lines of luminescent green on smoked glass, then looked down to the blouse crumpled on the seat beside me. I picked it up, shook it out, spread it on the steering wheel: a small, white blouse of no distinct style, strands of white thread where the buttons had been ripped away, and just above the pocket of decorative frill a ragged hole ringed with the rust of dried blood.

"I recognize them, Dr. Raj. I put them in the freezer right away." Good man. A patient. He had once seen Jan and Rohan at my office. This job at the Lopez City morgue—I didn't know. But it's a new job, he'd thought it'd be quieter, he hadn't known this would happen—but who did? There were too many, they were coming in too quickly, there was no space to put them all. I could do nothing for him, offered what I could: a clutch of bills and coins. Insult. "No, no, Dr. Raj, save your money, I ain't want it." But Jan and Rohan—he will look after them? He will not let them be thrown aside, stacked, like the others in the corridors, at the entrance? "No, no, Dr. Raj, don't worry. My word, you have it." A haggard man, impatient, teetering on the edge. But—they will be here when I come back for them, I don't know when? "Yes, yes, Dr. Raj, now go, is not a good place to stay." Can't I see them? "Go away, Dr. Raj, you ain't want to see nothing now." The stench. The buzzing clouds of fat and frenzied flies. I drove away in the suspicious glare of the men sheathed in blue, the men of the silver lightning.

I swept the blouse off the wheel, clutched it tightly in my right hand, after a moment stepped out of the car.

The coolness of the air surprised me. I had forgotten that, up here in the hills among the buildings of the ruined fort, temperature was cut by elevation and the moisture-laden breeze that blew in unobstructed from the sea. It was a fragment that had not survived the twenty years since my last visit here, and I knew then, with a kind of sorrow, that much more had escaped me, retreating to the little corner of the brain where virtue, battered, cowered in its own membrane of vulnerability.

The short walk to the parapet across the uneven lawn was refreshing. My head cleared, if only a little, the muscles in my thighs loosened, the blood diluted, began a smoother flow. Beside me an old cannon pointed its thick cylinder of black metal dramatically, if ineffectually, to the sea. The cannon—there were several, deployed at intervals along the parapet—had never been fired, at least not in anger or defence; they had become, from the moment of their installation, museum pieces. I thought grimly of the effort it must have taken the British to haul the pieces from the harbour, along what must have been, back then at the beginning of the nineteenth century, little more than rutted dirt roads, up the steep, winding, crumbling mountainside, which even today caused cars distress. I thought of the sweat and the pain and the bitter cursing that must have resounded into the dripping vegetation every step of the way; and, with pain, of all that useless effort, all that wasted power and ingenuity, that little thrust of empire that ended in a hilltop collection of crumbling buildings and spiked cannon and a seething, restless town on the plain below.

And I felt that, somehow, those men who had sweated and strained here, making their little play at fortification only, just over a century and a half later, to cut their losses and run in a well-orchestrated theatre of brass bands and flag-raising, were in no small measure responsible for the fact that my wife and my son were dead, that my home was a shambles, that Madera, gun in hand, was down there somewhere satisfying his bloodlust. Those men who had sweated and strained had had other, more valuable lessons to teach, but they had paid only lip-service to their voiced ideals, had offered in the end but the evils of their actions, had propagated but the baser instincts, which took root and flourished so effortlessly in this world they called, with a kind of black humour, *new*.

It was while looking at all this that I understood why I had come back, understood that in me too had sprung, without question, the intoxication of the offered evils. For I had come back not for Rohan, nor for my grandparents, nor for Kayso, but in order to build forts, redoubts from which to claim safely my share of the easy wealth. No matter how much I talked about doing my bit, about creating the dream, the fact remained that I would not have returned were the money not already there: no matter how much I gave of myself, I would always go away with more. Altruistic interest is, at its base, self-interest; to develop the undeveloped is to invest in future markets; to minister to the poor is to satisfy one's own emotional needs. Self, in the end, is the prime motivation. Nothing makes a bigger fool of a man more rapidly than rumours of wealth easily acquired.

I thought: So this is how the world shatters, with a peep at the soul.

Down below, the town spread across the oval coastal plain, ending off to the left in swamp and smoking garbage dump. On the highway and in the streets of the town nothing showed amiss. From here could be seen no activity, no vehicles moving, no smoke rising from conflagration. Calm, sleepy, tropical: here, in its camouflaging of a violent reality, was the true nightmare of the place. On my right, from behind the hills melding into the sea in cascades of cliffs and forest, the sky glowed red from the fire of the setting sun.

It's like a soup bowl broken in half. The sentence came at me from nowhere, as if the thought, riding the wind, had suddenly glided down into my brain, offering itself as vision. "Like a soup bowl broken in half." I whispered the words to myself. It was how we had tried to look at it back then in the days when flag, motto, anthem were yet untarnished. And of the island itself: *like an inverted teardrop.* We had tried to see beyond its smallness, to lend it an aspect larger than it could offer of itself: through image, simile, metaphor. So that the marshy flatness of swamp reclaimed or abandoned was seen as something else, a vision more acceptable. We had sought poetry; and where it could not be found, had sought to impose it.

But we hadn't been poets. We used words in their most dangerous capacity, not as tools of enquiry but as agents of concealment.

I turned my gaze from the town, turned my back on it, sat on the parapet, the stone hard and uneven under me. The lawn, rich, petering out only at its edges into a stone and gravel ugliness, rose gently on my left into a low mound, cracked concrete steps leading up its side to the signal hut, roof of blue shingles, wooden walls painted white, neat windows of clear glass, small porch enclosed by wooden railings. A charming building, charming in the way of tea and biscuits and gentle afternoons, it spoke of coattails and brass buttons, of lazy chess and leatherbound books in a distant outpost of empire, the kind of place in which colonial careers stalled or were dissolved in sinecure. The government had maintained it as a tourist attraction, along with the flagpole, the whitewashed mast of a schooner, that towered before it, the flag of the island, a geometry of green and red and blue, fluttering lazily from its cord.

At the base of the mound and slightly behind it, as if crouching in modesty or ignominy, was the squat, rectangular box of a stone building, its walls dark and wet-looking, tiny windows barred by thick, rusting iron bars. The door, of heavy wooden planks bound together by flat iron belts, had long been nailed shut. The building might once have been a storeroom or a jail, or both, set just enough in retreat to be neither oppressive nor impressive yet unmistakably present, like the faintest of bad odours.

Behind the buildings, as backdrop, loomed an impenetrable mass of green, vine and bush entwined with trees to create a thickness shadowed like that of night. Beyond and above the mass, with a grandeur that, looking as we had been taught to do always towards the sites of development and progress—our first skyscraper, all ten storeys of it, had been a focal point of excitement, despite Surein who, having seen London, kept saying, "It must be a damn low sky, boy"—we somehow never noticed, rounded hill tops rolled away in folds of green, lighter closer up, darker to almost black the farther they receded.

Twenty years. But I knew just by looking that the old fort was the same. Time had changed me, had made me unrecognizable— Mrs. McLean, spotting me in Salmonella one day soon after our return, had taken me for my father's younger brother, had called me by his name, and I, inexplicably embarrassed, distressed by the infirmities that age had brought to her, had picked up the charade, carried it off, fled without asking about Angela—but this place, older than everything but the land itself, had remained above it all, untouched, witness to the hopes of empire and the dreams of independence translated, over the years and through the shifting ideas of politics, into the despair of abandonment. Now, in the midst of this silence, of greenery and sunset, of time frozen, I longed for a time I had never known, when the world was less uncertain, when dreams and hopes were possible, when life was not yet an adventure played out.

I wanted to turn around, to let my feet dangle, to attempt to see the sea and the town through brighter, more optimistic eyes. But I couldn't bring myself to do it, could only turn my head for the briefest of moments: the plain, the smouldering garbage dump, the darkening sea, the town—objects, now, of terror. And in the distance the deepening night merged sea and sky so that there was nothing, nothing to reach out to. Tears filled my eyes and I knew that, at that very moment, I could let myself fall backward, could let myself tumble into a blur as ungraspable, as uncontrollable as events. Yet I knew, too, that it was not escape that I sought, not relief, but expiation. And that could come not by ending life but only by continuing it. Anything less would be pretence, a feint at action.

I raised the blouse to my face, rubbed it against my cheek—the fabric caught on the stubble, scraped sharply like sandpaper—then spread the frilled pocket on my open left hand. The bullet hole, neat, singed, the corona of dried blood stiff and crusted, was large enough for my index finger to pass through. Just around the heart, I estimated, maybe, with luck, a little above it, she hadn't bled much before it was ripped off.

But what did it matter? The little steel ball, hot and vicious, would have created havoc. What did it matter where precisely it had hit? The result, sooner or later, would have been the same.

My finger slipped from the hole, and with swift, businesslike motion I folded the blouse and placed it beside me on the cool stone of the parapet. The sun was gone, and in its indifferent afterglow, shadowless, chilling, I grew drowsy. My head spun. I stood up on legs hollowed, made my way unsteadily across the grass to the car, let myself fall through the open door onto the seat. My forehead hit the steering wheel, but I was beyond feeling.

As darkness closed over me, inky and inexorable, I thought: I have spent my life polishing shadows. It was the only truth, in that moment of extinction, that occurred to me.

The sky lightened, and from behind the arc of low hills to the east the red glow of sun began its timid ascent. I stepped stiffly from the car and walked to the parapet. The town below remained shadowed. I was not refreshed, felt calloused, rather, by a rested exhaustion.

When the light, soft and aqueous, at last reached the houses and the streets, when it drained the restrained power of the street lamps, I got back into the car, pulled the door shut and began my slow descent into the town, towards its restless and fitful slumber, towards its drama of splinter and crash. The blouse remained where I had lain it in the night on the parapet of cool stone. I had no need of it. There were cremations to be done. Thus would begin the expiation.

The men in green arrived unannounced, floating in on silk, clattering in from the skies, rushing onto the beaches.

And so ended one part of the story, with the wresting away of even the illusion of control. Later Grappler said, "Some people goin' to say they right, some goin' to say they wrong. But the way I see it, all they've done is to take away our right to kill each other wholesale. And maybe that's not a bad right to lose."

18

‸

When a dream is broken, turn your back on it, walk away from it, or the razor-sharp shards will slice you to pieces.

As a physician, I am trained to fight. To accept hopelessness, not to fight, is to accept defeat, but a defeat of a curious quality, a defeat that fuses both a weakness and a strength, weakness in its initial admission, strength in its final acceptance. It is a defeat that requires, too, a total trust: in the abilities, observations and deductions of oneself, in the abilities, observations and deductions of others. And it is this trust that is the Achilles' heel: take a view that is askew, put faith in the inadequate, make decision on the deficient, and even the slope seems flat, even the swamp seems solid.

Not only to have trusted as reality the distracting sideshow of sunlight dancing on primary colours but to have coddled it, fostered it, to have wanted it to be the reality; to have listened without challenge to all those could-have-beens and should-have-beens, all those sorrowed expressions of hope lost and possibility shattered: it was life swimming in delusion, life shimmering in fantasy, life in which the slope was flat and the swamp was solid.

A flight attendant, thin, of severe demeanour, walks down the aisle spraying bursts of insecticide from an aerosol can. The cabin stirs in anticipation of landing: bags rustle, clothes are straightened, hair combed and brushed and patted at. Below, through the darkness, through breaks in the high cloud, the distant lights of the city glitter like a quiet firepit strewn with diamonds.

I remember little from before the funeral. Phone calls offering whiffs of life at a time of death. Whispered conversations, words unimportant, the pure sounds of voice indispensable. Hands clasping briefly at the shoulder, bestowing mute sympathy with the incredible power of touch. Grappler, grim and greyed. Surein, recently released, thinner, hollow-eyed. "I'm sorry," he said, pronouncing as if with fear the hackneyed condolence. My Aunt Sylvia, torn between griefs, hugging me in a cloud of perfume, rushing off to her mother, my grandmother. And the house, Grappler's house to which I had been taken, crowded suddenly with people I knew and people I didn't know, people who knew me and people who didn't; the house, which after a while, in the noise and the heat and the subdued swirl of bodies, went airless, as if all the oxygen had been sucked out of it, and spun into a vortex of incandescent twilight.

And of the funeral itself: flowers, flame, sprinkled water and chants—*ooom-bugga-bugga*—over the bodies lying in their shallow coffins of dense styrofoam.

I remember the funeral pyres, staves of dried wood stacked five feet high beside the brown, sluggish river, steep banks thick with tall grass.

I remember the march from the hearse, the open coffins, protected underneath by folded, white sheets, lain five or six times on the earth, for prayers, for the surrendering one by one of the human senses.

I remember the lifting of the bodies to the top of the pyre. And then I climb up to join them, Jan and Rohan lying side by side, a sea of solemn faces turned upward at me: Who are these people, I wonder, and what are they doing here? I am alert enough to think her name when I spot Asha, sheathed in red, in the front ranks of the crowd, but too numbed to be more than vaguely aware of the other pyre not far along the bank on top of which my grandfather's body has been placed, Surein, shoeless like me, standing beside him. My uncles abroad have been unable to arrange flights. The airport, military domain now, remains closed to civilian traffic.

But suddenly there is no time to dally. The sun is boiling down with its oily heat, and in the east storm clouds are gathering.

The two pundits on the ground behind me—members of the family, one an uncle, the other a distant cousin, both unknown to me until this day—begin passing up to me open containers of clarified butter, each the size of a paint can, green with gold lettering. I know what is expected, sink my right hand deep into the butter soft and warm in the sun, scoop out dripping handfuls and smear it thickly on Jan and Rohan, masking their faces with it, caking their arms, their torsos, their legs.

"Don't forget the feet," says one of the pundits.

"Hurry, hurry," says the other.

"Put more, put more."

"Put it on t'ick."

"Put more on the feet."

"Cover the feet."

And then the sugar. Pour on the sugar, cover them with it.

"Not too much," says one.

"No, put more," says the other.

"Too much, and the bodies not goin' to burn."

"Too little, and the bodies not goin' to burn."

Then the rice on top of that. The bodies no longer recognizable except in indistinct form, individuality concealed.

"Sprinkle it, sprinkle it," says one.

"All over, all over," says the other.

Next are passed to me small, hard, white cubes of a material I do not know, but recognize from the collection plate my grandfather used to pass around at large prayer meetings: a brass platter, in the middle a fresh, red hibiscus, and scattered around it, among the offered coins, little pieces of this white, inflammable material, each burning a steady flame. I make to break the first piece, it is how I have seen it used, but the voices in unison urge me just to put them on the bodies. And, working in haste, following directions, I place the cubes on their eyes, on their chests, along their arms and legs, on their feet. Two more pieces are passed to me, but there is no place to put them, I have been careful, conscientious, neat.

"Put them in their mouths," says one.

I hesitate.

"Part the lips and put them in their mouths," says the other.

Horror. I reach down, dig with my fingers through the layers of rice and sugar and butter, locate the lips clammy and inert, force them apart, insert the cubes as well as I can.

All is ready. I straighten up, only now notice I am short of breath, am drenched in perspiration. My hands drip with rice, sugar, butter.

"Come down," says one.

I climb down, step onto hard, damp clay. Water is poured onto my hands from a brass vase. I wash them as best I can; there is no soap, they remain greasy. Grappler, standing red-eyed beside my shoes, gives me his handkerchief, but it is of little use, is too damp.

Then, flame. A torch, a length of white cloth wrapped around one end of a bamboo pole, dipped in kerosene and set alight, is passed to me.

"Walk around the pyre with it," says one.

I make my way around, the flame, vibrant and whipping, licking at my face, back to the two pundits. I notice sweat stains under the arms of their white cotton tunics.

"Put it in," says the other, indicating the closest corner.

The torch slips easily through a space in the stacked wood, the flaming head settling in the centre.

Another torch is passed to me.

"Walk around with it."

And I repeat the ritual—the walk, the insertion of fire—four times, until there is a torch in each corner of the pyre. The flame builds; smoke curls from the interior of the wooden structure.

A fifth torch is given to me.

"Light their mouths," says one.

Their mouths?

"Their mouths," says the other. "Look through the wood, find the faces."

I bend close to the wood, peer through into the growing flame, feel the heat on my face, my neck, my shoulders, my arms. The butter is melting on Jan's face, her profile sharpening: she looks as if she is sucking at the white cube between her lips. And for the first time in what seems an eternity, I realize what I am about—I realize that I am, with my own hands, burning my wife and son. My throat constricts, a gurgling fills my head, my eyes feel pulled apart.

A hand touches my back. "Light it, light it," says one. "Quick, son, quick," says the other.

With one movement, I insert the torch, lay the flame directly on her face. Two hands seize my shoulders, pull me insistently away from the intensifying heat. Grappler. He steadies me, helps me into my shoes.

The pyre is all flame now, thick smoke billowing into the darkening sky. I hope it will not rain, for what then? Will we have to repeat all this with half-charred bodies? I walk around the pyre, examine the vibrancy of its flame, take satisfaction in its avid consumption, turn my back on it, walk away, for I have no wish to stay. It is said that if you watch closely as the fire burns, as the wood blackens and thins, you can sometimes see an arm rise as if alive, or the skull bared as the flesh melts. Grappler catches up to me—I am walking more quickly than I know—and leads me through the crowd to the car just as my grandfather's pyre, too, begins to smoke.

There are other ceremonies to be performed, other rituals in the coming hours, days and weeks: the placing of food for the dead beside the funeral route; the ritual shaving, as a public sign of mourning, beside a river; the final ceremony of farewell to the souls. And they could probably find more, if I let them. But I want no part of it. Others can do them if they wish, and my family is full of those who will, believers and nonbelievers alike, superstitious all. I have done my part, feel strangely cleansed, understand better now the purification of fire. As for the other gestures, the other motions of appeasement, they are of darknesses too remote, of a past that has formed, but does not inform, me. Too much time has passed, too much space has been travelled. What began so long ago as flight from a dusty and decrepit village in India brings me now to a flight on a jet blasting its way through a cool Canadian night to the newest destination of highways and high rises. It has been a long journey, and not an easy one. Much has been jettisoned, much has been lost. But the important thing is to keep moving on.

The flight attendant gathers up my coffee cup and napkin, says, "We'll be landing soon, sir."

Down below, the city winks and glitters in an expanse that reaches to the extremes of the night. I think, with anxiety, of the visit I must pay to Jan's parents, of the news I must deliver, of the distress I must cause. But it is my final duty, and an unavoidable one.

Mr. Lal shuffles unsteadily by on his way from the washroom. He stares at me, as if in expectation.

I say, "How's she doing?"

"Dying, Doctor, dying." His expression does not change.

"And you?"

He shrugs. "About the same."

The plane banks sharply. Lights. Lights stretching into the distance, whites and yellows and reds, roads, highways, cars moving along.

The plane levels off, rumbles its landing gear into place.

I decide that, when we disembark, I will avoid Mr. and Mrs. Lal, I will avoid my distant relative. I decide I will run if I have to.

The lights grow bigger, our speed appreciable. The jet engines whine. We skim roads, fences, buildings, streak past red and blue lights.

Buildings.

The wheels hit the runway, settle. The airplane fights itself, struggles with its own power. The terminal building flashes by in a white, solid blaze. The airplane slows, exhales as if in relief. The engines relax.

I look out, into the familiar unknown where no one awaits me. Beyond the airport, the city breathes warm and welcoming, spreading its ardent anonymity in the endless necklaces of its lights. I think: It is like the first time. I have completed an open-ended circle, have come all the way around once more.

I go, like my forebears, to the future, to the challenge that lies elsewhere of turning nothing into something, far from the casual brutality of collapse, far from the ruins of failure, across thousands of miles of ocean.

So it has been. So it is. So it will remain.